Vermont
WEDDINGS

Vermont WEDDINGS

Three Romances Overcome Challenges in Small-Town Goosebury

PAMELA GRIFFIN

BARBOUR
PUBLISHING

Dear Readers,

Meet three extraordinary young men and three remarkable (but lonely) young women; linked together through their unusual association to a wise but mysterious advice columnist—Dear Granny. All of them hide similar insecurities regarding the diverse troubles they face, brought on by thoughtless words and the past actions of others. Yet, all is not lost. The road to happiness, love, and fulfillment waits just around the bend, with the help of a God who can heal the most broken of hearts.

And He's decided to use the small, picturesque New England town of Goosebury, Vermont for His background.

Take a walk with me through sugar maples groves and along covered bridges to a nostalgic community with flawed but lovable characters who will move into your heart and find a home there. Journey down a famous trail whose incredible scenery is no less magnificent than the coming together of two lost and lonely souls; bask in splendid vistas of mountains, farms, and streams; discover a place where family is essential, children are special, animals are treated with care, and God reigns supreme.

Give yourself a few hours and travel with me to Goosebury, Vermont. I think you'll find it well worth the journey.

Pamela Griffin

Dear Granny

Dedication

A big thank you to all my helpful critters and readers, especially to Heidi Gennaro for all her invaluable help relating to Vermont information. As always, this is dedicated to my patient Lord, who was tolerant with me whenever my heart rebelled against doing some unwanted thing. Yet once I yielded to Him, God worked through my obedience, often changing lives in the process.

Chapter 1

Leslie Edwards gaped at the cranky editor in chief of the *Goosebury Gazette* as if the man had addressed her in fluent Chinese. His diminutive height, sparse gray hair, and bony frame were misleading; his brusque words packed a wallop.

"Well, do you want the job or not?" he prompted.

"I, uh. . .couldn't you use me in some other department?" Perched on her chair edge across from his cluttered desk, like a nervous canary about to be gobbled down by a famished cat, Leslie swallowed hard. She unclasped her hands, then smoothed them over her knees and the linen navy skirt she'd bought especially for this interview at the local weekly paper. "I wouldn't even mind starting in the obituary section."

Not many reporters would claim that, but as a budding young journalist with little field experience, Leslie had been certain it was where she would wind up. That or reporting on city council meetings, new parking restrictions, or other mundane civic issues. Obits wasn't her first choice or second or third, but it had to be better than what Mr. Abernathy was offering!

"I need you as 'Dear Granny.'" The grim-faced editor fetched a stick of candy from a full jar on his desk. Holding the red- and white-striped peppermint between two ink-stained fingers, he stuck it in his mouth. "Fern Wallace wound up in the hospital at the last minute and left me in the lurch," he said around the candy as though Fern was the one at fault. "The column's been planned to debut this week for the anniversary celebration of the paper's fiftieth year. I need you to take Fern's place."

"I hope Ms. Wallace is all right?"

He removed the candy from his mouth and held it between two fingertips and a thumb, using his middle finger to tap it over a clean ashtray as if it were a cigarette. "Fool woman decided to up and paint her barn and fell off a ladder. She's in traction. Hurt her back."

Leslie made a mental note to seek permission to add Fern's name to the prayer section of her church newsletter, since she was in charge of getting the two-page paper out twice a month. Fern was a member of her church.

Mr. Abernathy rapidly flicked the candy over the ashtray so hard it clinked against the glass. "I'm a busy man, Miss Edwards. If you don't want the job, just say so. Plenty of reporters would jump at the chance."

"It would only be a temporary position? Just until Ms. Wallace returns?" Leslie sounded as if she had a frog in her throat and cleared it. If she chose not to accept this job, she could see her two-year dream of working at the *Gazette* going up in a puff of smoke.

"Sure, sure." He stuck the candy back in his mouth and used his heels to scoot his rolling office chair sideways over the tiles. "Start looking through these and have a final copy to me for proofing before five tomorrow." Bending, he retrieved an open, shirt-sized cardboard box from a shelf along the bottom of the wall and slapped it on top of her closed portfolio, then held both items toward her. He'd barely glanced at the portfolio, which contained clips of her writing she'd labored to put together.

"Since the column isn't due to release until the upcoming anniversary issue and there hasn't been publicity regarding it, these questions are from the paper's employees and their families." He pulled the candy stick from his mouth. "That'll change within days once the column airs and the letters start trickling in. Be selective, nothing corny. The *Goosebury Gazette* has a reputation to uphold. My father started this newspaper fifty years ago. I may have gotten stuck with it when he passed it on to me, but I'm not about to see it fold while I'm still owner."

Mutely, Leslie accepted the box, which she could now see contained numerous envelopes and notes of all sizes and colors.

"Miss Alden will show you to your desk and get you started. Oh yeah, and welcome to the *Gazette*."

The greeting might have seemed sincere if Mr. Abernathy hadn't immediately broken eye contact without giving Leslie a chance to reply. He propped his candy on the edge of the clean ashtray, took up the red pen on his desk, and hunched his shoulders, setting to work on some waiting papers.

Had she agreed to take the job? She didn't remember agreeing. Leslie left his office feeling a bit shell-shocked. She hugged the items to her chest, wondering how this had all come about. She, the boy-shy girl who'd had one date in her entire life—the prom didn't count since her cousin's mom bribed him into taking her when no other boy would—was about to give advice to the lovelorn and become the *Goosebury Gazette*'s own Dear Granny.

She doubted her life could get any crazier than this.

❧

Blaine Cartell rolled the wheelbarrow to the edge of what was once his mom's front garden and stopped to take a breather. Thankfully, the weather had warmed and the snow had finally melted, but he'd been warned not to expect a long summer. A week ago, Blaine had overheard one old man at the market-place tell a tourist, "Last ye-ah, summ-uh was on a Thursday."

Casually hooking his thumbs in his belt loops, Blaine studied his peaceful surroundings, again feeling as if he'd taken a nostalgic step back in time.

To his left and behind the two-story A-frame house he now called home, century-old maples and other deciduous trees stood scattered across a field of wild grass. Great gaps of space stood between them so that he could see the slopes of the distant Green Mountains on the other side of the miniature forest growing on his property. If what he owned could be called a forest. In addition to that, in every direction he looked, clusters of trees stood in all shapes and sizes, including towering pines. He liked their zippy, woodsy smell. And from where he stood facing north, he could just see one end of a red covered bridge.

To his right, the ground gently sloped upward. There sat his neighbor's home with its gray siding, similar to his own home except that hers was the shape of a long rectangle since it had once been a barn. A dirt road cut an angle about thirty feet past her home. The only frequent visitors to travel over it were Bradley, the friendly mailman, and old Tom Henry, a naturalist who sold organic vegetables and fruit from his orchard at Goosebury's market every Saturday. Blaine had other neighbors on the opposite side of the wood but didn't know much about them. Not that he knew anything about his closest neighbor, either.

From what he could tell, Leslie Edwards stayed holed up in her house most of the time. In the three months since he'd moved into this place his parents had bequeathed to him, Blaine had caught an occasional glimpse of her dark brown hair and almost boylike physique. Her legs must come close to the length of a giraffe's; she stood near his own height of six feet two. Yet she walked with grace, and he'd noticed she had a pretty smile the few times she'd hurriedly responded to his friendly waves.

Blowing out an extended breath, he removed his hat and wiped the sweat from his brow with his forearm. He figured he ought to get back to work and make good use of his day off. Since his move, he'd cleaned out and painted the shed in back—and the house could sure use a coat—but first he had to do something about the garden. It was an eyesore he couldn't stand any longer.

Dropping to his knees, he grabbed a spade and studied the flowerbed that ran seven feet along the right side of the front door. He'd only been digging a few minutes when he heard his neighbor's screen door slam shut. He turned his head to look.

Leslie stood on her porch, stared his way several seconds, then walked back inside.

Blaine hiked his brows. *What was that all about?* He set to work again, noticing he'd accidentally shoved the spade into a tall stalk of some kind of purple flower. It bent over, its petals brushing the earth.

The door slammed again.

"You're not digging up those flowers?" Her voice hailed him across the twenty or so feet that separated them.

11

Blaine turned his attention from the injured flower to Leslie. "What?"

"The flowers." She took the three steps off her porch and set a fast pace down the slope. "You're not digging them up to dispose of them, are you?"

"I hadn't planned on it."

Relief softened her expression. "I saw the wheelbarrow and thought you were." Her jaw was a bit square, her skin clear and fresh looking, rosy from her short jog. If she used makeup, she did so sparingly. He liked that.

"Your mom planted such a pretty garden," she explained. "The purple ones are irises, and the one now lying bent to the ground is a daylily. When I saw you with that spade, I thought you were getting rid of them."

"I'm weeding."

"With a spade?"

"Soil's hard. Garden's been neglected a long time."

She nodded, and her gaze went to her shoe tops. "Incidentally, I'm sorry for your loss. We've barely spoken with one another, and I just want you to know that your parents were well thought of in Goosebury."

The words were kind, yet Blaine felt the stab of loss prick his heart again. He kept his focus on his work. "Thanks, Leslie. Hearing about their train getting derailed and crashing into that other one was a shocker. But it helps to know they went together, since they did everything else together."

She picked up a forked tool from where it lay with other gardening implements in the wheelbarrow. "Mind if I help? I could use the exercise. I've been reading all afternoon, and if I read one more word, my eyes may dry up and wither away."

They did look bloodshot. Though he couldn't fail to notice they were a pretty hazel-brown. "Sure. Have at it. I appreciate the extra hand."

She knelt at the opposite end of the flowerbed and carefully began working the points of the tool around a weed between the flowers to loosen the soil so the weed could be pulled out. He watched her several seconds, then set to his own task. He wasn't the talkative sort, and apparently neither was she. The few casual questions he did ask, she shrugged off or gave short answers in reply.

Together, they worked in companionable silence until the bed was weeded. Then with a slight smile and a casual "Well, have a nice day," Leslie rose, brushed off the knees of her jeans, and strode back to her house.

Sitting back on his haunches, Blaine stared after her and watched as she disappeared inside. Since the day he'd arrived from Fort Worth, Texas, to this speck-on-the-map rural town of Goosebury, Vermont, he couldn't remember enjoying an afternoon more. Folks around these parts still weren't sure about him—he sensed that—and sometimes he got lonely. He wouldn't mind getting to know Leslie, but it sure would help matters if one of them were better equipped with verbal skills.

Restless, Leslie tried to resume reading the letters, selecting those she would use for the column. The loud mechanical buzz of a lawn mower cut into her train of thought. She moved to the window to close it.

While she pressed hard on the pane that didn't want to budge, she caught a glimpse of Blaine's back, tanned and muscular, as he pushed a mower across his lawn. The white cowboy hat he wore covered most of his hair, but she remembered on other occasions how his dark locks shimmered in the sun with a hint of auburn highlights and matched his semisweet chocolate brown eyes. The man really was too attractive for his own good.

Not that she was looking.

The glass finally gave way, and she shut the window, at last muffling the noise of the mower. Deciding she wanted a sweet snack before she continued her chore, she went into the kitchen to retrieve a sticky bun and a glass of chocolate milk, childhood favorites she'd never outgrown. Chocolate. Again reminded of her neighbor's eyes, she frowned and replaced the slim carton, pulling out the white version instead.

Five minutes later, settled into her comfortable beanbag chair, she relived her interview with Mr. Abernathy while taking a bite of her glazed pecan-laden bun. Yes, she had her own column, unheard of for a green reporter, but no byline. None bearing her name anyway. No interviews, no one-on-one contact with real people. Just letters rife with questions she had no idea how to answer. She would gladly trade places with any of the staff at the *Goosebury Gazette*, even young Robert, the gofer and editor's grandson. It didn't make sense. Why had Mr. Abernathy chosen her?

Resigned to her task, Leslie picked up one of the letters and unfolded it:

Dear Granny,

I've liked a guy I work with at the office for almost a year and think he could be "the one." We've become friends but nothing beyond that. I've done everything I know to get him to notice me. I even changed my wardrobe to reflect the styles he likes and bought a peacock blue sweaterdress, since he's partial to that color. I've run out of ideas. What else can I do to get him to really notice me?

Eager for Love

Leslie typed the question into her laptop, then punched out the first answer that came to mind:

Dear Eager,
Try dying your hair peacock blue.

13

Chapter 2

Try dying your hair peacock blue'?" Mr. Abernathy slammed the printout on his desk and speared Leslie with angry gray eyes. "What kind of fool answer is that?"

Without giving her a chance to respond, he snatched the paper up a second time. "And this one—'Dear Granny, my husband is addicted to old Westerns and watches them day in, day out. We rarely talk anymore, and I feel as if I'm losing him. Any advice?' Your helpful answer: 'Invest in a cowgirl outfit and buy a horse.'"

Leslie averted her gaze to her lap. It was no secret that the job she'd been given she'd labored at grudgingly, but she felt ashamed to hear her answers aired aloud. She really hadn't given this her all—not even a tiny bit of halfway.

Whatever you do, work at it with all your heart, as working for the Lord, not for men. Her nana's words from Colossians, years ago, gently chided her spirit.

"This kind of foolish tripe isn't what'll keep our readers buying the *Gazette*, Miss Edwards." He bit off the tip of his peppermint stick and threw it in the ashtray. "I'll give you one more chance to come up with something decent that'll be a credit to this paper. As a favor to your grandmother, I gave you a job. I read over your former clips and expected better. You've got until five today to get an acceptable piece of work on my desk to run in the anniversary issue."

Nana had called Mr. Abernathy? She must have, since she hadn't set foot off her property since Leslie's grandfather had died fourteen months ago. Leslie wasn't sure how she felt about her grandmother getting involved in her career, what little career she could claim.

"Thank you, Mr. Abernathy." Leslie meekly rose to her feet. The man stood almost one foot shorter yet still managed to tower over her. "I won't let you down."

"You'd better not."

His words rang in her ears all the way back to her cubicle. Leslie slunk to her chair, propped her elbows on her desk, and bowed her head, pressing palms to temples.

"Trouble in Big Chief's wigwam?" Carly Alden, a writer for the entertainment section, crossed her arms over the edge of the cubicle wall from her side. A lock of her shiny black hair slid past her shoulder and fell over the glazed glass. Her almond-shaped eyes glimmered with amusement.

"I'm just not cut out to be an advice columnist. But if I don't learn this job fast and please Mr. Abernathy, I can see my every hope for a career as a newspaper journalist whirling down the drain."

"Cheer up, Leslie. If Abernathy didn't think you could do it, he wouldn't have hired you. He's not the gracious sort."

"Can I ask a question?"

"Aren't you the one who's supposed to supply all the answers?"

"Funny." Leslie leaned back in her chair. "What's with the peppermint sticks?"

"Abernathy?" At Leslie's nod, Carly smiled. "He's a reformed smoker; his office used to reek of the stench from yesterday and beyond. After the non-smoking areas popped up in all the public places, he got complaints, too, but it wasn't until his doctor warned him his ticker couldn't handle any more tobacco that he stopped. The peppermint sticks are something the doc suggested as a substitute whenever Big Chief wants a cigarette. I've also heard they help his stomach problems. He goes through a jar of those candy sticks a day."

"At least he's doing something to try to break the habit."

"Oh, I agree. He's a grizzly bear at times, but he'd be missed around here if he weren't with us anymore. Okay, I've got to scoot if I'm to get that copy to Mike before deadline. Meet me for lunch?"

"I wish I could, but I only have a few hours to salvage the mess I made. And with no idea how to do it."

"I wish you all the best. Maybe we'll grab a bite together on Monday." Carly's head ducked down and disappeared.

Leslie mulled over her predicament. How was she supposed to come up with serious answers to all these questions when she had no foundation, no love life to call her own? A picture of Nana's wise face came to mind, and smiling, Leslie picked up the phone.

Blaine walked around the blue four-door sedan, rubbing his hand along the back of his neck as he inspected the car that was two decades old—and one year.

"She rides like a baby on a week's worth of Pablum," the balding old Vermonter who'd introduced himself as Mr. Meeker told him. "Can't see well enough to drive long distances anymore. Since my wife died, can't see much reason goin' into town neith-uh."

Blaine kicked the tires. Firm. Little wear. And the engine looked good, too. Ran smoothly when he'd started her up. But the paint was peeling, a crack ran two inches along the center of the windshield, and the upholstery was ratty. Plus, he'd really wanted to invest in a truck.

"Nice hat you got there," the man said, staring above Blaine's brow.

Blaine quenched a smile. "Thanks." The ten-gallon cowboy hat had been a going-away gag gift from his ex-roommate for Blaine to remember Texas by. As if he'd forget the state in which he'd been raised. He'd rarely worn a hat before leaving Fort Worth but used it now and then to keep the sun out of his eyes.

"Gets good mileage," Mr. Meeker offered.

"Not your usual gas guzzler?"

"Ah-nope."

"Runs on unleaded?"

"Ah-yup."

Blaine took another round-trip tour of the vehicle, checked under the hood once more, looked underneath the body to check for any oil leakage, then straightened and eyed Mr. Meeker.

"I'll give you seven hundred."

The man's whiskery jaw dropped. "I'm only askin' four." He motioned to the cardboard sign on the inside of the windshield and the numbers written in shaky red paint.

"All right, sir. You drive a hard bargain, but I can see why for a beaut like this. Seven-fifty and the hat." He pulled the white ten-gallon off his head and slipped it over the man's shiny pate. For the first time since Blaine arrived at the front of Mr. Meeker's rundown home, the old Vermonter smiled.

"You ha'd of hearin', boy? Though I always did want me one of them hats eveh since the day I saw my first John Wayne Western. Still, don't seem right, takin' all that money."

"The furnishings *are* worn, but the seats can be recovered. And the windshield'll need to be replaced. But I'm no swindler, Mr. Meeker. Unless I miss my guess, that engine is only a few years old."

"Come to think on it, I did have a new motuh installed five years back. More or less."

Blaine let out a resigned sigh. "All right, all right. One thousand dollars. And that's my final offer."

The old man's eyes lit up as though Blaine had offered him the moon and the stars to go with it. Observing Mr. Meeker's bent frame, Blaine wondered if the man received enough from his Social Security payments to eat a decent meal every day. Since his parents had left him the house and a comfortable nest egg, Blaine wasn't hurting for cash. But if he went any higher in price, the old man was bound to catch on to his strategy and be offended.

Mr. Meeker eyed Blaine like he had a screw loose, but he held out his arthritic hand. "You have yourself a deal, son."

"If I don't get the lead out now, I'll be late for work," Blaine said, shaking the man's hand. "But I'll come by during my lunch break to finalize the deal. Better yet, why don't you drive the car up in three hours, when I'm due for my break? I work at Milton's Pantry, just a few blocks up the road."

"Yup. I can do that."

Tucking in his shirt, Blaine traveled on foot up the two-lane street. At least Mr. Meeker was sure to have a good meal today; Blaine would see to that. There was something about the whimsical old man that reminded him of Grandpa Joe. Maybe it was in the youthful light of the man's blue eyes trapped inside a weathered face and work-worn body. His spirit was as alive as a boy's, and the smiles he'd given made him seem both humble and wise.

A dark green compact car drove past, crunching along the small rocks. He caught a glimpse of Leslie's profile as her car turned into Milton Pantry's white gravel drive.

Blaine grinned. This day was just getting better by the hour. Increasing his pace to a jog, he headed her way.

Leslie accepted the sacks containing the food order she'd called in to save time and thanked the cashier. She had to eat, but her deadline prohibited her the ability to enjoy the ease of dining inside the restaurant. Besides, this way her grandmother would get a good meal, too.

As she approached the carved wooden door, it opened wide. In the rush of sunlight sweeping in, she made out Blaine's handsome face and tall form, at least three inches loftier than hers, which was saying a lot.

He looked startled, then confused. "You're leaving?"

"Yes." Why should he care? Oddly enough, he didn't act surprised to see her but rather spoke as if he knew she'd be inside. "I'm on a pressing deadline."

"Oh?"

She nodded, feeling a bit silly holding the sacks and standing stationary while talking to him as he held the door wide open.

"I have a job at the *Goosebury Gazette*. Nothing much." Well, she didn't consider it much anyway.

"You a writer?"

"Trying to be."

"Blaine, close that door before you let in all the flies," the girl behind the counter called out in a cheerful voice. "Velma will be glad to see you. Kaye called in sick."

"You work here?" Leslie's brows rose.

"Sure do. I'm one of the cooks."

"I didn't know you could cook." Well, obviously he could cook *something* since he was a bachelor. Feeling as if she'd just registered a mark higher on the social-idiot scale, Leslie winced. "I mean, I didn't know you cooked professionally—for other people, besides yourself." Yikes. That sounded worse. She could almost hear the bell go *ding* as the scale rocketed to the top after her last brainless remark. "Uh, sorry. I really have to go. It was nice talking with you, Blaine."

"You, too." He held the door open for her, and she brushed past him with a faint "thanks."

Once Leslie was in her car, she shot a glance at the restaurant door, now closed, and chided herself for the disappointment that rushed over her. Of course Blaine wouldn't still be standing there. He had work to do. Besides, they were only friends, if that. If not for his parents' generosity, he could very well be her landlord.

When the Cartells had moved to Vermont eight years ago, they'd bought the property, fully renovated the barn into living quarters, and rented it out to Leslie. She loved her bedroom in the loft, which overlooked the sunny dining and living areas, and her little mudroom in the back, so much like Nana's. The Cartells had been great neighbors and landlords, and in their will, they'd stipulated that she was to have ownership of the property in which she lived. Upon hearing the news, she'd been stunned, wondering if any family members would come forward to contest the will. Blaine was their only son and had stated to his lawyer that if that's the way his parents wanted it, that's the way it stayed.

From the day the Cartells' lawyer relayed that message to Leslie, she'd felt sure Blaine must be a special person. Yet he considered her no more than a neighbor, at the most a casual acquaintance. Not that she was interested in any romantic notions, though the man had gorgeous eyes and a smile to die for.

Shaking herself from ridiculous notions, she drove the three miles to her grandmother's home and felt cheered when she saw the peaceful sight of the slow-moving river running past a white-shingled house with a gray roof. Nana had told her she'd be in the back, so Leslie didn't bother knocking on the front door, going through the gate leading to the garden instead.

"Hello!" she called out, a smile lifting her lips at the sights and smells that greeted her. "Nana?" She inhaled a deep fragrant breath.

The entire backyard was a flower-lover's paradise. Nana had certainly outdone herself this year.

Shades of blossoms in red, fuchsia, purple, and pink filled a good section of the entire south area, and tiny ruby-throated hummingbirds flitted among many of the tubular flowers, their wings going so fast they appeared as a blur. Some of the birds sat on twigs and leaf stems, resting, and looking adorable, like miniature figurines. Leslie had loved the tiny creatures ever since she had been a little girl helping Nana in her garden. The remainder of the area held a variety of blooms from other spectrums in the color wheel, the delightful aroma reminding Leslie of one of her favorite floral bubble baths.

"I'm in here." Nana's voice came from the open door of the mudroom. Leslie walked into the enclosed porchlike area her nana used for dirty projects. She spotted Nana's plump frame bent forward on a stool in front of the floor sink. Nana washed off a pair of mud-caked work boots.

Leslie set her purse and the bags of food down on the bench seat. "Take a rest. I brought lunch."

"You're a dear heart." Nana placed the rinsed boots on a nearby ledge. Pulling off her gloves, she rose to her feet with effort. "I just couldn't resist digging in the garden today. It's such a lovely afternoon, and the winter was so terribly long this year. As your grandfather used to say, 'It outlasted even itself.'" She chuckled.

Smiling at the memory of her grandfather's droll sayings, Leslie took the bags into the kitchen and went about setting plates and silver on the table. She knew Nana's home as well as her own. Leslie's parents had divorced when she was twelve, and though she often saw her father, who lived a county away, her mother had married a New Yorker with children younger than Leslie and had moved to that state. Once she'd turned eighteen, the seasons Leslie spent in busy Manhattan ended by her own choice. She had gently explained to her mom that she preferred to feel settled and not as if she were always being split down the middle between two states and two parents.

At least Mom called twice a month and came to visit during the fall, often bringing the rest of her family. But it was Nana, her father's mother, who'd been there for Leslie all through her young life and on into high school. She owed this woman the world and wished she could think of some way to urge Nana from her self-imposed, boxed-in existence, something Nana had adopted ever since the funeral. Her hair, once dyed a nutmeg brown when Granddad was alive, had turned back to its natural ash gray. While it looked fine on her and there was nothing wrong with gray hair, to Leslie it was just another piece of evidence pointing to Nana's exile from life.

"How can I help you, Leslie?" Nana poured tea for both of them. "You sounded beside yourself over the phone."

They prayed a short prayer to bless the food. As they ate, both women discussed Leslie's new job.

"Well, I never would've imagined Ronald would give you a position like that," Nana exclaimed. "Though I have every confidence you can do the job."

"Not without help. I'm not exactly an authority on love, Nana, and Mr. Abernathy hated my initial suggestions." Leslie related them to her grandmother, then took a bite of her juicy roast beef and tomato sandwich, not missing the amused sparkle in Nana's kelly green eyes. "So will you help me?"

"I'm not quite sure how, but of course you know I'll help in any way I can." Nana forked salad into her mouth, chewed it, and swallowed. "Tell me, Leslie, not to change the subject, but are you seeing anyone? I hear you have a handsome new neighbor and that he's single and a Christian, too."

Leslie's face grew hot. Likely Nana had learned that information from her friend Vivian, who called to check up on her once a week. "Blaine's a nice guy, but we aren't dating. In fact, he reminds me a lot of Jimmy."

"Jimmy? Oh, that's too bad."

"How so?" Her brother was a great guy, and she missed him a lot since he'd moved to New York.

"After what Vivian said about Blaine, I was hoping you might feel differently toward the man, other than just having sisterly-type feelings for him."

Leslie didn't answer, instead paying supreme attention to finishing her sandwich and corn chips. Nana's one flaw, to Leslie's way of thinking, was her habit of frequently urging that Leslie find someone to make her life happy.

Her life was just fine. Maybe not bursting-at-the-seams happy, but fine just the same.

She owned her own home, had a good-running car, and had landed a job at the paper, even if the beat wasn't her choice. One day, maybe, she would meet the right man. But until that time arrived, she didn't want to feel steamrollered into marriage.

After they'd eaten and the few dishes they'd used were rinsed and the table wiped off, Leslie read to Nana those letters she'd chosen to answer. Nana sat perfectly still for a long moment, her arms crossed across her stomach, her hands clasping her elbows. If her eyes hadn't been open, Leslie might have thought she'd dozed off. Suddenly Nana rose and returned with the big family Bible, opening it to Proverbs. Leslie drew her brows together in confusion, and Nana smiled.

"It seems to me, Leslie, if you're going to offer advice to those in need of wise counsel, then you'll need to refer them to the source of all wisdom. Now, let's see that first letter."

Leslie handed it over, wondering what her editor in chief would have to say about this.

Chapter 3

"M iss Edwards!"

Leslie jumped at least half a foot when Robert, the editor's buck-toothed grandson, invaded her cubicle and called her name. His gray eyes shone with excitement.

"Granddad wants to speak with you right away."

Heart still racing, Leslie was glad she'd set down her coffee so it didn't end up all over the front of her new, flower-sprigged blouse. Unable to stop shaking, she took deep, irregular breaths for calm and went to beard the grouchy lion in his cluttered den.

The anniversary issue had hit the streets yesterday, and she'd been waiting with barely contained patience to discover the public's reaction. When Mr. Abernathy first scanned the messages to readers her grandmother had helped formulate, he'd grumbled that the tone was too bleeding heart but was passable this once since there wasn't time to get anything else written and meet the deadline.

"Good luck," Carly said, never looking away from the words she typed. She'd acted strangely all morning, and Leslie wondered if one of those Dear Granny letters had been hers. The answers Leslie had concocted with Nana's help hadn't been tampered with, except she'd been disappointed to notice that almost all biblical references Nana had worked so hard to locate and jot down were edited out.

Mr. Abernathy waved a peppermint stick around as he spoke with someone over the phone. "Sit down," he mouthed to Leslie, then, "I appreciate your call, Mrs. Bloomington, and I certainly will pass along the message." He laid the receiver in its cradle, his eyes snapping with excitement as they shot to Leslie.

Immediately, the phone trilled beneath his fingers.

"Hear that?" he asked. "That's been going on all morning with no end in sight. A few feminists were offended and called to complain, which was to be expected, but for the most part, readers like Mrs. Bloomington love 'Dear Granny.' Forget what I said about how to write the article, Miss Edwards. You're doing a grand-slam job. Keep up the good work." He broke eye contact to answer the phone again.

A rush of breath swept from Leslie, and she felt a little dizzy. They liked it? That was it? That's why she'd been summoned to his office? Relief made her muscles weak, as if they'd turned to mush.

Considering herself summarily dismissed, Leslie rose, waited a moment to see if Mr. Abernathy would tell her to sit again, and then left his office. She returned to her cubicle, feeling as if she were riding a cloud. Her new boss not only approved her work but also commended her for it, and it was all due to Nana. If this kept up, surely Mr. Abernathy would reassign her to a better position. She just had to stick with it awhile longer until Fern Wallace was released from the hospital.

"Do you really believe all of what you wrote in there?" Carly approached Leslie, pointing with one salmon-colored nail to the top of the column where Leslie had addressed three readers at once. All three were concerned about outside appearances and what they could do to improve themselves so as to attract a potential boyfriend or respark the love-light in their husbands.

Leslie, with Nana's guidance, had written:

I sympathize with each of you dear ladies; in today's world, it's often difficult to know what to do in such a situation. Everyone thinks they have the answer. However, since you've come to me for aid, allow me to offer a beneficial piece of advice a wise teacher named Peter once penned: "Your beauty should not come from outward adornment, such as braided hair and the wearing of gold jewelry and fine clothes. Instead, it should be that of your inner self, the unfading beauty of a gentle and quiet spirit. . . ."

In Granny's words: While it's true men are attracted to the appearance of a woman (and there's certainly nothing wrong with keeping up your appearances, ladies, as long as you don't make it your prime focus!), relationships based solely upon this feature often last no more than a season. What will cause the man of your heart to desire to share a lifetime with you will be the issues arising from your heart. Especially addressing those of you who are married—a gentle word, a sweet nature, being a faithful companion. Difficult? Yes, it can be. But remember, those things that are of highest value require hard work to obtain and retain. And yes, to answer your unspoken question, it's worth it.

Love,
Granny

Leslie looked up from the column. "I do believe it, Carly." When she'd first worked with Nana in writing the answer, she'd also questioned how women of today would receive such old-fashioned advice. But seeing it in print brought an assurance deep inside her spirit that it was the right response to give.

Carly let out a soft laugh that seemed tense. "Maybe in the Middle Ages that sort of thing would work, but not in the twenty-first century. Mark my words, you're going to get a lot of flack from readers on this one. My advice? Stick to the peacock blue hair dye." She snatched up the paper and whipped around, heading back to her cubicle.

Leslie had definitely struck a nerve. Was Carly the girl in the peacock blue sweaterdress? She'd never seen Carly wear the color, but Leslie had been in the office less than a week. Or had Carly been one of the other writers? The anxious young teen who'd sought Granny's approval for an abortion, approval Leslie couldn't and didn't give. Or maybe she'd been the confused woman who'd just found out the flatlander she'd been dating for half a year was married. Leslie had gently advised the woman to get out of the relationship with the out-of-towner as fast as her two legs could carry her and that such an association could bring nothing but pain.

So many hurting people; so many difficult situations. Could she really be a help to any of them? With Nana's aid, Leslie felt she could, but Carly's curt reaction made her see the flip side to this job that she'd first thought of as pure fluff. People could and would hate her for her comments. For the first time since Mr. Abernathy had assigned her the role of Dear Granny, she was glad she was anonymous and didn't have her own byline.

She prayed Ms. Fern Wallace recovered quickly and was soon out of traction and the hospital. Despite Nana's help, Leslie wasn't sure she had what it took to continue as Goosebury's advice columnist. Still, it wasn't in her nature to quit. She only hoped that reader acceptance for the column continued and she didn't get fired.

After two weeks of hearing all the commotion, Blaine couldn't stand the curiosity that needled him any longer. During his next visit to town, after church on Sunday, he broke down and bought a copy of the *Goosebury Gazette*. He wasn't a subscriber, but he'd heard so much about a new column called "Dear Granny" that he had to see it for himself. Most of the people he'd overheard at church, the gas station, and the market had been wholly complimentary of the advice column, but there were a few snide comments about "ultraconservative mishmash" and "antifeminist garbage" he'd heard as well.

Inside his newly purchased sedan with its windshield now replaced, Blaine located the page number of the column and, using the steering wheel as a newspaper rest, spread out the *Gazette* until he found the right page. With curious interest he read Dear Granny's answers to five reader letters. Kind, old-fashioned, sincere, from the heart—the replies reminded him of something his own grandma or mom might have said. Both dear women were in heaven now, and Blaine missed their shrewd counsel. He pictured the author of "Dear Granny" as they'd been: wise in their years, busy beavers at home, always looking out for their families' best interests. Favoring a rocker, Granny probably wore printed housedresses and kept her silver hair pulled back with a hair clip or in a bun. At the nostalgic thought, Blaine smiled.

On the drive home, he toyed with an idea. He wasn't good at relationships, or rather, at how to keep them going. The few girls he'd dated soon grew tired of his lack of social skills—"stunted," one had called them—and all eventually turned down further dates. Not that he minded so much; he had yet to find that one special woman with whom he wanted to spend the rest of his life.

As clouds drifted lazily overhead, his mind drifted to Leslie. He'd like to take her out sometime. The few occasions he'd crossed her path since they'd worked together in his mom's garden had been pleasurable enough, though certainly not chatty. Leslie was no social giant either, and Blaine knew he needed all the help he could get if he didn't want to botch things during his first attempt to ask her out, as well as during the date itself. His last date with a woman, in Texas, had been a full-fledged disaster. He'd taken the city gal to a local rodeo, where her pricey heels were ruined, she'd had a close run-in with an ornery cow, and she'd complained about the stink the whole afternoon. From the way she dressed, she'd expected their date to include a steak dinner at a fancy restaurant, not corn dogs and a soda. But Blaine just wasn't a fancy sort of guy.

Once he arrived home, he made a beeline for his mother's antique wooden rolltop secretary and sat before it. Retrieving the scented purple stationery with dim yellow and blue flowers splashed over the page, Blaine thought twice about what he was doing. If anyone found out, he would be the laughingstock of all Goosebury.

He smiled wistfully, his eyes clouding as he thought of the woman who'd bought this feminine paper. Mom had liked flowers so much. After the double funeral, Blaine had spent the freezing winter inside, using this very stationery to answer condolence cards and send thank-yous for flower bouquets. Leslie's grandmother had also sent a nice card along with a green plant he now kept in the mudroom. He'd learned the woman had become a shut-in after her husband passed away and she'd recently been sick, so he had jotted her a short missive beneath his note of thanks, telling her he would pray for her health and happiness.

His momma would have been proud to know the good manners she'd laboriously taught her young son had somehow settled in over the rough spots in recent years. Still, Blaine might've never thought to write the thank-you notes if he hadn't run across her stationery when he began boxing up his parents' things. A difficult chore he had yet to finish.

Blaine let out a long breath and dashed the tears from his eyes with calloused fingers. Mom and Dad were happy in heaven; he knew that. The past was past. It was time to get on with the future, his future. Or at least the upcoming weeks. Picking up a pen, he mulled over what to write, then bent over the paper and busily set to his task.

Dear Granny. . .

Chapter 4

O h, Nana! You planted a butterfly garden. When did you do this?"
Leslie moved toward the north end of her grandmother's backyard.
Like sky ballerinas, numerous creamy white and lemon yellow butterflies fluttered with dainty grace in the fragrant air amid the trees and over the
flowers. As if she were a child lost in a land of make-believe, Leslie slowly twirled
in a full circle among them.

"Do you remember when I planted one just like it when you were twelve?"

"I'll never forget. That was the most difficult year of my life because of
Mother and Daddy splitting up, and then I came here and saw the garden." She
smiled at the memory. "I lived in it the entire summer. You showed me how to
tend the flowers so the butterflies would live on and multiply, and you also taught
me that if I was going to do a job, I should do it well. And always for the Lord's
pleasure."

Nana grew meditative. "I did say that, didn't I?"

Again Leslie decided to try to interest her grandmother in reentering the
real world. "According to Carly, the town's craft fair is coming up in two weeks.
She's in charge of the entertainment beat at the paper. I could pick you up for
church on Sunday, and we could go together afterward to look at the items on
the sidewalks. Not to shop, since I know you don't approve of doing that on
Sundays, just to look—"

"No, Leslie, I don't think so. Not yet." Nana turned toward the house. "Did
you bring any more letters?"

Leslie sighed. "Yes. Quite an interesting assortment to choose from this
week." How many times had she tried to get her grandmother to go with her
somewhere? And how many times had Nana refused with a vague answer of "not
yet" or "someday"? Too many to count.

"The postman brings about ten to fifteen letters from readers each morning," Leslie said. "I weeded out the really weird ones and disposed of them, but
I brought the rest for us to choose from." After the frenzied race to meet her
deadline for the first issue of "Dear Granny," Leslie had changed her weekly visits to Nana's to Tuesdays by asking for that day off so she would have more time
to get the column put together.

Three chairs stood near the house overlooking the garden. Nana claimed
one, Leslie another.

"So let's see what you've brought as hopefuls for this week's installment." Nana picked up a small Bible that sat on the third chair's cushion and laid it on her lap.

Wordlessly, Leslie retrieved the batch from her oversized handbag and handed them to her grandmother. She watched as Nana plowed through a pile of white and beige envelopes to retrieve a lilac one bearing the fragrance of the flower.

"Well!" Nana exclaimed and withdrew the letter. "This one might prove interesting." Leslie was aware of a faint sparkle lighting her grandmother's eyes. A sparkle that had been absent for a very long time.

" 'Dear Granny,' " Nana read aloud, " 'I'm not the social type, and neither is my neighbor. We've barely spoken to one another. But from the little time we've shared, I can tell my neighbor is someone special and someone I'd like to see on a more personal level. I've bitten the dust in past relationships, if you could call them that, mainly because I'm not much of a talker and, from what I've been told, don't know the first thing about dating or how to please a date. Could you give me some tips for success?' It's signed, 'Hopeless in Love.' "

Granny chuckled, surprising Leslie, who looked up from the letter to stare. A huge smile lifted her grandmother's cheeks, which seemed a shade pinker.

"Well, now. I think this one deserves a special reply," Nana said thoughtfully. "A very special reply indeed."

Leslie again eyed the lilac stationery with the faded peonies sprinkled across the page and the spidery handwriting. Did Nana know the woman? With the way she was acting, she seemed certain of her identity. "You know who wrote that, don't you?"

"I might."

"Well?" Leslie waited, the reporter in her eager for the full story. "Aren't you going to tell me?"

Nana sobered, though the belying twinkle in her eyes gave evidence of her continued amusement. "Why, Leslie, it wouldn't be ethical of me to say, nor is it ethical of you to ask."

Oh, yes, she definitely knew who it was.

Disgruntled, but knowing Nana was right to withhold the information, Leslie poised her pen above her notebook. "Okay, fine. I suppose silence is best. Your response?"

Nana closed her eyes as if she were praying, then opened them and gave her answer. Leslie jotted it down in shorthand, later intending to form it into her own condensed words fit for the column. She was surprised at the tone of the reply: so different from all the others Nana had given with previous reader mail.

"You're absolutely sure about this answer, Nana?"

Her grandmother's smile could only be described as sly. "Oh, yes. Perfectly sure."

Blaine heard Leslie's car pull into her drive. Looking out the window, he caught sight of the sun reflecting off the car's green paint and took in a steeling breath. The gist of the response Dear Granny had sent in reply to his letter last week was, "Man the torpedoes, full speed ahead!" and Blaine was about to give it his all-out, Texas-sized best.

"Hey, Leslie," he called once she'd exited her vehicle. She turned, shutting the car door with the motion. "Can you come over here a minute? I'd like to ask you something."

She stood motionless for long seconds as she stared his way. Realizing he still wore his mom's apron, which he'd tied around his waist from habit due to his job as a cook, he tore it off, and she began the walk toward him. *I really should invest in a more masculine white chef's apron soon.*

"Everything okay?" She came to a stop in front of him.

"Sure, sure. Everything's fine. I, uh. . ." Courage perched on the edge of its roost, preparing for departure. "I just wondered if you'd help me test out my new stove."

"Test out your new stove?"

He laughed at his own idiocy. "Well, what I'm making in it, not the stove itself." Oh, boy. This was bad. "I had Mom's old stove replaced with a current model that's easier to clean, and I cooked a pot roast for its first tryout, sort of like a christening dinner. Would you help me sample it? The pot roast." Okay, that was a little better.

"You're inviting me to dinner?"

"Uh, yeah, I am." She looked thunderstruck, and he quickly added, "You were such a help with the weeding, since I know next to nothing about flowers. I wanted to make you a special thank-you dinner."

"But you've mown my grass twice since then, Blaine. And again, thanks for that. Any debt you think you owe me has been more than repaid."

"Yeah, I know. But what are neighbors for if we can't get together and chew the fat now and then?" At her mystified expression, he realized he was beginning to sound like Grandpa Joe. "It's an old Texas saying—I didn't mean we'd really chew on fat." *Someone throw me a life preserver; I'm sinking fast.*

He cleared his throat and planted his hands on his hips in what he hoped would appear a relaxed manner. "Fact is, I'm not crazy about leftovers, and I can't eat the whole thing myself. Well, I could try, but it wouldn't be half as much fun as it would be if I had company to share it with."

There. That was a good save, though she kept staring at him strangely as if he still wore his mom's apron. Maybe he should have risked getting gravy on his new gray trousers and white shirt rather than having had her see him in the frilly, flowered yellow thing. He was tempted to toss it to the ground in a quick underhand behind him, but then she spoke.

"Sure, Blaine. I'll help you test your new stove." Her gaze briefly pitched to the grass in an almost shy way, and he grinned.

"Food'll be ready in about half an hour. Why don't you go on home, get freshened up if you want, and come back over then?"

Leslie inspected her blousy, plum-colored top and white slacks, hoping she looked "freshened" enough, then slid her hands in the pockets of her beige sweater and pulled the edges closer around her. Not for the first time, she wished she had feminine curves instead of the washboard chest, bony hips, and too-long legs she'd inherited. Not that Blaine was interested in her as a potential girlfriend. After all, he'd said this was just a neighborly meal. Yup. She'd definitely been around Nana too long; of all things, was she actually thinking of this as a date?

Shaking her head at her foolishness, Leslie knocked at his front door. Seconds trailed by. A strident-sounding alarm went off somewhere inside. Worried, she knocked harder.

Blaine threw open the door, his manner tense. "Leslie. Right on time. Come in." The acrid smell of smoke made her nostrils twinge.

"Did something burn?" She stepped inside, immediately noticing the smoke pouring from the kitchen.

"Yeah." Blaine hurried that way. "Stove burners run too hot—they're those glass-ceramic kind. All flat surface. Simmer is more like high heat—either that or something's wrong with the wiring. All the liquid evaporated in the pots. I'm used to working with gas stoves, but there's no hookup for gas here, so I had to go with electric."

Not knowing what else to do, Leslie closed the front door and followed him into the cozy yellow- and cream-colored kitchen with its pine cabinets. She hadn't been inside this house since he'd moved here. Gray smoke poured from the tops of two pots on the new stove by the posy-papered wall, and though a nearby window stood open, the smoke alarm was in full reveille.

Leslie acted without being told. Grabbing a pot holder, she made for the stove and pulled pots off burners, though all dials pointed to the "off" position, then set them in the chrome sink, since she couldn't spot any warming pads to place them on. Blaine flapped a wet dish towel, working to get the smoke headed out the window. Regardless, the strident buzz overhead continued. He disappeared from the room. The abrupt silence that followed proved to Leslie he'd finally shut off the alarm.

Perspiration dripped from his face and neck and dampened his hair; disappointment clouded his eyes.

Leslie looked into the pots. "I think these beans can be salvaged. It appears as if only the bottom ones burned. The top ones look fine. Same with the carrots. Rinse off what's left of the glaze, add fresh sauce, and they'll be as good as new."

His expression relaxed into a grateful smile. "Hey, who's the chef here?" He opened the oven door and frowned. "Not much of one. The roast got burnt, too."

Leslie stooped to peer in. "You'll just need to slice off the top. Those baked potatoes look good."

"You sound as if you've done this before."

"Yup, I've had the occasional burnt meal." She tilted her head. "Why are you smiling at me like that?"

The look in his eyes was kind. "I like to hear you talk. How you Vermonters drawl out your vowels and drop a lot of your R's."

"And you Texans drawl all your R's—and all the other consonants and vowels besides." Leslie laughed.

"Yes, ma'am, I reckon we do." He purposefully drew out the words in a slow, lazy manner. "But it's the little differences that make life more interesting, don't you think?"

The statement made Leslie wonder if more lay behind his casual words. Or was she only hoping it did? Again, she reminded herself this was no date. Too bad it wasn't. Blaine seemed like a good sport, and for the first time in a long while, she felt drawn to a man. In the half hour that followed, they actually kept a conversation going throughout dinner, comparing all the various and droll Texas and Vermont sayings they knew of and chuckling over both.

"It took me half a day to figure out what Mr. Meeker meant by a 'dooryard,'" Blaine admitted with a grin as he wiped his mouth and threw his napkin on his empty plate. "I'd never heard of it as being the yard just outside the front or back door before that."

"You should have heard my grandfather's old sayings. I think he made half of them up on the spur of the moment."

"He would've been in stiff competition with my grandpa Joe. I'll never forget him telling me, 'A feller ain't got no business swattin' flies that ain't in his own kitchen.'"

She grinned. "That's a good one. What exactly does it mean?"

"I was just a boy when he told me and didn't have a clue. But I reckon it means not to stick your nose into your neighbor's affairs."

" 'I reckon,'" she teased, loving his southwestern drawl. "At least they'll keep each other good company in heaven."

Blaine agreed. "How about taking a walk with me? I've wanted to check out that covered bridge near here ever since the weather warmed."

Leslie blinked, surprised by his swift change of topic and that he would want to prolong their time together. But then, so did she.

"First, let me help with the dishes."

"It can wait. I want to grab what sun we have left. Just let me run upstairs a minute. I'll be right back."

Leslie watched him go then surveyed the kitchen. As long as she had to wait for him, she may as well rinse the dishes.

Blaine doused himself with his dad's cologne, since Dear Granny recommended his appearance be at its top-notch best. He winced at the acrid scent. Did cologne get more potent with age, or was that how this stuff actually smelled? Hoping to rid himself of the majority of it, he scrubbed a damp towel along his neck and jaw. He'd run out of his own cologne last Sunday but wanted to mask the faint odor of smoke and sweat that now traced his skin and clothing. In any other situation, he would take time to jump in the shower and clean himself up, but he didn't want Leslie to get the idea that he'd forgotten about her. Instead, he changed into a bright red sports shirt.

So far, everything had gone pretty well with the date, save for a few blackened beans and carrots. Of course, he should have tried out that new stove first and gotten accustomed to it before inviting Leslie over for dinner. No use thinking about it now. The biggest surprise was that they hadn't run out of things to talk about. Maybe all those years of storing up his words had created a gusher, like an oil well suddenly struck. Stranger still, Blaine found he enjoyed talking with Leslie, something he couldn't say about the majority of his former dates, not that there had been all that many. But the real reason he'd initiated and carried the conversations had been due to what Dear Granny wrote in reply to his letter—that for a date or even a relationship to succeed there had to be some form of frequent verbal interaction between the two parties. "Just relax and be yourself" had been a piece of advice Granny had given.

Her answer rang with truth. How else could two people learn about each other without communicating? He just hoped the gusher would continue to flow and not suddenly be capped.

Leslie's smile faltered as Blaine approached, but she found it again and pulled on her sweater. "Are you sure you want to walk all the way to the bridge? It's almost two miles."

"What's two miles?" He shrugged it off.

"Okay, I'm game if you are. I also know of a shortcut through the trees, if you want to take that, but the ground's not always even there." She cupped one hand over her nose and mouth and gave a weak cough.

"I can handle a few hills or rocks." He noticed as she walked with him outdoors that she covered her mouth and coughed again. "I hope you're not catching a cold. Or is it allergies?"

"No." She glanced down as if embarrassed. "I'm fine."

After at least five minutes of silence during their walk that took them farther into the trees, Blaine scrounged for a new topic. "How's your grandma doing?"

Leslie looked at him in surprise. "How do you know my grandmother?"

"I only know of her. I overheard a few ladies at church talking about going to visit. From what I understand, she doesn't get out much."

Leslie shook her head, her face clouding with worry. "Not at all, not since Granddad's accident fourteen months ago." She heaved a sigh. "If you've heard people talk, you probably also know he was only a few blocks from home when it happened. A car ran a stop sign and broadsided him. Nana might have been able to get over that, but then an old friend of hers died in a car accident not a week after Granddad's. She hasn't driven or ridden inside a vehicle since his funeral."

"That must be tough. She stays inside all the time?"

"No. She enjoys working in her garden, so she does go outdoors. Just not off her property. And she seems happy when I visit every Tuesday, but the truth is she's withdrawn from everyone, from life itself." She bunched her hands in the pockets of her sweater, drawing it around her middle. "Those friends of hers who've known her a long time and do go see her tell me later that she's changed and isn't like they remembered at all. Some quit visiting because it was hard on them to see her like that. I call every night, just to check up on her and see how she's doing or if she needs anything. But she rarely wants to talk for long."

"It must be hard on you, too."

Leslie shrugged, as if she didn't want to talk about it. She looked beyond a cluster of trees. "See that river over there? It's the same one that runs by my grandmother's. Her house is right next to it."

"Maybe she'd agree to a ride in a boat."

Leslie only looked at him.

"I wasn't trying to be funny. If you have one or know someone who does, that might be a step toward getting her over this slump and helping her ditch any fears to step foot off her property. Suggest an outing next time you visit. It couldn't hurt."

"Hm." Leslie seemed to mull over the idea. "There's a private dock behind her house that Granddad always used for his fly-fishing. You might have something there."

They continued their trek through the woods. After about five minutes, Blaine saw a nice spot beneath some trees and suggested they rest. He wasn't tired but noticed during their walk that Leslie cupped her nose and mouth and coughed a few more times.

"Let's sit down for a breather." He headed for some red maples about thirty feet from the river.

She stayed on the trail. "You're tired already? You'll never last all the way to the bridge and back at this rate."

"I'm not tired, but it wouldn't hurt to sit back and take in the scenery. We've got plenty of time to get back before sunset."

Leslie studied the ground, her expression doubtful. "I'm wearing white pants."

"Not a problem."

Blaine pulled off his denim jacket and shook it out for her to sit on slapping the material against the hollow of a tree he'd chosen for their shade in the process. He spread the jacket on the grass. "There. That should protect your pants." He swatted at something buzzing around his neck.

Leslie halted her progress toward him, her eyes going wide. "Blaine. . ."

A needle prick punctured his neck below his ear. "Ow!" Something buzzed near his left shoulder. Another sharp sting punctured the inside of his arm.

"Bees!" Leslie cried. "Run for the river!"

Swatting at the winged creatures, who'd multiplied as the buzz grew louder, Blaine ran for all he was worth, not stopping until his feet splashed through water and it closed over his head.

Chapter 5

His hair and clothes damp, Blaine eyed Leslie as he sat at her kitchen table and she doctored his stings. He looked pitiful.

"I wish you would let me take you to the emergency room." Leslie swabbed the lumps with a pain-relieving cream containing tea tree oil, after having washed the areas with soap and putting ice on them per doctor's instructions. The minute he'd waded out of the river, she had helped him scrape off the stingers. Only the expected amount of swelling appeared evident on his arms and neck. Nothing pointed to an allergic reaction. At least he'd relented and allowed her to call old Dr. Freisen, a friend of Nana's, who'd grown accustomed to making house calls to her shut-in grandmother, something unheard of in this day and age. And the doctor hadn't minded giving first-aid directions to Leslie over the phone, either.

"I've been stung by bees before. I'm not allergic."

"Yes, but have you ever been stung by so many at once?" Leslie eyed the six angry red stings, then noted the humiliation that made his shoulders slump. "It could have happened to anyone, Blaine. You didn't know there was a hive in that tree."

"I should've been more careful when I heard the buzzing or at least taken better notice of my surroundings. Can you believe I was once a Boy Scout?" He shook his head and gave a self-derisive laugh. "At least the river water washed off the stench of Dad's awful cologne."

Leslie looked up in surprise. "You didn't like it either?" Embarrassed that she'd blurted the words, she set about screwing the lid back onto the jar of antiseptic cooling cream. The bitter stench of his cologne had made her cover her nose as much as she could during their walk while pretending to cough into her hand.

Blaine smiled, his first since the few seconds before he'd been attacked by bees and had sloshed out of the river. "This has been some first date, hasn't it? Burnt food. Toilet-bowl cologne. And the attack of the honeybees."

Leslie's heart gave a little jump as she pivoted to face him. He studied her eyes, which must have registered her shock, and gave a slow nod.

"Yeah, you heard right. When I asked you over, I meant this to be more than neighborly chitchat. Trouble is, I'm just not any good at asking for dates or at not having them bomb. And tonight's disaster could probably be recorded as one of

33

the top ten worst dates in history."

"It wasn't all that bad."

Blaine grinned upon hearing her hesitant words. "Thanks for sparing my wounded ego and trying to make it all better." He took gentle hold of her hands, one of which still grasped the cream-coated cotton ball. "If you'll give me another chance, I'd like to try a second time."

"Really?" Her word came out as a quick breath.

He nodded. "How about this Friday? We could visit that craft fair you were talking about earlier."

A strange bout of little-girl shyness swept through her, and she glanced down at the tiles before returning her gaze to his. "I'd like that, Blaine."

He looked at her a long time, his eyes going more serious, his jaw softening. "I should go," he said, his voice deeper than usual. "It's late, and we both have work tomorrow."

Leslie nodded, the power of speech eluding her. She had the strangest feeling he'd been about to kiss her.

"Thanks for being my nurse." He released her hands much to her disappointment and dispensed with the damp towel hanging around his shoulders, setting it on the table. He then grabbed his denim jacket lying on a chair nearby, and she walked with him to the door.

"The doctor said to take some aspirin if the pain gets bad. And don't hesitate coming over if any reactions appear and you need me to drive you to the emergency room. I mean it, Blaine. Even if it's late."

"I promise I'll come knocking down your door."

She couldn't help but return his playful grin. "Despite all the things that went wrong, I really did have a good time."

"So did I. I'll see you on Friday."

She closed the door after him, slowly spun around halfway, and pressed her back against it. Her smile lifting higher, she laid her palms flat against the wood.

Never, *never* would she have dreamed that Blaine Cartell would be interested in her! For the first time since he'd moved to Goosebury, Leslie admitted, if only to herself, that the interest was mutual. She had never allowed herself to imagine such a thing as dating Blaine, so mentally had denied any attraction toward him, other than platonic. But now that he'd made his feelings known. . .

A thought, like an invading bee, stung her bubble of joy. What if their relationship did progress and at some point he should ask for details about her job? She could never tell him she was Dear Granny. Not just because of her own mortification to be stuck with such a beat, but also he might think her a big phony if he was to discover just how mismatched she was to her vocation. Yet even if she did want to tell him the truth, Mr. Abernathy had made it clear that Dear Granny's identity mustn't be revealed.

Furrowing her brow, Leslie headed to the refrigerator for a glass of chocolate milk. They hadn't even had a second date, and she was already plotting how to deceive Blaine. No, *deceive* was too strong a word. *Withholding information* sounded better. She'd just gloss over the subject of work when and if he brought it up, but she would never lie to him.

෴

"So tell me about what you do at the paper," Blaine said to Leslie as they walked along the inside of two rows of booths that lined the closed street. Each booth, many with awnings, displayed a wide mixture of artisan crafts. Pottery, miniature sculptures, paintings, and more—all were laid out along three sides of the booth for any interested customers to buy. Food stalls were interspersed every five booths or so, and mouthwatering aromas of roasted hot dogs, spicy pasta, and caramelized popcorn all worked to create a wide mix of tempting food choices for the craft fair visitors.

She stopped walking suddenly as if perplexed by his query but seemed to recover and again kept pace with him. "It's just another beat."

"Beat?"

"A position. Journalist talk."

He nodded. "You like what you do?"

"No." Her gaze flew to his. "I mean, it's too early to tell. I'm still new at the *Gazette*."

Curiosity piquing, Blaine scrunched his brows together. "Exactly just what is it you do there?"

"Oh, you know, this and that. Have I told you about Carly? She works the entertainment beat and has the cubicle next to mine. She did the write-up on this craft fair." Her attention zipped to a nearby stall. "Oh, look, that's exactly the gift I want to get for my grandmother. She mentioned the other day that she's wanted one of those for years."

Blaine watched her uncharacteristic gung ho behavior as Leslie approached the artisan behind the stall, her hands flitting from one enamel clock to a similar one in a different color. She seemed nervous, talking more than usual, purposely veering off topic. Maybe she was one of those who preferred life's personal details to remain private. He could respect that, since he acted much the same way toward those people he didn't know well. But he sure hoped as their relationship progressed—and he had every intention of it doing so—that she would eventually trust him enough to share the details of her life with him.

Her purchase made, Leslie walked with Blaine farther down the street. A stall caught Blaine's eye with the sign "maple candy" tacked to it, and he paused. A pretty girl in a pink sweater was telling a tourist how they made the candy from maple syrup.

"Ever try a piece?" Leslie asked.

Blaine shook his head, and Leslie urged him to take one of the butterscotch-colored sample candies in leaf shapes that lay spread out on a platter. The pleasing smell of maple syrup and creamery butter tantalized his senses, and he readily complied. Sweet and rich, the soft sugar candy melted in his mouth. He complimented the candy maker and bought a box, then turned to rejoin Leslie. She spoke with a young woman whose pretty features, straight dark hair, and almost black eyes had a strong hint of Native American to them.

He walked their way, noticing Leslie seemed a bit tense. "You bought some maple candy. Great. It's the best." She glanced at the woman, then at him. "Blaine, this is Carly, a friend of mine."

Carly's head dipped in greeting.

"Pleased to meet you." Blaine stuck out his hand. Carly seemed surprised, then shook it with a grin.

"You're the Cartells' son, aren't you? From Texas. Of course you are; your accent gives you away." Her smile didn't disappear but faded as her expression grew serious. "I was sorry to hear about your parents, Blaine. I didn't know them well, but I met them a time or two. They donated to some of the worthier charities in Goosebury and often helped put on these fairs."

"Really?" Blaine didn't know that. He couldn't picture his sports-loving dad at one of these artisan stalls. "Leslie tells me you work at the paper and have the entertainment beat?"

"Why, yes." Carly's eyes danced. "Though I don't know why she would mention me in conversation." She turned her grin on Leslie. "Surely there are more interesting things to discuss than what *I* do at the paper? Like what you do, for instance?"

Leslie's gaze shot from Carly to Blaine, then down to the ground. She shoved her hands deep into the pockets of her sweater, bunching it around her middle.

"Relax, Les. I was only teasing." Carly shrugged. "I guess it's just my nature."

Leslie offered a wan smile, but the uneasy look didn't leave her eyes.

"Listen, I'd better scoot. My date is probably looking for me. See you in the funny pages, Les. Nice meeting you, Blaine." With a flip of her hand in a wave, the vivacious woman took off in the opposite direction.

"Your friend reminds me of my cousin," Blaine said, aware that Leslie still seemed uneasy. "She's a real go-getter. Works on a ranch."

"Did you? Work on a ranch?" The stiffness left her shoulders as they resumed walking.

"Naw. I once ran a chuck wagon when some area ranchers held a weekend roundup. One like they had in the old days, when the West was young. I was their traveling cook."

"That sounds interesting. Tell me more."

For the next several minutes, Blaine did, surprised at how easy it was to talk to Leslie. The pleasing sound of stringed instruments soon reached their ears, and they approached a small crowd who watched a group of four musicians play. Blaine quit talking so they could listen.

"Did you hear on the news about what happened this morning?" a blond teenager standing near Blaine asked her circle of three friends. "About forty miles south of town, some carjacker took a woman's car with her in it. She said on the news she was so scared. But she remembered something she'd read that Dear Granny wrote in her column about how to 'be bold when adversity hits, refuse to be fearful, and stand up for what's right.'"

"You mean the Dear Granny in the paper?"

"Uh-huh." The girl took a sip of her drink through a straw before continuing. "She said Granny's reply was related to something someone else asked the column, about how to talk to a daughter regarding a bad boyfriend or something. But anyway, when that guy's gun was on her, Granny's answer was all that came to her head, and it helped her get through the ordeal."

"That is too weird," another girl said.

"That's not all," the first teenager inserted. "She began talking to this guy about God and Jesus and stuff, and he ended up turning himself in to the police."

"You're kidding! I'll bet that'll get the paper publicity."

The second girl frowned. "The column is just a bunch of Bible talk. My mom said it's a way the *Gazette* is using to try to force religion down people's throats. She's read every issue."

The first girl turned on her. "But you have to admit, Trina, what happened with that carjacker is awesome stuff. And no one's forcing anyone to buy the paper. Your mom doesn't have to read it if she doesn't want to. My parents take the *Goosebury Gazette,* and they have horoscopes in there and stuff, but I don't read them."

"I've got to go," the girl named Trina said, looking put out. "My parents will come searching for me if I don't get back soon."

The girls said their good-byes and departed. Blaine looked toward Leslie, puzzled by the sad look in her eyes as she stared after Trina.

She seemed to shake herself out of whatever stupor held her bound. "Blaine, I've had a great time, but I think we should call it an evening. I need to get home."

"Feeling okay?"

"Sure. I just have a load of laundry needing to be done before tomorrow, and a few other chores to tackle besides."

Blaine was disappointed but agreed. Still, he couldn't help but feel that Leslie was bothered by something—and it didn't have anything to do with household chores or laundry.

As they walked toward the car, Leslie thought about the teenagers' conversation. She was astonished to hear the column was having such an impact on the town but sobered that some of the people probably felt as the girl Trina did. She knew Trina was Carly's cousin and wondered if all their family were against God.

"So what do you think about the 'Dear Granny' column?"

Blaine's question took Leslie by surprise. "Me?" Frantically she sought for something equivocal to say. "What's to think about it?"

"For or against?"

"Oh, that. For. Definitely for."

"Yeah. Me, too. The old lady's pretty smart."

Leslie gave a muffled sound of agreement and swung her attention to the nearest stand. She needed to divert the topic, fast, before he started delving into Leslie's knowledge regarding Dear Granny's identity. It stood to reason he would, since he knew Leslie worked at the same paper.

"Before we go, I'd like one of those soft pretzels with mustard. Want one?" Her stomach clenched in protest at the thought of another bite of fair food, but she managed what she hoped passed for an enthusiastic smile.

"Uh, sure." He looked at her strangely, probably wondering why she should be so hungry after having just had fajitas thirty minutes ago. "I'll buy."

Before she could step toward the counter, Blaine moved forward and bought two pretzels, also grabbing packets of mustard.

In the car, little was said between them as they each ate their pretzel and he drove them home, but like the time in the garden it was a comfortable silence. How long could such camaraderie continue? Not long, she was sure. She perpetually felt on the defensive about him finding out she was Dear Granny, though she'd managed to field his questions with something resembling ambiguity.

Once they arrived on their street, Leslie instructed him to park in his double garage and she'd walk to her house. She noticed his parents' old sedan sitting inside.

"Engine coughed her last a few weeks ago," Blaine explained as he pulled in. "I'm keeping her for spare parts."

"I wondered why you bought Mr. Meeker's old car," she admitted. A grin tilted her lips at his obvious surprise that she knew of the previous owner. "No one could fail to notice his new ten-gallon hat, since he wears it everywhere he goes. That was nice of you."

He looked away, evidently embarrassed. "Well, to tell the truth, I don't wear them all that much, so I can't say I miss it. My dad, on the other hand, now he wore baseball caps all the time."

"I remember." She didn't fail to notice how he casually dismissed his act of generosity toward Mr. Meeker—she'd heard both about the hat and Blaine paying more than the old sedan was worth.

They exited the car, and Leslie glanced at the stacks of cardboard cartons along the wall.

"I have so much stuff I need to get rid of that was Mom and Dad's," Blaine explained, "but I don't know what to do with most of it."

"If you'd like, I could help," she offered as he came around the back end of the car to join her. "There's a tag sale coming up in a few weeks—it's a big town event—and I could help you sort through the cartons to prepare for it. If you want to join in, I mean. Proceeds can be kept or used for charity."

"That sounds like a plan." He nodded. "I'd appreciate it."

"Well. . ." She shifted her gaze toward her house. She didn't want their time together to end, but knew she should go. A big stack of Dear Granny letters awaited her, not to mention the skirt and blouse she had to wash.

"I'll walk you home."

"That's not necessary, Blaine. I only live next door."

"Halfway then."

"Okay." She wasn't about to admit her relief that he'd pushed the idea.

"The garden looks nice," she said as they slowly walked by it. "I love those lavender daylilies with the ruffled edges."

"Most of the credit goes to you for the way it looks." He moved toward his flowerbed and hunkered down. "This the one you meant?" When she saw his intent, she bridged the short distance and put her hand to his shoulder.

"No, Blaine, leave it. The flowers are too pretty. If you break that one off its stalk, it will soon wither and die. I'd much rather see it every day, thriving in your garden, than for just a few days in a vase on my table."

He stood and turned, putting them within inches of each other. Her heart quickened a beat at his nearness.

"Leslie, you're one special woman. Anyone ever tell you that?" Boldness overtook his manner even while the expression in his eyes softened. "I'd sure like to kiss you."

Stunned but wanting the same thing, she barely nodded.

His warm fingers wrapped around her hands, and gently, slowly he tugged her close against him. As their lips met, his eyes closed, and she did the same with hers. Butterfly light, tender, warm. Her first kiss was all she'd ever dreamed it would be.

Within seconds, his lips lifted from hers. A moment of shyness hit, and Leslie's face heated. She glanced at his shirt collar, then, finding courage, up into his eyes, hoping for another kiss as sweet as the first. For a second, she thought he might have read her mind. His stare intensified, and his eyes grew darker, sending her thoughts into a whirl. His thumbs brushed over her palms, producing tingles that danced all the way through her.

He lifted their clasped hands between them. She felt the quickened beat of his heart against her fingers.

"I should let you go home," he said, "though I confess it's the last thing I want to do right now."

Her mouth felt too dry to speak. Her heart thudded hard against her rib cage when he lifted their clasped hands higher and slightly dipped his head to touch his lips to her fingers. "Good night, special lady."

Before Leslie's numbed mind could form a reply or she could find enough breath to answer his hushed words, Blaine released her hands, gave her one of his lazy, close-lipped smiles, then walked back to his garage.

Leslie let out a slow, shaky breath, watching until he disappeared from sight, then turned toward her own door. She may have no past love life with which to compare her current situation, but she knew enough to recognize she was falling hard and fast for Blaine. Yet in withholding information from him as she'd done all day and planned to continue doing, she worried that her landing could end up being painful. The question uppermost in her mind was if her job was worth that risk. At least Mr. Abernathy had promised her that her position as Dear Granny was only short-term.

Chapter 6

Leslie sat in her cubicle, looking over her rough copy for the obituary section. Besides "Dear Granny," she'd also been given obits. Wryly she recalled her first day here and how she would have jumped at the chance to work the obituaries and avoid being Dear Granny. Now she had both jobs.

Her eyes bleary, she averted her gaze to the cubicle wall and the calendar picture showing a field of flowers. Again her mind relived the tender moment with Blaine. Had he really kissed her, kissed her hand? Or had her skin-tingling interaction with the gentleman-cowboy been a dream? No, not a dream. A memory this vivid could only have stemmed from reality. Not mere imagination.

"Since Big Chief dispensed with smoke signals long ago," Carly said, breaking into Leslie's reverie, "he said to tell you he wants to talk to you." Despite her tongue-in-cheek announcement, Carly frowned.

"You okay?" Leslie asked. "You seem a bit miffed."

"Abernathy didn't like the way I handled an interview. No big deal. I'm thinking of quitting and finding another job, anyway."

"Oh, Carly, no. You're the only real friend I've got in this place."

Carly leaned against the cubicle. "I'll be around. We'll still see each other in town now and then, I'm sure. It's small enough. And anyway, I'm undecided about my future here. I might stay on awhile."

"I hope so. We still have to do lunch some day soon, remember. So how about today?"

A flash of surprise lit Carly's face, followed by doubt. She slid back onto her chair. "Can't. I have an appointment."

"Oh. Okay. Another time then."

Attributing Carly's curt answering nod to whatever just went on with their boss, Leslie gathered her wits about her, stood, and walked to Mr. Abernathy's office.

He looked up from writing something and smiled. It was the first real smile she'd ever seen on the man.

"Miss Edwards." He laid his pen down and stood, an abnormal gesture of courtesy he'd never shown until today. "Please sit down."

Please? Leslie hadn't realized her boss's vocabulary contained the word.

He resumed his seat after she took hers. "I'll come straight to the point. Since 'Dear Granny' has gone into print, sales have almost tripled. Tripled!" He clapped his hands together and rubbed them. "Thanks to you, we've had subscribers from as far as Montpelier and Rutland. They're coming from everywhere. And now we're looking into airing the *Goosebury Gazette* over the Internet. It's time this paper entered the twenty-first century and the cyber world."

"That's really great, Mr. Abernathy." Leslie managed a smile. Despite his enthusiasm—or maybe because of it—she felt a sense of impending doom.

He reached down to drag from the desk where it was propped a large burlap postal bag, plowed his hand inside its confines, and withdrew a packet of envelopes. "These are all yours. And there are more like it in a similar bag."

Leslie gaped. "Surely those aren't all letters for 'Dear Granny'!" She would never get finished reading and choosing from them before the next issue was due to circulate.

"Letters, yes. But not all are letters seeking advice. The majority is fan mail, Miss Edwards. I took the liberty of looking through a number of them, of course."

"Fan mail?"

"Yes, fan mail. In light of the rave reviews and massive amount of publicity the column's received during the past weeks—in good part due to the statewide newscast about that lady and her carjacker—I've made a decision."

Leslie swallowed. "You have?"

"Your beat as Dear Granny is permanent as of today, and to go along with it, I'm issuing you a two-dollar-an-hour raise." Smiling, he leaned back in his chair and stuck a peppermint stick between his teeth as if assured of her thrilled response.

"Permanent?" Leslie gripped the chair arms. "Oh, no. I couldn't do that. You told me when I first started working here. . ." She sought for a more logical way to phrase her objection.

"Is there a problem, Miss Edwards?" His gaze grew steely, the smile slipping from his face.

"What about Fern Wallace? I can't take her job away from her. This was only supposed to be temporary until she recovers."

"Ms. Wallace decided to take a leave of absence. The injury has literally put her on her back for a long time. When and if she should return to the *Gazette*, there'll be another job here for her."

Leslie continued shaking her head. "Oh, no. No. Please, Mr. Abernathy, I can't do this." She swallowed hard, knowing what she was about to reveal could cost her any future position at the paper. "The truth is, I didn't write those replies."

"What?" The chair protested with a loud squeak as he sat forward.

"Oh, I didn't plagiarize or anything like that—but I did take Nana's words and make it more journalistically appropriate." She sounded like a blithering idiot. "What I mean is, she gave me advice on how to answer, and I wrote the replies down using my own words."

His gaze grew reflective as he stared at his candy stick. "Yup, now that I think on it, I can see a lot of Lily in there." He chuckled fondly, then shifted a glance toward Leslie, whose mouth had dropped open in astonishment that he not only knew her grandmother's first name but also used it so casually. And had he actually chuckled?

He cleared his throat. "I'm not overly concerned with the methods you use, Miss Edwards. Reporters have done worse to get a story, and what you did wasn't so bad. What I *am* concerned about is that you have the column ready and on my desk before five o'clock Saturday."

"But, Mr. Abernathy. . ."

"You *do* want to work here, don't you, Miss Edwards?"

Leslie hesitated. Did she? If it meant a permanent beat as Dear Granny, she wasn't so sure.

His expression smoothed into one almost fatherly, and she sensed he was about to change tactics. "Think about it over the week. I advise you not to make snap decisions regarding your career. This column could be the ticket to your advent as a world-renowned journalist. Think about that. Should you decide to leave the paper years from now, it would be one of the best clips you could present to a prospective employer in that scrapbook of yours. Of course, I'll provide you with a glowing recommendation should that day arrive. Now, I have business to get back to." He changed his tone to its usual gruff self. "Those bags are too heavy for one person to carry. Give me the keys to your car, and I'll order a couple of men to put them inside the trunk."

Order. A word that fit Mr. Abernathy to a tee. The role of a dictator would suit him well. Wordlessly, Leslie returned to her desk to collect the requested keys. Her thoughts, on the other hand, scattered far and wide.

🜏

Blaine approached Leslie's front door, hoping his neighbor wouldn't think him the type to swat flies that weren't buzzing around in his own kitchen, as Grandpa Joe would have said. But during his morning prayer and cup of coffee, as Blaine sought the Lord for leading concerning his relationship with Leslie, he'd felt led to proceed with what they'd discussed on their first date.

Seconds after his knock, the door swung inward. Her dark brows rose and her bottom lip dropped in surprise. Over one arm, she carried a large tote. Keys jingled from her other hand.

"Heading to your grandmother's?" he asked.

"Yes, how'd you know?"

"You mentioned your Tuesday visits when we walked in the woods." He bolstered his courage. "Today's my day off. Mind if I come along?"

"Come along?" She remained motionless, but wariness lit her eyes as if she'd taken a huge mental step backward.

Was she regretting their kiss and now felt nervous in his company? Had he been too reckless? Maybe so. But after staring into her warm, hazel-brown eyes that evening, he'd been unable to help himself.

"I don't think today would be a good idea, Blaine. Some other time maybe."

Disappointed at her reply and wondering if she was trying to avoid him, he held up a plastic shopping bag. "Mrs. Vance asked me to drop these gardening books off at your grandmother's. She said she wants them ASAP."

"Mrs. Vance?" The expression that crossed Leslie's face could only be described as flabbergasted.

"Yeah. I swung by her house this morning."

"Why?"

"Come with me, and I'll show you." He smiled in entreaty.

She stepped outside and locked her front door. "I can only give you a few minutes. I'm late as it is."

"Fair enough." Sliding his free hand casually into his jacket pocket, he led the way down the path through the woods. The morning had been overcast, and the temperature had taken another dive, but now it was pleasant, and the sun shone high in the sky.

"Blaine, just what is this all about?" He watched Leslie take in the familiar, timbered landscape all around her as if trying to hunt up a clue to her question. Her long legs easily kept stride with his rapid pace.

"It's a surprise."

"What kind of surprise?"

"You'll see."

He didn't fail to notice her little huff of exasperation. But there was a sparkle to her eyes that had been missing before; so then she did like games.

Soon they reached the river's edge where he'd docked the small aluminum boat at a short pier. Obviously clueless, Leslie looked his way.

"I borrowed Mr. Vance's fishing boat. I figured today was as good a day as any to take your grandmother out on the river."

As his meaning dawned, her face slackened, and the look in her eyes softened. "Blaine, that's so sweet of you. But I have to be honest. I'm not sure this idea of yours will work."

"We won't know unless we try it, right?" He stepped into the four-person boat, which rocked with his movements, and offered her a hand.

Still she hesitated. "She might get upset or think we're interfering."

"Leslie, I'm not going to put a gun to her head and force her into the boat. I'm not going to say a word except to introduce myself. I'll let you do all the convincing." He grinned.

Her lips flickered upward in reply. Still, she cast an uncertain look at her cloth tote, then back at him. Finally, she took his hand.

"If you're worried about your bag getting wet, I can store it in the tackle box. It's a big one, and I think there's room." He held out his hand for it.

"No." Leslie clutched her bag closer to her hip as if it contained gold nuggets. "I mean, thanks, but it'll be okay."

Blaine mentally shrugged. Women and their purses. "Then we're off," he said as he took his place at the back near the outboard motor and she slid into the plank seat in front of him.

"It would appear we are." Her smile seemed less than eager, and he wondered about that, but at least she'd agreed to come along. As he handed her a required safety flotation device and buckled his around him, he hoped her grandmother would be just as agreeable.

Chapter 7

Over the thrumming of the motor, Leslie considered her plight. Her rational-thinking mind must be turned off for her to have agreed to this outing with Blaine. She had a deadline to meet, and the "Dear Granny" letters she'd fished from the postal bag still in the trunk of her car would now have to wait.

Holding her tote closer to her body in an effort to protect its contents from the spray, she realized her mistake. She should've left the bag with the letters inside her house, but of course she'd had no idea what Blaine planned. Doubtless, she would need to return to Nana's once this river excursion ended. But she couldn't fault Blaine for his considerate gesture. Rather, she admired him for it.

Leslie had worried for months about her grandmother's abrupt departure from a normal life. At first, Leslie explained Nana's behavior away as an expression of grieving, but fourteen months of self-imposed seclusion was just too long. When Leslie realized more than grief plagued Nana, that a fear of driving or riding in road vehicles also attacked her, this caused Leslie great concern. She didn't understand how a woman who'd always been considered a pillarlike Christian could be tricked by such a fear, and daily Leslie prayed for her grandmother's peace of mind. As far as Leslie could tell, it was the lone weakness Nana suffered.

If this idea of Blaine's worked, relief seemed a weak word in comparison to what Leslie would feel. Her deadline came secondary to Nana's well-being. Besides, she reminded herself, this outing was only a delay, not a substitute for working on the letters. As Blaine said, it was definitely worth a try.

"You'll have to tell me how to get there." Blaine raised his voice to be heard over the motor once he'd maneuvered the boat past the pier and headed for the center of the river.

Leslie called instructions over her shoulder. Within minutes, the back of Nana's house came into view.

Evidently Nana heard the motor, for as they drew up close to the short dock Leslie's grandfather had once used, the garden gate swung open and Nana appeared. With her hand on the crown of her wide-brimmed straw bonnet, she set a quick pace across the grass to the river's edge.

"Leslie," she exclaimed. Her eyes briefly turned to Blaine, then back again in curiosity. "When you were so late, I was worried. What's this all about? Did you have car trouble?"

"Sorry about being late, Nana. Mom phoned, and of course, I had to take the call. And no, no car trouble."

"How is your mother? And the family?"

"They're well. The girls went to summer camp last week." She cleared her throat. "It's such a nice day, and we thought you might like to enjoy it with us. This is my neighbor Blaine. He moved here from Texas in January."

"Hello, Blaine," Nana said with a slight nod, obviously still curious.

He gave a friendly nod in return.

"The truth is, Nana. . ." Leslie halted that remark. She didn't want to sound too logical; that might put Nana off. Silently she rephrased her pitch. "We thought you might like a break from it all. Since the sun came out, it's so nice outside, and we thought you'd enjoy a ride on the river."

"You want me to ride in that thing?" Nana looked at the little moss green fishing boat as if it were an alligator that had swum all the way from Florida just to gobble her down for lunch. "I couldn't possibly."

"I've had a lot of experience maneuvering these," Blaine inserted smoothly, his hand still at the tiller. "In Texas, my grandpa Joe and I took his motorboat out to the lake every summer. And there's not a soul on the river today. Probably because of the rain earlier. I dried off the seats so you won't get your clothes wet. Of course, we have a life vest for you, too."

A look close to longing entered Nana's eyes. "I don't know. . . ."

"We could stop at the restaurant near River Road and have lunch there. My treat." Leslie knew how her grandmother liked their crab salad topped with layers of sliced smoked salmon and grated cucumber. "It's only a short walk up the path from the pier."

"But I'm not dressed for such a thing, Leslie." Nana looked down at her jeans and flowered, button-down shirt.

"It's casual dining this time of day. I'm wearing jeans, too." She could feel her grandmother beginning to waver and said a prayer underneath her breath.

Nana doubtfully eyed the trace of water at the bottom of the boat. "Are you sure that thing doesn't have a leak?"

"No leak," Blaine said. "I checked."

"Well, maybe just this once. I suppose I should go get my Wellies on so I don't get my shoes wet."

Leslie almost cheered. "We'll wait right here."

"Before you go inside," Blaine inserted, "Mrs. Vance asked me to give you these gardening books."

"Oh—thank you!" Enthused, Nana took them from him. "I saw them listed in a mail advertisement flyer and asked Margaret to get them for me."

"But you are coming right back?" Leslie didn't want the books to give her grandmother a convenient excuse not to join them.

"Of course. I said I would, didn't I?"

While her grandmother walked to her house, Leslie moved to the seat by the pointed bow, thinking Nana would feel safer seated in the boat's wide middle. Blaine gave her a big, close-lipped smile as if realizing her intention. His approval pleased her.

Nana was gone so long Leslie wondered if she'd changed her mind and was poring through the books, but soon she walked outside and across the wooden dock. She'd put on a crocheted sweater and carried a vinyl purse over one arm. Blaine took her hands, helping her inside. The boat tipped waterward as she stepped aboard but righted itself when she scurried to the bench seat near the middle. Leslie handed her a life vest, and she snatched it from her hands, quickly pulling it around her. The boat rocked as Blaine returned to his place at the back.

Nana gripped the seat hard. "Perhaps this wasn't such a good idea."

"Relax, Nana," Leslie soothed, helping her fasten the preserver around her waist. "It'll be fun."

"Your idea of fun and my idea are entirely different, Leslie Anne." But as the minutes passed and they glided over the waters with the wind blowing strong in their faces, Leslie darted a look over her shoulder and saw her grandmother had relaxed. Even smiled.

"I see the Landons built onto their house," Nana called over the roar of the motor.

"They felt the need after Sharon delivered twins." Leslie didn't mention the addition had been completed last year.

Another backward glance showed Nana observing her surroundings with interest, as a tourist might who'd never visited the area. Leslie also studied the scenery, trying to see it as her grandmother did.

A glimpse of the Green Mountains spread out before them, miles in the distance, and on both sides of the wide river, tall stands of pine grew intermingled among sugar maples, poplars, birches, and many other hardwood trees. In late autumn, Leslie loved to watch showers of red, orange, and yellow leaves flutter onto the silver water's surface and pad it, making it seem like a brightly printed bedspread covering the ground. Now that early summer was upon them, the trees offered a thick, endless scope of green broken by the occasional timbered house.

After several minutes, at Nana's request, they stopped to just listen and watch, allowing the river's gentle current to carry them. Leslie pivoted around on her seat to face Nana and noticed Blaine held one of the oars. Probably to have ready in case they drifted too close to shore.

"I'd forgotten how peaceful this area is," Nana said quietly while they were treated to the sight of a powerful bull moose, its antlers barely grown, drinking at the water's edge not thirty feet away. The massive beast seemed unconcerned with his watchers and lifted his great head to look directly at them, then slowly turned to reenter the forest.

Her forearms resting on her knees, Leslie relaxed, taking in God's artistic rendering in their small corner of the world. Since Blaine had cut the motor, all was quiet except for nature's sweet song. Birds sang a melody around them. Insects chirruped from the trees nearby. The water gently lapped against the boat, providing a sluggish, sleepy sound and feel. No one talked, and Leslie enjoyed the calm interlude.

After a long while, Blaine lazily spoke. "If I don't get something to eat soon, I may just lay back and catch a few winks here. Anyone else hungry?"

Leslie and Nana agreed, and within twenty minutes they sat at a small table in the restaurant, enjoying the delicious food. Leslie was amazed at the number of people who'd come by their table to talk to Nana, expressing their delight at seeing her there. Even the manager, whom Nana babysat when he was a boy, insisted her meal be on the house.

The only alarming moment occurred when Blaine brought up the "Dear Granny" column, commenting on a few of the more recent letters and asking what they thought about her advice to Living in Fear, a frightened young girl in an abusive marriage. Leslie fished for a way to change the topic. To her surprise, Nana beat her to it, glossing over her agreement with the reply given, then going on and on about how good the crab and salmon salad was. Blaine seemed satisfied and thankfully didn't reopen the topic.

As she ate her order of cornmeal-crusted rainbow trout, peppered just the way she liked it, Leslie's mind returned to the letter. Nana had admitted upon reading it that she'd felt a strange unease in answering, but Leslie couldn't ignore the poor woman's plea for advice on how to protect her children and save her marriage. She knew Nana's discomfort must stem from the fact she'd once befriended a lawyer's wife who'd lived in an abusive marriage, but that family had moved away years ago. With Nana's help, Leslie advised the reader to take her children and flee from what could easily be a life-or-death situation, also directing her to locate a women's shelter for aid and not to consider returning to her husband unless he received and completed all counseling needed. No woman or child deserved to be beaten.

The food Leslie previously enjoyed seemed to curdle in her stomach at the thought. Blaine rose from his chair to pay the bill, resisting Leslie's efforts to pay for her food. He insisted lunch was on him since he owed her a meal to make up for, in his words, "the charcoal offerings" of their first date.

As soon as he walked out of earshot, Nana reached across the table and squeezed Leslie's hand. "Give it all to the Lord, Leslie. All we can do for that woman and her family now is continue to pray for them."

Leslie returned the squeeze. How well Nana knew her. "I wonder how many more are out there like her, though. I never knew giving advice to the lovelorn would end up being such a significant task. I'm not sure I'm up to it—even with your help, Nana."

"When the situation seems too difficult, just keep saying, 'I can do everything through him who gives me strength.' That verse from Philippians has held me up more times than I can count."

"Pastor Neil talked about that last Sunday." Leslie picked up a curly fry and bit into it. "You should come with me to church next week. Everyone asks about you."

"Not yet." Nana concentrated on eating her seafood salad. "I enjoy watching church services on TV. Since I got that Inspiration Channel with the cable, I have it on all the time, so I don't feel as if I'm missing out on any important spiritual messages."

"But Pastor Neil made it clear how important it is to fellowship with other believers. Without that, we can't get the encouragement or support we need from fellow Christians."

"I have you, don't I?" Nana smiled. "And a few ladies from church come now and then to visit. Not to mention my weekly visits from Jeremy, the boy who delivers my groceries. I'm doing fine."

No, she wasn't, but Leslie didn't argue. Instead, she took a sip of her lemon water. Leslie surmised that since the church didn't sit beside the river like this restaurant and could only be reached by car, it was all that held Nana back from attending. She wondered why Nana didn't apply the verse she'd quoted toward her own fear, then scolded herself for the thought. Nana might not yet be able to rid herself of any psychological fear—what her doctor pegged it as being—but God could certainly deliver her from it. At least she'd taken this mammoth step by agreeing to the boating excursion.

"You did enjoy today, didn't you, Nana?"

"More than I thought I would when you invited me. And if you two wouldn't mind dropping me off at Margaret's for an hour or so, I'd love to surprise her and come by for a friendly face-to-face chat. Then you youngsters can putter away for some time alone together without an old, decrepit lady like me along to intrude." The look in Nana's eyes was positively crafty.

Leslie laughed. "You are anything but old and decrepit! And your mind is sharper than anyone's I know. I sense you're trying to pair us off."

"I like Blaine. And he likes you."

"You really think so?" Embarrassed by her eager reply, Leslie concentrated on tearing a smidgen from her buttery roll and popping it into her mouth. "I don't know. He's probably just being kind. Neighborly."

"Neighborly? Anyone with eyes in their head can see he's interested in you, Leslie."

"Maybe. I just wish I knew how to tell the difference between platonic friendship and personal interest." Despite Blaine admitting he wanted to be with her and his parting kiss of last week, Leslie was still unsure. She'd seen couples kiss who later protested they were just friends and that the kiss didn't mean anything, and she felt too inexperienced to tell the difference between casual and serious relationships. Maybe he meant he wanted to spend time with her as a friend. He probably only offered the kiss because he thought it was the way she'd wanted him to end their evening together.

And he'd been right.

She let out a long sigh. "I'm just so not used to any of this, Nana."

"Any of what, dear?"

"A man's possible interest in me." Self-conscious, Leslie used the napkin to wipe off her fingers. "I mean, I'm not exactly considered a great catch."

"Oh, *poff.* Somebody's obviously filled your head with a lot of nonsense. You're sweet, thoughtful, talented, and cute. What more could a man ask for?"

"And you, dear Nana, are terribly prejudiced. But I love you for it." Leslie sobered. "I suppose while we have the chance, we really should be discussing when we'll work on those letters."

Nana seemed to think a moment. "Leave them with me. I'll call tonight with my answers and save you a trip back."

"That sounds like a plan." Leslie darted a glance toward the front lobby and the cashier and saw Blaine sticking his wallet in his pocket. "I almost choked on my water when he brought up the column." She snatched up her tote and quickly retrieved the bundle of letters she'd wrapped with a rubber band.

"Do you plan on ever telling Blaine about your job as Dear Granny?" Nana took the letters and placed them in her own bag.

"Are you kidding?" Leslie rethought her hasty reply. "Even if I wanted to, I'm not allowed. Mr. Abernathy made it clear no one's to know. He feels it will help public interest to remain high."

"Ronald and his schemes." Nana *tsk-tsk*ed. "He hasn't changed a bit."

Leslie let her mouth drop open slightly, just as she'd done in Mr. Abernathy's office when he called her grandmother by her first name. "That's right. You went to school with him, didn't you?"

"Yes. Your grandfather, Ronald, and I shared a class at Goosebury High. Once, many years ago, he and your grandfather fought for my attention. But that was another time and another place."

Sensing her grandmother's approach toward melancholy, Leslie rerouted the conversation. "There must be close to thirty letters in that packet I gave you. I just grabbed a handful from the top of the mailbag. You decide which five to answer."

"Mailbag?"

"I'll tell you later. Blaine's coming back."

Smiling, he approached them. "You ladies ready?"

"First, I want to call Margaret and make certain it's all right with her that I drop by. I'll be with you shortly." Nana scooted out of the booth and headed for the pay phone near the restrooms.

Blaine hiked his brow. "She's going for a visit?"

Leslie nodded. "She would like us to drop her off for an hour. You were right, Blaine. This boat outing was a great idea."

"Glad I could help and that the plan worked."

"I just hope we aren't taking too much of your time. She mentioned wanting to spend an hour at Margaret's, and you must have more important things to do with your day than to waste it all on us."

He shook his head slowly. "Leslie, I would never consider a day with you as time wasted."

She offered a weak smile. Were his words delivered in a spirit of friendship or something else entirely? She wished she could tell, but since she didn't know, she decided it safer to put emotional distance between them.

Maybe he shouldn't have said what he did.

Blaine glanced over at Leslie, who had seemed unwilling to look at him ever since they'd left the restaurant and dropped off her grandmother at her friend's home. Silence he could handle. But uncomfortable silence was another matter altogether. What should he do? He remembered Dear Granny's advice that he should just be himself. But was it good enough? His inexpert attempt at conversation had apparently landed them in this edgy atmosphere.

Easing the tiller left, he steered the boat past a grouping of rocks near the shore. They glided along a narrow bend in the river where the current moved more slowly, and the covered bridge came into view. An idea came to him, one that made him smile. He slowed the boat, pulled alongside the bank, and cut the motor. Finally, Leslie looked his way.

"We didn't get the chance to walk along the bridge on our first date because of my run-in with bees," Blaine explained. "We're here now, so we might as well give it a shot. What do you think? Are you game?"

She looked at him as though he'd suggested spraying the historical landmark with buckshot. "You mean for us to just leave the boat here and climb that embankment?"

"Why not? It's not that steep, and those rocks up the west side look like they could be a natural stairway."

"There isn't a dock nearby."

"I have rope. We could tie the boat to that tree over there. And the water is somewhat shallow here."

She shrugged, clearly undecided, and cut a glance to her white sneakers.

He tilted the motor up, stepped into the cold water that came to his jean-clad knees, and pulled the boat ashore, tying it safely. After he turned, he saw that Leslie now stood and eyed the riverbank as if she might try to leap across the few feet of water to prevent her canvas shoes from getting wet. Without a word, Blaine sloshed into the clear water, put his hands on either side of her waist, and swung her from the boat and to shore. She stumbled as he set her upon her feet, her eyes wide in surprise. An embarrassed smile flickered on her lips, and she thanked him and turned away.

Together they hiked up the embankment, discovering the stones did provide a natural stairway of sorts. On the road, Blaine stepped over the shin-high guardrail and took hold of Leslie's hand, helping her to do the same.

About the length of two train cars, the town's restored Sophia Bridge had originally been built in 1870, according to the wooden sign above the portal. What Blaine had learned was called *town lattice truss* made up the sides of the dark red bridge, which sported a gray, sloped roof of slate. The road still received a fair amount of traffic, busier during certain times of the day, and during the bridge's restoration, a pedestrian walkway had been built alongside it, one of the few in Vermont. Blaine chuckled as they approached the portal, and he lifted his gaze to see an old-timey sign nailed below the one with the bridge's name and year of construction. It warned: ONE DOLLAR FINE FOR A PERSON TO DRIVE A HORSE OR OTHER BEAST FASTER THAN A WALK, OR DRIVE MORE THAN ONE LOADED TEAM AT THE SAME TIME ON THIS BRIDGE.

Without letting go of Leslie's hand, Blaine took the lead inside the narrow, covered walkway. Diamond-shaped patches of outside light shone through the lattice, breaking up the shade. When they approached midpoint, he stopped to admire the craftsmanship of the inside wooden lattice of the ancient bridge, then turned to look through the added-on lattice of the walkway facing the river.

Leslie withdrew her hand from his to tuck her hair behind one ear. "Do you know the story behind this bridge?"

"No."

"The man who oversaw its construction had a young daughter, Sophia, his only daughter, and he doted on her. Despite her mother's insistence that such a thing was inappropriate, he often brought Sophia to watch the bridge being built." She gave him a sad smile of explanation. "I wrote an article about it when I was in high school. That's how I know all about this. The year of the bridge's completion, Sophia drowned about a mile from here where she was swimming with friends. Her father named the bridge for her."

"And is it supposed to be haunted like Emily's Bridge in Stowe Hollow?"

"How do you know about Emily's Bridge?" Leslie asked in surprise.

"Mom had a picture book of Vermont's covered bridges. I'm halfway through it and have been reading all the lore written about them. I'd like to visit as many of those nearby as I can. Texas doesn't have any. Doesn't need to since the winters aren't as cold or harsh as New England's."

"I've lived around covered bridges all my life so never thought much about them one way or the other, though I've heard this one has always been a popular kissing spot for teenagers—" Her words cut off, and he glanced at her. She evaded his gaze. "Walkers and joggers take advantage of its shelter during sudden rainstorms, too," she quickly added.

"You only heard about it?" he asked, addressing her first comment. "Didn't any of your old boyfriends bring you here?"

She was silent a moment. "I didn't have any boyfriends to kiss me here or anywhere else for that matter. Not that it's a big deal or anything. It's not."

Blaine noted her rigid jaw, which said otherwise. Her gaze latched onto the green-leafed branches of the nearby trees as if she were remembering a painful past.

All former doubts regarding how to act around her or what to say disappeared, as if carried away by the gently moving current below. More than anything Blaine knew what he wanted at this moment and hoped she felt the same.

With his hand he slowly nudged her shoulder, turning her toward him. "Can I be the first?"

At his low-voiced question, shock entered her eyes, followed by something close to embarrassed self-defense. "I wasn't hinting that you should kiss me, Blaine."

"I know. But to be honest, it's been uppermost in my mind since I laid eyes on you this morning."

"It has?" What looked like hope softened her expression. Her lips gently parted.

"Yeah." He began to lower his head. "And I kinda like the idea of being your boyfriend, too." His last words came out in a whisper, before he captured her stunned breath with his warm kiss.

Chapter 8

For the past two nights, Leslie had been unable to retrieve the mailbags from the trunk of her car and had resorted to snatching a handful of letters to read at a time instead. The first night, after her river outing with Blaine and Nana, it had rained, and last evening, the ground was muddy. Tonight promised dry ground, a full moon, and plenty of light by which to see.

Leslie went to the mudroom and opened the back door of the house, stepped through, then silently shut it behind her. The air, chilly and moist, made her give a little shiver. She darted a glance through the thinly spaced pines toward one of Blaine's top windows, noticing a light shone from there. *Must be his bedroom.* She would have to be careful he didn't spot her. If he did, knowing Blaine, he would probably come outside with an offer to help.

Feeling much like a spy on a top-secret mission, she almost gave a nervous chuckle at the absurdity of the situation. Regardless, she used stealth as she crossed the grass to the caked ground of her drive, then proceeded to her car, eased the key into the lock, and turned it. The trunk hatch gave a protesting, elongated creak as it slowly rose. Had it ever been so loud?

Leslie shot a glance to Blaine's lighted window. A shadow crossed the curtains. She darted behind a rear wheel and ducked down, wishing her legs weren't so long and it wasn't so difficult to hide.

Hide? Yup, she'd lost it. She was acting like a nut.

Determined to be done with her task, she rose none too slowly, grabbed the bag she'd not yet opened, and hoisted it out of the car. It landed on the drive with a muffled thump. Taking hold of the drawstring cords, she walked backward, dragging the mailbag across the grass and wincing at the loud rustling the action made. Afraid of being caught and seeing she was almost to the steps, she tried to move at a faster pace. In so doing, she lost her footing and fell flat on her rear.

"Ouch!" The painful exclamation automatically left her mouth as the bushes she fell next to cracked against her upper back and head. Her gaze zipped to Blaine's window. The curtain parted.

Jumping to her feet, Leslie grabbed the drawstrings and pulled the uncooperative mailbag awkwardly up the stairs and through the entryway. Relieved to have made it indoors, she propped it against the mudroom wall, not certain if she had the fortitude to fetch the other one tonight. Besides, her mission had just been jeopardized; her only plan now was to abort.

Hurrying outside to close her trunk, she no longer bothered with silence. With the trunk hatch slammed closed, she U-turned back to her house, the deed acted out in almost one fluid motion. Once she reached the safety of the mud-room, she shut the door, but not before catching a glimpse of Blaine's silhouette at the window.

What on earth is she doing?

Blaine rubbed a towel over his damp hair as he stared out his bedroom window and wondered if Leslie would reappear. When he'd heard the rustle and faint cry then looked out of the glass to see that she'd fallen, his first instinct had been to rush downstairs and out the door, despite the fact he wore only sweat-pants and was barefoot from a recent shower.

Reassured she hadn't sprained an ankle or otherwise hurt herself when she jumped to her feet, he then watched her lug what appeared to be a canvas sack bigger than a rolled-up sleeping bag over her two back stairs and into her house. Why had she waited until nighttime for what was apparently a difficult task—why not tackle it during daylight hours? It didn't make sense.

From this angle and the position of their homes, his second story was only a little higher than her first floor, so he'd seen inside her trunk before she'd rushed outside to slam it closed. The moonlight coming down through the tree branches spotlighted that specific area. Having seen what looked like a similar canvas bag, Blaine wondered what they could contain.

Since it didn't appear as if she was coming outdoors to retrieve the second bag, she obviously meant to let it sit in the trunk overnight. Leslie was a capable, independent woman who preferred her privacy; from his encounters with her, Blaine knew that. But after witnessing her struggle tonight, he felt she might welcome a man's strength next time. Or would she consider his help unwanted? He wished he knew her well enough to figure out the answer to that question. Of one thing he was positive: He wanted to know her better.

Blaine smiled when he thought about the soft feel of Leslie in his arms the day he'd kissed her on the covered bridge. Innocent, alluring, she was all that and more. Their return boat ride to Margaret Vance's to collect her grandmother had been quiet, but it was a peaceful quiet, unlike the previous trip to the bridge, and Leslie had smiled his way twice, making his heart give a funny twist each time.

To coincide with Leslie's day off, Blaine had asked his manager for the day off from work tomorrow. He and Leslie planned to visit a neighboring county and the five covered bridges scattered throughout the area, then eat dinner together. For once, Blaine had called ahead and located a nice restaurant not far from the last bridge they planned to visit. He looked forward to spending the day with her tomorrow. But before they left, he would be sure and remember to offer to carry that remaining bag.

Leslie poured herself a glass of chocolate milk—for a reward concerning her recent ordeal, she made it a tall one—and reached for the last sticky bun in the package. She caught sight of the maple sugar candy box Blaine had given her and chose that instead. He'd brought it over after their river outing, explaining he'd forgotten to give it to her the day of the craft fair. He was such a thoughtful man, and the two times he'd kissed her had made her anticipate more.

Reluctantly, she brought her mind to the sack of mail, which she'd dragged to her beanbag chair. She winced as her sore bottom made contact with the cushy foam. If she hadn't acted like a trespassing thief out committing a crime instead of a rightful homeowner retrieving her property, she wouldn't have fallen and bruised her hip. A long bubble bath before bedtime should ease the ache and help make her more comfortable.

Looking forward to that pampering, she bit off a leaf edge of the creamy candy and dove into the mailbag, withdrawing a few handfuls of letters. Some had been slit open. Evidently Mr. Abernathy had taken a peek, as was his right. She skimmed through them, sorting the glowing fan mail to be read later, maybe during her bath, into one stack, and the letters with possible questions to be answered into a second one. Into a third pile, she placed derogatory letters, and there were a surprising number of those. The praise far outweighed the criticism, but for some reason, the negative comments were all she could focus on at the moment.

Three letters from the last pile had similar envelopes but no return address. Upon investigating, she saw the writing was the same, too—a woman's, she would guess, because of the fancy loops. But the pretty script was deceiving. The negativity contained in the letters sliced Leslie to the core, attacking her on a personal level. Some of the accusations hurled insults regarding her very Christian character. Words like *narrow-minded bigot* and *mealy-mouthed hypocrite* jumped out at her in a message cluttered with foul and crass language.

Leslie's first reaction was to be offended, to dispose of the letters by tearing them up in small pieces and tossing them into the wastebasket. How could this person be so cruel as to make such false accusations when she knew nothing about Leslie? She hoped this reader received her comeuppance at some point in life.

After chugging down half her chocolate milk and biting into two more candies, viciously chewing on them, another thought intruded on her previous unchristian one: *Whoever sent those letters must bear a lot of personal pain to strike out at a stranger so cruelly.*

But I tell you: Love your enemies and pray for those who persecute you.

The Bible's golden words that had been buried in the treasure trove of her spirit reminded Leslie of what she should do. Still, she didn't see how she could pray for someone who not only attacked her work—a piece of herself—but also attacked her as a person, calling her abusive names when she was none of those things listed.

"You must forgive this woman and all of them who strike out at you, child. Forgive, as you have been forgiven. I understand your hurt, for I experienced betrayal and persecution during My walk upon the earth as well."

The words gently wafted into her mind, bringing with them moisture to her eyes. What her Lord went through was so much worse than this. Still. . .

Carefully, she folded the letter and slipped it into its envelope, setting it atop the third pile. Sighing, she ripped her gaze away from the letter after long moments had passed. "Lord, I know I need to forgive. I want to. It's just. . . hard."

Stowed away but not entirely forgotten, memories of previous school days came back to trouble her. Taunts from peers about her boyish body which, as she approached and entered womanhood, never achieved the feminine curves she'd so desired, silently repeated their pitiless chants. Recollections of the cruel pranks played against her rose up, barbs in her mind.

One prank was instigated by a girl in her sophomore class, whom she'd wrongly judged to be a friend, and had centered on a boy named Nate whom Leslie had had a crush on. When her so-called friend had captured Leslie's avowal of love on tape without her knowing it and played it over a loudspeaker during a basketball game at halftime, Leslie had been utterly humiliated. After that black event, instead of trying to fit in socially, she had put all her efforts into class work and discovered journalism.

She'd excelled and been encouraged by teachers' praise. After graduation, she considered college, but with no scholarship, it proved impossible. Instead, she'd taken a few online writing classes. Short-term jobs as a fast-food waitress and later working in a movie rental place hadn't appealed. Nor had her social life improved. The one date she'd shared with a coworker had been a disaster; she soon realized he was on the rebound after just breaking up with his girl, whom he talked about the entire night. Then came her job at the *Goosebury Gazette*. . . and Blaine.

She softly smiled when she thought about Blaine and what they'd shared, but too soon her gaze again landed on the small stack of hurtful letters, as if compelled. Disgusted with herself, she rose to rinse out her glass and put it on the draining board. Other small kitchen tasks didn't relieve the memory, and as her hands rested in the silky dish-washing soap bubbles, one reality became clear. Many of those wrongs done to her were outdated material. But until she forgave *all* those who'd hurt her, she would never be completely free from the pain.

Chances were good that the writer of the poison pen letters never forgave her persecutors and the bitterness had eaten through to her heart. If Leslie held on to her unforgiving spirit, might she become just as bitter, to the point that one day she would injure others with similar words?

Bowing her head, she gave up any so-called right to hold on to justifiable anger from past or present hurts and instead prayed for those who'd inflicted them upon her.

Afterward, she felt better and continued her chore. While she rinsed the dishes, again her mind drifted to Blaine. Within her, a powerful knowledge arose that she needed to speak to him about her job. First she should request her boss's permission to tell him the truth, since Mr. Abernathy had requested it remain private knowledge. Yet she wasn't exactly sure how to bring up the subject to either man so, once again, conveniently pushed it back upon her mental shelf.

⌒☜

If the weather were a good forecast of upcoming events, this day would be terrific. The sun shone, dazzling from a cloudy blue sky, and the temperature was warm with enough of a breeze to be stimulating. Still, something didn't feel exactly right.

Leslie had seemed distant all morning, though she'd offered a smile or two Blaine's way. Why her smiles should seem tinged with guilt is what puzzled Blaine.

Remembering his plan, he approached her where she stood near the back of her car. "Before we leave, I'd like to help you with that sack in your trunk. From what I could tell, it looked pretty heavy."

Leslie froze in her action of digging through her purse. Her gaze shot to his. "Sack?"

"Uh, yeah. I saw you last night lugging a huge sack into your house, and I couldn't help noticing there was one like it in the trunk. The full moon was so bright it was easy to see, and it shone right down on it," Blaine explained with a sheepish smile when her brows arched upward in disbelief. "Guess that sounds like I was being somewhat nosy, huh?"

"Maybe a little." The smile she offered was faint, her mind obviously still on whatever plane it had been on since he arrived. She looked into a zippered pocket of her bag and withdrew her keys, giving a little murmur of relief. "Really, the help's not necessary, Blaine. But thanks for the offer."

Before he could respond, she moved away. Since his sedan was in the shop, the seats currently being reupholstered, they were taking her car. She slipped behind the wheel before he could think to follow and open the door for her. Wow. She was moving fast today, as if she were out to report a four-alarm fire and not going for a leisurely drive in the countryside. Shooting a curious glance to the closed trunk, he moved around the back of the car to the passenger door.

Ten minutes into the drive, the atmosphere grew considerably more relaxed. Blaine studied the scenery, appreciating the low mountains and green ocean of tall trees all around.

"This really is pretty country," he mused aloud. "I used to wonder why Mom and Dad stayed up here and bought a house instead of returning to Texas. Now I know."

Leslie glanced in his direction then turned her attention back to the road. "Your mom once told me her original idea was to spend time with her mom after she was put in the assistance center. After she died, she just didn't want to leave New England. She mentioned she was raised in this county and missed the place."

Blaine nodded. "And Dad was the type to give her whatever she desired. She liked Texas—met him during a vacation there as a matter of fact. But she often told me how much she missed the Green Mountains of her home." He studied her. "You and Mom were close?"

Leslie's smile was one of wistful remembrance. "When I began renting the place from them two years ago, we swapped sweet bread recipes at first, then offered each other gardening tips. Within weeks, she was inviting me over to share dinners with them on Sundays after church. I think she was worried I might starve." A soft chuckle escaped her lips, and Blaine liked the airy sound of it.

He nodded. "Sounds like Mom."

"Since she grew up in the area, she was often full of questions about all the events that had happened in her absence. And since my mother is living in New York with her other family, your mom was often the listening ear I needed when small problems arose. I didn't want to worry Nana, not after all she'd been through when Granddad died, so I guess you could say your mom became something of a surrogate mom to me."

"I'm glad, Leslie. I remember her writing about you in her letters."

"She wrote about me?" Her surprise was evident.

"Yeah. She thought of you as the daughter she never had. But she failed to say what a fantastic lady you really are. She just said you were sweet."

He grinned, but Leslie kept her face turned toward the windshield. "I'm curious. What made you stay in Texas? Why didn't you move up here with your parents eight years ago?"

Blaine took time to think about that. "I was seventeen then, just finding my way in the world and trying to figure out who I was and what I wanted to be. At that time, I couldn't imagine leaving Fort Worth. Besides, I figured Grandpa Joe needed me more, and after talking it over with my dad, he agreed to let me stay awhile. My grandma was sick, and I helped Grandpa Joe on the farm," he explained. "When Grams died the next year and Dad and Mom flew down for the funeral, I told them I felt I should stay on with Grandpa Joe. He seemed so lost sometimes, and I felt he needed me, especially to help around the place. It was hard on Mom, since I was their only child. When Grandpa died, he'd already sold most of the land to pay my grandmother's hospital bills and other bills. By then, I was in my twenties and had found a job as a cook at a steak house. It seemed pointless to pick up and leave then. My mom often asked me on the phone when I was planning to fly up for a visit, but there was always something going on, and it just didn't seem like a good idea to leave. Now I wish I'd taken up her offer. Good thing they flew down to see me twice a year, so we did see each other some."

Leslie grew thoughtful. "Do you ever plan on going back to Texas?"

"Funny thing. When I flew up here in February, my only plan was to put the house up for sale and settle their affairs. Of course, it was way too cold and snowy to do anything except stay inside, wrapped from neck to foot in blankets, and try and keep warm. But now the days are nice, I'm not all that sure I want to leave. I haven't got any family to go back home to."

"So you *do* plan on making Goosebury your permanent residence?"

Her voice sounded almost wistful, or was it his imagination? A glance in her direction showed her attention riveted to the road.

"I thought I might. I have a good job, a nice home. Don't get me wrong, I still have ties to Texas. In fact, I'd like to vacation there sometime and visit friends—preferably during the winter months." Seeing the corner of her mouth tilt upward, his smile grew wider.

A lengthy span of comfortable silence passed between them, and Blaine thought over their conversation.

All this talk about family brought a sudden thunderbolt of revelation lighting up his brain. His parents had left Leslie the renovated barn and him the house. For the first time, Blaine wondered if the action had been deliberate. As a method his mom had used to ensure Blaine would come to Vermont, whereby he'd meet Leslie. . .and hopefully fall in love with her? The prospect sounded far-fetched—but exactly like something his mom might have planned. Of course, she couldn't have had any way of knowing just how soon the time for meeting her Maker would come, but trust it to her to leave nothing unfinished. Since she hadn't been able to bring the two together to meet while she'd lived on this earth, what if his mom had formulated a plan so that the task might be accomplished when she was gone?

Dazed, Blaine slowly shook his head as the implausible became logical. In all his mom's letters, she'd asked Blaine if he'd found a girl he was serious about yet, and then, he now remembered, the next paragraph always contained a sentence or two mentioning her "sweet renter, Leslie."

Good ole Mom. Well, this time she'd been right.

Blaine glanced Leslie's way. His pretty neighbor likely had a lot to do with his decision to make his home in Goosebury.

⤬

Leslie enjoyed the afternoon with Blaine, though they didn't converse much. Yet with Blaine, that didn't present a problem. For the most part, she felt comfortable with him whether they talked or not, even if there had been that awkward moment at first concerning the mailbag still in her trunk.

He'd brought a digital camera, and at each covered bridge they visited, he asked her to pose beside its portal. At first she'd laughingly protested, insisting she was no model, but he'd been just as adamant, stating he wanted her in all the shots. "Makes it more personal," was his comment. "Gives the pictures feeling they wouldn't have if I just snapped shots of the bridge itself."

She'd raised a curious brow at that but complied. Each bridge they visited, they hiked down an embankment to get a picture of the side of the edifice. Often it was difficult ground to travel. Yet Blaine never failed to help her over the rough spots, which made Leslie feel special. His mother had raised a real gentleman.

At Emily's Bridge, Leslie sensed a strange eeriness about the place but explained her unease away as being psychological and stemming from legends surrounding the historic structure. She didn't believe in any ancient ghost that reputedly shook the bridge at times or clawed its supposed hapless victims, as folklore claimed. Still, she was glad to leave the place.

Thinking of life's real victims, her mind went to the letter she'd read last night from a reader known only as Desperate. Like the sender of the lilac stationery, this person had chosen to remain gender anonymous. Leslie had no idea if the person was male or female, though from the artistic way the gloomy words were written on the lined notebook paper, she assumed it to be the latter.

The note was a cry for help, almost suicidal, not at all resembling the usual questions about relationships she generally received. Only a post office box had been hand printed for a return address, no name above it, and the postmark bore the name of Mendleton. A town conveniently on their route today.

Next, they visited Fisher Bridge, set over some railroad tracks, and Blaine walked along the rails inside the Town-Pratt double lattice bridge, fascinated by the cupola that ran its full length along the top. "I read in that book that the cupola was used to let steam from the trains out of the bridge," he said, his gaze running the length of the top as he continued to walk.

Leslie smiled at his boyish enthusiasm. She could imagine him as a child.

"You ought to join our local Covered Bridge Society," she joked.

He looked at her seriously. "Hey, that's a good idea. I haven't found a way to really fit in with the folks in Goosebury yet, and that just might do it." He crossed his arms in a mock-teasing way. "Don't laugh, Leslie. I can tell you're on the verge of it with the way you're grinning. But think about it. These bridges aren't only necessary to the community for practical purposes; they're also monuments of history. They remind us of simpler times when life was slower-paced, with wagons and horses, and the beginnings of civilization as we know it were just being carved from the wilderness."

"Why, Blaine"—her words came out surprised—"I didn't know you were a romantic."

By the way his eyes shifted downward and his face flushed a shade darker, she could tell she'd embarrassed him and was immediately sorry. After picking his way along a few more railroad track ties, hands in his pockets, he turned around to look at her again. "I never considered myself one, but maybe I am. Is that okay? Or is that a trait in men you don't like?"

"N–no, it's fine." Now it was her turn to be nervous. He looked at her as if her opinion actually mattered. Suddenly uncomfortable, she chose to change the subject. "I came across some adhesive labels the other day and thought they'd do great to price your parents' items for the tag sale. Is it all right if I come over tomorrow? The tag sale will be a good place for you to blend in with the community, since you said you wanted to do that. It's basically a town-sized yard sale."

"I have to cook for a catering event that night, a wedding, but I'm free before five."

"That'll work for me." He continued to stare at her, and she looked away. "Well, I guess we should make tracks." Her laugh was a little high-strung at the unintended pun, and she moved toward the car. She still felt off-kilter from their previous conversation.

"Leslie."

At the guarded way he spoke her name, as if he had something weighty to discuss, her heart gave a painful little jump. She turned to look at him.

"I appreciate your offer to help me. When I first moved up here, I wasn't sure if the majority of folks in Goosebury would accept me or not. Sometimes, I still wonder."

Worry gave way to sympathy, and she softened her voice. "Blaine, please don't take it personally. It's just our nature. We're a staunchly independent folk, and it usually takes us a little more time to roll out the welcome rug to strangers. But we're a friendly town when you get to know us. And you will."

"I know *you* are. Friendly, I mean. Your offer to help me weed my garden was the first show of true friendship I'd received from anyone." His low words stirred her heart. "Leslie, before we leave, can I be honest with you? 'Cause I think we're both a bit strung-up today, and it might help if I spoke."

Curious, Leslie looked at him. He seemed nervous, glancing away, then back to her again.

"Fact is. . ." He slid the sole of his boot along a railroad tie. "I'm not all that used to steady dating either, at least at taking a woman out more than a couple o' times. So if I say or do something that makes you mad, could you let me know? In a nice way, of course."

The unexpected words surprised her, but she gave a slight nod. "Sure."

He seemed relieved to have gotten it off his chest. "Good. Well, I guess we should be heading back." He looked up at the sky. "It'll be evening before we know it."

Leslie walked with Blaine to the car. She couldn't imagine him making her angry and wondered what must have been wrong with those women he'd dated. Even more amazing was the fact he felt as apprehensive as she did about making a mistake. She would never have believed it before today; his manner had been so casual, so easygoing, so smooth. And when he'd kissed her, her head and heart had spun into a pleasurable whirl. The thought that he, too, shared this dating anxiety strangely calmed her, made her feel closer to him, and she was able to fully relax in his company as she'd never been able to do before.

Back behind the wheel, Leslie looped around and headed south. They talked little, and Blaine crossed his arms over his chest, tilted his head back, and closed his eyes. She spared a glance or two in his direction, appreciating his attractive profile. The moderate slope of his forehead, the more prominent thrust of his nose, his lips full and gentle, and his chin, strong and sure. Could such a man really be interested in her? It seemed unbelievable.

On their return, she noticed a sign she hadn't seen before, and her mind skipped ahead to the locale. MENDLETON: EXIT 2 MILES

"I'd like to stop for some coffee," she said, wondering if he was still awake. "Is that okay with you?"

"As long as it doesn't spoil your dinner."

"Dinner? I didn't know that was in the plans. Where are we going?"

"You'll see." He opened his eyes and turned his head her way. His smile sent her heart into overdrive.

No, she could never be upset with Blaine Cartell.

❧

Blaine looked around the Wayside Café, noticing how intently Leslie focused on her surroundings. He didn't see anything extraordinary about the wooden paneling and floor, nor the decorative attempt of the antique copper pots and pans lining the walls. Old-fashioned, hand-lettered signs, appearing as if they belonged to another century, hung between the cookware and advertised food items at incredibly low prices. Lower than today's menu.

Leslie preempted his suggestion to sit at a small table by heading straight for the long counter. A conversation was in progress between one of the locals, an old man in a plaid work shirt and cuffed dungarees, and the middle-aged waitress behind the counter. Besides Blaine and Leslie, they were the only two people in the building.

The woman walked toward them to take Blaine's order of two coffees. Leslie also ordered a sticky bun, adding that she only wanted a small one, afterward murmuring to Blaine that she promised it wouldn't spoil her appetite for dinner.

At this, the waitress chuckled. "By your accent I assume you're from these parts, but you"—she eyed Blaine, not unkindly—"sound like a flatlander."

"Yes, ma'am, born and raised in Texas. I live here now."

The waitress arched a shaggy brown eyebrow. "Oh, yes? I lived in Oklahoma for five years. Near Tulsa." As she poured their coffee, she shot a glance at the digital camera hanging from a strap around Blaine's neck. "So you're out takin' pictures of the scenery?"

"Yeah, something like that."

Rosemary, as her name tag clearly showed, laid a saucer with Leslie's sticky bun in front of her. The minutes passed as Blaine and Leslie finished their coffee in relative silence. Before leaving, he looked the waitress's way. "Excuse me. But is there anything in town worth capturing on film? I'm especially interested in covered bridges."

"In Mendleton?" Rosemary laughed. "Place is so small the shade doesn't bother t' waste time growin'."

At the quirky saying, Blaine and Leslie shared an amused glance.

"But if you would've come around here yesterday, now that's a different story. If you were a reporter, that is."

"Oh?"

She gave a slow swipe of the countertop with a wet dishcloth, then leaned on one hand propped against the counter, as if assured she had a captive audience. Blaine noticed Leslie bend forward, intent on hearing what might be said.

"Ned Porter brought from his farm a zucchini that resembled a melon. More or less. The size of it could've won a blue ribbon at the fair."

"Oh." Leslie gave a faint laugh, sounding disappointed. "I thought you meant a crime had taken place or something like that."

"We don't get much crime here in Mendleton. Except there was that one episode last week. . . ." The woman frowned as if reexperiencing it.

"Rosemary," the old man on the other end of the counter admonished, "you ought not be talkin' about things that aren't your business."

The woman turned her scowl on him. "Honestly, Lyle. It was hardly a private matter, what with the way Mark Lester chased Sharon through town with a rifle. It was the topic of conversation in Mendleton for days."

"Rifle?" Leslie asked.

"Yup. Poor woman took the kids and left that monster she married," Rosemary said on a little sigh. "Thank the Lord she got away. Sharon worked for me last year, a sweet girl. And her three children are just as sweet, though the boy barely talks anymore. Who knows what went on in that household."

The old man gave a disapproving grunt, then asked her to refill his coffee cup.

"We should be getting back on the road," Blaine urged Leslie once the waitress moved away, none too happily. The talk disturbed him, and he assumed Leslie must feel the same way as somber as her features became.

She gave a distracted nod and popped the last of her sticky bun in her mouth. Seeing that the two locals were in low, heated conversation, Blaine left a five-dollar bill next to his empty cup, more than the price of both coffees and the bun.

Soon they were on the road again. Yet as distant as Leslie seemed, Blaine couldn't help but feel as if she had stayed behind, back at the Wayside Café.

Chapter 9

The week flew by for Leslie, the high points being her three meetings with Blaine. Saturday, she'd spent hours helping him sort and price those items he'd chosen to put aside for the tag sale. Clothing and other basic necessities, he'd put in cardboard boxes to drop off as donations to a charitable organization; she'd driven him there since his car was still in the shop, needing more work. Then on Sunday, she'd been surprised and pleased when he'd slid into her pew at the white-steepled community church they both attended. Afterward, they grabbed a bite to eat at a local restaurant—nice, but nothing quite like the surprise Leslie received when he had taken her to an Italian restaurant after they visited the covered bridges and she discovered they shared a passion for Italian food. He'd surprised her by again showing up on Tuesday and taking her and her grandmother on another river outing, this time in a rowboat. While they'd waited for Nana to change clothes, Leslie discreetly left another batch of letters on the table for her grandmother to read later, then showed Blaine the garden.

Now Leslie sat in her cubicle, sorting through the latest letters Mr. Abernathy had given her. Since receiving the two mailbags, thankfully the inflow had died down considerably, and Leslie attributed the previous popularity boost to the weeks-old news report of the lady and the carjacker that had aired statewide. She still received mail every day and hadn't yet sifted through all the envelopes of the second bag, but it wasn't anything she couldn't handle.

"What's this mean?" she murmured as she saw a familiar long, white security envelope.

"Something wrong?" Carly wheeled out from her cubicle, leaning back in her rolling chair to look at Leslie.

"Hm? Oh, no. Just someone I'd written to." Mr. Abernathy's final inclusion hadn't included Desperate's question or Leslie's answer to the reader in the *Goosebury Gazette*, so unknown to her boss, she'd written to the post office box with a private reply. She just couldn't ignore Desperate's pain and had wanted to do what she could to help. Often, since visiting Mendleton, she wondered if that woman could have been Sharon Lester.

She sliced open the envelope and withdrew a single page of notebook paper. As she read, her heart dove bottomward.

"Bad news?" Carly asked.

The letter strongly threatened suicide.

Leslie folded the page and looked at the clock on the wall, glad to see it was almost quitting time. She reached for her purse. "I need to leave early. There's someone I have to find. If Mr. Abernathy wants me, tell him I'll have the copy on his desk tomorrow."

"Wait a minute. This sounds as if it could be interesting. Just who are you rushing off to meet so fast?" Carly arched her dark eyebrows. "Blaine?"

"Why would you think that?"

"Oh, come on, Leslie. You're always together. Who else could it be?"

Leslie shrugged, uncomfortable with Carly's intent stare. She wasn't yet ready to confide in anyone—especially since if Mr. Abernathy caught wind of her plan, she could be in danger of losing her job. This might not be her favorite beat, but it did pay the bills and fill her cupboards. And the word *fired* on a résumé wouldn't help her to gain new employment, either.

"It's not Blaine. Just someone I have to find and talk with," was all the explanation she gave her curious coworker before heading out the door.

Blaine checked the tuna and, assured it was achieving perfection, stirred ingredients together for the relish. His boss had recently mentioned she wanted to expand the items available on the catering menu, bringing more diversity by introducing a few gourmet dishes, and Blaine had offered to dust off his cookbooks from the culinary school he'd attended years ago and whip up a few samples for her to try, experimenting with a few of his own ideas. Some dishes he made at the restaurant, others at home. Since Leslie was due here any minute for dinner, he decided to treat her to a first taste of grilled tuna with pineapple relish and didn't think she would mind him using both of them as taste testers. The aroma coming from the grill made his mouth water, and he breathed in deeply.

For a table centerpiece, he chose a basket of purple and blue flowers—silk ones of his mom's, since he remembered Leslie's preference that flowers stay alive in the garden. Her long-ago admission had touched him, giving him a hint of what a compassionate person she was. The last few weeks of knowing her had underlined that fact. So why, fifteen minutes after the time she should be here, hadn't she called to explain her delay?

Frowning when he saw the food was past the stage of being ready and having no chafing tray to keep it warm, he turned the oven to its lowest temperature and slid the fish inside, hoping the succulent, flaky center wouldn't dry out.

While he waited for Leslie to show, he relaxed in the den. Sprawled out over a recliner, he closed his eyes and considered his past. Years ago in high school when he'd told his co-op teacher he wanted to be a chef and had taken home economics, his friends had ribbed him. He didn't understand why cooking food couldn't be considered masculine—fearless hunters did it long ago. All men liked to eat. It seemed a sensible job. And he enjoyed grilling, cooking, and mixing things together to come up with desirable entrées.

Blaine lifted heavy eyelids and realized he'd been asleep. Checking the clock, he saw that Leslie was now forty-five minutes late. He went to the window and pulled aside the curtain, but her car wasn't there. He wished he had thought to get her phone number. Hungry, he gave up and went into the kitchen for something to tide him over. A jar of peanuts seemed like a good choice.

Ten more minutes trickled by like the slow drip coming from the faucet. Blaine wrenched the handle hard to stop it. Another look out one of the kitchen windows proved that Leslie's car wasn't there yet. Maybe she'd had engine trouble.

Flipping through the phone book, he found the page Leslie should be on, but her number was unlisted. Locating the number for the *Goosebury Gazette*, he asked to be connected with her extension.

"This is Carly Alden, how can I help you?"

Surprised when her coworker answered the phone, he hesitated. "I'm calling for Leslie Edwards."

"She left here about forty minutes ago."

"That's funny. She's not home yet."

"Sorry, I don't know what else to tell you. She got a letter in the mail and went chasing after some guy."

Some guy?

"Well, at least that's what I assumed." The girl's voice sounded penitent when he didn't respond. Another short pause ensued. "Uh, is this Blaine?"

"Yeah."

"Listen—Blaine—I don't really know why she left so fast. She wouldn't tell me where she was going, and I'm just guessing about the guy. I shouldn't have said what I did. Do us both a favor and forget it. Okay?"

He made himself relax his grip on the receiver. "If she shows up, could you tell her to call me?"

"Sure."

"Thanks." He ended the call, refusing to believe Leslie would two-time anyone. His grandmother made that mistake once, and it almost ended her marriage to Grandpa Joe, but he'd eventually forgiven her and accepted her back home, where they'd shared three happy years together before she died.

Blaine took in a deep breath and exhaled, letting the air whiz from his teeth. Leslie and he were hardly engaged or even serious. She could see whom she wanted, he supposed, though the thought of her going out with someone else didn't set well with him. Not at all. And he never would have believed her the type to stand him up on a dinner date.

Resigned to a solitary meal, he pulled the fish from the oven. The fish's center had gotten dry. Even the relish didn't help sweeten the experience, and Blaine's attitude remained sour.

❧

Envisioning a long, hot bath, Leslie drove past the sign welcoming her back to Goosebury. Her mission hadn't been successful. Upon arriving at the Wayside Café, she realized how foolish she'd been to expect to find the reader Desperate, especially without any type of real game plan to go by. But a tragic experience in junior high, when a fellow student committed suicide and Leslie wondered for months if she could have said something to prevent it, had propelled her actions.

Rosemary had been openly curious when Leslie asked if she recognized the return address on the envelope, and her shaggy brows lifted even higher when she'd seen the name *Dear Granny c/o The Goosebury Gazette* scrawled on the front. Thankfully, she appeared to accept Leslie's hurried explanation of "I work at the same office as the columnist—at the *Goosebury Gazette*—and I'm trying to locate this person for her." Not exactly a lie, but nothing to give herself away either.

Rosemary was able to pinpoint the general direction of the rural box, recognizing the first two digits of the return address, but when Leslie finally found the road, she couldn't find the box number, which soon led her to believe it was a phony and didn't exist. She drove around the area for another ten minutes, just to be sure, before coming to the conclusion she'd been had in some sort of immature prank. Either that, or Desperate didn't want her whereabouts known. After stopping at another roadside restaurant for a meal, deflated but ravenous, she'd headed back to Goosebury.

Sighing with relief to be home, she spotted Blaine's well-lit house through the trees. Headlights cut up the darkness in front of her as she turned onto the road leading to her driveway. Her shoulders and back hurt from being tensed most of the day, and after stepping out of her car, she stretched to loosen them.

Footsteps rustled in the grass, and she turned to see Blaine heading in her direction.

"Are you okay?" With the cloudy night sky behind him, he appeared almost formidable. "Where were you?" The words held an edge to them, so unlike Blaine, and she did a double take.

"Where was I?" The minute she asked the question, she remembered. "We had a date!" Wincing, she groaned. "Oh, Blaine, I'm sorry. I forgot."

"You forgot." The repeated words sounded as if he didn't believe her.

"Yes, I was doing something important concerning my job."

"Carly said you weren't at the office."

"You called the *Gazette*?" Leslie couldn't believe he would do such a thing and felt uneasy that he was digging too deep. "Why'd you do that?"

"Because I was worried." He raked a hand through his hair, his countenance grim. "You're never this late. I didn't know if something had happened to you or what. And Carly told me you'd run off—"

"Yes, I thought it necessary."

"To chase some guy."

"What? Carly said that?" Leslie would have to have a serious talk with her coworker. "Well, I wasn't. Okay? I don't chase guys."

Highly uncomfortable with the path of their conversation, she slammed her car door shut. "It's been a long day, and all I want right now is a hot bath. I'm dead on my feet. Can we talk about this another time, please?"

She walked off, her low heels making rapid clacks on the small rocks, but she noticed Blaine didn't move from his spot.

"No, I want to talk about it now. What are you hiding, Leslie? Why are you running from me?"

"I'm not running from you. There's just nothing more to discuss."

"Don't you think I'm at least entitled to know what made you ditch our date and where you ran off to for over five hours?"

In wearied frustration, she whirled to face him. "Look, I'm sorry about dinner. Something came up. I had somewhere I needed to go, and I just forgot. Can't you accept that?"

"Meaning you're not gonna tell me where you went or who you went to see?" He braced his hands on his hips.

Leslie's mouth firmed. "Meaning I'm not going to tell you."

"Great. That's just swell, Leslie. Thanks a heap for the vote of trust. I thought we'd come further than that. I thought—" He opened his mouth as if to say more but instead closed it and shook his head.

Her heart raced at his unspoken words, but rising irritation held any further apology at bay. "I told you weeks ago, we're staunchly independent here in Goosebury. And we don't like people meddling in our affairs. You asked me then to tell you when you made me angry. Well, Blaine, you're balancing that beam right now."

Hurt struck his eyes, making her wish she could retrieve her hasty words. His jaw hardened. "Point well taken. Enjoy your independence, Leslie. I won't bother you anymore." He turned on his heel and marched across the lawn to his house.

"Blaine!" Not wanting him to leave on such a bitter note, she stepped to the edge of her drive as if she would follow but didn't. "I couldn't tell you if I wanted to. Please understand!"

Instead of stopping and turning back to her like she'd hoped he would, he kept walking until he disappeared into his house.

Stubborn man. Hot, angry tears burned the rims of her lashes as she made tracks for her own home. Why couldn't he take her words at face value and leave it at that? When he'd first come over tonight, she had almost wished she could tell him the truth regarding her hopeless search for Desperate and even about her role as Dear Granny. But after being the recipient of his bullying manner, she was doubly glad she hadn't. As upset as he was, departing as he had, Leslie doubted he wanted anything more to do with her. The thought sat heavy in her chest, as if a sharp stone lodged there.

Leslie spent a long, lonely week missing Blaine. The day after their argument, when she was more alert and calm, she'd realized if the roles had been reversed and he had been the one who was a no-show at a dinner date for a meal she'd prepared, she would have been just as upset. Maybe more.

The one time she'd seen him outside, retrieving his mail as she hurried off to work, there'd been no time to talk. He had met her gaze, hesitated as if unsure what to do, then lifted his hand in a wave. She had returned the gesture, wishing she could take the time to bridge the distance across their lawns and try to mend things between them. She hated this separateness. He had come to mean a lot to her, she realized, and she missed being around him. As soon as she saw him again, she would do what she could to speak with him.

Now she sat behind a table she'd brought for the tag sale, with her offerings on top. All up and down the town square, people had brought tables, blankets, and even used the back of two pickup trucks to display the many and varied items for sale. Seated on her stool, Leslie scoped the area for Blaine, but he wasn't there.

Disappointed, she straightened a stack of old writing magazines and smiled at a couple who stopped by her table. She accepted a five-dollar bill another elderly tourist handed her for an eleven by thirteen acrylic framed painting of Vermont's woodland in the yellows, oranges, and reds of fall and slipped the purchase into one of the paper sacks she'd brought from home.

Children played, chasing each other and laughing in the grassy park area directly behind her. Three tables down, a portable stereo set on the oldies station played popular tunes from the '60s. A cool breeze teased tendrils of hair back from her face, making the day a pleasant one.

Footsteps whispered closer in the grass behind her. Expecting one or more of the children to approach her table and eye the battery-operated, fiber-optic mini fountain, as they'd done all morning, Leslie waited. Suddenly, from above, a ribbon-tied cellophane bag of candy descended down several inches away from her face, suspended by a male hand.

Her mouth dropped open in surprise, and she spun around on the stool. "Blaine!" Her smile was as enthused as her voice.

His lazy, boyish grin sent her heart into a crazy dance; how she had missed it! "I come bearing gifts," he said. "Two dozen sweet ones."

Leslie accepted the bag of maple sugar candy. "Thank you. I haven't finished the box you gave me weeks ago, but I can't see this going to waste. Want one?"

The steady look in his gorgeous dark eyes suddenly made her nervous, and her hand shook as she untied the bag.

"Sure." He paused, shuffled his feet. "Leslie, I acted like a real jerk last week, and I just want to say I'm sorry."

She looked up, the bag open in her lap. "You're forgiven, Blaine. If the roles were reversed, I might have done worse. Maybe even thrown the ruined dinner at your head."

The remark was said in jest—she never would have done such a thing—but it made his lips lift in a smile. Teasing glimmered in his eyes. "I'll have to remember that for future reference."

Future reference! The thought he still wanted to see her sent waves of happiness wafting through her, making her feel light as air. At the same time, she knew it was important to reintroduce the touchy topic so as to prevent any possible replays of that night.

"But please understand, Blaine." She worked to frame her words. "There are just some things I can't talk about right now, especially concerning work. Maybe one day. Just not now."

She could tell he was disappointed, but he nodded. "I'll take note of that and try not to trespass." His manner took on a more casual air. "So, mind if I set up next to you?"

"I'd love the company."

First asking a nearby seller to watch her table, she then helped Blaine carry the three cartons containing household decor he'd decided to sell. He popped out the metal legs of a card table and soon was in business.

The rest of the morning passed in comfortable camaraderie, though long spans of time elapsed where not a word was exchanged between them. Still, Leslie didn't mind. Differences now mended, their lack of conversation was comfortable, even peaceful. A number of locals came by their tables throughout the morning, and Leslie introduced Blaine to those who didn't know him. Michael Alden, Carly's uncle, mentioned his membership in an organization that helped to beautify and restore covered bridges. Within seconds, Blaine was hooked.

While the men talked, Leslie excused herself to take a turn around the street and see if anything interested her. A book on one table caught her eye: *God's Answer to a Life without Fear*. Thinking of her grandmother, she paid the two dollars for it.

"Hi, Les." Carly's voice broke her attention, and she turned to see her coworker walk toward her. "I see my uncle is talking to Blaine." Her words and expression were grim. "And poor Blaine doesn't look as if he's getting a word in edgewise."

"Are you and your uncle having problems?" Leslie knew Carly had been raised by her mother's strict sister and husband and that the home situation wasn't always a good one.

Carly shrugged. "He's not happy I've decided to quit the paper. Says I'm acting recklessly with my future."

The news didn't cheer Leslie either. "I'll miss you."

"Well, we could get together for a lunch date, if you're still willing. I can't believe we haven't done that yet. Again, I'm sorry I said what I did to Blaine when he called the office last week. But do you ever plan on telling him the truth, about you being Dear Granny?"

Leslie sighed. "Maybe. I don't know. I feel caught between a rock and a hard place. I don't want to cause any further misunderstandings between us, but Mr. Abernathy did tell me to keep quiet. If things progress between me and Blaine, I guess I should tell him, though."

"Yup, you should. He really likes you. I heard it in his voice and could tell he was worried that day over the phone." Carly's smile flickered, as if confused. "You know, when you first came to work at the paper, I wasn't sure about you. At first, the answers you gave in the column made you seem flippant, as if you didn't really care all that much; then I pegged you as a judgmental holier-than-thou. But maybe I was wrong." She focused on the table beside them, seeming unusually nervous. "Leslie, I should tell you something. . . ."

"Leslie Edwards, how lovely to see you here!" An elderly fellow churchgoer moved toward Leslie. "How's your grandmother? We certainly do miss her at our seniors' meetings."

To Leslie's dismay, Carly quietly excused herself as the woman continued to talk. Leslie tried to keep her mind focused on the conversation yet couldn't help but wonder what Carly had been about to reveal.

Chapter 10

When the third letter from Desperate came, Leslie was almost expecting it. She slipped it inside her purse, intending to read it at lunch when she was away from all eyes. Knowing that Blaine didn't work until the evening shift since today he'd traded slots with a fellow worker so the girl could go to a wedding, she headed for Milton's Pantry. Since it was close to the office and fairly empty this time of day, despite it being one of the best places in town, the restaurant should offer her the privacy needed.

She was beginning to feel guilty for withholding her job title from Blaine and always working to avoid the topic the few times he brought it up, but that was just how it had to be. For now. Still, in these past weeks, she and Blaine had grown closer, and they spoke with each other every day—over the phone for a few minutes if they didn't meet or go out together. It had begun to feel as if Leslie were doing more than withholding information. The word *deceive* often echoed in her mind. Yet she just wasn't ready to reveal to him her role as Dear Granny. Maybe when she felt more confident with the beat, she'd ask Mr. Abernathy's permission and do it then. She knew she should tell him soon.

Inside the red vinyl booth, Leslie sipped at the ice water a waitress brought her, mulling over the letter's surprising contents. Desperate begged for a face-to-face meeting, expressing the need to talk to someone who cared, stating her fear and weariness that kept her from wanting to go on living, and she claimed Dear Granny might be able to help.

Reflective, Leslie scanned the letter a second time. Again she sensed Desperate must be a woman and, from the letter's contents, one who still planned to take her life if she didn't get the help needed. Leslie felt she should go, try to reason with her, encourage her, but she wondered if the decision were a wise one. Desperate's suggestion to meet at a halfway point near Emily's Bridge sent warning chills up her spine. Still, she felt compelled to help somehow.

"Leslie!"

One hand on each side of the paper, she jerked in shock and almost ripped the page apart upon hearing the familiar voice.

"Rhonda told me you were here. I'm glad you came."

"Blaine?" She twisted her upper body around. Her ears hadn't deceived her. From a few feet away, Blaine was striding in her direction, a white chef's apron covering his clothes and a big smile stretching across his face.

Leslie zipped back around to the table. Fingers flying, she grabbed the envelope from where she'd propped it between the salt and pepper shakers. Her purse—on the bench seat against the wall, with more than a foot between them—seemed an island away. Dropping envelope and letter onto her lap in an attempt to hide both, she shifted forward until her midriff came in contact with the table's edge and tried to assume a nonchalant air.

The letter fell from its precarious perch. Floating in a sweeping sideways arc, it hit the bottom of Blaine's pant leg as he stopped beside her table, then came to rest atop his shoe.

Leslie almost swallowed her tongue.

ᴄ᷍ᴀ

"Don't bother," Leslie blurted. "I'll get it!"

"That's okay. I got it."

They knocked heads as she dove for the paper at the same time Blaine bent down to retrieve it.

"Ow!" they both said, but his fingers latched onto the lined page with blue handwriting before hers could. He picked it up and straightened, handing it to her.

Her face was flushed with color. She continued rubbing her forehead near the hairline where they'd made contact and snatched the letter from his fingers with her other hand.

O–kaaay. He wished now he'd gotten a good look at that letter. Her eyes flashed up to him, then downward again, almost as if guilty. Why was she acting so strange?

"Reading up on family news from New York?"

She shook her head and deposited both the letter and an envelope into her purse. "I thought you had the evening shift." Her words seemed to accuse, but the slight smile on her lips seemed friendly enough.

"Rhonda called me to come in early. One of the girls called in sick, so I'm working two shifts."

Her expression softened even more. "That's nice of you."

"Well, at least it's given me the opportunity to cook you a decent meal and not one basted in ashes. Tell me your favorite, and I'll have it fried, baked, or pan broiled before you can make a decision on what movie we'll watch tomorrow night."

"So, you're the cook *and* waiter now?"

"Only for you."

She relaxed, her lips winging upward into a genuine smile. "Why are you always so nice to me, Blaine?"

"Because you're worth it." He shifted, became more businesslike. "Sorry to say, I only have minutes to spare since I just got off a break and the usual lunch crowd of what generally amounts to all of a dozen people will be swarming in soon.

So what'll it be? Meat, fish, or vegetarian?"

She laughed. "Vegetarian is Carly's preference, or so she's said. Not mine." She looked at the plastic-coated lunch menu and jabbed a nail midpoint. "I think I'll have the half-pound bleu burger with everything on it. And"—she appeared embarrassed—"could you ask the waitress to bring me a glass of chocolate milk, too? I know my choices probably sound horrid, since you're a chef."

"Blue cheese burgers and chocolate milk?" He grinned, then dipped his head to drop a hasty kiss to her lips. "Leslie Edwards, you're a girl after my own heart."

Leslie felt little more than a girl as she drove to meet Desperate. Many times this past week she had questioned her decision. Yet if she didn't go, she would never forgive herself if the poor woman took her life.

All day she'd felt an uneasy check in her spirit and had hurried through her morning Bible reading, giving little time to prayer afterward. Asking and interceding instead of being silent and listening—partly because she was afraid to hear the answer, partly because she was afraid the answer would cause her to have to make a choice that didn't seem like an option.

Uncomfortable with agreeing to Emily's Bridge as a meeting point, she'd written back the day she received the letter, suggesting they get together at a park midway between towns instead. She preferred the encounter be held in a public place where people were sure to be this time of year. For Desperate to suggest a "haunted" spot like Emily's Bridge made Leslie wonder about the woman's mental state. On the other hand, if Desperate were at the end of her rope emotionally, as she'd implied, then suggesting such a place as the bridge wasn't so unusual.

Days later, Leslie received another letter with only two lines of reply: "Meet me at the park at noon on Wednesday. At the bench between the water fountain and children's play area."

High noon.

Picturing a ghost town with two gunfighters facing one another and eerie drawn-out whistling music in the background, Leslie fought down a hysterical giggle at the over-the-top, dramatic scenario that formed in her mind. She was being ridiculous, and maybe she shouldn't have watched Blaine's choice of that shoot-'em-up TV Western last night. What was it with men and Westerns anyway? Especially in Goosebury, lately the theme seemed to have spread like wildfire. Maybe because a former Texan had recently joined the populace?

She softly smiled at the thought of Blaine, then forced her mind back to the task at hand. Spotting the sign leading to the turnoff, Leslie switched on her right blinker, her heart beginning to thump hard and fast. Maybe if she'd shed her own adolescent uncertainty and had been more talkative with the round-faced girl whose desk had been behind hers in eighth grade, she could have prevented Dorothy from taking an overdose of her mom's pills. Maybe if she had focused less on her own shortcomings then and had been able to help change Dorothy's history, she wouldn't feel so compelled now to try to have a hand at changing this present set of circumstances.

Leslie pulled her car into the rocky drive fronting the park. No other cars sat in the lot, but she heard a child's squeal. Through the gaps between the leafy green sugar maples, she glimpsed a little girl's slight form on a wooden jungle gym not far away. Another child swung on a swing behind her.

With a wistful smile, she thought back to the carefree existence of her own childhood at that age. Fly-fishing in the river with Granddad and swimming there on hot summer days. Baking iced sugar cookies with Nana and playing dress-up, while holding tea parties with her dolls in Nana's wonderful butterfly garden. And when she was older, playing soccer with her brother over the lush, green field that edged the forest by Nana's house. She missed Jimmy and hoped he would like Blaine. Since they were a lot alike, she was sure he would.

Locating the designated bench, she took a seat. She looked first to the right, then to the left, but no adult walked along the one dirt path in evidence. In fact, no adults were present at all. Another drawback. The park was smaller than she'd thought it was on the day she and Blaine drove by during their covered-bridge outing, and now she wished she had suggested a busy restaurant instead. After a while, the sound of a motorcycle's rumbling engine grew closer, then stopped somewhere nearby. But after several minutes, no one had come into view.

The little girl's squeal again captured Leslie's attention, and she shifted her focus to the child. A boy now climbed the playhouse wall behind her. They both looked about eight or nine years old and had white-blond hair. With dexterity born of youth, the two scrambled up the side until they reached the playhouse's top and stood on the flat roof with gables on each side. Hands on her hips, the girl looked in Leslie's direction, her stance tall, proud, the conqueror-princess of her castle. Leslie could well imagine her thoughts.

Spotting Leslie, the child wildly waved, and Leslie waved back. She wasn't so old that the thought of joining the two in play didn't provide a temptation, but she remained seated. One day, maybe she'd have her own daughter or son to climb castles with. A child whose dark hair bore a reddish tinge when the sun hit it and who had gentle brown eyes and a heart-tugging smile just like. . .Blaine's.

At the thought, her face heated, but she faced the reality head-on. She'd fallen deeply in love with Blaine.

The crunching and scattering of small rocks alerted her to someone walking her way. A man who appeared to be in his thirties with greasy hair growing to his shoulders and wearing a dirty plaid jacket approached. His hands remained buried in his pockets. Something about his riveting stare, dilated and unfocused, sent an alarm bell ringing through Leslie's brain. He stopped beside her bench, looked at her, and then glanced around as if searching for someone.

"Desperate?" she whispered, immediately wishing she hadn't blurted the name. If this was her reader, she didn't want to meet with this man alone.

Surprise flicked across his face before his eyes narrowed. "You're Dear Granny?"

Before she could respond, he stepped close, bending near her. The acrid smell of beer fouled his breath, and the sickly sweet grassy odor of marijuana cloaked his clothes.

Instinctively, she drew back, though there was nowhere to go. She glimpsed his hand make an underhanded swing as sunlight flashed off metal. Hot pain pierced the area over her stomach.

Giving a surprised gasp as he drew back, she clutched her middle and looked down, then pulled her hand partly away. The sight of red made her shocked, queasy. She looked up at him in horrified question.

"If it weren't for you, my wife never would've left me and taken my kids," he rasped in a whisper, retreating a quick step back, almost as if he, too, was shocked by what he'd done. "That'll teach you to stay out of business that's not yours." With that, he turned on his heel and sprinted away.

Leslie fought down rising panic. *Lord, how could this have happened to me? Why?* Help. . .she must find help. Quickly. She didn't think she could walk or drive. She must call someone.

Hand trembling so badly she could scarcely get her purse open, tears of pain and fear clouding her eyes, she dumped the bag's contents for her cell phone, but when she flipped it on, she couldn't get a signal. No! From the parking lot the roar of a motorcycle revved up, then tore away.

"Lord, please help me!" Using one hand, she pushed herself off the seat, still pressing her other hand hard over her white blouse. She would not just sit here and die on this bench. She must make herself walk, find help. Determination forcing her onward, she staggered in the direction of the distant playhouse, using tree after tree for leverage. The children had turned from their play to watch her. The little girl's mouth formed a wide circle of horror.

"Please. . .get help," Leslie called to them.

The boy jumped down, fell to his knees in the dirt, then shot up and ran for a distant house, the windows and roof of which Leslie could now make out through the trees. The girl scrambled halfway down before she also jumped to the ground and took off at a run, following him.

"Mama, Mama!" the girl's faded cries reached Leslie as the child neared the edge of the park and what must be her own backyard.

Faintness robbed Leslie of breath, preventing her from walking any farther. She braced her hand against a tree trunk and doubled over. Legs giving way, she slumped to the ground.

Chapter 11

Blaine glanced at the clock again, telling himself not to overreact or worry. Last time Leslie didn't show up, he'd blown everything out of proportion by his Neanderthal behavior once she pulled into her drive. True, he'd been worried and a lot of the verbal anger he'd expelled that night had been due to relief at seeing her alive and in one piece. But the last thing he wanted was a repeat of that night. Feelings between them had strengthened, though he had yet to tell her he loved her. He sure didn't want to wreck things between them by acting in haste.

Due to that long-ago argument, he found it hard to believe she would forget to call him now. The previous evening, when they'd planned tonight's date as they watched a TV Western, she'd told him she would be home shortly after five. She usually pulled into her drive at five fifteen. And this morning, before they'd each left for work, she seemed sincere when she'd shouted across the distance that she would be sure to call if anything came up.

At least he now had her number. Twenty minutes before six, he gave in and phoned her house. After ten rings, showing her answering machine wasn't picking up, he took a deep, steadying breath, pushed down the hang-up button, then dialed her number at work and asked for her extension. Carly answered the phone, sounding distracted. Feeling an uncomfortable sense of having gone through this before, Blaine asked to speak to Leslie.

"Oh, Blaine—you haven't heard? Leslie's in the hospital. Abernathy got the call shortly before one o'clock. She was stabbed at a park thirty minutes from here. No one's even sure why she was there."

Fear and horror ripped through him. "Is she. . ." He took a deep, heavy breath. "Is she okay?"

"She's out of surgery. That's all I know. I plan to head there as soon as my deadline's in. Could you do me a favor and contact Leslie's grandmother, in case it hasn't been done yet?"

"I'm already on it." Blaine grabbed a phone book, rapidly flipping through its white pages. "Tell me what hospital she's at, and I need directions how to get there, too."

Carly relayed the information, and Blaine scribbled everything down, grabbed his cell phone and keys, and headed out the door.

With difficulty, he pushed away every frightening image his brain conjured up of Leslie hurt—or worse—and concentrated on the drive. Under his breath, he sent up a prayer.

Groggy, feeling misplaced, Leslie opened her eyes to an unfocused world. Her stomach hurt, and her whole body felt drained. Turning her head where it lay on a pillow, she blinked at the red sunset streaming through a nearby window. An IV stand and a host of other electronic equipment met her eyes.

"Leslie." A wealth of relief sounded in that one soft exclamation of her name. "Well, dear heart, leave it to you to find a way to get me into a car again."

At the soft, familiar voice and mildly teasing words, Leslie spied the beloved form of her grandmother rising from a chair close by.

"Nana?" She was surprised at the weakness of her own voice. Bits and pieces of the day played tricks with her mind, and she focused on the white sheet covering her body, trying to think.

"You were in surgery, but the doctor says you're going to be fine." Nana came close and covered Leslie's hand with her own. "I've called the leader of the prayer chain at church. Everyone there is praying for your speedy recovery."

The words brought with them a handle to a memory. "I was crazy to meet...to talk with him. Desperate...and he—Nana, he had a knife!" Moaning, she tensed as fear sliced through her wooziness and gained a strong foothold.

"There, there. The police want to question you later, but for now you need rest. You haven't been out of surgery all that long. You're still under medication, I think." She turned in her chair. "Blaine, will you go get the nurse?"

Blaine. Leslie closed her eyes, peace chasing away the panic and coddling her like a warm blanket as she again succumbed to the mind-numbing effect of the medication. Nana was there, and Blaine was there. She would be all right.

Once Blaine passed along the information to a nurse that Leslie had awakened, he took off in the direction of the elevators. He needed time to think, time to regroup and sort things out.

Seeing Leslie like that, vulnerable and hurt, and knowing something of what she'd gone through shook him up badly. But hearing her rambled words about being crazy over the guy who'd hurt her about bowled him over. At first. Now, upon thinking about it, nothing made sense. Leslie wouldn't have hooked up with an abuser like the guy who'd stabbed her. Stabbed her...

Blaine couldn't grasp the fact. Who in this peaceful county would want to hurt Leslie? Whoever it was, Blaine hoped he got what he deserved. Right now, Blaine felt about as far removed from Christian thinking as Texas was from the North Pole and wished he, himself, could get his hands on the jerk to teach him a lesson.

Leslie had said she didn't have any former boyfriends, and she'd told Blaine he was the only one she was seeing. She'd once mentioned she wasn't the type to chase after guys. So why had she been "desperate" to meet this weirdo at an out-of-town park? Why hadn't she told anyone where she was going? And the million-dollar question: How did this guy figure into Leslie's life? Too many questions with not an answer in sight.

Pushing his hand through his hair and sliding his palm to the back of his neck, Blaine tried to think. Tried to make sense of all that had happened today. There had to be a logical explanation. He just couldn't figure out what it was.

At least something good had come about from all this. He now realized how deeply he cared for Leslie. And if she would have him, he meant to tell her of his feelings and propose soon. The unexpected thought of marrying her stunned him a moment, making him question if he was really ready for such a monumental step. But the thought of a life without her was one he couldn't tolerate.

Blaine pondered an idea that came to him. He needed wise advice on how to go about all this. Should he wait until she was better? Or tell her how he felt now? It might cheer her up; then again, it might not. Especially if there *were* some other guy in the picture.

Blaine's heart felt crushed at the thought. No, he trusted her. But the very thought of avowing his love and proposing—foreign to Blaine up until now— made him go hot and cold all over. Especially if she turned him down.

His mind a battleground of conflicting thoughts, he entered the empty elevator and pushed the ground-floor button. Leaning his head and shoulders back against the wall once the doors shut, he closed his eyes. Then again, maybe he was moving too fast. Not for the first time, he wished his parents were still alive. Even a male friend would be nice to talk to right now. A thought struck, making him open his eyes and straighten from the wall as the elevator pitched downward and his stomach dipped. *God, I need help. I need wise counsel and feel You appointed that lady columnist to Goosebury since she sure sounds like a Christian. Should I write her one more letter, seeking advice?*

Carly had mentioned she planned on coming tonight; in fact, she should be here any minute. And someone at this hospital was bound to have paper and an envelope Blaine could use. He could write the letter now before he chickened out and pray about it more over the next few days. A decision such as this one required a lot of prayer. Still, it wouldn't hurt to write the letter and give it to Carly to hand-deliver to Dear Granny.

Hopefully, the advice to him would be printed soon. If his letter was one of those chosen at all.

❧

Despite the fact her arm was sore from a tetanus shot, and her entire middle ached from the metal staples holding her together after surgery, Leslie was forced to get up and walk the next morning. When Nurse Freid had changed her dressing earlier, Leslie commented, "My stomach looks as if it's been closed with a zipper." The friendly nurse had laughed. "Yes, we've come a long way from the buttons we used to use." She'd winked at her in jest, and once she finished tending her, she'd gotten Leslie out of bed. Leslie's body protested every laborious step.

While blowing into something called an incentive spirometer to keep from having her lungs collapse, she was told, Leslie pushed the awkward IV on wheels with her sore arm. She wished she had wheels on the bottom of her feet, too, and could get this torture walk done and over with so that she might return to the comfort of her bed. Still, for all the misery the nurses and doctors consistently put her through—"necessary misery," Nana gently chastised her—she was grateful to be alive and thanked God each time she opened her eyes.

Surely, if there were such a thing, she should receive the trophy for Goosebury's Idiot of the Year for the crazy and dangerous stunt she had pulled, meeting a stranger in the park alone, whose letters pointed to emotional and mental instability. Even the police had looked at her as if she were missing a few rafters upstairs when she'd answered their questions and told them her reasons for going.

At least God had brought some good out of the situation, and Nana had surmounted her fear enough to ride in a car with Blaine to the hospital. Leslie wasn't sure what she would have done if Nana weren't there and told her so as she entered her room and the nurse helped her back into bed.

"I'm just thankful I *am* able to be here for you, Leslie," her grandmother comforted once the nurse had gone. Nana fussed over her, tucking the sheet around her as if she were a child. "That book you gave me on how God sees fear helped me to view matters in a different light than I had before. I learned the type of crippling fear I was experiencing was because I was putting faith in the wrong thing. Instead of trusting God, I placed my faith in the idea that a feared crash would come to pass the next time I rode in anyone's car. But to be honest, if this hadn't happened to you, I'm still not so sure I would've gotten into a car anytime soon. When Blaine told me you'd been taken to the hospital, the old fear did creep in. But I was so concerned about you, this time I was able to squelch it, especially since using a motorboat wasn't an option." She grinned.

"So you think this is the first of many outside steps your house?" Leslie shook her head. The medication was causing her tongue not to coincide with her brain again. Or maybe it was due to exhaustion of mind and body from her torture walk. "I mean steps outside your house."

"Yes, I think so. Blaine's already offered to pick me up for church on Sunday, since my driver's license is expired. After what happened, I feel a strong need to go. Anyway, now that I've read the book you gave me, I'd like to give it to someone else. Would that be all right with you, dear?"

"Who?" Leslie racked her brain for someone they knew who might benefit from such a book.

"I'm not sure. I want to be open to the Lord, but it will definitely go to someone in need of it."

"Nana, the book's yours. Do what you want with it. I'm just glad it helped." They carefully hugged, and for the first time in a long time, Leslie felt as if Nana was going to be okay.

About an hour later, as Leslie watched an old sitcom on television, Mr. Abernathy walked into her room, holding a laptop and a handful of letters. He seemed edgy, as if he wanted to get out of there. "Glad to see you looking well."

Leslie wondered what his definition of *well* was.

"When you're up to it, I'd like you to go through some of these letters and e-mail me your replies. Deadline's tomorrow."

The bathroom door opened, and Nana stepped out, pulling it shut behind her. "Ronald, what are you up to?"

"Lily?" He seemed genuinely surprised to see her. "I'm sorry your grand-daughter got it into her head to pull such a crazy stunt as meeting that maniac in the park, but I still have a paper to run."

"And you couldn't find anyone else to take her place for this one issue?"

He shrugged. "You could help if you wanted. I learned you've been doing a lot of that, more or less. You always did have a soft heart, Lily." He smiled. "It's good to see you again."

"Hmph. You haven't changed one bit. Still as stubborn as the day is long and as business minded as ever." She crossed her arms over her ample chest, but an answering smile flickered at the corners of her lips.

Leslie grinned to see Nana's cheeks go so rosy. "If I'm feeling better later, I promise I'll get to them, Mr. Abernathy."

Before she'd finished her sentence, another visitor walked into the room.

"Carly!" Leslie smiled and shifted, trying to sit up, then winced as the skin pulled a bit from the staples. She couldn't wait to get them out. "Weren't you here night last, too?" Her pain medication was making her sound like a moron.

"Yes, but you were way out of it. Sounds like you're still hinging on the edge. Feeling any better?" Carly walked toward the bed.

Mr. Abernathy cleared his throat, shuffled his feet, and said his good-byes, quickly making his exit. Nana excused herself and followed him out the door.

"I'm really sorry this happened to you," Carly said.

Leslie concentrated on speaking slowly and choosing her words so they didn't jumble. "Maybe if I'd told you where I was going, you could have talked me out of it. You're a lot smarter than me sometimes."

"Not so smart." Carly looked down in shame before her gaze met Leslie's again. "I do dumb things, too, things I regret. I just hope we still can be friends once I tell you. I gave a weak try that day at the tag sale, but now I want to get it off my chest."

Leslie waited with no idea what Carly could mean.

"I wrote...after the anniversary issue came out." Carly exhaled a deep breath after a few false starts and dove in. "All right, here it is. I wrote some awful letters to you after reading your first issue of the column. I was hurt and upset, but I shouldn't have taken it out on you, and I'm sorry."

Leslie collected her thoughts. "You're the poison pen writer?"

"Ouch." Carly winced. "I guess I deserve that. But you didn't deserve having your character ripped apart like I did, or me calling you a poor excuse for a Christian, either. Since I'm not one, I wouldn't even know the genuine article if it came up and bit me on the nose." She gave a weak chuckle. "But if I did believe in a God and had to call anyone a Christian, I'd say you're it, Les. Actually, you're one of the sweetest people I know."

Leslie dredged up a faint smile. She had prayed for the poison pen writer every day since receiving those three letters. Several other letters from other readers had also been detrimental but not like those three. Now that she knew it was Carly, she waited for bitterness or betrayal to rise up and was surprised when it didn't. Instead, she felt only a rush of relief to learn the truth.

"Can I ask a question, Carly?"

"Sure."

"What did I write that made you so mad?"

Carly hesitated. "I was one of the initial letter writers, one of those you first gave advice to."

"I thought so. The peacock blue sweaterdress?"

"No." She shifted her feet. "Actually, you know what? I'd rather not talk about it. I'm trying to forget that entire episode in my life and keep a fresh perspective on things. I just want you to know that I now stand beside you. That is, if you even want me there."

She pulled an envelope from her shoulder bag. "The other reason I came, besides to lay my head on the confession chopping block, was to bring you this. Since Abernathy's being his usual lovable self and is pushing you back to the grindstone from your hospital bed, if you *do* feel up to working on the column, I suggest you give this letter top priority."

Leslie looked it over. "No stamp or postmark?"

"It was hand-delivered."

"You mean personally?"

"Uh—yup. And that's all I'm going to say." Carly made the motion of locking her mouth shut with one hand and tossed the imaginary key over her shoulder. She gave one of her signature carefree grins. "Well, now that that's done, I need to scoot. I have a job interview in the a.m. Don't let them stick anything up your arm without knowing what it's hooked to." She grinned to show she was teasing and headed for the door with a flip of a wave. "Try to have a restful night."

"Carly?"

The perky co-worker halted and swung a look over her shoulder, her long dark hair swinging with the motion.

"We're still on for lunch, right? Say in two weeks, when the doctor says I'll feel more like myself again?"

Dawning realization glimmered in Carly's eyes, along with what Leslie suspected was a tear or two. A smile stretched across her face, proving she knew she'd been forgiven.

"You bet. And I have a couple of great, loose caftans you can have to putter around the house in while you heal." She hesitated. "Thanks for the second chance."

"Besides Nana, you've become my only ally."

"Newly converted to the 'We Love Dear Granny' Fan Club, but at least it's something, eh? By the way, do you plan on telling Blaine your true profession soon? I'd bet my entire paycheck he would make another great ally if he knew."

"I should've asked Abernathy's permission while he was here, but I forgot. I'm still out of it and not thinking clearly."

"Do it soon, Leslie. I mean it. You wouldn't want to lose a great guy like Blaine by not being totally up-front with him. And all because of some unmerited loyalty you feel toward the paper."

Struck by Carly's sudden serious attitude, Leslie was left speechless as her friend exited the room.

Chapter 12

"Nana, could you hand me those letters, please?" Leslie set down her apple juice, something she'd ingested a lot of during this clear-liquid diet phase the doctor had put her on, and pressed down the button to raise the top of the bed a little higher.

"Are you sure you want to do this now?"

"I think I'm up to looking through them, at least, and we still have time before the deadline. Mr. Abernathy brought a phone cable to hook up to the computer, so I can e-mail him the answers straightaway. I'll let you type them."

"It'll be a matter of hunting and pecking on the keys, but you know I'll help however I can, dear."

After much thought, Leslie had decided, at least temporarily, to continue her job as Dear Granny. But she had learned her lesson and would never meet with a reader again.

She glanced through the batch of letters and chose the hand-delivered one Carly had labeled top priority, deciding to read it first. She tore open the flap and withdrew the paper.

" 'Dear Granny,' " she read aloud so Nana could hear, " 'I wrote to you once before and used your advice, but since then complications have developed in our relationship. Ever since that first date with my neighbor, I've fallen in love with her—I think I might've even loved her from the start—but now I have reason to suspect there's someone else in her life. We've been seeing each other on a steady basis for weeks, and I've reached a point where I want to propose marriage. But now I feel maybe I should just hold off since I don't know half of what's going on in her life. A lot of strange things have been happening lately, and talking to her about them doesn't seem to work. She refuses to tell me what's going on, so I've stopped pressing her. What advice can you give me? Should I tell her how I feel now? That I love her? Or should I just keep quiet? I don't want to botch things up even worse than I did one night when I was upset and she wanted my trust—but I walked away and wouldn't give it to her.' It's signed, 'Hopeless in love.' "

"Oh!" Awareness made Leslie lift her head. "This is from the reader with the purple stationery. Only it's a man, not a woman like I thought. That's the second time I've made a mistake concerning gender. I thought Desperate was a woman, too." The last two sentences she added to herself, under her breath.

"Leslie, I'm ashamed of you."

At the stern note in Nana's quiet voice, Leslie looked up from the letter in surprise.

"You're not a stupid girl. I know that for a fact, since I practically raised you. But these past few months you've acted like a total lunkhead, as your brother Jimmy would say."

"What? Why?" Leslie was baffled by the abrupt attack.

"You've strung that poor man along all this time without letting him know your true feelings for him? And you've refused to tell him the truth about your position? Leslie! While I do understand your concern about clearing the matter with your boss first, I think in this case you've carried your subterfuge entirely too far."

Leslie blinked. The new medication didn't alter her thought processes as it had before. Nevertheless, she felt far removed from reality. She wondered if they were even on the same planet.

"Nana, what on earth are you talking about?"

"You really don't know, do you?" Nana shook her head. "Read the letter again. Slowly, this time. And think about the words."

Swallowing over the sudden lump in her throat, feeling as if a chink of light had begun to enter the door harboring her ignorance, Leslie read the letter a second time. The words seemed to jump out at her, revealing themselves in a blatant way when before they'd been hidden. *Oh, my. . .Hopeless in Love is Blaine! How could I not have seen it before? And. . .he loves me? Wants to marry me?*

Stunned, she looked up. The expression on her face must have been enough to prove her discovery, for when Leslie focused on her grandmother, Nana nodded like a wise sage. "Yes, it's Blaine. I recognized his handwriting and the stationery the first time from when he sent a thank-you note after his parents' funeral."

"And you didn't tell me?" Leslie still worked to latch on to clear thought. A roller coaster of emotions dipped and peaked inside her.

"It wasn't my place, and you didn't need to know at the time. But I thought surely you would explain about your job to him once your relationship progressed. It's been months, Leslie. You could've spoken to Ronald at any time to clear it with him. Why didn't you?"

"I don't know." Leslie moaned and clutched her hair on both sides of her head. "Or maybe I do. Maybe subconsciously I didn't want Blaine to think any less of me when he found out about my job, so I didn't tell him. You know I thought of it as pure fluff at first and was embarrassed to get stuck with it. Oh, Nana. I feel so stupid. I'm the last person who should be writing this column and giving people advice. I've made such a mess of my own life!"

Her grandmother moved to lay a comforting hand on Leslie's arm above the IV needle. "Don't be too hard on yourself, dear. Wisdom comes with age. And with it, experience. You're still young. Give yourself time to grow and learn and make mistakes in the process. Everyone does; it's all part of growth. And while it's true you did make a mess of things, I don't think it's too late to work it all out."

"You really think so?" Leslie swiped at a tear that dripped past her lashes.

"Of course. It does make the situation a bit more difficult since he was one of the letter writers, but the problem shouldn't be insurmountable as long as you deal with it quickly and set things straight right away." A smile lifted the corners of her mouth. "So am I correct in assuming that for answering this letter you won't need my help?"

"Yes." A surge of excitement swept through Leslie. "I know exactly what I want to say, and I need to type in this reply myself. Can you help me with the table?"

Nana cleared off the lunch tray and laid the laptop within Leslie's reach before excusing herself from the room in what Leslie knew was a method to give her some privacy. Typing hurt, and she couldn't do it for long, but Carly was right. This was one letter that deserved her sole attention. And as an exception to her new rule, this was one reader she *would* meet with face-to-face. She only hoped she wasn't too late.

❧

Nervous, Blaine rode the hospital elevator up to Leslie's floor. He hadn't brought flowers, since she preferred they remain in the garden, and he'd given her enough candy to enable him to try out for a part as Willy Wonka. At the gift shop, he'd found a small white bear that seemed like something Leslie might like, so he bought that instead. Dear Granny had advised him in today's column to talk to his neighbor with all haste and not to withhold any of his feelings when he did. That he might be surprised by her answer.

Blaine hoped so. He also hoped the idea of proposing to her before she left the hospital wasn't a mistake, but Granny had urged him in that regard, too. After two days of seeking the Lord's guidance, Blaine knew Leslie was the woman with whom he wanted to spend the rest of his life.

Walking into her room, he noticed her sitting on the edge of the bed and wearing a loose pink dress, her hair all combed back and tied in a pretty ribbon. Her grandmother and Carly were there, too, but all Blaine could see was Leslie. Her eyes shone as she looked at Blaine and smiled, her gaze dropping to the bear he held by one paw.

Blaine shifted nervously. "This is for you." Well, of course it was. He was already sounding like an idiot, and he hadn't even asked his most important question. Mentally grabbing onto the coattails of boldness, he cleared his throat and walked closer. "Leslie, there's something I need to talk to you about. This really wasn't the way I'd planned it—in a hospital, with you barely back on your feet—but what I have to say is important enough not to wait any longer."

Her grandmother and Carly made their excuses and quickly cleared the room, leaving Blaine alone with Leslie. Her eyes seemed to sparkle even more, her expression soft, expectant.

"Yes, Blaine?"

"The truth is, I love you and have for some time now. I'm not sure what that was all about at the park, or why you were even there, but I'm hoping you can learn to trust me enough to tell me some day soon. I'm also hoping there's no one else you're going out with right now, because I find I don't want to share you with anyone." He shook his head at his garbled sentences, which seemed out of order.

"There's no one else, Blaine." Her tone sounded hopeful.

"The guy at the park?" The question came out before he could stop it.

"A stranger. I didn't even know him." Her lashes flicked down. "Um, I don't really want to talk about that right now." She looked up at him again. "Believe me, there's no one but you."

The elation he felt by her admission battled with his misery regarding her exclusion. But maybe she was right; now didn't seem like the time to ask about the park. He was still stunned by her last words, and they emboldened him to move closer. "Leslie, what I'm trying to say is I want to be more than your boyfriend."

Realizing he still held the bear and wanting to hold her hand instead, he set the plush animal on the corner edge of the nearby table. The bear almost fell, and he pushed aside some envelopes stacked by her laptop in order to make room for the toy. The first two letters slid out of place. The words *Dear Granny* caught his attention, and he reached for the stack instead.

"What's this?" Confused, he shuffled through the letters, noticing they all bore the same address of the *Gazette*'s office. His recent letter lay at the bottom of the pile.

She gave a sharp intake of breath. "Blaine, I can explain. I'd planned to. . . . I just wanted to wait to hear what you had to say first."

Understanding hit him like a swift blow to the gut, and his gaze shot to her anxious one. "You're Dear Granny."

She closed her eyes and offered one swift, brief nod in return.

The unexpectedness of her betrayal twisted his heart. She must have known it was him all along—how could she not? The letters gave him away; his love for the girl next door, their mutual lack of conversation, even glossing over their fight when he'd stalked off that night.

He stared at her in hurt disbelief and let out a disgusted, self-deprecating laugh. "I should've known." He looked back at the letters in his hand. "Man, you must've pegged me for a total fool!"

"What? No!"

He paced to the window, looked outside. He had just bared his heart to her, had just opened up to her in a way he'd never done with any other woman. And in the span of seconds, she'd blasted him without a word via his discovery of her game; what an idiot he was.

"What was I to you, Leslie? Some cheap publicity gimmick? A plan you and your boss hatched to bring in more readers to the column? Did your reasons for going out with me include the idea of eventually publishing our dating disasters so all of Goosebury could get in on a good laugh?" Upset and hurt, he turned back to her and tossed the letters on the end of the bed with a quick flick of his wrist.

She jumped, though they came nowhere close to hitting her. "Blaine, it wasn't like that at all. I liked you. That's why I went out with you."

"Liked me? How can I believe you, Leslie? You haven't been straight with me from the start. What else am I to assume but that you had a personal, ulterior motive since the day we met?" He set his mouth into a grim line. "So, was it worth it? Didja get a good laugh, Leslie? Huh? Did you enjoy trying to make me feel as if I was finally beginning to fit into your town, when behind my back you were doing what you could to ridicule me?"

"No, Blaine, it wasn't like that at all—"

"Did you read my letters aloud to Carly and did both of you get a good laugh over the lame-brained, word-shy Texas flatlander who had the stupidity to fall in love with his Vermont neighbor? Or was that all part of the gimmick, too—to make me love you?"

Tears made her eyes shine and trickled past her lashes. The sight disturbed him, and he averted his gaze to the little white bear. How different he'd thought this morning would turn out when he'd bought it!

"I know I should've told you, b–but I couldn't. I was embarrassed. I didn't want you to think any less of me, a–and if you found out what my beat was at the paper, you might have."

Her tremulous words knifed through his heart, but his pride was badly wounded, and he refused to bend. "So you really thought deceiving me would make me feel better about you as a person? That it was perfectly all right to tell me how to proceed and give me advice, knowing all along I was the letter writer. But then never telling me the truth about yourself?" He shook his head in disbelief. "Sorry, Leslie. Your reasoning just won't wash."

"I didn't even know you were Hopeless in Love until yesterday. You must believe that, Blaine."

"Why? Because you've been so honest with me so far?"

She dropped her head as if beaten.

He wanted to stay mad, wanted to keep his defense strong. But the sight of her jaw trembling and seeing how hard she worked to hold back the tears was making him soften fast.

She betrayed you, a dark thought interrupted, *betrayed your love. Played with your feelings in a callous way that made a mockery of what you'd thought was beautiful between you. She doesn't care. You're just another unwanted flatlander to her.* The notion stung like sulfur burning a hole through his heart.

"Please, Blaine, I do care about you. Honest," she said as if she'd eavesdropped into his private thoughts. "I meant to tell you. This whole thing just got so out of hand—"

He lifted his palms to face her, to prevent her from saying more, then shifted his focus to a few feet below her entreating face. The room now felt stifling, suffocating. His feelings raged too strong, and he shook his head, knowing he needed out of here. Fast.

"Sorry, Leslie. I've just got to get away from you right now." Not trusting himself to say another word, Blaine quickly exited the room.

The tears Leslie tried so hard to contain escaped once Blaine left. She grabbed the white bear, bending her face to it as she dampened its plush fur with her tears.

She had ruined everything! Her foolish pride concerning her job title and the fear she would be ridiculed had robbed her of the man she loved. Surely ridicule wouldn't have stung so badly.

"Leslie?"

Hearing Nana enter the room, Leslie worked to stifle her tears and crying little gasps. But when her grandmother's arm went around her, she almost gave in to them again.

"I've lost him." She sat up and looked Nana in the eye. "I acted like the fool Proverbs always warns about, and I've lost him, Nana."

Concern etched furrows in Nana's brow, but she shook her head. "No, I don't think so. He's just mad right now and hurt. Often those we're closest to are the ones who hurt us the most."

Leslie sniffled and wiped the tears from beside her nose. "You talked to him?"

"Only briefly. He asked Carly to take us home."

Leslie gave an abrupt nod. "See? He doesn't want anything more to do with me, and who could blame him? He thought I'd held back telling him who I was because of some publicity stunt I'd hatched with the paper and that it somehow involved him."

"*Tsk, tsk.* Oh, Leslie." Nana laid her palm on her shoulder. "Nothing hidden stays that way. The truth always comes out in the end. But once the dust settles and he's had time to think it over, you'll see him again. I'm sure of it. All couples have their little tiffs. Your grandfather and I certainly had our share."

"This seemed like a lot more than a 'little tiff,' Nana. It was more like 'the end,' like a good-bye. I just don't seem to be making any wise decisions lately.

I should've told him I was Dear Granny first instead of waiting for him to speak. Now I feel like a complete fool."

"I'm sure it's not the end, Leslie, and you're not a fool. In these past months we've been writing the 'Dear Granny' column together and basing a lot of suggestions from the book of Proverbs. If you've learned nothing else, I hope you've learned what we found from that."

Nana shifted to pull from her tote the Bible she carried. "The source of all wisdom is to be found in here. *All* wisdom, Leslie. Because God is the only One who's entirely wise. Fools despise His Word, even mock it, and they mock those who present it to them. Proverbs tells us only the wise can give good advice, but fools can't."

Leslie looked down at the Bible that Nana had raised to make her point.

"This is why the advice we've given for the column was widely accepted by many but rejected by others. Fools can't accept it, meaning those who are opposed to God. So you see, you're no fool, dear, because I know you love God and read His Word. But these priceless words are nonsense to fools. They turn against those who give them, sometimes in a violent way, like what happened to you in the park. You didn't heed that check in your spirit not to go, and you acted foolishly, but that doesn't make you a fool."

"I just wanted to help." Leslie hung her head. "I feel like such a failure: first my stupidity of going alone to meet an unknown reader without telling anyone, then my deception with Blaine. Sometimes I wonder if I'm really any good for anyone."

"Actually, you are."

A woman's voice suddenly came from the door, and both Leslie and Nana looked that way in surprise.

"I'm sorry," a pretty blond said, her face flushing. She stood with one foot in the room, one foot still in the corridor. Her eyes darted to and fro, as if she were suddenly embarrassed to be caught eavesdropping. "The door was open, and I thought it would be all right for me to come in. I shouldn't have intruded." She turned to go.

"Please—wait." Leslie half stood to stop her. At the sudden rush of weakness, she regretted standing without aid and sat back down. "I'd like to talk with you."

The woman hesitantly turned. Of average height and build, her features appearing as if she had Swedish ties, she had an astonishingly pretty face, dainty, almost china doll-like. Leslie assumed the woman to be in her early twenties, like her. Her platinum blond hair looked natural and hung to her jaw in spirals.

"Have we met?" Leslie asked.

"No." The woman still seemed uncomfortable as she took a few steps inside. With both hands, she clutched the handle of her purse hanging down in front of her. "You don't know me, but I know you're Dear Granny."

A hint of alarm made Leslie's eyes go wide. "Please close the door and have a seat."

The woman did so. Once seated, she nervously smoothed her canvas beige skirt over her knees. Her clothing looked old, worn, as did the faded peach-colored T-shirt she wore.

"Why have you come to see me?" Leslie asked. "Who are you?"

The woman looked up after a few seconds elapsed, her sky blue eyes solemn and wide. "I'm Sharon Lester. The wife of the man who attacked you."

Chapter 13

At the woman's startling announcement, both Leslie and Nana continued to stare at her.

"I—I had to come," Sharon explained. "You told me something I already knew through your column—that I had to leave Mark and get help. But I was too scared to act before. I was the reader who wrote as Living in Fear. You probably don't remember me; I'm sure you get hundreds of people writing to you."

"Actually, I do remember," Leslie said. Hers had been one of the more disturbing letters.

Obviously nervous, the woman gave a slight nod before she went on. "When Mark was hitting only me, that was one thing. Believe me, this isn't my first visit to this place." She paused to look around the walls of the hospital. "But when he turned on our five-year-old son. . ."

A fierce protectiveness shone from her eyes, and she firmed her shoulders. "I just couldn't let that happen again. I took your advice and found a shelter. I asked the lady who runs the safe house where the children and me are staying to bring me to see you since the paper said you'd be discharged today. She's waiting for me outside in the hall. I knew Mark wouldn't be stupid enough to show his face around here. And I wanted to help you, since you've helped me so much. And to thank you for what you've done."

Leslie waited for the woman to continue, uncertain of what to say.

"I told the police it was Mark who attacked you. He has a motorcycle, like the newspaper said, and the physical description fits, too. When he found out I'd written you and you'd given me advice to leave him, he was angry—and that last day with him, he said he would find out who Dear Granny was and get even if it was the last thing he did."

Sharon inhaled a deep breath, briefly glancing down and pulling at the edge of her bottom lip with her teeth. "But you should know something. I came forward because what Mark did was very wrong and he needs help. As crazy as it sounds, deep in my heart I still love him. He's the father of my children, of the baby inside me now, and he wasn't always mean. That only started after he got fired and couldn't find another job once our last child was born. That's when he began smoking pot and doing other drugs—crystal meth and stuff. I just want him to get straightened out."

"That's admirable of you, Sharon. I'm not sure many women in your place would be so forgiving or so loyal."

"Oh, I'm no saint, er. . ."

"Leslie."

"Leslie. I'm still hurt by what Mark did. And sometimes when I think about our home life these past few years, I get so angry I want to scream or spit. Anyway, I just wanted you to know where I stand in all this. I'm not turning against Mark or seeking revenge or anything like that. I want him to get the help he needs, and I think the only way that's going to happen is if he's arrested and forced to get some kind of counseling."

Leslie mulled over the woman's words.

"I guess that sounds strange to you. But I learned some time ago that the important things in life are worth fighting for. My marriage is important to me—still is—and my children are important. And I'll move heaven and earth to take care of what I've got."

A knock sounded at the open door, and the doctor strode inside. At the interruption, the defiance slipped away from Sharon, and she bowed her head meekly.

"So, Leslie," the doctor said, "are you eager to go home?"

"You bet."

"I've taken enough of your time," Sharon said, rising. "Thank you for seeing me."

"Sharon," Nana cut in, "while the doctor confers with my granddaughter, may I speak with you in the corridor?"

The woman looked puzzled but nodded, and both Nana and Sharon left the room.

As the doctor gave instructions about caring for the wound while she was at home, Leslie nodded each time he paused, but she couldn't stop thinking about what was going on in the corridor. She wished she were a fly on that wall.

Once the doctor left, Leslie collected the "Dear Granny" letters Blaine had strewn over the end of the bed and tucked them in her tote. At the memory of how she had so obviously hurt him, tears threatened again, but she held them back.

The metal staples had been removed, and Steri-Strips of threaded adhesive tape were in their place, which the doctor had told her would eventually curl up and peel off. Yet she couldn't help but feel as if her wounded heart needed stapling together as well. Sighing, she finished packing and wondered if there was such a thing as emotional sutures.

⌇

Blaine shoved a second T-shirt deep inside his roll bag.

All week, he'd purposely stayed away from home now that Leslie was back. Her grandmother had temporarily moved in with Leslie to help out, and from her, Blaine had learned about the attack in the park and the cause of it. Leslie's carelessness both alarmed and exasperated him. But her deception still stung as badly as it had that first day, and he didn't want to see her.

It wasn't so much that she'd neglected to tell him her job title; it was her reason for withholding that information. She'd purposely omitted the fact, and Blaine now remembered the many times she'd hedged or quickly changed the subject when the "Dear Granny" column was introduced into conversation. Why? It didn't make sense, unless her motives were selfish. She'd once told him her goal was to be a star reporter. Maybe to her, their dating fiascos—and writing articles about them on the side—had just been a stair step in reaching that goal. True, he'd never seen one published, but this theory was the only reason he could think of as to why she'd kept silent.

The phone rang, and Leslie's voice came on after the answering machine beeped.

"Blaine? Are you there? Please pick up if you are."

The sudden urge to pick up the phone was strong, taking him by surprise, but Blaine held back and forced himself to continue packing instead.

His manly pride had been badly beaten that day in the hospital room. Yeah, maybe he was acting immature in not answering her call or in not going over to see her since she'd come home, but her betrayal still smarted. He'd bared his heart in those letters, written his deepest feelings to a person he'd thought was a sympathetic, gentle-hearted old woman, a stranger—he'd written words he could have never said aloud to anyone he knew, especially the object of his desire. To realize it had been Leslie who'd read his failings and insecurities about women—and worse, knew who he was the whole time—felt invasive, as if she'd trespassed into a personal journal. All along she must have known he was the reader Hopeless in Love, despite her denial of it at the hospital last week. If that didn't reek of deceit, he didn't know what did.

The phone rang again, but this time the caller hung up and didn't leave a message. Blaine finished packing, then grabbed his jacket and walked through the rooms, making sure all windows were locked and everything was off. Upon further consideration, he'd decided not to sell this house and move back to Texas—his initial plan as he'd stormed from the hospital that day. But he had asked for a week's vacation from work with the intent of driving through Vermont and visiting places of interest, as well as the covered bridges throughout the state. Those points of contact made him feel closer to Mom, since she'd collected items with a covered-bridge theme. Once again, he wished he had a family member he could confide in.

He swung his duffel bag into the backseat and slid behind the wheel of his refurbished car. If he'd been better prepared, he would have hiked the Long Trail, which went from southern Vermont all the way up into Canada. To Blaine's surprise, one of the guys from church had invited him to tag along with a group a few days earlier. But he didn't have the required camping gear and wanted some time alone right now anyway. A drive through the Green Mountains should give him exactly what he needed. Some peace and quiet to sort out life's present issues.

At least, for the first time since he'd moved here a season ago, the ice was beginning to thaw between him and the locals and a hand of friendship had been extended. One he would gladly accept upon his return. Too bad things were now so rocky between him and his neighbor, though.

You can change that, a gentle voice seemed to whisper inside his head. *All you have to do is put the past behind you and forgive.*

He pulled his car out of the garage and hesitated, his gaze swinging to Leslie's house. Maybe sometime soon he would try to make amends. But that wouldn't stop the hollow pain stemming from the knowledge that Leslie obviously didn't care about him as much as he'd come to care for her. He'd been an assignment to her, a rung up the job ladder.

Shaking his head, he drove off, leaving Goosebury behind.

"Heard from Blaine?" Carly asked as she walked inside Leslie's house, a small paper sack with what Leslie assumed to be letters in her hand.

"No." Leslie still wasn't recovered enough to return to the office, so Carly visited each day and brought any "Dear Granny" letters that came.

"Cheer up. Like your grandmother said, he's just spending a little time blowing off some steam. A few days ago he told my uncle he was going to take a week off to tour the countryside. I doubt he's moving, since he also told my uncle he's planning on joining his covered bridge club."

"Really?" Hope flickered inside Leslie, and she managed a smile.

"Really. You know what you need? An outing. Feel up to hitting Milton's Pantry?"

"Oh, Carly, I'd love to. But I'm behind in getting the column ready. Though I sometimes wonder if I shouldn't just resign from my job and let Mr. Abernathy give it to someone else."

"No, don't do that." Suddenly serious, Carly sat on the couch catty-corner from her. "The advice you and your grandmother concocted helped a lot of readers."

"It wasn't us concocting anything, so much as using the Bible for a guideline. 'The eternal words struck a chord in readers' hearts,' as Nana once told me."

Carly shifted, looking uneasy. She and Leslie had grown closer since her confession, but she still avoided the subject of God.

"If that's how you think, then why are you talking about quitting?" Carly asked.

"Because I feel so inept at times. Nana should take a journalism class so she can take the beat. She fits the role perfectly. Much better than me."

"But it's your know-how and talent with words that draw readers to the column, Leslie. If you left, it wouldn't be the same." She paused, as if struggling with what she was about to say. "I know I said I didn't want to speak of what was bothering me, but maybe I was wrong not to say anything. Maybe you should know where I was coming from when I wrote you those letters. But please don't tell anyone else. In this small town, I'd probably be looked upon as if I wore a scarlet letter or something."

Her gaze plummeting downward, Carly played with the tassel of a pillow. "I was the reader who wrote about dating the flatlander who was married. Only I didn't know Jake was married; he'd led me to believe otherwise. Only when I went to an art gallery to conduct an interview did I see him there with his wife."

"Carly." Leslie reached out to lay her hand on her friend's arm. "I'm so sorry. That must have hurt a lot."

"The hardest part is that I'd gotten so serious about him. When you wrote what you did about giving him up, part of me knew that was the right thing to do, but the other part of me—the part that wanted his love—rebelled against your words. About a week ago, I completely broke it off with him, and I hang up when he calls now. If my uncle or aunt were to find out about my affair, they'd throw me out of the house for sure. They say I'm just like my mother more times than I can count, and I know about her only from what I've heard from them, since she dumped me on them when I was two. Even though I know it's high time I find my own place, I don't want to be forced into the position by getting kicked out."

Leslie considered a moment. "I have plenty of room here. Would you like to move in with me?"

For a moment, something like hope crossed Carly's features, but she shook her head. "I appreciate the invite, but I'd drive you nuts within a week. Don't worry about me, Leslie. I'll figure something out. As long as my secret scandal stays safely buried, I'll thrive in Goosebury."

"You know I won't tell a soul."

"I know." She smiled. "I trust you."

"I wish other people did." Leslie's attempt at a carefree smile felt fake.

"Give him time. He was hurt, but can you blame him?" The words were sympathetic, the look in Carly's eyes soft. "You should have told him the truth weeks ago, when I said to."

"I know, I know. You don't think I haven't kicked myself in the head for not doing so every day?"

Carly grinned. "That brings an interesting picture to mind. Seriously, Les, he'll get over it and will be back on your doorstep in no time."

"I'm not so sure. I read in an article recently that the one thing you're never supposed to do to a man is injure his pride. He bared his heart to me in those letters, thinking I was a complete stranger. Even worse, those letters were about me." She sighed. "I should just try to let it go and forget about him, I guess."

Carly sailed to her feet like a rocket, surprising Leslie. "Leslie Edwards, I can't believe I just heard you say that. Okay, so you made a mistake. Big deal. You're only human. But I didn't think you'd be the type to give up so easily in things that really mattered. Look how you've stuck it out by taking on the beat of 'Dear Granny' when you didn't want the job. How many times did you tell me you wanted to quit? But instead, you went to your grandmother for help, you persisted, and it paid off. If Blaine's worth it, and I think he is, isn't your relationship that much more important and worth fighting for? At least go see him and try talking to him again once he comes home. Don't throw in the towel yet."

"We hardly have anything serious enough to label as a real relationship, Carly. I mean a serious one. We've only been dating a few months." Still, to Leslie it had become serious, and that's why she suspected the pain of the breakup stung so badly.

"What I saw in his eyes was serious when he was looking at you. And didn't he say he planned to propose in that letter he wrote? That sounds pretty serious to me." Carly sank to the cushion next to Leslie, the fight in her gone and sympathy again coming to the surface. "Just don't give up, Leslie. You've got what it takes to win him back, because you've got his heart."

Carly's words brought with them the memory of Sharon Lester's similar words, and how that woman was all set to fight for what was important to her.

Ashamed that she'd been ready to give up so easily on any hope of a continued relationship with Blaine, Leslie uncovered new strength within herself. With God's help, she was determined to do all she could to mend things. And the idea of how to do it came so swiftly it almost took her breath away. It was perfect. She was just surprised she hadn't thought of such an approach sooner.

❦

All around Blaine, people gathered at wooden tables inside the rustic restaurant, seated with families or friends, chatting as they ate. Sitting by himself at a table for two, he felt loneliness sharper than the taste of the lemon he sucked on from his tea.

Peace and quiet? Ha! Not with his thoughts and memories constantly jabbing at him right and left. Sure, he could get in the car and drive away to a solitary place in the mountains, but he couldn't escape himself. And he was getting mighty tired of his own company.

Without Leslie, life was sour. It just wasn't fun viewing the sights alone. His thoughts jumped back to the day they'd shared visiting bridges when they first started dating. Seeing them alone didn't have the appeal that looking at them together once did.

"You should've handled things better, Blaine," he muttered to the lemon slice in his hand. "Should have thought things through before you acted, ignoramus that you are. But did you listen to common sense and exercise self-control when you needed to? No. So whose fault is it now that you're feeling like scum growing atop a millpond?" His gaze suddenly lifted to the table beside his and the semishocked stare of a woman sitting there. She regarded Blaine as if he were a mental patient escaped from a ward.

Another problem about spending hours alone, day after day, when he was accustomed to sharing them with Leslie in some manner. He'd begun to talk to himself—and answer his own questions. He gave a halfhearted smile of acknowledgment to the woman, who quickly focused on cutting her already-sliced meat into even tinier portions.

Now that he thought about it, he supposed he must look like he'd made his home in a cave. Jaw unshaven, hair mussed from the wind, eyes likely still red from lack of sleep. Nor had he been able to escape the memory of the awful way he'd treated Leslie that day in her hospital room. Yeah, she was at fault for omitting a few rather important facts from him, but he'd gone off the deep end in his accusations toward her, fueled by hurt pride, he guessed.

No wonder pride was such an issue with God. It spawned a chasm of unforgiveness and affront when said pride was pounced upon. Still, Blaine didn't consider himself better than anyone else, so he began thinking on the flip side.

He was angry with Leslie for not admitting she was Dear Granny and for learning of his feelings for her through his letters. But come to think of it, hadn't they each withheld information the other should have been privy to? He had been evasive in sharing his true feelings; she had concealed her true role. Both of them had been informed of the truth through that one letter.

Blaine groaned at the revelation, earning him another alarmed glance from the lady diner. Maybe he was just as much at fault for keeping quiet and not sharing his heart with Leslie these past months as she was for publishing his letters regarding her and not being more open with him.

"Ready to order?" A cute blond waitress stepped up to his table, pad in hand, and gave him a sunny smile.

"I'm not that hungry tonight. I think I'll just have a steak sandwich, large serving of onion rings, and a glass of milk."

"Milk?"

"Yeah." A thought made him grin. "Make that a tall chocolate one."

Her nose stopped just short of wrinkling into a grimace, and he thought he heard her say *gross* as she walked away.

Grinning at the remark, he turned his head slightly as he continued to watch the biased-about-food teenager return to the kitchen. Blaine could eat anything, loved to experiment, and often did. A trio of newspaper stands near the register suddenly caught his attention. Unable to quench his curiosity and feeling the lady diner's continued stare, he sought temporary escape and walked over to scan the front pages. He was disappointed to see the *Goosebury Gazette* wasn't one of those displayed for sale.

Well, what did he expect? He was in a different county after all. Still, he'd heard that the *Goosebury Gazette* had brought in readers from all over the state. He wondered how hard it would be to find a copy, then wondered why he should want to.

Leslie looked up from the pages of her Bible and stared out the window at the white clouds sliding across the treetops. Recalling her difficult day, she frowned. She had needed to point out from the police lineup the man who'd assaulted her. Mark Lester's face had been easy to spot; it sometimes chased her in her dreams, and she would startle awake, heart pounding fast.

At least Carly had gone with her for support, as had her grandmother. Ever since Nana had reentered the world, she hadn't retreated, and Leslie was so grateful to God for that. Still, she wished she could rewrite a good deal of the past. Why was it that it often took a tragedy for people to wise up and do what they were supposed to do from the start? How had Leslie failed so?

She sipped her coffee and looked back down at the verse in Proverbs she'd just read: "Plans fail for lack of counsel, but with many advisers they succeed."

All these months, she'd been giving advice to people, instructing them with Nana's help on how to best deal with issues concerning them. Yet she'd never once sought advice concerning her own problems. Not from Nana, not from God. Instead, she'd blindly struck out on a path of her own choosing, never stopping to consider the haste with which she acted.

Sure, she could explain away her actions as only doing what she thought was right at the time, but it didn't make it right. A verse from Isaiah 55 came to her as she dwelled on the idea: " 'For my thoughts are not your thoughts, neither are your ways my ways,' declares the LORD."

How true.

It hadn't been God's intent for her to go to the park; the uneasiness she'd felt in her spirit that morning was put there for a reason. If only she had heeded God's warning then, she wouldn't be in the fix she was in now.

"Are you still browbeating yourself over what happened?" Nana asked as she brought Leslie a sandwich and set it before her.

Leslie shrugged. "I don't know. I just wish things had turned out differently, is all."

"It does no good to foolishly wish for things that can never be. What's happened has happened. Now it's time to go forward. Learn from your mistakes, but don't let them control you, Leslie."

Propping her elbow on the table and resting her chin against her hand, Leslie observed her grandmother. "Nana, how did you come to be so wise?"

Her grandmother laughed and sat down across from her with her own sandwich. "Perhaps it's the one good thing that can be said about growing old."

"I doubt Mr. Abernathy sees you as old."

A becoming flush colored Nana's cheeks, and Leslie smiled.

Perhaps romance was in the air. If so, Leslie was glad. For herself, she could only wait and see what the week brought, since the letter to her readers was now in print. Her boss hadn't been at all happy with Leslie's decision, but since the attack, she'd found herself less meek where Mr. Abernathy was concerned and, for once, had politely stood her ground.

God, it's all in Your hands now. Where I should have put it from the start.

Tired of watching a nature series on African wildlife, Blaine flicked through the channels of the TV in his room at the rustic inn. He supposed he should just go to bed but had tried that intelligent idea once without success. The rustle and soft thump of something hitting against his room door startled him. Had he been asleep, he doubted the noise would have awakened him. As alert as he was, with the volume of the TV turned down low so as not to wake any of his neighbors, he'd heard the thump well.

Curious, he moved to the door and opened it. A recent copy of the *Goosebury Gazette* lay on the flat brown carpet at his feet. Relieved that the woman at the desk had been able to locate the newspaper he'd requested, he picked it up and once more got comfortable on his bed. Without hesitation, he opened to the "Dear Granny" section, then frowned, perplexed. This was different.

Dear Readers,

This past summer, you've graciously allowed me into your homes, asking difficult questions, expecting helpful answers. To the best of my ability, I've provided aid or encouragement whenever I could. Yet in one matter I failed most dreadfully. I gave you counsel but didn't seek advice when I myself needed it. In so doing, I failed at my own relationship and hurt the man I've come to love by shielding the truth from him.

A shrewd king named Solomon once wrote this proverb: "Listen to advice and accept instruction, and in the end you will be wise." Given recent events, I can hardly call myself wise. Therefore, I think it best I resign from my post as Dear Granny. I'm hardly experienced enough for the important job of instructing you in your lives when I've failed so miserably in my own.

Take heart, the column will continue, and I've been assured my replacement will be just as wise (hopefully more so than I). Before I conclude this letter, I wish to address a very special reader one last time—

Blaine read the snippet below the column, and a painful lump formed in his throat, spreading to his heart:

Dear Hopeless in Love,
       Forgive. She never meant to hurt you.

Chapter 14

I can't believe we're finally getting to eat lunch together." Carly laughed. She finished the last of her huge chef salad.

"Me, either. It seems like each time we tried, something came up." Leslie smiled. "I'm sorry about last time."

"What's to be sorry about? I knew it was important that you and your mom talk. And I'm sure you had a lot to talk about."

Carly was right. Leslie's mom had been frantic ever since she'd arrived at her New York home after being out of town a week and learned of Leslie's attack. They'd ended up talking on the phone for over an hour, followed by a call from Leslie's worried father who'd also been away, on a business trip.

"We did have a lot to discuss," Leslie agreed. "Talking about the attack led to talking of other things and airing a lot of buried feelings I've had since their divorce. As a result, we were able to get some things straightened out between us. Actually, I think the call drew me closer to my mom than I've ever felt before."

"I'm glad to hear that. I wish I could say the same about my aunt and uncle." Carly stabbed a cherry tomato with her fork and popped it into her mouth. "But I'm still being punished for the sins of my mother."

Leslie sympathized. "One day, I'm sure you can work it all out with them."

"Maybe." The word was heavy with doubt.

"Well, I guess I should be getting back home."

Carly glanced at her watch, quirking her mouth to the side as if considering. "How about hitting a store or two first—if you're up to it?"

"Well. . ."

"Crandell's is having a preseason sale."

Leslie laughed. "Okay, you've convinced me."

They visited the store, but Leslie didn't see anything to interest her. Carly tried on almost every outfit in her size from the two round sale racks and then decided to purchase only a scarf in shades of blue and green. At least there was a chair for Leslie to sit in when she grew tired.

Once they left the shop, Leslie thought Carly would take her home, but soon she found herself standing beside her friend at a vegetable and fruit stand Carly just couldn't resist as she drove by. Here, Carly was more willing to part with her money and, after carefully inspecting each vegetable or piece of fruit, bought two cartons of food. Afterward, she said that trying on all those clothes and hunting through the vegetables made her hungry again, and she stopped at an ice-cream place for a frozen-yogurt cone.

Leslie was starting to get edgy. She was tired—this was her first day out, after all—and she wanted to go home, but she bit back a taut reply and politely agreed. Carly didn't usually act so selfish; maybe she was just excited they were finally getting to spend a girls-day-out together, and she didn't realize Leslie was about ready to drop.

"Leslie," Carly said thoughtfully, after she licked the peak of her vanilla mound. "If Blaine were to forgive you and would want to renew your relationship, would you consider it?"

"Of course. If I didn't, I wouldn't have written what I did."

"About loving him?"

Leslie's face grew hot. "Yes."

"What if you two were to get together, and he should ask you to marry him someday in the future? Would you?"

Taken aback and a little flustered with the direct line of questioning, Leslie paid supreme attention to crunching into the last of her chocolate cone. "You're rushing things quite a bit. Right now, he won't even talk to me."

"Hm. Guess you're right." Carly concentrated on her cone, a slight smile forming at the corners of her mouth. "But just suppose it did work out. Would you marry him?"

"I don't know. I might." Leslie concentrated on wiping each finger individually with her napkin.

"Okay, okay. I'll change the subject." Carly's grin reminded Leslie of a mischievous child about to thrust a grass snake at her face. "I hear Abernathy wants you back."

Leslie relaxed. "Yeah, it was the strangest thing. You would think that the letter I wrote would have ensured that the readers wouldn't want me as Dear Granny anymore."

"You were good at what you did. Even I have to admit that. Why do you think the column is so popular?" Carly reached in her purse for her lipstick and smoothed the dark pink shade on in three swift strokes, using the mirror in the lipstick case as a guide, then pressed her lips together. The action brought her dimples into prominence. "I may not have always agreed with you one hundred percent, Les, or even fifty, but I could tell you cared about the people you wrote to, and after that first writing disaster when you were new on the column, you came to care about what you wrote. Your advice helped a lot of people."

"Thanks to Nana."

"Don't discount your way with words. Both of you play a big part in the column. And isn't it fantastic that Big Chief offered your grandmother a paying role in all this? You think she'll take it?"

"I hope so. The column's helped her focus on other peoples' problems, which helped to take her mind off her own. I really think it was good for her. In a way, it was partly due to the column that she found the strength to get over her fear of driving or riding in cars and to come to the hospital. If I hadn't been Dear Granny, I wouldn't have gone to the park that day."

Carly sobered. "Yeah, that was something. Have you heard anything more from that girl?"

"You mean Sharon Lester?" At Carly's nod, Leslie sighed. "No, but Nana told me she gave her a book that I'd given her, and I think it'll help. I'm sure she's safe, since her husband's in jail."

"I guess you'll have to testify?"

"I imagine so."

"At least you can't say your life's been boring."

Leslie laughed at Carly's teasing words. "That's the truth. Since I became Dear Granny, my world has tilted on its axis."

"You know, there's another good thing about it you haven't considered. . . ." Carly grew meditative. "I doubt Blaine will object to your keeping the 'Dear Granny' beat. Now that he knows who you are, I'll bet he'd even support you in it. He must've thought it was a good column, since he wrote you two letters asking for advice."

"Are we on that subject again?" Leslie felt rattled. Carly obviously had more faith than Leslie that things would work out with Blaine. It had been three days since the newspaper with her letter to the readers had been circulated, and except for Nana's calls and Carly's, her phone remained silent.

"Cheer up," Carly said, grabbing her purse and rising from the table. "It'll work out. Aren't you Christians always the ones talking about living by faith?"

The words weren't snide, but they surprised Leslie, nonetheless. Usually at any mention of God, Carly changed the subject. Leslie could hardly believe she was introducing it.

"You're right. Thanks for getting me back on course, Carly. I gave the circumstances to God while I was at the hospital. I just need to let Him work it all out and trust that He'll do what's best for both of us. Easy to say, hard to do."

Carly's smile wasn't as wide as usual, but it seemed more sincere than any to date. "Let's get you home. I've kept you out long enough. I've seen you yawn twice, and I wouldn't want your nana to give me an earful."

"Nana's not there." Leslie eyed her friend strangely. "She's not coming over until tomorrow night."

"Oh." Carly nodded once as if remembering. "Right."

Their trip back to Leslie's house was quiet. Carly's mind seemed stuck in another world.

They pulled onto the dirt drive fronting Leslie's home, and the car rolled to a stop in front of the house. Leslie's mouth dropped open, and she stared, closed her eyes for a few seconds, and then opened them again. She *must* be dreaming.

Parallel rows of gorgeous blue and purple flowers paraded in a long border up to her front porch steps. All along the front of her house, flowers of the same color along with taller yellow, blue, and red blooms spread out in glorious profusion.

"What. . . ?" she breathed when she could speak.

"Well, Les, I'd like to stay, but I can't. I've got plans for the night. So I'll just drop you off here."

Leslie's attention snapped her way. "Don't you see all the flowers?"

Carly's expression was deadpan. "Well, of course I do, silly. I'd have to be blind not to. It looks like instead of the usual red carpet, someone rolled out a carpet of flowers for you." Her gaze flew to the porch, and her grin became positively naughty. "And oh, look. There's that someone now."

Leslie turned to see. Her heart gave a little leap as she continued to stare. *Blaine!*

"If your jaw drops any farther, it'll be in your lap," Carly teased. "Get on up there. He's waiting for you."

Leslie fumbled with the latch and somehow managed to open the door. She wasn't sure how her legs moved the distance up the walk and was glad when Blaine met her halfway.

With a honk and a wave, Carly drove off. Blaine waved back, thankful for her help in diverting Leslie's attention for the past few hours. It had taken every minute of that time to transplant the flowers from his mom's garden, front and back, to Leslie's yard.

Her focus still dreamlike, she looked from his face and down to the colorful rows of flowers, then back again. "How did you. . ."

When her words trailed off, he finished for her. "Manage to do this before you got back? I had help." He looked over his shoulder to Leslie's front window, where her grandmother stood looking out at them. The woman lifted her hand in a slight wave, then moved away from the curtains. "And she brought some of her own to plant, too," he said as he faced Leslie again.

"I just. . .I can't believe this."

"I'm just not sure why I didn't think of doing it before."

"It's all so beautiful, Blaine. My home's never looked nicer." Her gaze was soft but still seemed unsure. "And you were so thoughtful to do this for me."

"A simple apology didn't seem like enough this time." He felt suddenly nervous. "Besides, you're the one with the green thumb. I just toss up the dirt. Croissants, not crocuses, are what I do best."

She shifted her weight to one foot as if uncomfortable. Small wonder. She'd only been out of the hospital a week and a half.

"Would you like to sit on the porch?" she asked quietly.

"That's a good idea."

They sat on the top step and stared ahead at the stone walkway. Neither said a word.

He may not be a silver-tongued Romeo, but surely he could get out the words he needed to say somehow.

"Leslie. . ." He moved his head to look at her and was met by the heart-stirring sight of her wide hazel eyes as she turned toward him at the same time. Something seemed to lodge in the middle of his throat. "I read your letter. In the paper."

She gave a faint nod. "I hoped you would. That's partly why I wrote it. I really didn't know you'd written those letters, Blaine. Not until I was in the hospital and read that last one. Even then, Nana had to point it out to me. She knew all along. Like I said, I'm just so sorry, and I wish I could turn time back. But I can't."

"I'm sorry, too. For the way I blew up at the hospital that day."

"It's perfectly understandable, though it did make me wonder if I'd ever see you again."

Her statement gave him the boldness he lacked. "Would you have been too disappointed if you hadn't?"

"Very." The sincerity in her eyes made his heart pick up a beat.

"The flowers weren't just meant as an apology, Leslie. I wanted to give you something that was mine. Something I knew would make you happy. The look on your face when you got out of Carly's car made it all worthwhile." He took her soft hand, cupping it in his. "Leslie, the truth is, I want to share everything I have with you. These past days have given me a lot of time to think. And I want to marry you someday."

Her intake of break was quick. "Oh, Blaine, you really mean it?"

"Yes."

Wariness replaced the joy in her eyes. "I resigned as Dear Granny in that letter in the paper, but oddly enough, the public wants me back. Mr. Abernathy has been getting calls and letters since it went into print. Seeing as my grandmother will be given a paying job for her help now, I've already told him I would continue with the column."

"Okay." Blaine was unsure why she would bring up such a sudden switch in topic at this pivotal time. "I think it's a great idea. The advice you both gave readers was top-notch."

"Then it wouldn't bother you if I continued giving advice to the lovelorn?"

So that was it. Relief made him grin. "Not as long as you don't go chasing after any more readers."

"Yes, that was a bad idea."

"Leslie, you can turn to me any time. A couple shouldn't hide important things from one another."

"I agree." She looked down a moment, then lifted her head again. "I was unsure about a lot of things before, including myself and what you'd think of me if you knew what I did at the paper, especially after what I'd told you that time at the bridge. That I'd never dated. But after what happened in the park, well, I guess coming so close to death gives a person a different view on life. I feel I've matured a bit since then. I've stopped harping on things that are of little importance—like the fear of what people may think—and I've learned to be less passive about a number of things. Including making decisions and sticking to them."

"There's still one decision you've yet to make," Blaine reminded, trying to keep his tone casual, though his pulse raced. "Regarding the question I just asked. Will you marry me?"

He read the answer in her shining eyes, her soft smile, her breathy little sigh. "Yes, Blaine. Of course I will. I think I've loved you since the day I discovered that you'd mowed my lawn without me knowing it."

"Really?" A sense of amused disbelief made him chuckle. "That was the same day I fell in love with you. When you came over and helped me weed the garden."

"And now you've given me all your beautiful flowers." Her gaze momentarily went to her colorful lawn, then back to him.

"I want to give you so much more, Leslie. . . ." Blaine leaned toward her, bending his head at an angle so he could caress her mouth in a kiss. "So much more."

His lips met hers softly at first, then more firmly, and as their arms went around each other, he gave her his heart.

Epilogue

The day was bright with promise. Leslie adjusted her wedding veil, a simple rim of white silk rosebuds and seed pearls attached to a waist-length veil, then nodded to Carly, her maid of honor, that she was at last ready. They hugged carefully so as not to muss the long white gown or Leslie's carefully curled tendrils that hung to her shoulders. Then along with two other bridesmaids— Leslie's stepsisters—they hurried out the door of the church alcove.

Taking her father's arm, exchanging a quick smile with the dear man who'd reared her and stood by her countless times throughout her life, she then turned her attention toward the narrow center aisle, her eyes and heart going to her future husband. Blaine literally took her breath away. Standing tall, wearing a black silk tux with a white rosebud in his lapel, he exemplified her every dream of the perfect man.

His beautiful brown eyes glistened with love and admiration as she joined him to take her place beside him. Nervous and excited, Leslie barely was able to follow the ceremony, but she was sure it must have been wonderful since both Nana and her mother had helped to plan it. Sharon Lester sang a solo of "I Will Walk with Thee," her voice clear and angelic, hauntingly beautiful. It had been a year since the trial and her husband's imprisonment, and in that time, she and Leslie had become good friends. Leslie had also had the delight of leading Sharon to find real safety in beginning a relationship with Jesus. She had been like a dry plant desperate for living water, soaking up God's message of love.

Once the time came for vows to be spoken, Leslie had no difficulty focusing on the cherished words Blaine spoke or in remembering her part. Staring into his gentle eyes made it easy to speak from her heart and to hear his. Everything else—the guests, the church—seemed to fade away. In the year and a half they'd known each other, they'd graduated from falling in love to abiding in love. Through life's troubles—which always came—they'd learned to trust and to confide in one another. As a result, their love had become deeply rooted and blossomed as beautifully as a sweet red rose. Through the watering of the Word and their nurturing words to each other, acting upon them, and weeding out any minor spats, which often proved inconsequential, they learned to tend their relationship as meticulously as a gardener looks after her flowers. With love, respect, and diligent, tender care.

Now as Blaine slipped the gold wedding band onto her finger, and she did likewise with the matching one for him, Leslie rejoiced that they were truly one. The grin she loved so much lifted his lips before he captured hers in a delightful kiss that lasted several seconds and made a child in one of the front pews titter. Pulling apart, she and Blaine grinned at one another, then stepped down from the altar, husband and wife.

As they hurried toward the back doors and the waiting limousine that would take them to the lodge where the reception was to be held, she spotted Nana with their boss. He had insisted Leslie call him Ronald, ever since he'd started dating her grandmother half a year ago. Leslie suspected another wedding would soon follow and was glad Nana was happy again. She blew her grandmother a kiss while her other hand remained firmly linked in the crook of Blaine's arm.

Turning her attention to the street, she caught sight of the limo driver, who looked their way as they hurried down the few steps of the church. Quickly, he folded his newspaper and stepped outside to open the back door for them. A sea of guests flocked outside, and for a moment, Leslie thought they might be showered with iridescent bubbles, but then she remembered that was something saved for later, when they left the lodge for their honeymoon trip to the Southwest. Blaine had said he couldn't wait to show her Texas and introduce her to his friends. And Leslie was looking forward to seeing her first rodeo.

Blaine ducked into the car after her, and the driver closed the door. They waved at those guests who'd flocked to watch them before hurrying to their own cars and the reception to follow.

"Just think," Blaine teased, taking her hand in his as they drove off. "If it hadn't been for your close ties with Dear Granny, I may have never scrounged up enough courage to ask you out on a date, and we may have never gotten this far." He winked, and she felt her face warm pleasantly.

"More like Dear Nana," she corrected under her breath, thankful for her grandmother's intervention.

"Dear Granny?" The driver perked up. "Did you folks say something about Dear Granny?"

"Yes. I was just telling my bride here that a big part of the reason we're together today is because of Dear Granny."

"Is that a fact?" The driver slowly shook his head in amazed amusement. "Well, now, way it appears to me, that Dear Granny is one right smart lady. Right smart. She talked sense into my daughter and advised her not to leave her husband. Emmy called me yeste'day and said she's decided to try to make a go of her marriage after all." He peered into the rearview mirror. "And you folks say you know her?"

Blaine looked at Leslie, his grin absolutely mischievous. She felt her face go hotter. If she were the blushing sort, her skin would be tomato red by now.

"Oh, yeah," he said to the driver, his sparkling eyes never leaving Leslie's.

"I know her very well. And I have to agree with you, sir. She's one of the best there is."

With that, Blaine slid his hand along Leslie's jaw and kissed her tenderly, thoroughly, editing out all thoughts of the column and bringing her loving focus only on him.

Long Trail to Love

Dedication

A special thanks to Therese Travis and Adrie Ashford for their invaluable crits. And to my Savior, who protected and led me down the long trail to eternal life, I give You my all.

Chapter 1

The telephone's shrill ring interrupted Carly's conversation with Leslie and Jill, her best friends and the only two people in Goosebury who would have anything to do with her at the moment.

"Aren't you going to answer it?" Leslie asked when the insistent bell clanged through the room a third time.

"No." Carly pursed her lips in disgust. "Why should I? It's him. I know his ring."

"His ring?" Leslie shared a look with Jill.

"Okay, maybe that sounds crazy, but he hasn't stopped calling since Mrs. Vance caught us arguing in the park two days ago." *And heard every disparaging, condemning word aired.*

"You weren't to blame, Carly," Leslie soothed. "We know that. No one thinks any less of you for what happened."

Carly knew better. "I feel as if everyone in town has branded me with some sort of scarlet letter. In line at the post office this morning, two old women were whispering. They mentioned my name and kept darting glances my way. And yesterday when I popped into the news office to see if you wanted to do lunch, everyone looked at me, then became real busy, though a few told me 'hi'—nervous 'hi's,' I might add."

"I think you're seeing things that aren't there." The gentle flow of Jill's Australian accent helped soothe Carly's nerves, nerves the jangling phone attacked as it rang once more. "You did used to work there, and after that row you had with Abernathy, I imagine they were surprised to see you. Don't worry about what others say or think. The bush telegraph will judge how it wants to in any case, and that's the way of it—the town gossips," she inserted when Carly looked at her stupefied. "Once news of a more shocking nature comes along, this will be forgotten."

"You're right, Ju-Ju," Carly said with a wry twist of her lips. "The vultures will gather once a new corpse has been found in someone else's closet. What about you?" she asked Leslie. "Does Dear Granny have any pearls of wisdom for me today?" She gave a rueful shake of her head. "If I'd just taken your advice, I might not be in this jam." Leslie had often spoken to her about God in the year and nine months they'd known each other. In her top-secret profession as Goosebury's advice columnist to the lovelorn, Leslie gave biblical advice with the aid of her grandmother, advice that at first annoyed Carly. However, as the months progressed, she and Leslie looked beyond their differences and became good friends. Carly had known Jill less than half that time, but they, too, had become close.

Leslie's eyes held sympathy. "I think Jill's right on with this one, Carly. Nobody at the office has been gossiping about you, not to my knowledge. And if a few old ladies have nothing better to do than to run people down, well, that kind of thing has been going on for centuries. Don't let it get to you; it's not like you to get so upset."

Frustrated with the entire situation, Carly swept the receiver up as it shrilled a seventh ring—"Hello!" Warmth crept over her face at the stern greeting she received. "Oh, hi, Aunt Dorothy. . .No, he's not home yet. . .Okay, sorry about that. . . Yes, all right, I'll tell him."

"That was my aunt," she needlessly explained as she hung up the phone. "She wanted to know if my uncle Michael was home."

"See, you worked yourself up over nothing," Leslie gently chastised. "Jake has probably given up chasing you."

"You don't know how much I've wanted to change this phone number these past two days!" Carly groaned and slumped into a chair. "Always having to sprint for the phone before my family could pick it up hasn't been easy. My aunt must know about Jake from all the gossip—I'm amazed she hasn't confronted me with it yet. But if she knew he was calling me, still trying to see me. . ." Carly sighed.

"Can't you just explain matters to her?" Leslie asked.

"Are you kidding? My aunt wrote me off as a bad seed the moment they took me in. She's always treated me as the unwanted child; not that I care. I don't." She ignored the prick in her heart that told her otherwise.

"Why didn't you just bail out once you came of age?" Jill asked.

"I should have, but life intervened. The year I graduated, I'd planned on getting an apartment with a classmate, but that was also the year my aunt got sick with the tumor, so I stuck around here to help out. Trina was too young to do much for her mom or take care of the house, and I felt obligated since they'd given me a place to live. My uncle hasn't been so bad, but my aunt sometimes looks at me as if she hates me."

Carly knew the reason for the woman's hatred but didn't voice it, still ashamed by what her aunt said her mother did all those years ago. Before Carly even knew of such things, Aunt Dorothy had claimed that a mother's sins became the daughter's and had placed Carly in the same despicable class as her mother. If Aunt Dorothy learned of this situation, everything she'd ever accused Carly of would be justified.

Leslie broke the silence. "I've talked to Blaine, and we've decided to move into my loft and rent out his house. We don't need two places, especially since they're next door to each other. Would you be interested?"

Carly smiled at her friend's thoughtfulness; she'd never understood how Leslie could be so tolerant toward her, when she'd been so undeserving of her forgiveness during those first months Leslie started work at the *Goosebury Gazette*. Blaine had been Leslie's neighbor before they married, and both shared the trait of a protective attitude toward others.

"If I still had my job, I'd jump at your offer, Les, but I have no income to afford my own place. I am a complete dolt—what's that word you use, Ju-Ju? For a fool that's duped?"

"A mug." Jill looked sympathetic.

"Yeah, that's what I am. A mug."

"Since Mr. Abernathy is my boss and has married my grandmother, I could put in a good word for you," Leslie suggested.

Carly winced at the memory of her last outburst at the *Gazette*. Over a year ago, when she'd first discovered Jake's lies, she had created a scene while conducting an interview. Her boss had given her a fiery tongue-lashing but also a second chance. Always restless, and unhappy at the *Gazette*, she'd wanted to quit then but had needed the income and couldn't find another job that suited. This last time when she'd learned she'd been deceived, while taking a phone call at the office, she'd had a meltdown and Abernathy had had enough.

"I doubt I'll get good references from the Big Chief," Carly said. "Or a third chance. And anyway, I don't want to get you involved in my problems."

"You're my friend. That makes me involved already."

Carly didn't know what she'd done to deserve these two, but she was grateful for friends like Leslie and Jill.

"Say. . ." Jill's blue eyes looked thoughtful. Carly had seen that expression enough times to recognize her friend was cooking up a plan. "Some of my mates from church are joining me and Ted to hike up the Long Trail into Canada in two weeks. You're between jobs and want to distance yourself from Goosebury until things cool down. Why not join us?"

At the word *church*, Carly inwardly cringed. Ironic that her two best friends in the world were Christians, since Carly wanted nothing to do with Christ. "Will there be a lot of preaching?"

"We'll hold a Bible study and have devotions each night before we turn in, but we won't tie you to a tree and force you to attend, Carly."

Carly chuckled at the sparkle in Jill's eyes. She'd never been on the Long Trail, though she'd promised herself she would attempt the extensive hike someday. As she listened to Jill gush about the exquisite scenery, the scope of mountains, and the experiences she'd shared with her husband when they'd section-hiked the trail, an idea came to Carly. She had made a living as a writer. Maybe she could document her experience and write a guidebook for beginners by a beginner. That idea might reel in the readers, especially those interested in the outdoors.

Still, she hesitated. "Is there a list of items I'd need? I can't invest in anything extra right now."

"I'll get you the list tomorrow. Anything you can't afford, I might have a spare. Ted and I have done a lot of hiking over the years, so I have heaps of gear. You can have my old tent—it's ace, not a thing wrong with it; we just needed a bigger one after we married." Jill fairly bubbled with enthusiasm. "You'll only need what you can carry in a backpack, along with a pair of good sturdy shoes. The sporting goods store is having a corker of a sale from what I saw in an ad this week, so no worries there, either. And you'll have plenty of time to break them in. Oh, this is exciting! Ted's bringing his mate along, and now I'm bringing mine."

"Ted's bringing a friend?" Carly felt her internal radar go on the alert.

"Oh, no worries about Nate. He's fair dinkum."

"Uh, yep, I'm sure he is." From her experience, Carly doubted any guy was genuine or trustworthy.

"You two are making me jealous," Leslie complained with a sad chuckle, putting a hand to her six-months-pregnant stomach. "I would love to go hiking. It seems as if it's been forever since Blaine and I went anywhere, even to visit covered bridges."

"Oh, poor you." Jill threw a semimocking glance her way. "If I could, I'd exchange places with you in a heartbeat."

Leslie's face reddened, and remorse swept over Jill's features. "Oh, Leslie, I didn't mean that the way it came off."

"I know. But you're right. I should count my blessings instead of complaining about what I can't have."

Sensing unease in the atmosphere, and knowing Jill's frustration stemmed from being married five years and not having the child she desired while Leslie became pregnant within three months after her marriage to Blaine, Carly voiced her decision.

"All right, Ju-Ju, you've convinced me. I'll invest in a pair of hiking boots and take that 270-mile journey down the long, long, *Long* Trail."

They all laughed, but restlessness still coiled deep inside Carly.

Knowing Jake, he would make another appearance in Goosebury soon, determined to see her. He hadn't given up the first time, and she doubted he would retreat this time either. She needed to get as far away from him as possible. The next two weeks couldn't go by fast enough.

❦

Nate stuffed as few articles in his backpack as he felt he needed for the month-long hike.

"So you're really going then?"

At the unexpected voice, he jumped and turned toward his door. His father stood in the entrance. At Nate's look of surprise, he explained, "I knocked, but the door was ajar."

Nate gave a short nod. He must not have closed his apartment door all the way when he'd come home, loaded down with shopping bags. The air currents in the outside corridor had a habit of pushing the door open if it didn't stick, but his frustrations didn't end there when it came to this place. He really needed to find somewhere else to live, but it was the only place available in his price range when he had been looking. Still, if a reporter and not his dad had been standing there, Nate would have been cornered.

He eyed his father in his gray suit with navy tie, his silvering hair distinguished and brushed back from his face in a confident manner, his entire appearance calculated to assure clients he remained the man in control. But today his father didn't look in control. New lines creased his brow, and a defeated hunch bowed his shoulders.

"Dad, I just need some time alone. To put distance between myself and Bridgedale and to sort things out."

"She wasn't worth it, son. I know it hurts, but any woman who won't stand by her man doesn't merit the money it takes to afford her lifestyle. You're better off without her."

Nate sensed that, but the reminder didn't help right now. He had thought he might propose to Susan once upon a time but had held back. Now he was glad he had. Losing his job, several of his so-called friends, and his girlfriend within a twenty-four-hour period had been tough. Dealing with the newscast that sent his family's life whirling into upheaval would have been that much more difficult if Susan had thrown his ring back in his face, too. Nate retrieved his camera from a shelf and stuffed it inside its protective carrier. He planned to take plenty of pictures while he connected with nature and, he hoped, rediscovered the peace that notoriety had wrenched from his life.

"Your stepmother is heartbroken. I don't know what to tell her. I never had a teenager become so rebellious, and I have no idea what to advise her concerning Brian."

Nate's jaw clenched. The last thing he wanted to talk about was his felon of a stepbrother or the social-conscious woman who sucked his father dry of funds at every chance she could. Rail about the two of them, yes. Maybe that would ease the frustration packed inside him like a time bomb ready to go off. But seeing the once-proud attorney reduced to such a torn, humbled man twisted Nate's heart, and he withheld his true feelings.

"I'm sure you'll work things out, Dad. You always do."

"This, I'm afraid, is beyond working out." His father took a seat on Nate's bed and shook his head.

Nate sympathized with his father, but he'd heard once that an empty vessel didn't do much good at filling others' pots, and his was as dry as a bone. None of the Bible promises he'd read during his long-ago studies seemed to float to mind, and he hoped that these weeks away would improve his connection to his Savior. Lately, he felt like the line between them crackled with static.

"I can't say I blame you for leaving," his father said. "The media can be merciless, but Julia wanted to stay close—though after that sad excuse for a preliminary hearing and the mob bearing down on us like baying hounds on the courthouse steps. . ." He sighed, breaking off his thought. "I was afraid she might have a breakdown. I should have taken her on a cruise months ago. Since my last client dropped me, I don't know why I don't." He bowed his head into his hands. "She blames me for not representing Brian, though I've told her I'm not a criminal attorney. Even if I were, I couldn't act in his defense because of the conflict of interest."

"Maybe you *should* take that cruise. You need some peace, too." Nate clapped a hand to his father's shoulder in a show of support, all he could offer at the moment. "I'll be back long before the trial starts. I'm not running out on you."

"You've always been dependable, son. I know I can count on you. Your mother would have been proud."

The reference to his mom made Nate think of his sister, a mirror image to the first Mrs. Bigelow. "At least Nina lives in Connecticut and is immune to all this."

His father slapped his leg in frustration. "It just isn't right. You shouldn't have been made to suffer so; none of this was your fault."

"Yeah, well, life's not fair. Never has been, never will be." Nate shrugged into his backpack, adjusting the strap. "But we have to struggle along and make the best of things somehow—isn't that what you always told me?"

His father let out a dry chuckle. "I never knew you were listening."

"I always listened."

The two men shared a look charged with emotion, each of them letting the other know without words that he was important.

"Just don't make the same mistakes I did, son."

Nate gave a slight nod. "I'll keep that in mind, Dad."

Chapter 2

A short trek from the road where the bus dropped them off led Carly and her group to the state line bordering Massachusetts and Vermont, the beginning of the southern boundary of the trail. In the hazy sunlight, under a covering of beech trees, the group assembled. With walking sticks in hand, they toted backpacks and looked like the serious hikers they would need to become. Carly studied the other six in the group, a man and his daughter, a newlywed couple, and Jill and her husband, Ted. Ted's friend hadn't shown up, which made Carly breathe a sigh of relief.

A rugged wooden sign with painted yellow letters marked their welcome onto the Long Trail, calling it "A FOOTPATH IN THE WILDERNESS." Instructions underneath offered helpful information on the painted blazes marking the path—white for the main trail, blue for side trails. Below that came information on the Green Mountain Club, the organization that had created the trail decades ago. Carly took a picture of the sign with her camera, thinking she would want to supply photos for the guidebook she planned to write.

Ted Lizacek, Jill's husband and leader of their motley group of seven, stood with his hands on his hips and eyed them with all the aplomb of a drill sergeant mustering his troops. His stint in the army had had lasting effects, apparent in the rigid set of his jaw and shoulders and in his no-nonsense demeanor. "I hope everyone here has spent the past weeks conditioning for this hike. The trail starts out easy but gets rougher as the days progress. A good thing, too. It'll strengthen those leg muscles and get you sluggards into physical, mental, and emotional shape. Once we hit the north end toward Canada, the hike becomes more difficult. The terrain gets treacherous and will involve a lot of climbing, sometimes requiring hands as well as feet. The path is always rugged. It's not for the faint of heart."

Across from Carly, a pretty blond teen with thick glasses that magnified sky blue eyes shot an anxious glance toward her father, a man of similar coloring. He gave her a reassuring wink, but his smile seemed faint.

"What a way to rally the troops, luv." Jill put her hand to Ted's back. "If you don't curb your welcoming speech, it might turn into an address of farewell. This isn't like when we traveled into the outback. At least we'll reach shelters on this trail, and signs are posted so we can't get lost."

Carly heard a deep, quiet chuckle behind her and looked over her shoulder, startled. A pair of blue-gray eyes in a bronzed, masculine face caught and held her attention. The owner of the eyes looked in her direction, and she turned her head back around so fast she almost gave herself whiplash. She pressed her hand to the burn zipping along her neck. Great. The last thing she needed was a muscle spasm. She wondered where he'd come from; she hadn't seen him on the bus.

"It's important that everyone understands the difficulties we'll come up against," Ted countered.

"Which is why we gave out detailed information weeks ago, and I'm sure everyone has read their brochures by now," Jill mollified.

"All right, maybe I went a little overboard."

"A little overboard?" Carly heard the man behind her mutter in amused disbelief. "Try more like taking a bungee jump off a high cliff." She felt her lips twitch but kept her focus on their hiking leaders.

Ted straightened, evidently having heard his heckler. His gaze speared the man behind Carly. "Well, well, well. You got something to say, slacker? Come out from hiding and speak up so everyone can hear."

Like an unruly child facing a stern instructor, the man stepped out from behind Carly, and she got her first good look at him. Slim and well toned, he wore a blue plaid shirt with the sleeves ripped off over a long-sleeved gray flannel shirt and blue jeans. Sandy brown hair hung shaggy and windswept to his nape, feathering in soft waves in a long sweep over his forehead and angling in shorter waves at the sides. He stood several inches taller than her five feet six. Realizing she stared, she shifted her attention to Ted, who crossed his arms across his barrel chest.

"What have you got to say for yourself, boy?" Ted addressed the man as if he were years younger, though Carly thought they appeared near the same age.

"Well, now," the stranger spoke with unhurried ease, "I thought I'd signed up for a pleasure hike along the Long Trail, not a grueling, thirty-day workout at Ted Lizacek's Boot Camp."

Uncomfortable silence filtered through the group. All Carly could hear was the wind rustling the leaves and the sounds of other hikers in the distance as they readied for their departure.

Ted's eyebrows shot up. "Something wrong with that idea?"

"Maybe not for a PC game or for one of those so-called reality shows. As for real life, I think I'll just stick to enjoying this hike—minus the drills, Sarge."

Ted glared at the unflappable man seconds longer before bursting into laughter and slapping his heckler on the back. The mock tension broke as they smiled at one another. Carly shook her head, realizing their little joke.

"Nate, man, it's good to see you! When did you sneak in? Everybody, Nate here is my old hiking buddy. We section-hiked this trail for the first time together when we were juniors in high school."

"And you were just as overbearing then as you are now," Nate said good-naturedly.

"Yeah, but you wouldn't recognize me any other way," Ted joked back. "I want you to meet the group. Jill, you know."

"G'day, Nate," she said, giving him a hug. "Good to see you again."

"And this is Kim and her dad, Frank Melby," he addressed the teenager and the man beside her.

Nate shook the man's hand and gave the teen a smile and nod. Carly noted his even, white teeth made the smile swoonable, which would explain Kim's pink face.

Swoonable? Man, I've been out of a job too long. I'm getting rusty in my vocabulary. Maybe I should create a dictionary of ridiculous adjectives and try to sell that. Before she could break from the thought, Nate moved to stand in front of her, his steady, blue-gray eyes making contact with hers. She drew a swift breath, which she quickly related to embarrassment at just connecting Nate to her crazy new word for the day.

"Nate, this is Carly Alden," Jill said, an undertone of exuberance that hinted at matchmaking, evident where it had been absent in previous introductions. Carly shot Jill a warning glance, then looked back to Nate.

"It's nice to meet you," she said in a noncommittal manner.

His smile edged up a notch at the corners, suggesting he also heard the undertones and they amused him. "Likewise."

She pulled her hand from his warm grasp and averted her gaze to the next available face. It turned out to be Jill's, and her traitorous friend had the audacity to wink.

Ted and Jill continued down the line with introductions, with Nate between them. Needing time alone to sort out her thoughts and knowing Ted intended to start the hike soon, Carly took the opportunity to sign the register.

Maybe coming on this hike had been a mistake, but she had to avoid any chance of running into Jake again. He wasn't the type to tolerate waiting for long; nor was he the type to accept rejection. He pushed the buttons and expected everyone to hop when he said hop. Given that he was CEO of his own company, his attitude wasn't much of a surprise.

Her mind switched to Nate, and she observed him without his noticing. He laughed at something Frank said and turned to Bart, the other guy on the hike. She'd heard only good things from Jill about Nate for the past two weeks without really learning anything personal about the man. That alone made her skeptical. She wondered if she was the only one in the group who found it odd that Ted or Jill hadn't introduced Nate by his last name. Maybe because the three were friends, they missed the fact others wouldn't know it. Not that she cared one way or the other. The less she had to do with the male species, the better, and at the first opportunity, she would stress that fact to Jill. As for Nate, the absence of his last name aided Carly's desire to keep him at arm's length.

After more than an hour on the bus, her muscles felt cramped, and knowing their supercharged drill sergeant was eager to get started on the twelve-mile hike to the first shelter, Carly set down her backpack and stretched her legs with slow, easy lunges. Her body was well toned thanks to daily aerobics, and she'd spent the past weeks walking every morning and evening, increasing her mileage each time to prepare for what promised to be a grueling but stimulating month.

"Hi!"

Carly turned to see Kim smile as she approached. In her gray sweatshirt bearing the name of a well-known pop group emblazoned in pink across its middle, and with the remnants of baby fat pleasantly rounding her pink cheeks, the girl looked thirteen or fourteen.

"Hi." Carly straightened from her stretch.

"Can you believe this day finally got here?" Kim's bright features matched her eager words. "I thought it would never happen. I've been putting red Xs on my calendar forever!"

"I take it you're just a tad excited?" Carly joked.

"Well, yeah!" Kim laughed. "I mean, this has been like a dream of mine ever since I was little and heard how my grandparents hiked the trail when they were young. I read that not everyone makes it. Since the trail first opened in 1930, only about twenty-six hundred hikers have made it to Canada—at least I think that's how many." Kim pulled her eyebrows together. "Anyway, whatever, a lot dropped out along the way because they just didn't have the strength and endurance needed. But I'm going to make it—me and my dad."

Carly smiled. "I'll bet you are, Kim, and I'll be rooting for you all the way."

"Hey, thanks. You, too! Well, I guess I'll talk to you later. I know Mr. Lizacek wants to go soon." With a slight wave, Kim returned to the group.

Carly liked the exuberant teen. So far, everyone seemed like they would make good companions for an extended hike. They hadn't started preaching to her the moment they saw her, as she had half suspected they might, and she'd found common ground with a couple of them. The newlyweds, Bart and Sierra, shared her lifelong love of historical Native American culture and art, and they'd conversed during the bus ride. Carly and Jill were good friends, despite differences in their beliefs, or rather Carly's lack of any. And though she and Ted never talked much, he always treated her with respect.

She looked over the group, her attention going to the newcomer. With a start, she noticed Nate looking at her. She thought she read a sort of watchful amusement in his eyes but realized, from a distance of at least thirty feet, it was impossible to tell.

She broke eye contact. Well, at least *most* of her group seemed like they would make good companions. Uneasy, she turned her back to Nate and continued her warm-up lunges, her defensive nature waving warning flags inside her mind.

Four miles into the trail, Nate began to relax. The stress from the upcoming court case and his family situation eased away the deeper he forged into the endless tunnel of greenery. A mix of abundant hardwoods, towering evergreens, and copious overgrowth that spanned the entire length of Vermont, the thick forest traveled along the spine of the Green Mountains.

He took deep breaths of the bracing air, rich with the earthy aroma. An earlier rain sharpened the scent. Today's hike wasn't strenuous, but Nate knew he wasn't in the same shape as he'd been the last time he and Ted had hiked this trail. Not that he was out of shape, but riding his tour-guide cart around on his last job hadn't been physically challenging.

Carly, who ambled ahead about ten feet behind Frank, suddenly stopped and aimed the camera hanging around her neck toward one of many trees. Nate knew that Ted wanted to reach Congdon Shelter and get situated before dark. They were behind schedule, and this had been the third time Carly had stopped to aim her digital. Nate came up beside her.

He looked in the direction she aimed, at the tree on which a ring-eyed furry observer perched. "You might not want to use all your shots our first day out. You'll see plenty of raccoons and much better scenery farther up the trail."

She lowered her camera. Her night-dark eyes seemed to glimmer with contained steam. "Maybe, but I won't see *that* particular raccoon again." She raised her camera and compressed the shutter.

O-kay. Nate studied Carly, not sure what to make of her. By her body language—the haughty tilt to her chin and the straight set to her shoulders—he sensed her hostility but didn't understand the reason for it. He'd tried to be nice to everyone, but she seemed to want no part of his company. Not that he looked forward to anything other than friendship these upcoming weeks.

Her sleek hair was almost coal black, and she had pulled it high into a ponytail that brushed the center of her shoulder blades. Her khaki shirt set off the olive tones in her smooth skin, complementing her exotic beauty, whether Latina or Native American, he wasn't sure. Incredibly full lips that rimmed a large mouth above a more delicate chin and high cheekbones did nothing to detract from the appealing picture.

"Yes?" Clearly miffed, she turned to catch him staring. "Was there something else?"

Maybe her exotic blood originated from the Arctic, what with the frost he was getting.

He decided to shrug off her attitude. "We should catch up to the others.

It looks as if we're going to get more rain before this day is through, and that'll slow us down."

"Don't let me stop you." She pushed a button on her digital camera to view her shot.

"Well, see, that presents a problem." He knew she wouldn't like what he had to say, and he respected her obvious independent nature. But he also knew this was the church group's first time on this particular trail, and they were unfamiliar with what to expect.

"Really?" She regarded him with a sort of lofty disdain as if he were a black fly she'd like to swat away.

"Yes. I told Ted I'd help out when he first invited me to come along, and he asked if I would take up the rear during our hikes."

"Okay?" she inquired impatiently, waiting for him to elaborate.

"Well, if I leave you behind, that pretty much takes away my designated spot."

"In other words, don't be a slacker?"

He couldn't help but grin. "I wouldn't put it in Ted's words, but that's the gist of it."

"Okay, fine, whatever." She shut off her camera.

"We just want to keep everyone together and don't want anyone lagging too far behind. They have those white blazes to mark the trail, but it's still possible to get lost."

"No problem. I understand." Her terse words showed her irritation, but she began walking.

It didn't take a woodpecker drilling the info into his head for Nate to figure out he wasn't welcome company to Carly, but if he stayed behind her and walked any slower, he would be taking baby steps. Still, the need to walk single file impressed itself upon him, so he moved in closer, hoping to speed her up a little. She shot him a glare that stifled anything further he might have said.

Withholding a sigh, he dropped back a few feet. The trail had been aptly named—this was going to be one long hike.

Chapter 3

Near Seth Warner Shelter, Jill convinced Ted to stop for a lunch break. They were halfway to their night stop, but Carly had a feeling if Ted could have gotten away with it, he would have continued the remaining six miles and forced everyone to chow on granola bars and trail mix while they plodded ever onward.

"Everyone needs a breather," Carly heard Jill tell her husband. "You're used to a heap of physical activity, but this is their first day out. We need to call it quits, or someone could strain a muscle."

Ted gave in with reluctance, and Carly mentally applauded Jill. Carly had practiced carrying her forty-pound backpack when she trained on the lane near her home, but she'd never carried one for so long, and her shoulders and lower back burned. A break to sit and rest would be welcome, and as the others dropped their backpacks and walking sticks on the ground with relieved sighs, Carly knew she wasn't the only one who thought so.

Her gaze wandered to Nate. A flush of embarrassment shot through her to see him look up from setting down his pack to catch her watching him. She looked away.

Since their slight altercation, Carly had worked harder to push ahead, walking faster, though after a couple of miles, her shins and thigh muscles complained at the mistreatment, and she acknowledged her foolishness. She couldn't explain her irritation with the man, since Nate had only followed Ted's orders in watching out for those green to the trail, but she felt her unease had something to do with how Nate stared at her. She darted a glance his way. He was still staring at her.

She took a seat on the platform of the three-sided shelter, which was damp, but she'd been forewarned that rain and getting wet were givens on this hike. Retrieving a package of freeze-dried vegetable crunchies from her backpack, she also pulled out her mini recorder to recount her first day on the trail so far. The all-encompassing forest of greenery refreshed her soul, as did the scent of rain.

Sierra joined her, asking what she was doing. When Carly admitted her former job as a journalist and that she wanted to compile information for a book, Sierra asked questions regarding writing and the publishing business, stating that she'd thought about submitting some poetry to a publisher. The two talked until Ted rallied everyone to resume the hike, and the break ended.

Instead of relieving her aching muscles, the rest had made them feel worse. Carly groaned as she slipped on and buckled her backpack around herself.

"The first days are hassles," Jill sympathized. "It'll get better once your body adapts to the new routine."

Carly hoped Jill was right and only the first days were bad; no matter how hard she tried to keep to the front, her flaming shins and aching lower back had her lagging toward the rear, until she again trudged in front of Nate. She felt his eyes burn through her scalp, and she lost her footing. Her arms flew out as she struggled to regain her balance.

Nate grabbed her arm before she could fall in the mud. "Watch out for those tree roots."

"Thanks." Her face flushed hot, but she didn't make eye contact with him.

The remaining miles awkward, Carly forced herself to concentrate on the tree-lined view and the path while thinking of ideas to add to her book. By the time they reached Congdon Shelter, gray clouds loomed above, shot with orange from the evening sun. Ted instructed the group to pitch their tents before the deluge hit, and Carly hurried to do so, pleased that regular practice in her backyard now had her looking like a pro. Satisfied, she straightened and brushed off her hands, noticing Nate watching from several feet away. He'd already pitched his tent about fifteen feet from hers.

"What? Didn't think I had the brains to do it?" she asked.

A burst of air left Nate's mouth, sounding like an annoyed half laugh, and he shook his head. "No, Carly, I didn't say a thing."

She crossed her arms. "You may not have said it, but you thought it."

"And just how would you know what I thought?"

"Because you have that look on your face. Superior and all knowing. And you're male. All men think the same thing—that women are incompetent creatures who rely on a man's input for every single thing."

Nate stared at her a moment as if he had no idea what planet she came from, then put up his hands in surrender. "I concede. You're right—"

"Aha!"

"I *am* male. But I have no idea what you're talking about or where you get your ideas. And the look on my face was admiration for how fast you put that tent up. Jill told me this was your first time camping overnight."

Carly felt a niggling irritation that Jill had spoken to Nate about her. "I've been on day hikes before. And I've camped out at cabins."

"Not exactly the same thing."

Carly couldn't argue with that. At least the shelter had a privy—but not much else.

A smattering of raindrops struck her cheek and head, and she looked up at the same time Nate did.

"You better duck inside your tent," Nate said. Then as if sensing her bristle, he added, "Just a suggestion if you don't want to drown. Not an order."

"Drown?"

"Never mind."

The faint smile on his face as he moved to his own tent needled her, but she resisted the urge to demand an answer. She ducked into her tent and zipped it closed. With hardly enough room to move, she decided against cooking one of her one-dish meal packets on her portable stove, choosing instead to eat nuts and dried fruit for dinner.

The rain splattered against her tent, then slammed into it in a deluge.

"Carly!"

Surprised to hear someone outside, she unzipped the partition partway. Jill stood in a rain slicker and handed her something.

"Heyo. I brought you a prezzy I thought you could use."

Thunder rocked the trees behind as a zigzag of lightning flashed through the sky. Carly undid the zipper all the way and pulled Jill inside the cramped tent.

"Are you nuts? You shouldn't have come out here in this!"

"This? This is nothing. One thing about weather and the trail—you can't wait out the weather, or the weather will outwait you."

"Huh?"

"Something Ted said. The weather always changes, and on a hike like this, you're the one who has to conform. I've been in worse Down Under. Heatstroke and bush fires aren't something you want to tangle with, though a small bush telly would come in handy right about now!" She shrugged, laughing. "I came to bring this. It's exceptional for sore muscles."

Carly unscrewed the top from the tube of ointment and flinched as the heavy menthol odor infiltrated her nose. "Oh! Between that and the bug repellent, I'll be a candidate for the worst-smelling hiker on the trail. Then again, maybe I should patent the combination. I might have come up with a great new scent guaranteed to repel men—Keep Away."

Carly laughed, and Jill shook her head at her silliness.

"It is bad, but you won't regret using it. Ted won't go on hikes without it."

"Ted?" Carly's picture of the strong, unflappable outdoorsman didn't include an image of a man with aches and pains.

"Too right! For all his bluff and bluster, he's oversensitive when it comes to sickness or pain. All men are, from what I've seen." Jill winked and smiled, making Carly laugh. "But Ted is also one of the best mates I've known, an ace leader, and smart when the need arises. He may be gruff on the outside, but he's really a big koala bear and one of the nicest blokes I know. I was filming the roos, and he swept me off my feet—after he smashed into my Jeep."

"I remember months ago you told me the story of when you met in Australia, but I forgot all of it."

"I was doing a nature film, a hobby I had, filming home movies, and out of nowhere Ted came barreling into my life. You should have seen him, Carly. At first I thought he had a few kangaroos loose in the top paddock." She tapped her head. "He kept yabbering an apology, then invited me out to dinner. At first I steered clear—I thought he was a big galoot. But later I realized he wasn't such a bad bloke, after all."

"Too bad there aren't more guys like Ted filling the earth," Carly mused.

"Nate's blood is worth bottling." At Carly's lost look, Jill laughed. "I mean he's an ace bloke—and helpful, too."

Carly shot her friend a warning look. "Not interested, and I really don't think there are any ace blokes." She realized her words might offend. "Well, except maybe Ted. But my uncle's a loser, my dad—whoever he is—is a loser, and of course it goes without saying that Jake was."

"You can't generalize the entire male population into 'loser' status, Carly. It's not fair to good men like Nate. Give him a fair go. Just as a good mate—a friend—nothing else."

"Why should I? I'm not here to start a new relationship. I'm here to escape an old one. Partly. I also wanted to gather info for a book, but I told you about that. And that's all I want, so please don't try to hook us up."

"I'm not suggesting that." Jill let out a soft breath. "I understand your reasons, but I hate to see you close yourself off when someone as beaut as Nate is around."

"Jill. . . ," Carly said in warning.

"Okay." Jill put her hand up as if making an oath. "Even though it goes against my wish to see two of the nicest people I know become good mates, I promise not to interfere."

"Thank you."

"I better get back before Ted thinks I made a boat and sailed away. Get some good sleep. Oh." She stuck her hand in her pocket as if just remembering something and pulled out a handful of sweets. "Want some lollies?"

Carly took a cinnamon disk. "You're going to get cavities with as much candy as you eat. I'm surprised you took up room to pack them."

Jill left laughing, and Carly settled down for the night.

As the rain pummeled the weatherproof tent, she reflected on their conversation. Jill had vowed not to interfere, but remembering the tone of her voice, Carly became uneasy. Jill wasn't the type to go back on her word, but Carly sensed her friend had something up her sleeve.

Nate couldn't figure Carly out. After the incident at the shelter, he resolved to steer clear of her. Yet as their second day on the trail progressed, he found himself watching her more than he should. Of course, since she was often the one to lag to the back of the line, that wasn't hard to do.

The climb up Harmon Hill wasn't so bad, and the clear view of the green valley refreshed them after all the rain, but from there, the trail made a steep descent by means of a natural stone staircase that seemed to go on forever. Another cross over Maple Hill and then another descent further challenged tired muscles.

Because of the shelter spacing and the need for water, they had to hike fourteen miles that day. After they'd been on the trail a number of hours, Nate could see Carly lagged even more, and he reduced his pace. He opened his mouth to ask if she needed a rest, then thought better of it. He felt relieved when Ted broke for lunch once they reached Hell Hollow Brook. An anomaly to its name, the water rushed clear and refreshing over smooth rocks of all shapes and sizes. Abundant fronds of tall greenery bordered the narrow brook, reaching almost to touch at the center in some points.

His friend looked as weary as the greenhorns on the trail, and Nate held back a chuckle. The first few days were always the toughest in hiking a trail like this one, but it satisfied Nate to see their robust and vital leader struggle with the same problems, since he had bullied them so.

"Guess that's not a very Christian attitude," he muttered to himself. "I shouldn't wish upon my team leader the same pains we're all having."

Carly stopped and turned. "What?"

"Nothing," he said, surprised she'd heard him. "I wasn't talking to you. I was talking to myself."

She gave him a skeptical, accusing glance. He shook it off and took a seat beneath one of the maple trees on a smooth boulder, one of many that filled the trail. This one felt surprisingly comfortable. He took a long draw from his water bottle and squinted against the sunlight as he watched Carly take a spot yards away under another group of trees. Kim joined her, and Carly smiled, her attitude friendly.

At least she opened up to the other hikers, though Nate noticed she never went to them. They always came to her. As she tossed back her long dark hair, which she'd pulled out of a ponytail, and threaded her slim fingers through it, Nate dwelled on the enigma of Carly. Did she think herself too good for everyone, or was she shy? No, not shy. And with the amenable and laughing conversations he'd witnessed between her and Jill, her and Sierra, and now her and Kim, he didn't think she thought herself superior to anyone, either. Yet for all that, she still seemed to hold herself aloof, as if she bore an invisible sign that said, TRESPASSERS WILL BE SHOT. And she'd made it abundantly clear Nate fit into that category.

He shook his head, reconciled to the idea, and concentrated on tearing his teeth into his beef jerky while appreciating the scenery. Fog hovered above the trees in the distance. He hoped they wouldn't get more rain.

Seeing the water in his bottle was low, Nate squatted down by the creek to refill it, dropped in a water purification tablet, and screwed the lid back on. Hearing a stir in the grasses behind him, Nate looked over his shoulder.

"Thought you had a good idea," Ted explained, unscrewing his own water bottle. He struggled to get down so he could submerge the bottle, and winced. Nate felt bad about his earlier vengeful enjoyment that they were going through mutual aches and pains.

"Trail getting to you there, buddy?" he joked.

Ted snorted. "Don't tell the others, but I'm not exactly as young as we were when we hiked it in high school."

"Really? Never would have guessed. The way you were leaning on your walking stick, I just thought you were trying it out as a pole for a high jump."

"Yeah, ha-ha, very funny. I'll be twenty-nine in a few weeks, but today I feel like fifty."

"Twenty-nine isn't so old." Nate grinned. He was two years younger.

"Thanks," Ted said dryly. "I guess it wouldn't be so hard if Jill wasn't wanting a kid so bad. I do, too, but not as much as she does."

"Did you talk to a doctor? You said you were going to."

"Yeah, both of us are okay. Not sure what the holdup is."

"Well. . ." Nate used his walking stick to help him straighten. Today his shins burned like crazy. "You're always telling me God's plans don't fit into our timetables, so maybe that's all it is. It's just not time yet." He shifted his gaze to the right and felt a jolt of shock to see Carly staring at him. She looked away, back to Kim.

"Could be." Ted straightened, following Nate's gaze. Nate detected a smile in his voice. "You know, it wouldn't hurt you to settle down. Plenty of nice girls in Vermont to choose from. Some right under your nose."

Nate swung his head around to see Ted grinning at him like a maniacal Cheshire cat.

"Yeah, well, the interest has to work both ways. Don't want anything one-sided."

"Maybe it does."

"What are you talking about?"

"What are *you* talking about?"

Nate wasn't about to fall into that trap. "What I felt you were talking about."

"Don't you mean who I was talking about?" His focus went to Carly. "She's a real looker; likes the outdoors, too. And you're sharing the same trail for the next month. You couldn't do better if she were hand-delivered to your door."

Nate snorted. "Except for one small point."

"What's that?"

"She has no interest in me."

"I doubt that."

"What makes you think she does?"

"I've watched her watch you. People not interested don't stare."

Nate thought that over. "Maybe she's plotting my demise."

Ted grunted and rolled his eyes. "When did you get so stupid? You were always smart in school."

Nate decided to let that one go. "What do you know about her?"

"Not much. She's Jill's friend—met her at a vegetable stand of all places. But she's nice. And she's had a rough time. Her ex-boyfriend did her wrong, but that's all Jill told me. I think the real problem is that you represent the entire male community in her mind, and right now, she's targeted man as her enemy."

"I noticed that when she talks to you, she doesn't look like she's plotting where to hide your body."

Ted laughed. "Yeah, but that's because I'm spoken for. I don't represent a threat to her. You do."

"I try to be nice."

"It has nothing to do with nice. You're young, single, and out looking."

"I am not out looking. I just broke up with Susan, remember? Or anyway, she broke up with me."

"Buddy, before marriage, every man is out looking, whether he'll admit it or not. You may not know you're looking, but tell the truth. When you meet a girl who attracts you, isn't one of the questions going through your mind, 'I wonder if she's the one'? And I'll bet you thought that about Carly, too."

Nate didn't want to admit Ted was right. At twenty-seven, with most of his former classmates married, he'd thought a lot about settling down. He'd wondered if Susan might be the one, before three months of getting to know her and discovering what she was like. From knowing Carly two days, he didn't even need to ask the question. Without a doubt, she wasn't the one for him. They couldn't exchange a few sentences without her thinking he harbored ulterior motives.

"I think maybe you need something more than water purifier tablets," Nate muttered. "Some microorganism must have gone to your brain and made you a little nuts."

"Mark my words," Ted said, walking away with a chuckle. "By this time next year, you may just be asking me to be your best man."

"Make that a lot nuts," Nate called after him as he walked behind Ted.

"You want some nuts?" Jill asked, coming up to him. "I've got chocolate-covered peanuts."

"Thanks." Too embarrassed to correct her as to what he meant, Nate accepted a handful and ignored Ted, who was laughing so hard he sounded as if he might come apart at the seams.

Chapter 4

The farther they walked through this part of the trail, now thickly wooded and giving off a feeling of extreme isolation, the more grateful Carly was for her walking stick—though every so often, the staff became stuck in the slurping mud and she had to pull it out. The traction on the bottom of her heavy hiking boots helped her keep her footing on slippery ground, and two pairs of socks prevented blisters. But at times she longed for the freedom of bare feet. Still, the positives outweighed the negatives.

Earlier, the group had taken several levels of stairs up the Glastenbury fire tower to see the sun paint the Taconic Mountains with early morning gold, and Carly hadn't been disappointed. Staring at such an impressive vista, Carly could almost believe God existed.

"Look!"

Kim stopped on the path and turned sideways, her pink face alight. Carly followed her gaze to see a small porcupine bristle through the undergrowth.

"Look at it walk." Kim giggled. "It waddles like an overblown pincushion on rickety wheels."

Carly smiled. It did look funny. She grabbed her camera and readied it, then noticed Nate come up beside them.

"Permission granted?" she asked dryly, not failing to see Kim's blue eyes widen behind the lenses of her glasses.

"Whatever." Nate gave a grunt mixed with a less than amused half smile. "Don't get too close, Kim," he warned the girl, who'd also taken her camera out and edged closer to the trees as the porcupine waddled away.

"I was just hoping to get a shot from the front," Kim explained, disappointed.

"Better safe than sorry. If you advance, you might scare it into thinking you're a predator. And you don't want to get on the wrong end of a porcupine's quills. They're loose, and if it lashes out its tail, it can hit you, embedding the quills in your leg like darts."

"Too bad I don't have quills to lash out and discourage advances from predators of the two-legged variety," Carly muttered under her breath once Kim resumed walking.

"What?" Nate turned a sharp glance her way.

"Nothing." Carly smiled sweetly and continued her trek. "I wasn't talking to you. I was talking to myself."

"Sure you were," she thought she heard him say but didn't look back to ask. She chuckled under her breath, so busy giving herself a mental two points that she didn't think to step around the large puddle like Kim had and instead sloshed right through it. The tip of her clunky hiking shoe caught on a tree root hidden beneath the inches-deep muddy water, and she went sprawling forward to land hard on her hands and knees.

Nate came up beside her. "You okay?"

"Yeah. Just dandy." Embarrassment that he should see her in such a humbled position put a bite to her words. She moved her hands to get better traction, but the mud and the weight of her heavy backpack made her slide forward, drenching her shirt even more.

He held out his hand. "Need a lift up?"

"No." She gritted her teeth. "Thanks. I can do it myself." This time she planted her hands in front of her and pushed her right foot forward to boost herself into an upward lunge. Despite the traction of her sole, she slipped hard and fell farther into the mire with a splash. She spit out muddy droplets in disgust.

"You're doing a great job of it so far."

She heard the thread of amusement in his voice and glared. "Don't you have anywhere else to go, or do you get your kicks out of annoying me?"

His eyebrow arched, and she felt a moment's remorse. She knew he was only trying to help, but her pride stung worse than her body. Had anyone else witnessed her dilemma, it might not have wounded so bad, but that it was Nate made it feel like alcohol on a cut.

"Just. . .please. Go. Really, I can handle it."

"Suit yourself."

His light words and merry whistle as he walked off didn't surprise her half as much as the fact that he'd actually left her alone on the trail. Sure, that was what she wanted. But what happened to his claim of needing to take up the rear to watch over any laggers? She guessed he wasn't as sincere or genuine as Jill had tagged him.

Planting her walking stick in the sludge and using it as a brace, Carly struggled to her knees and finally to her feet. With care, she stepped out of the puddle, then surveyed herself, letting out a heartfelt groan. Her whole front looked as if she'd been dipped in a vat of milk chocolate. Maybe if it were milk chocolate, it wouldn't be so bad. Of course, the bugs might then feast on her despite the noxious repellent she wore.

She took the bend on the trail and stopped in surprise.

Nate stood off to the side, his camera focused on the summit of Glastenbury Mountain, just visible through the trees.

"Glad to see you made it okay," he murmured.

Suspicious, she studied him, not failing to notice the slight quirk of his lips when he turned and took in her appearance.

"I thought we weren't supposed to loiter behind and take pictures along the trail."

"That was only because of the rainstorm. No danger of rain on the trail right now. . .though of course there's always danger of getting wet."

She wanted to remain aloof, but his deadpan words struck her as funny. She could feel the corners of her telltale mouth edge upward in a smile. Astonishment swept over his face before she turned away, resuming her trek.

"Speaking of water, the sooner I find a body of it to immerse myself in—preferably clean water—the better."

"Don't take it so hard." He fell into step beside her. Here the trail was wider, though most of the time they had to walk single file; the pamphlet Jill had given her said that to prevent erosion, hikers should stick to the middle. She opened her mouth to remind him, but he spoke before she had a chance.

"Falls are a natural part of life when hiking. Skinning knees, scraping hands—I imagine every one of us will do it many times before we reach Canada. Shedding a little blood is a given with as rough as this trail can get."

Strangely, his quiet words reassured her, didn't make her feel so awkward or humiliated, and she cut him a glance.

"I think the worst for me was when I fell down some rocks and scraped one side of my face and side. For days, I wasn't a pretty sight—unless you like red, black, and purple as a color combination."

She took note of his profile, his straight nose, and his strong, lean jaw. His skin had undergone a slight burn, especially the bridge of his nose and his cheekbones, but was unmarred. She couldn't imagine him unattractive. When she realized where her mind had taken her, she forced her attention away from him and onto the hike.

He fell back into step behind her, and she wondered if he had just remembered the single-file rule or if he had given up trying to steer her into conversation. Regarding Nate, Carly felt nonplussed and uncertain, and she didn't like anything that threatened her independence and self-control.

A few nights later, Nate grew reflective as he gathered with the others in a circle, using the remnants of the flaming sunset for light. Of all the summits they'd crossed, the one today was a favorite of Nate's: Bromley Mountain, with a spectacular view of the landscape in all directions.

Fire rings were allowed at some camps, but the wind blew too strong that evening to build one. Nate relied on his slim pocket flashlight once the red and gold in the western sky gave out. This was the first evening they'd reached the shelter early enough to set up camp and still have time for group devotions before sunset. The shelter housed eight, and five new high school graduates occupied it, so Nate's group had needed to pitch tents. After the other young men and women introduced themselves, they dove into their sleeping bags and zipped themselves in, exhausted. This had been the first evening Nate's group hadn't just wanted to let their aching bodies tumble into their sleeping bags after having said a communal prayer of thanks for making it to their destination alive and in one piece yet again. At long last, they felt acclimated to the hike.

Nate flipped to the seventh chapter of Romans in his pocket Testament and listened as Ted's strong voice seemed to shake the air as he read. A snapping twig diverted Nate's attention to the trees across from him. Carly stood at the edge of the clearing, her stance rigid.

He watched her until she turned her head, her gaze meeting his. The same jolt of awareness hit as it always did when they seemed to connect. Then to his disappointed frustration, she turned on her heel and walked back to the shelter and, he assumed, the latrine.

He had trouble concentrating on the discussion afterward, but he made a monumental effort to keep his focus on the topic.

"I find it interesting how Paul said he always wants to do what's good, but he winds up doing those things he doesn't want to do instead." Kim let out a sigh. "That makes me feel better. To know someone like the apostle Paul dealt with messing things up, too, well, I don't feel like such a hopeless case. So I guess the question I have is this: What was his secret? How did he overcome all that to be able to be so strong in prison and through all those beatings and the torture?"

Amazed, Nate stared. He had never figured the bubbly teen, who giggled constantly and talked about pop bands at all the breaks, would have so much depth.

Jill smiled at Kim. "I think the answer is that we must build our spirits, put the ol' flesh man to death—the one that always hassles us and craves sin. The only way we can tackle that is by spending significant time in God's Word and in prayer."

Nate listened with half an ear. Carly came into view again, and he focused on her, waiting for her to rejoin them. He was surprised when she went to her tent instead.

"Jill's right," Ted said. "This hike is a great chance to get in tune with our Creator and get closer to Him. I encourage all of you to do that. I like to pick a time of day when I can be alone and just go off a short distance to look at the mountains and meditate on God."

"So then, we *can* wander from camp?" Kim sounded puzzled. "I thought that we're supposed to stick together. Especially after we saw that sign on the road."

Everyone grew quiet. Nate recalled the sign that the U.S. Forest Service posted with photographs of two backpackers who'd been killed and an appeal requesting the public's assistance in identifying the perpetrator.

"Everyone needs some time alone. Just don't stay away long or go far. No more distance than a half block. Tell someone before you go that you're leaving, as well as what direction you're heading. And always take your backpack. That way you'll have your compass, your flashlight, and anything else you might need."

"You mean if we get lost?"

"You shouldn't get lost if you don't go too far." Ted's words became abrupt, a sign he now felt boxed in by Kim's worried attitude. He had never developed good people skills.

"Why do you think they call this Lost Pond Shelter?" Bart asked, not helping matters any. "You think someone got lost here once? I read on a Web site there have been people who signed the register and took the trail but were never heard from again."

"Thank you, Major Suspense," Sierra joked, rolling her eyes.

"What?" He looked at his wife. "I'm just curious."

"Kim." Jill's voice was gentle. "Whenever you need to take some time off, give me a nod, and I'll walk with you most of the way." She looked at her husband. "Since you, Nate, and I have taken this trail and all the others are new to it, I think we should use the trail-mate system in such cases."

"Assign all the greenhorns expert buddies?" Ted wanted to know.

"We could do that." Jill nodded. "I'll be stuffed; I'm not sure why I didn't think of it before. That sounds like a corker of an idea."

"I'd like to be assigned to Kim," her father said. "I've had experience hiking along the Appalachian Trail."

"Sure, Frank." Ted gave a nod of consent.

The young newlyweds shared a smile, and Bart winked at his wife. "We'd like to be trail mates," he said, turning to Ted.

"I think," Jill observed, "since you're both new to this trail, it would be better if I take Sierra, and Ted takes Bart."

"That sounds doable," Bart agreed.

"So, I guess that leaves Carly for Nate."

Hearing the words jarred Nate, though he saw it coming the minute the topic had switched to assigned buddies.

"That okay with you, partner?" Ted asked.

Even in the dying light, Nate detected the amused glint in Ted's eyes. Thinking of the curt treatment he'd already received from the independent spitfire, he sent Ted a look that promised payback.

"If it's okay with Carly. Sure."

Sending a resigned look to her tent, he wondered who would convince *her* of the new plan.

Chapter 5

O nce Carly buried all remains of breakfast—a preventive measure to keep from attracting animals—she brushed her hands off on her canvas walking shorts and looked up. A quiet groan escaped when she saw Nate headed her way. Couldn't the man just leave her alone for once?

"Yes?"

"Good morning to you, too," he responded cheerfully despite her abrupt greeting.

A hint of embarrassed warmth flashed over her face. "Morning," she mumbled, heading back to her tent to finish packing up.

"If you have a moment, I'd like to talk to you."

She sighed and turned around. "Yes?"

"Last night, the group decided to employ the buddy system."

Mystified, Carly eyed him. "The buddy system?"

"Where no one goes off alone, but everyone travels in pairs."

"I do know what the buddy system is." She hoped she had been assigned to Jill, but from Nate's uneasy behavior, she suspected the worst.

"Great. And, well"—he spread his hands wide—"you're looking at your new trail mate."

Terrific. First she'd ripped the packet of her granola and blueberries cereal too fast and too wide, spraying the contents of her breakfast all over the ground; next, she'd been attacked by swarming black flies during her latrine run because she'd forgotten to apply her bug repellent; and now this. The start to a perfect morning.

"Thanks, anyway, but I'll pass."

"Well, it's not exactly an option."

"I don't need an escort. I can do fine on my own."

"Everyone has a trail mate. It was Ted and Jill's idea."

She would just bet it was Jill's idea! "Maybe so, but I don't need one. I've done some camping, and I do know enough not to go wandering off and get lost, contrary to the helpless female you think me to be."

"What I think you to be?" He shook his head as though flummoxed. "How did this get into a discussion of my hypothetical opinion of you as an individual?"

She shrugged. "That's what it amounts to, doesn't it? Even if you don't come right out and say it, you think I can't cope."

"I never said—"

"Oh, you don't have to say it. You've got it written all over your face. So, are you one of those men who think a woman's only place is at home, preferably at the stovetop or in whatever room happens to interest him?"

"*What?* How did you come up with that?"

"Never mind. You don't have to answer if you don't want to. I understand. Personal views tend to put people in sticky situations."

He settled his hands on slim hips and studied the treetops as if trying to find his bearings, shot her a baffled glance, shook his head, and walked off.

A smidgeon of remorse niggled a hole in her triumph. Jake and her uncle did hold such outdated views; she and Jake had fought about it. But maybe she shouldn't have been so hard on Nate since she didn't know him or his personal opinions. On the flip side, if she kept pushing him away, he might soon get the message and not be inclined to pursue her to "buddy up."

Frustrated, Carly used unnecessary force to roll her sleeping bag and fasten it to the backpack. No man could be as "ace" as Jill claimed Nate was; the man was sure to have his faults. No admirable man existed on the planet. Not Jake, not her uncle, not even her father, whoever he was. . .though sometimes she felt she knew.

She stopped packing and grew somber, staring at the trees without seeing them. Her high school beauty-queen mom had gotten pregnant as a senior, given birth to Carly, then two years later dumped her off onto her childless married sister with the explanation that she needed to go and "find herself."

Carly wondered if after twenty years her mother had found herself yet.

They hiked down to Big Branch River, where a suspension bridge stretched across and led into an extensive clearing. From there, they began a gradual climb up to Little Rock Pond. Nate smiled when Jill and Sierra oohed and ahhed over the peaceful area with its tranquil waters, so clear they could see all the way to the bottom of the deep pond. Rimmed by low mountains covered with thick forests of trees, the pond invited weary travelers to rest, and the women asked if they could. Ted agreed and called an early lunch.

"From this angle, it's mysterious," Kim said, "almost gothic, with the way it's hidden and protected in shadow, like something you might see in England or Scotland."

"Have you ever been to either of those places, Kim?" Nate asked.

She gave a self-conscious grin. "No, but I've seen pictures."

"I agree," Sierra said. "It gives off an aura of mystery, especially with the mist. It inspires a poem; if I had a few hours, I'd give it a shot."

"What about you, Carly?" Noticing she'd taken a seat a few feet away on a partially submerged boulder at the edge of the pond, Nate attempted to pull her into the conversation. "What are your views of Little Rock Pond?"

She looked away from the pond and unscrewed the top of her water bottle. "It's nice."

Nice. Well, what should he expect after the silent treatment she'd given him all morning? At least she'd spoken those two words to him. She acted as if he was the one responsible for incorporating the buddy system into their group—which Nate considered a good idea, regardless of what Carly thought. He just had no idea how this trail-mate idea would pan out; somehow, he had to find neutral ground with her these next few weeks.

After their break, they made a short descent before climbing the summit of White Rock Mountain. A downhill spur led them to the awe-inspiring White Rock Cliffs. They climbed to the top, and Nate watched Carly move toward the edge.

"You might want to drop that heavy backpack before getting too close," Nate suggested.

She shot him an annoyed look but did as he said.

The cliffs plunged straight down into a sunlit valley, with distant peaks beyond. When Carly's shoe sent some loose pebbles plummeting over the edge, Nate barely restrained himself from grabbing her arm and instead only murmured, "Watch yourself."

She didn't answer, and he worked to bury his impatience with her attitude; this silent treatment was really getting on his nerves.

The rest of the day went much in the same manner. Clarendon Gorge, with its steep descent and narrow suspension bridge that swayed in the wind, had been dedicated to a hiker who'd met his end there before the bridge was built. Carly drew close to the edge to peer the eight hundred or so feet to the rocks and creek below. Did the woman have a death wish? Nate clenched his teeth to prevent himself from calling out words of caution.

Hungry for real food, they made a short detour that led to a popular restaurant for hikers.

Nate wolfed down his steak and eggs. He noted Carly equally enthused about her vegetable salad and shook his head at her food choice but noticed she didn't hesitate to order strawberry shortcake for dessert. So, she had a sweet tooth. He ordered the same, and their eyes met across the table a moment, before she pretended extreme interest in a children's coloring menu left on the table by the last patrons. It wouldn't surprise him if she picked up a crayon and played connect-the-dots to avoid a conversation with him. Noticing a blue crayon by the salt shaker, he was tempted to hand it to her.

At their prearranged food drop, they loaded their backpacks with supplies that should last them until the next place. Those who wanted to made phone calls and mailed letters and postcards to family and friends. Nate wondered how his father was handling the situation at home, but that brought his spirits low, and he concentrated on the reason he'd come here: to get away from the outside world and all its problems.

Once they resumed their trek, the climb became extremely steep; the path led out of the gap and resembled a rockslide, with ferns hanging from cracks along the stone walls. The high humidity didn't help, either.

Nate regretted the full meal he'd eaten, and from the groans he heard, he wasn't the only one. Even Ted set a slower than usual pace. By the time they reached Clarendon Shelter, everyone felt hot, exhausted, and sweaty. Little daylight remained, and Nate found himself in a funk. His sole desire was to stock up on water, pitch his tent, grab some chow, and dive deep into his sleeping bag for an early night.

He crossed the far-reaching carpet of green grass that fronted the three-sided shelter and left his heavy backpack there. Setting off for a nearby stream, he experienced a dark gratitude to be alone. He groaned when he saw Carly had arrived there first. Hearing him, she turned and shot him a suspicious look.

"Are you following me?"

"Why would you think that?" About at the end of his limit, Nate didn't feel up to Carly's verbal jabs.

"Because it seems whatever I did today, you were always behind me, breathing down my neck."

"Maybe if you exercised a little more caution, there wouldn't have been a need."

She frowned. "I was fine both times; I knew to be careful on the summit and the bridge. And I don't need a buddy."

"You say that, but—"

"I do have a brain, you know. I'm not a complete ignoramus."

Nate gritted his teeth. "So you've told me."

"But with the way you act, it's like you've got some misguided, outdated concept that you have to play valiant hero to my helpless heroine. Only I'm not helpless, Nate, contrary to your narrow-minded opinion of me and probably of all women in general."

"I never said—"

"I mean"—she gave an exasperated upward sweep of her hands—"you're always lurking in the shadows, as if this buddy-system thing has gone to your head. Even before that, you were watching my every move like you planned to rush in and cart me off to safety at the least little slip. Well, guess what? I don't need saving! I did great before I met you, and I can do fine on my own now, too."

Seconds of silence crackled between them before Nate swooped down and grabbed her beneath the knees, his other arm looping around her shoulders. He swept her off her feet into his arms. Carly gaped at him, too stunned to speak.

Held close against his strength and warmth, his compelling stare drilling her, she found it hard to move her tongue to speak. He straightened, his blue-gray eyes burning inches away from hers.

"Good, it worked." His smile came grim, determined. "I had a feeling this was the only way I could shut you up long enough to actually listen to what I was saying and not just hear what you wanted to. First off, I have the utmost respect for women and don't think they're a weak-kneed, unskilled sex as you're always accusing me of thinking. Second, I've never once said a deriding word about you or how I feel about you, and contrary to what you think, you cannot read my mind."

"What's third?" Her voice cracked in a whisper.

"Third?"

"There's always a third."

"You want a third? Okay, here it is—the buddy system stays intact whether you and I like it or not. And unless you can learn to shed some of that prickly independence and not always bare your teeth at a hand offered in friendship, then lady, you might find it hard to keep your feet on solid ground." He set her down hard as he said the last, and her soles hit the soil with a thump.

Immediately, he stepped away, and she pitched sideways, working to catch her balance. She gaped at him like a grounded fish, her eyes bulging, her mouth wide open.

Good. She seemed to have gotten the message.

Without another word, he retraced his steps to the shelter, deciding he would refill his water bottle in the morning.

145

Chapter 6

All night, the wind had howled through the trees, but the morning dawned mild. Fog shimmered in the sunlight, cloaking the area in damp mist. Nate hunched down at the brook as he refilled his water bottle and allowed the breeze to blow away from his mind the clutter of yesterday's fiasco. For the first time in a week, he had snapped, reacting instead of thinking. Now that he'd had time to cool off, he regretted his impulsive actions. If Carly had disliked him before, she must now rank him high on her ten-most-hated-men list.

Hearing a twig snap, he looked over his shoulder. Carly approached, a silver packet in her hand. From the way her gaze darted to him, to the water, then back again, she seemed uncertain.

"Good morning," she said at last.

"Good morning." Nate wondered if she was deliberating giving him a push into the creek.

"I, um. . ." She brought her hand forward with the silver packet. "I brought you a peace offering. I didn't have any of Jill's candy, so I made do with this."

Nate took the protein shake, eyed it, then her. "Thanks." Feeling uneasy but thinking he should take a sip, he did so, trying not to grimace. A recollection of his youth flashed across his mind. He'd never excelled at board games, and his older sister and her friends had taken advantage of that, letting him join in when they played. They made the loser drink a "death drink" composed from any and all contents of refrigerator and cupboards that they could find to make the taste as appalling as possible. Nate always lost. Years later when they were teens, Nina confessed how she and her friends cheated to get Nate back for always tagging along.

Looking at the silver packet, he wondered if and how Carly had managed to filter grass and dirt through the hole with the straw.

"It's not much." She shrugged. "I had some left over when we got to the food drop."

He could understand why.

Before she could walk away, he spoke. "About last night." She looked at him, and he sighed. "I was way out of line, and I'm sorry. Maybe not so much in what I said, but with the way I said it and what I did."

"I had it coming."

Her answer shocked him. He never knew what to expect from her.

"I came on this hike, fresh from ending a relationship that went very sour very fast."

"Sorry to hear that."

"Yeah, well, it wasn't your fault or anyone else's. You've been nice no matter what a grouch I've been. So, I'm sorry, too."

Nate could think of a few occasions when he'd made a comeback, saying something he shouldn't have, but at the thought of peace between them, he decided not to bring them up.

"Anyhow." She nodded to the silver packet in his hand. "You'd better drink the rest if we're going to be trail mates and you plan to keep up with me." Her lips curled into a smirk before she headed back to camp, and he wondered if her words were deliberate and she knew exactly what sacrifice she asked of him in drinking the brew.

He also wondered if squirting the awful-tasting contents into the creek would kill any of the fish. Maybe he was overdramatizing; he took the barest sip to find out if he'd imagined it. Less than a minute later, after making sure Carly wasn't watching, he emptied the contents of the brown shake onto the ground, then folded the packet and put it with the rest of his garbage he would take with him so as to leave no trace that he'd been there.

He hoped the concoction wouldn't kill the grass.

After a short morning prayer, the group set off for their seventh day on the trail.

A gradual uphill climb near the summit of Beacon Hill and passage through open fields gave Nate a chance to talk to Carly, which he hoped might spur a friendship. Despite her tendency to withdraw to a corner, she possessed an independent, free-spirited quality that drew Nate to her.

"So, tell me," he said as they approached a high ridge above a brook that sparkled with the few coins of sunlight the trees allowed through their branches, "is there part gypsy in your blood?"

Carly laughed, and Nate thought it nicer than any sound he'd heard on the hike thus far. Now that she relaxed around him, she was pleasant to be with.

"Gypsy? No. Nothing Bohemian about me except for some of my clothes. According to what little my aunt has told me, I'm supposed to be descended from an Abenaki chief who made his home in these mountains centuries ago."

Nate studied her proud bearing and exotic features. The idea of Native American princess fit her well.

She looked at the trees. "I think I would have liked to have experienced life back then, but only for a few weeks, maybe a month. I'm too attached to home appliances to want to have lived in historic days."

"Well, you seem to be doing okay without electricity."

"Don't get me wrong—I love it. Like I said, a few weeks in the wilderness is great, and the length of this hike is perfect. Those packet meals aren't half bad, though I miss cooking from scratch. And the protein shakes were a good investment, too."

A wash of warmth swept up Nate's face, having nothing to do with the exertion of the hike. "Uh, yup."

"If nothing else, they make great fertilizer."

He shot her a sharp look at her wry words. Busted. He shook his head. "How'd you find out?"

"Nate, even the few guys I know who avoid meat wouldn't drink that stuff. Could be because of the alfalfa grass or maybe the kelp. Who knows?"

He stopped in shock. "Kelp? Meaning the green algae that grow at the bottom of ponds?"

She gave him a sweet smile and walked ahead.

"And don't horses eat alfalfa?" So she *had* been trying to feed him grass! "I knew you were trying to kill me," he muttered softly enough so that only she could hear.

She didn't look back, but her laugh brought about a reluctant smile.

❧

The next day took them to Killington Spur. A steady rain started, and everyone decided it best to forgo the climb to the second-steepest summit in the state and head for a popular inn for skiers and hikers. To the group's deep gratitude, Ted had made previous reservations, and all were eager for a short overnight stint to wash off the trail dust—or in this case, trail mud—and take a breather. They all knew that the farther the trail went on toward Canada, the more difficult it became, and it had already proven a challenge.

Close to evening, they arrived, weary and beaten, at a charming lodge with gleaming hardwood floors and a convivial stone fireplace in the cheery common area. Each went to their assigned rooms. Once in hers, Carly threw her backpack off, stripped down to nothing, and stood under a hot shower for a good ten minutes. The stress and pain of days on the trail melted away as the reviving needles of water did their magic and massaged tense muscles. Carly released a deep sigh of pleasure, shampooing her hair three times until she felt completely clean. She knew the results wouldn't last, but it was nice to get all the dirt off for at least one night.

Afterward, relaxed and refreshed, she changed into a T-shirt and clean hiking shorts—her only clean clothes—promising herself she would do her laundry before bed. Right now, her stomach growled. She headed to the main part of the lodge to meet with the others for dinner, not all that surprised when Nate alone rose from the sofa in the community area. He'd also showered and changed into a soft plaid shirt, a dark green one with long sleeves rather than the usual torn ones.

"Where are the others?" Carly asked.

"The newlyweds are in their room, Kim wasn't feeling well, and Ted and Jill went off to find a phone and run a few errands."

"So, in other words, it's just us." The last three words gave Carly a strange tingle in the pit of her stomach.

"Looks like it. You hungry?"

"Famished."

"Then what are we standing here for? Allow your trail mate to come to the rescue—just this once." He gave her a mischievous grin and crooked his elbow in a formal manner she'd seen in old movies. She chuckled, relaxing as she took his arm. They found a table for two, and a waitress gave them menus.

"The corned beef with cabbage looks good. . . ." Nate trailed off at the look Carly gave him. "Sorry, I forgot you don't eat meat." He glanced at the menu. "No salad here, either. We can go somewhere else, if you'd like. There's a pub nearby that serves food."

"That's okay. I do eat more than salads." Carly thought it sweet of Nate to offer. Maybe she had pegged him wrong. He really wasn't such a bad guy, but it wasn't until he'd swept her off her feet the other night—literally—that he'd rattled some sense into her brain so she could see it. The memory of their close encounter made her cheeks hot, and she closed the menu.

"I think I'll have the French onion soup and the stuffed mushrooms. Two appetizers should fill me up." The one vegetarian entrée loomed too far out of her price range.

"I still can't believe you fed me grass."

Carly laughed. "Perfectly-good-for-you grass, it was, too. Not a thing in the world wrong with it."

"If you're a horse."

She giggled again at his sober teasing, and conversation flowed easily. Once they gave their order and the meal came, he bowed his head in silent prayer, and she glanced out the window, a bit uneasy. She had realized he was a Christian like the others the night she'd spotted him with his Bible at the group's evening prayer rituals—or whatever they did. But he hadn't tried to shove its contents down her throat at any time this past week or point and call her a sinner, and that helped her to relax. Jill's friends were a lot different than she'd thought they would be. It felt good to be around them.

"So, Carly, tell me—what's your story?"

"My story?" She set down her spoon in the soup bowl and raised her eyebrows. "Now you're the one sounding like a reporter."

He stopped short of taking a bite of his sandwich and peered up at her. "You're a reporter?"

Did she imagine it, or did his words seem tense? "I was. With the *Goosebury*

Gazette, our town paper. I handled the entertainment section, current events, that sort of thing."

"Oh." He took a hefty bite, but she sensed something still troubled him. "So, what's Goosebury like nowadays? I lived there a couple of years during high school but don't remember that much about it."

She gave a sharp laugh, capturing his attention again. "Sorry. This isn't the best time to ask me that question. Any other day, I'd say it's your usual charming New England small town, filled with its covered bridges, scenic spots, and the like."

"And on the other days?"

She shrugged.

"Any family?"

"An aunt, an uncle, and a cousin. And to save you the trouble of asking, since it always follows, my mom took off when I was barely out of diapers, and I don't know where my dad is, much less who he is." She hoped he didn't hear the tremor of bitterness in words she tried to deliver in a bored monotone. But given the fact that Nate now gaped at her, again ignoring his sandwich, he must have.

He collected himself. "That must have been hard, growing up without parents. My mom died when I was just a kid, and my dad remarried five years ago." His jaw tensed, and he set down his sandwich and took a drink of soda before returning his attention to Carly. "You said you worked at the *Gazette*. What do you do now?"

"I'm between jobs."

"Funny, so am I."

"I got fired." She might as well be honest.

He grinned. "Me, too."

Her eyes opened wider. "You're kidding?"

"Dead serious."

"Wow, talk about odd—us being in the same boat. I'm not sure it's something I want to talk about, but I have to admit it's good being in like company."

"Same here." His smile switched to full-blown and knocked Carly a little off-kilter. The guy was attractive, likeable, and nice, but, she reminded herself, she didn't want a relationship.

"As for what I'm doing now, I'm gathering information to write a guidebook for beginners, by me—a beginner—of what to expect on the Long Trail."

"I wondered what that mini recorder was for; I figured you were recording things for a personal journal. A lot of hikers do that sort of thing."

"Nope, I'm formulating a guidebook. I know there's a market, but I'm hoping my inexperience as a hiker won't cause problems in selling the idea. I doubt my old boss would give me the time of day as far as references go after the chewing out I got from him—long story; I don't want to go there. But I have other connections in the publishing industry and the media, so we'll see."

This time, she couldn't mistake his reaction. Nate became withdrawn, almost detached. He polished off the rest of his sandwich and his side of red potatoes in silence, and Carly concentrated on her meal, too. The stuffed mushrooms were zesty with garlic, just the way she liked them, and the soup was rich and smooth, perfect to take away the chill in her body. Too bad the warmth didn't reenter their conversation.

Nate wiped his mouth. "I should call it a night. I'm beat, and we need to get an early start tomorrow."

"Sure." Carly floundered, a bit disconcerted by his abrupt behavior. "If you're still feeling bushed tomorrow, I always have an extra protein shake."

The answering chuckle he gave was weak, and as she went to her room to take care of her laundry, she scolded herself. So what if he didn't want to spend the rest of the evening talking with her? That was what she wanted—her own space and no unwelcome advances. He seemed to have received her oft-repeated message loud and clear. So since everything now pointed in her favor, it made no sense that Carly should feel upset that he'd done exactly as she'd asked him.

The next day, the trail grew narrow, the overgrowth looming high along the sides, the path shooting up then down with what seemed neither rhyme nor reason. At lunch, they stopped at one of the shelters and met some AT hikers, those hiking the Appalachian Trail. Since both it and the Long Trail traveled the same path for one hundred miles, Nate was surprised these were the first AT hikers they'd met. The robust, middle-aged married couple were hiking the trail for their twenty-fifth anniversary, and Nate admired their courage in tackling it.

Carly seemed distant, which for once made Nate glad. The trail lay cluttered with countless rocks and massive tree roots, requiring every bit of attention.

Last night, when she had confessed she was a reporter, warning bells had gone off inside Nate, and the tragedy of his family's dilemma attacked him full force. He didn't appreciate the unwanted reminder, though he realized Carly wasn't to blame. She couldn't have known his story. No one did except Ted and Jill, whom he'd sworn to secrecy. And Nate planned to keep it that way.

He was sure Carly's journalistic blood would simmer to a boil if she knew that one of the most sought-after and evasive sources of recent headline news to hit southern Vermont hiked a few feet behind her. No longer would she avoid him; he would be running from her. Remembering his narrow escapes from the media, his "running" might become reality. And he couldn't let that happen.

He needed this hike. He had started to feel a closeness to God he hadn't experienced in months. For some reason, his town had marked his entire family as outcasts for one man's sins. Nate would never understand that, but he'd felt the full brunt of their bitter rejection. Here with Ted's church group, Nate enjoyed acceptance and anonymity; he didn't want to lose that.

When they reached the shelter where they would spend the night, a group of hikers who'd arrived before them invited their group to share in a weenie roast. While Carly didn't eat their food, she did participate in the light conversation as they all gathered around the fire and compared experiences they'd had while on the trail. She sat across from Nate, and he found his gaze wandering to her often. When she would suddenly look at him, he would shift his attention to something else like a misbehaving kid.

Kim excused herself, and soon after that, Carly left, too. Nate hesitated when she headed away from the shelter. Should he follow or just trust that she wouldn't wander too far in the dark and would know to stay out of trouble?

The answer, from previous experience, made him quietly groan, and he excused himself and set off in the direction she'd taken. He moved around the shelter and almost jumped out of his skin as he came close to mowing down both Carly and Kim.

Both girls squealed in shock, and Kim beamed her flashlight into Nate's face.

"Looking for someone?" Carly asked, her brow lifted, her tone steady.

As he worked to regain his bearings, Nate blocked the light from his eyes with his hand. He gave a disgusted chuckle and shook his head. "You would think I'd know better by now. Could you please shine that thing somewhere else?"

"Hey," Carly's tone came softer, "I was just teasing."

Kim lowered the light, and it flickered. "Rats. Looks like I need new batteries. Me and Carly were just about to play cards. We could make it a game of Hearts if you want to join us."

About to refuse, Nate noticed Carly's expression, what he could see of it. Was the twilight playing tricks with his mind, or did she actually look hopeful that he might agree? He thought it over; a game of cards wasn't a journalistic interview, and he needed to unwind.

"Maybe just one game."

"Great," Kim enthused. "I have a candle, too. I'll get it." She scampered off.

"A candle?" Nate arched his brow.

Carly laughed. "Well, we can't exactly play by the light of the moon since there isn't one tonight."

"Good point." They walked to the front of the shelter.

Kim met them with a lit candle, using her hand to shield the flame.

"Why do you think the front is fenced in like a half gate?" Kim asked about the shelter as Nate opened the gate for her and Carly.

Nate didn't want to speculate, but he knew about recent bear sightings, and in the winter, porcupines made a nuisance of themselves. "Probably to keep out the animals."

"But animals are everywhere," Kim insisted. "It just seems sort of weird, is all."

Two campers not from their group lay sound asleep, huddled in a far corner. Kim dribbled wax on an old boxlike crate to secure the candle. Carly dealt them each a hand. Even with the flickering light, it wasn't easy to see the larger-than-usual numbers or colors of the cards, but Nate didn't care. The two girls were chatterbugs when together, though they spoke in quiet murmurs so as not to awaken the other hikers. Nate enjoyed hearing more of Carly's past when Kim asked her specific questions. From the little he remembered, Goosebury was a nice town. At least some small towns were nice.

Realizing the direction his thoughts had twisted, Nate pushed them to a back corner of his brain and concentrated on the good company. The lazy buzz of cicadas filled the night, and Kim rubbed her eyelids behind her glasses and yawned. "Well, that's it for me. My eyes hurt, and I'm beat—though not at cards." She laughed.

"That's right, rub it in," Carly joked.

"I'll walk you to your tent." The fence around the shelter bothered Nate more than he cared to let Kim and Carly know.

"You don't have to."

But Nate had already risen to his feet. Carly also stood.

"We have another long day ahead of us tomorrow. I think I'll call it quits as well."

Because Kim's tent was closest, they dropped her off first.

"Keep the candle." She handed it to Carly. "You can give it back tomorrow. It's creepy without a moon. Dangerous, too."

Wishing his slim flashlight wasn't behind in his backpack, Nate walked with Carly to the tent she'd pitched farther down the line. They seemed to have run out of things to talk about, and Nate wondered if Carly also felt an odd stirring in the air, a sense of awkward anticipation. He shot her a sidelong glance.

She held the candle at shoulder level. The flame illumined her already exotic features, giving her an almost otherworldly glow. Nate held his breath at her beauty. All she needed was a beaded dress and studded headband to look the part of a real Native American princess.

She turned to face him as they reached her tent. Nate detected her uneasiness as she finally lifted the gaze of her huge, dark eyes to his. He could get lost in those eyes and not mind it one bit.

"Nate, I know we didn't hit it off from the beginning, again my fault. But during this week of getting to know you, I've come to realize I do want your friendship. I can't help but feel, what with the way you've been acting today, that I did something or said something to upset you at the inn. So, if I did, I'm sorry, and I'd like to be trail mates again."

"Meaning no more veiled thoughts of pushing me into a creek?"

She grinned. "As long as you don't hoist me up and dump me in it first."

Nate couldn't help but return her soft smile. "Carly." He laid his fingers against the sleeve on her upper arm in a manner meant to reassure. "Just so you know, my behavior today had nothing to do with anything you've done. I've been going through some hard times, and last night brought it all back."

Carly gave a nod. "I can understand that." She moved the candle between them, her fingers almost touching his chest. "Any time you want to unload, I make a decent listener."

"I'll remember that." His words came quietly, his mind spinning to another track. Standing so close to her, he felt connected. Her eyes drew him; her lips parted. If not for the chance of scorching his chin with the flame from her candle, he would have leaned forward to kiss her. Even more shocking, she looked as if she wanted him to.

He gave a slight shake of his head and retreated a step. "Well, I need to call it a night. Dawn will be here before you know it. So, uh. . .yeah, good night."

"Do you need the candle?" Carly called after him.

"No, I can make it."

Seconds later in the pitch dark, he stumbled over a tree root and fell flat on his hands and knees.

"You okay?"

At the worry in Carly's voice, he hurried to his feet and brushed off his jeans. "Sure. I meant to do that."

She giggled at his silly response, and Nate's heart gave a light jump at the unexpected sound of her velvety laughter, but he continued his trek toward his tent. He wasn't about to return to collect any candle, because this time he would give in and kiss her. And Nate had no idea how to handle this sudden, mind-boggling switch from thinly veiled hostility to open friendship. He'd wanted her friendship, sure, but nothing else. And as far as he knew, the powers that be hadn't written a guidebook on the best defense against falling for another person.

Falling for another person. . .the thought almost made him trip again. No way was he falling for Carly. No way. . .

He readied for bed that night with more force than necessary, unzipping his sleeping bag so fast he felt grateful he hadn't knocked the zipper off the metal teeth. Nate had come on this hike to get away from complications and to get in tune with God. Though the latter had brought results, the former still needed improvements.

He had no desire to start a romantic relationship.

Chapter 7

Over the next few days, the hike turned rougher, the trail steeper, filled with copious natural stone steps, many of them uphill. But where there was uphill, downhill must follow, and Carly wondered when the trail would level off, if ever. At times she had to use her hands to climb exposed ledges. Still, despite the strenuous workouts, the blisters she nursed, frequent rain, and thick clusters of black flies and other insects near all bodies of water, she was glad she'd come. The alpine region through which they trekked made her grateful for the warm clothes she'd packed, and the brisk, clean air brought new life to her lungs. The awesome views at the summits of each mountain were masterpieces to her eyes, and she took so many pictures, she was glad she'd invested in a second camera card. The sensation of being secluded safely away in nature's quiet corner helped Carly to relax and forget about the real world for a while.

She and Nate had become true "trail mates," and she found it curious he hadn't been nearly as talkative with her today as in recent days. A slight tension sizzled between them, though his attitude toward her remained friendly and helpful.

Their lives had produced a pattern. During the days, they hiked, climbed, and sometimes fell or otherwise banged themselves up. During the evenings, they relaxed, ate, and got to know one another better. Carly had also become good friends with Kim, amazed at how intelligent the girl was. She talked about the regular things all teenage girls enjoy—favorites in music, fads, and boys—but at times when they played cards, their conversation took a deeper route, and Carly got a good look inside the girl's mind. For herself, she hadn't shared much beyond the basics of her personal life, and she intended to keep it that way. She never mentioned Jake's name; just thinking about him put a sour taste in her mouth.

"Carly."

The presence of Nate coming up behind her so abruptly and murmuring her name threw her, and she startled.

"Hold still. Don't move."

The words themselves brought all manner of terrible visions to mind. "What is it?"

"Just hold still." Nate's hand made a quick swipe through her hair, and she did all she could not to scream.

155

"A bug? There was a bug in my hair?" The inchworms falling from the trees the other day had been bad enough to try to avoid.

"A spider."

Just the name gave her shivers. She and the eight-legged creatures didn't get along well—she always gave them their distance. Regardless that she knew the vicious invader was gone, she swept her fingers through her hair.

"It was pretty small. About the size of a nickel, with legs."

"You are not helping any." She gave up combing her fingers through her hair and bent double, flipping her hair over to whisk her fingers through as if washing it.

"I did get it out."

"I know, but it might have had babies."

"In your hair?" She heard the amusement in his voice.

"They carry them in a sac, you know. My aunt stepped on one once—hundreds of tiny babies went scurrying all over the floor." Just saying it gave her another dose of shivers.

"Well, no worries. I see no more creatures running through your hair. Tiny or otherwise."

"Thanks." The word came out droll.

"So, I take it you don't like spiders?" Nate had the audacity to grin, and Carly could have cheerfully pushed him down the rock step they'd just climbed.

"Name one person who does," she shot back.

"Spiderman."

His crazy answer made her roll her eyes. "Those people not belonging to the fictional world of Marvel comics."

"I'm impressed. You know your comic books."

"Not really. My cousin grew up on them."

"Any sisters, brothers? I hardly know anything about you."

"I'm an only child. And anyway, you know all that's important to know, and more besides." Carly shrugged, uneasy with the turn of conversation and her memory of spouting off about her parents. "Whereas I know next to nothing about you. How come?"

Nate looked ahead on the path. "We should catch up to the others."

"Well, that was an evasive answer if ever I heard one."

"Not much to tell." He didn't meet her eyes, instead showing extreme interest in their surroundings. "But I guess we could resume this conversation at lunch if you want."

"I'll hold you to that."

And she did.

As they gathered at Birch Glen Camp, Carly put aside her noonday habit of reciting notes into her mini recorder and, hands clasping her thighs, she sank to her knees in front of Nate.

"I'm all ears," she said, her manner pure innocence.

"What?"

"For the story of your life."

He groaned. "You have a good memory."

"I have a great memory. So how about it?"

Nate took a long swig from his water bottle and capped it. "Well, to begin with, I was born."

Carly's brows arched. "Why does this sound strangely like an intro to *David Copperfield*?"

Nate laughed. "I'm surprised you recognized it."

"I'm a writer, Nate. I have an interest in books. But I'm surprised you brought up a classic. Somehow you don't strike me as being a literary bug."

"You're right; I'm not. Old memories still lodged in there from high school, I guess. I had to write a report on that book. I almost sweat drops of blood over that paper."

Carly laughed. "Ah. That explains it. So, I know you were born, and that your name is not David Copperfield. What about your family?"

Did she imagine it, or did Nate tense?

"A father, a married sister, stepmother, stepbrother. Like I said before, Mom died when I was a kid, and Dad remarried several years ago." He shrugged. "Not much to tell."

"You're too modest; I'll bet there are a lot of interesting things about you." A flash of heat swept over Carly, and she noted his surprised look at her telltale words. "I mean, everyone has stories of interest. So let me help you along a little. What did you do before you got fired?"

"You're a curious sort, aren't you? Is this an interview?"

"No, strictly off the record. I guess you could say curiosity runs deep in my blood." She shrugged as if that explained it. "Besides, I told you my former job title, so it seems only fair you should reciprocate. Isn't that what buddies do—swap jokes and trade woes?"

"Oh, so *now* you want to be my buddy," Nate said in mock amusement. "Now that the spotlight is trained on me."

She gave a sweet, not-so-innocent smile, and he snorted.

"Okay, *buddy*, I was a tour guide for a small organization in southern Vermont. I basically carted people around the countryside to places of interest."

"And you don't call that interesting?" Carly could see Nate as a tour guide; he had that friendly quality with people, even strangers. And he was careful to watch out for others getting off on the wrong trail—literally. Carly remembered when he'd stopped Kim from using a side trail. She hadn't seen the blue blaze marking the tree. Maybe that's where he'd gotten his protective nature, from his job.

Or maybe it was just a part of who he was.

"What?"

She made an effort to stop grinning. "Just thinking you would have made a great tour guide, is all."

"A compliment, coming from you?" He gathered his brows in pretend amazement. "I think someone must have slipped something into your mud-protein shake."

She laughed. "Okay, okay. I know I was pretty hard on you at first, but maybe I was wrong about you. Give a girl a break."

Hearing footsteps, Carly swung her head around. "Hey, Kimmers."

The teen waved back, but Carly noted her face seemed tense as she walked on into the shelter and sat down at a table there. Maybe she'd had words with her dad; Carly had spotted them in intense conversation earlier that morning.

"Do you give everyone nicknames?" Nate asked. "I've heard you call Jill Ju-Ju, and Sierra, Cat."

"Only my friends. Jill got dubbed Ju-Ju because of her desire to always fix things. Like Zuzu's petals." She looked at him when he only stared. "From the Capra movie *It's a Wonderful Life*."

"Oh, right."

"And Cat, well, with her pretty auburn hair and green eyes, she just looks catlike. Kim became Kimmers because the word reminded me of glimmers and shimmers; she's always so bubbly." Carly tilted her head and stared at Nate in deep reflection. "I guess since we're trail mates now, I need to think up a name for you, too. *Trail Mate* just doesn't cut it." She grinned wickedly. "Maybe Alfalfa...Kelpie. Or Shadow would work. Creek Scourge or Brook Rogue are options, too."

"Cute." Nate reached over to tug a hank of her hair, as if they were children.

"Hey—only kidding!" She laughed. "And no one touches my hair."

"Right, I'll remember that for the future."

"You'd better," she said in a menacing tone.

"Does that order count in the case of any future arachnid dwellers?" His grin teased. "Or do I have permission then?"

She couldn't help it; she swatted his arm.

"Hey!" Nate pulled back, laughing.

"Hi, you two." Sierra walked up to them. "Ted wants everyone to gather for a short reading. Since Jill's sick, we're camping here, and we won't be having discussion tonight."

"Ju-Ju's sick?" Alarm wiped the smile from Carly's mouth. She hoped her friend hadn't gotten hold of some bad water.

"Yeah, probably a twenty-four-hour virus. With all this rain we've had to hike in, it's a wonder all of us aren't sick."

True, but rain only augmented an illness; it didn't start one. And they'd been wearing protective rain gear.

"Ted said this might set us back a day. We won't know if she can manage the hike until tomorrow morning."

Carly shrugged off her worries for Jill and stood to her feet. The only part of this group hike that made her uncomfortable had been the devotional readings with discussion following. Most nights during the onset of the hike, she'd sought escape in her tent, but not wanting to be rude to her hosts, she had joined the group on other occasions.

She felt like an interloper during those times Ted or another person read Bible passages aloud, followed by conversation, sometimes intense, as each gave their views. She didn't believe in any of what they said, had never been raised to accept it, so she couldn't take part and sat silent, a reluctant observer. But at some point, something infinitesimal had metamorphosed within her in such a quiet way she'd hardly noticed when her feelings had begun to change.

Before this hike, she had doubted the existence of God and argued such a viewpoint to the ground when anyone brought it up. Being so attuned with nature and absent from the continual distractions of town life and the electronic devices that were part of her existence had quieted her mind and made her think. Here, she experienced a different world; maybe not a better world than the one she knew in Goosebury, but one that offered mental peace and emotional solitude, as well as physical challenge. A world where she could stand on summits so elevated that if she reached up, she could touch the sky and then look over the panoramic landscape far below and all around her. A world clustered amid trees and rocks and water, riddled with snow-peaked mountains and hidden valleys. A world where it became more and more difficult to accept her belief that life had come into being by chance.

As Ted read aloud, Carly watched a shaft of afternoon sunlight stream through the branches of nearby trees. A flash of orange streaked through the light, and she saw a fire salamander dart over the ground from under a log and race through the tall grass.

How could this all have just happened? She'd never really thought about it, just went along with her family's ideas; but the detail in each leaf, each flower, each creature, diverse and beautiful in its own way, had to have been crafted by a master hand.

Shivers went through her as her mind began to open up to the concept she had always denied.

There is a God.

From what she'd witnessed of her friends Leslie and Jill and seen of their lives, she was ninety-nine percent certain this all-Supreme Being was the God of the Bible. The God who had made a heaven and a hell. And knowing that, Carly experienced a stirring of personal doubt, guilt—and fear.

If they were right and Carly was wrong, then she was in even worse trouble than she'd thought.

The next day, Nate questioned his decision to ask Carly if she wanted to tag along for a short, four-mile spur down a side trail, but the words shot out of his mouth before he could reel them back.

"Sure." She looked at him, curious. "I'll get my backpack."

Nate didn't blame her for her surprise. One minute, he retreated from her; the next minute, he invited her company. At breakfast, he'd barely talked to her. But he didn't want to make the trek alone for more than just safety's sake.

"How's Jill doing?" he asked when Carly returned. "I saw you go to her tent earlier."

Carly finished buckling the strap around her. "She's a trooper, though I know she hates to hold everyone back like this. But she hasn't been able to keep anything down and is too exhausted to move. Sounds like that virus that was going around Goosebury before we took off."

"She shouldn't feel bad about holding anyone back. This is a much-needed diversion. Ted has been running everyone too hard, trying to get so many miles in each day. It's nice to kick back for a while and rest. Especially before tackling the Camel's Hump. That mountain has challenged the best of hikers."

"And we're going on a short hike to relax?" Carly grinned.

"Okay, well it's nice for the others who are new to this sort of thing. Me, I can't sit still for long. If I do, my muscles may atrophy."

"Same here." Carly cast a glance up and sobered. "But the sky looks like rain."

"So when have we ever let a little moisture stop us?"

She laughed again. "Agreed. Should we invite the others?"

"I did. They'd rather rest, and Ted is busy taking care of Jill."

They'd only traveled about a mile before the rain hit. Nate pulled up the hood of his rain gear, and Carly did the same with hers. Instead of the mild shower he'd hoped for, the precipitation became a deluge, hindering their ability to walk.

Carly grabbed his arm and pointed off the trail to an area where the trees formed a canopy. "We could stay there until this passes."

"Under the trees? I don't think that's a good idea."

"There's no lightning, and even if there were, on a mountainside covered with so many trees, the chance of a strike are about one in a million."

She took off without waiting for him to answer. "Lady, do you always flirt with danger?" he called after her.

Shaking his head, Nate had no choice but to follow. The other option that flitted through his brain—dragging her back to camp—didn't seem a wise choice.

Once under the thick, sheltering boughs, which let in scant droplets of rain,

Nate had to admit it was nice not to have to clear his vision by continually wiping water out of his eyes. With a little smile, Carly tipped her head back against the trunk, her eyelids sweeping down as if to absorb her surroundings and the few drops that landed on her skin.

Nate took the liberty of studying her face. Her lashes wet, they still had a curl at their tips, thick and lush, as natural as the gentle arch of her eyebrows. On this wilderness hike, the women didn't bother with makeup, and Nate knew all he saw of Carly was natural. Rain only accentuated her beauty as the clear beaded drops played with the light, emphasizing her high cheekbones, the gentle slope of her forehead, the smooth line of her nose, which ended in a soft rounded tip. Underneath, her lips were full and moist.

A strange sensation knotted his throat, almost painful, as he stared at her mouth, then back up to her closed eyes.

"You're staring at me," she said. "Stop it."

Surprised she realized it, he felt a bit disconcerted. "So, what, now you have radar in your eyelids?"

At that, her lips curled into an amused smile. "All women do, didn't you know?" She opened her eyes, and Nate wondered if it was his recent scrutiny of her features that made him notice how shimmering dark they were and how big. "It's the only way we can keep ourselves armed against unwanted attention."

"Right." Nate looked back out at the trees. What was he doing? What was he thinking? Of course, Carly didn't want anything to do with him on a more serious level; he also had no desire to take it further. They were trail mates on the path to friendship. Nothing more.

For the remainder of the downpour, Nate focused on the range of trees surrounding them and their diversity of textures. Thick hardwoods and slender pines stood with one another, opposites in traits but equals in their cause for existence. Each trunk maintained its own space, not allowing the other trees inside its circle, but still, they all somehow managed to work together in harmony to give the mountainside beauty, the animals shelter and food.

"Nate, listen." Carly looked toward the west. "Do you hear that?"

Broken from his wry musings, he struggled to listen. The rain had lessened, and he could hear what sounded like a faint bawling, almost a bleating.

"Whatever it is sounds as if it's in trouble." Carly moved toward the sound.

"Carly, I wouldn't do that."

Regardless, she continued her course.

"Woman, don't you ever listen to anyone?" he muttered in frustration, following her.

She stopped at the edge of some overgrowth, pulling it back. Even above the sounds of trickling water, he heard her gasp. "Nate! Come look."

He joined her, looking over her shoulder. A cream-spotted fawn nestled on the grasses, its head low. Its frail body was no more than the size of a large housecat, and its soft, pointed ears lay to the side as its huge black eyes watched them.

"Oh, Nate. Isn't she the most adorable thing you've ever seen?" Carly's voice became soft, wondering. "And the poor baby's shivering. Do you think she's cold or scared?"

Nate watched Carly lean forward as though she might pet it.

"Carly—don't." He grabbed her arm, this time not allowing her the choice of going against him. "I know it's cute and it's tempting to pet, but you shouldn't touch any wild animal, especially a baby." Releasing his hold on her, he studied the fawn, whose bleats had grown more frantic. "It looks like it's only a few weeks old."

"Where's the mother?" Carly scanned the area as if hoping to spot a doe, then turned back to the fawn. "You don't think the poor thing has been abandoned, do you?"

"No, that's how a doe treats its young. It hides them somewhere safe and returns when the fawns need to feed."

"But what if she doesn't come back? What if this poor little girl is left all alone without her mother to take care of her? Look at her now. She's so fragile, so vulnerable. She looks as if a strong gust of wind might blow her away. What if a bear finds her?"

"The pelt helps to camouflage the fawn against would-be predators." Nate watched doubt and compassion play across Carly's face, noting how she'd instantly labeled the fawn a female and not a male.

Carly swung her head around to pinpoint him with flashing eyes. "We can't leave her here all alone!"

"There's nothing else we can do, Carly. We can't take it back with us. We need to respect the wildlife. And hard as it may seem when things look bad, we can't tamper with nature's order, much less violate state laws that forbid anyone other than a wildlife rehabilitator from intervening with sick animals."

"That just seems so wrong," she fumed. "So let me get this straight, according to the system, we let a helpless creature, no more than a few weeks old, die because man's law says we must. That's just not right." Tears shone in her eyes, astonishing Nate. "Under extenuating circumstances, I think some laws need to be vetoed or rewritten."

"This is more than just about the fawn, isn't it?" he asked softly.

He watched her lips part in surprise, watched her clamp her teeth and her jaw grow firm as a hard glint shone in her eyes while she struggled to maintain composure. Struggled, and lost. To his bafflement, she bowed her head, and her shoulders shook. He'd never seen Carly so vulnerable, like the baby fawn.

Compassion urged him to move forward and take her in his arms, while common sense warned him to back away while he still could. His heart triumphed in the battle with his mind, and compassion won.

He pulled her close, and she stiffened as his hands gently pressed against her back. "It's okay, Carly. It's okay."

She relaxed against him, little by little, dropping her forehead to his collarbone. Along with his sympathy for whatever brought on her mute sobs, Nate couldn't help but realize he enjoyed the soft feel of her in his arms. As she released quiet tears mixed with the gentle sprinkle of rain, Nate smoothed a hand along her slick hair. Her hood had fallen away at some point, and just as he thought about plucking it up and replacing it, she lifted her eyes to look at him. Glazed with tears, they'd never appeared so beautiful, so soft. Her lashes curled in gentle spikes, her lips trembled.

"I'm sorry, I—"

"Shh." With a slight shake of his head, Nate moved his hands to cradle her jaw, then leaned in to kiss her.

Her lips were cool, soft, wet from the rain, and what Nate had told himself he intended to be a token of gentle reassurance turned into much more. He brushed his lips over hers and heard her gasp. He couldn't remember when he'd last felt like this, or why he'd been avoiding it. Stunned, he pulled away a fraction and looked into her slightly unfocused, night-dark eyes.

"What are you doing?" She breathed a little faster, her features soft, uncertain, her lips that he'd just touched with his parted and trembling.

"I don't know, but if you figure it out, don't tell me," he whispered before leaning in to kiss her again. To his shock, Carly whimpered and pressed against him, sliding her hands up around his neck as their kiss altered into one of mutual need. He moved his hands to her back and responded with equal fervor, until suddenly she pressed her hands against his chest and broke their kiss, pushing away. He released her.

She retreated a few steps, wouldn't meet his eyes. Nate stood motionless and couldn't keep from staring at her.

"I shouldn't have done that," he said after a taut silence elapsed.

"I shouldn't have responded."

"But you did, and I did." Nate's voice was low. "So where does that leave us, Carly?"

She shook her head in frustration. "Don't ask; I don't know. Maybe we should just call it a mistake."

"A mistake is something never meant to happen. Neither of us may have expected this just now, but I think if we're honest with each other, we've both felt the currents all along."

Carly shut her eyes, and her lips parted, revealing to Nate he'd been correct. "I don't want a relationship, Nate. Not now. I just came out of a really bad one."

He didn't want a relationship, either, so why was he pushing her? He shoved his hands in his pockets. Another minute passed before he spoke.

"Mind telling me what that was all about earlier?"

"You mean my crying jag?" The cynicism crept back into her voice. "I thought you would have figured it out after what I told you at the restaurant. My mom abandoned me on my aunt's doorstep when I was a kid, remember?" She shrugged as if it didn't matter. "Call it a sudden weakness that overcame me when I saw the fawn. I'm really over those days, and I have no idea why I carried on so."

Nate doubted she was as emotionally invincible as she wanted him to believe. "Carly, it really is okay to cry."

Her brow arched wryly. "Are you speaking from experience or just saying what feels right at the moment?"

"Both."

She didn't answer. After a moment, she looked away from him and to the fronds that covered the baby deer. "What about her?"

He knew he would regret the words that formed in his mind, but they escaped regardless. "I guess we could stick around for a while, out of sight, and wait to see that the mama comes back. With the way the fawn was bawling, if the doe is nearby, she'll be coming soon."

Carly's smile brightened the day, making him glad he'd suggested it.

"Thank you, Nate."

Together, they moved away from the fawn and among the trees closer to the trail, hidden from view of the fawn's bed but still within range to spy. Nate wondered how long they would have to stand there until Carly's hopes were satisfied; he didn't want to wait for hours. Worse, he had no guarantee the mother would return. The doe might have been hurt or killed by a carnivore. Yet Nate had a feeling Carly wouldn't budge from her observation post until the doe made an appearance.

As the minutes passed, he thought of a multitude of questions he wanted to ask but reasoned it better to leave such things unspoken at this point. Normally, he enjoyed the sounds of nature and didn't always like to talk, but their earlier words felt as if they'd been left teetering on a precipice, undone and unfinished. His only worry was that if he said too much, he would push her over, along with the conversation.

"Nate, it's okay. Really."

"What?" Startled she had spoken, he looked at her.

"You're wondering what to say to me about my mother. Or maybe you're wondering if you should bring up our kiss. So let me save you the trouble; I'd rather not talk about either."

"You know, Carly, it baffles me how you always think you can read my mind."

She offered him one swift glance at his somber words. "So, was I wrong?"

Nate didn't want to admit that this time she was dead on target. But the thought of continued silence oppressed him. He fished about in his mind for the right words, but those that came to him seemed too trite. Those he longed to speak, too personal. What did someone say to a woman like Carly in a situation like this?

"Nate." Her excited whisper broke through his frustrated musings. "Look."

At the edge of the trees where he had kissed her, a doe moved with wary grace, then stopped and sniffed the ground. He hoped the delicate creature wouldn't be able to discern their scent, that the rain had washed it away. If the doe didn't return to the fawn, Nate wasn't sure what Carly would do.

As they watched, the doe lifted her head, alert. The fawn bawled louder as if sensing its mama nearby. After another tense wait, the doe moved to the tall fronds where she'd hidden the fawn.

"A happy ending," Carly breathed with a wistful smile. "That was worth every second of standing in the rain to see." She looked at him. "Again, thank you."

He smiled and nodded. "Are you ready to return to camp?"

"You don't want to continue the hike?"

"The others might get worried if we're gone too long and send out a search party." Nate was only half joking. "Ted's pretty upset about Jill, and I don't want to add to his troubles by not showing up for lunch."

"I've been worried about her, too," she said as they started the hike back.

"Well, it's like I told Ted, she has nothing that a good amount of loving, prayer, and rest won't cure."

Carly didn't respond, and Nate wondered which of the three she didn't agree with. He doubted it was the second, since she was with a church group, and didn't think it could be the last. Everyone complained at one time or another that Ted pushed them too hard. So that left loving, and considering the glimpse she'd given him into her past and the knowledge that she'd just come out of a bad relationship, Nate had a sneaking suspicion Carly had rarely been on the receiving end of any real affection.

The sudden thought that he might be the one to change all that sent an unexpected rush of adrenaline through his veins. One minute he fought the idea of a relationship with her; the next, he welcomed it. She was fire and water, ice and wind—her passionate nature, her free spirit attracting him like no other woman had done. He had enjoyed the times they'd conversed on friendly levels, and a part of him had been drawn like a moth to her flame when they'd exchanged heated banter. She confused him, exasperated him, magnetized him, and fascinated him.

He was beginning to feel as mixed up as Carly acted.

Chapter 8

That night as the others gathered around the campfire, Carly held back. She couldn't explain why on other occasions she hadn't minded joining the group devotions so much, even if she did feel as if she was on the outside looking in, but tonight she not only felt like an outsider but also a hypocrite.

Her mind still whirled with her earlier conversation with Nate, not to mention his kiss, which she'd been shocked to find herself not only accepting but returning, and she didn't feel as if she could paste a smile on her face one more night and pretend something she didn't feel.

She tended to her needs, hoping Kim might still be up and would want to talk. The teenager had left the group earlier, complaining her eyes hurt.

Carly poked her head in the shelter, where Kim and her father had opted to stay because of all the rain, but even in the dark, she could see that Kim's sleeping bag lay flat. Confused, Carly looked back toward the latrine. She had just come from there and would have passed Kim on her return, but she checked again anyway. It, too, was empty.

Before she created a panic, Carly walked around the shelter on the outskirts of the trees, searching for Kim. The increasing darkness made it difficult to see, even with the light from the fire ring that three other campers huddled around.

She glanced toward the small group in front of Ted's tent. Jill sat by his side, and Carly was relieved to see her friend must be feeling better. The moon washed the circle of hikers in its glow, and someone had placed a camp lantern in the middle, providing more light. A sweeping glance in their direction was enough to tell her that Kim hadn't rejoined the group.

She hurried toward them, and they all turned to look.

"Kim's missing."

"What?" Her father, Frank, tensed, then shot to his feet. "What do you mean 'missing'?"

"She's not in her bedroll or anywhere else. I checked."

"That's not possible—she knows better than to go off by herself." Even as he said the words, Frank grabbed the lantern from the middle of the ring.

"Maybe she's just hanging around at the back of the shelter," Sierra suggested.

"Why would she do that?" Frank insisted.

Sierra shrugged. "Just an idea."

"She's not there; I looked already," Carly inserted.

They all gaped at one another, then moved into action. A quick search of the immediate grounds and a short interrogation of the other campers brought no success. Clouds now covered the moon, dimming what little light it gave. Frank looked about ready to come apart, and Jill took his hand. "First, we pray. Then, we search."

A little disconcerted, Carly didn't pull away when Sierra took one of her hands and Nate the other as they formed a circle. She looked around at everyone's bowed heads, then dropped her head as well, though she kept her eyes open, peering at their faces in the faint firelight.

"Lord, we ask You to keep Kim safe and help us find her. We trust You to watch over our young friend and give us wisdom in this situation. In Jesus' name, amen."

"Amen," the group echoed, and Carly whispered her own amen, feeling she should say something, too. She wasn't sure what to believe anymore. But that these people, all of them intelligent and normal, did rely on a higher power and first turned to God in their time of crisis shook her, made her think. She may not understand the source that propelled their actions, but she respected the sincerity she witnessed in their expressions. They believed what they preached; not only that, they lived it.

"We split up with our buddies, each of us taking a different route," Ted said. "No one goes alone. Frank, you come with me." He clapped a hand to his shoulder in silent support.

The three hikers not of their group came up to them. "We overheard you talking, and we'd like to help."

"Thanks," Ted said. "We can use every pair of eyes we can get. If you'll backtrack up the main path and search there?"

"Sure."

The three men left, armed with their backpacks and flashlights. Ted assigned the rest of the group areas in which to search.

"Be sure and take your backpacks. You never know when you'll need them."

Frank's expression grew grim. "Kim doesn't have hers." He shone his light on the dark blue canvas painted with pink neon hearts.

A pall of silence descended before Jill spoke. "We'll find her, Frank."

"Are you sure you shouldn't stay behind, love?" Ted said. "With the camp emptying out, if Kim does return, someone should stay here to tell her what's up."

"What happened to 'every pair of eyes we can get'?" Jill's words were light and serious at the same time. "I'm better, not so crook. Kim's gone walkabout, and I want to search, too."

Jill might not feel so sick, but her face was still too pale, and she'd hardly touched her dinner. Jill was stubborn when it came to certain ideas like wanting to fix things for others, so Carly treaded with caution, deciding it best not to focus on her friend's sickness, but only on Kim. "Ted has a point, Ju-Ju. Kim might get scared if she comes back and no one's here. She might try and look for us. If someone stays behind, that won't happen."

Carly looked up to see Nate watch her with approval. That shocked her; she'd never had approval from any man. But it lifted her spirits, though she wasn't sure why she should care whether he approved of her or not.

Jill finally agreed, her reluctance obvious.

Ted eyed the group. "Whoever finds Kim, blow the whistle we gave you the first day. One, if all is okay. Two, if you need help." He said the last with a dismal sideways glance at Frank. "Don't worry about waking anyone since the other campers joined in the search, too."

"But they don't know about the whistle signals," Sierra said.

"I'll tell them; they're still within sight." Bart ran to catch up to the three.

Carly shrugged into her backpack and buckled it. Nate came up beside her. "You ready?"

She nodded, and together they walked to their assigned section in the east, combing the trees.

Carly and Nate used their slim flashlights in a wide sweep and stayed no more than a few feet apart as they moved through undergrowth, pushing branches and bushes aside as they called Kim's name. In the distance, they heard the rustle and calls of the others and saw pinpoints of light to each side of them. Minutes ticked by, and Nate sensed Carly's fear heighten by her jerky movements. Despite his own worry for the teenager, he tried to reassure her.

"Kim knows better than to go too far."

"She also knows better than to go anywhere alone without her trail mate," Carly shot back, concern lacing her voice.

"She's a bright kid. There must be a logical explanation for this."

Carly didn't respond.

"Any minute now, we'll hear a whistle blow or stumble across her ourselves." As dark as it was in these woods, the flashlights didn't help much.

"That's what I'm afraid of." Her words wavered.

"What?" He looked her way.

"I keep remembering that sign we ran across, about the two murdered hikers. What if someone's out there, and he's gotten hold of Kim?"

Nate took a moment to respond, since the same thought had flashed through his mind. "Hey." He reached out, slipping his arm around her shoulder, then pulled her into a one-armed hug. "None of that." Staring out at the black woods, he dropped a light kiss in her hair when she let her head drop to his shoulder. "I can't have my trail mate falling apart on me."

"You're right." She lifted her head, swiping at her eyes with her fingers. "This is getting us nowhere. It just hit me how very alone we are out here in this wilderness with no police to turn to, no emergency aid, no one really. Anything could happen."

"Carly, there's no use borrowing trouble. More than half of a person's worries never happen. We just have to trust God that this is all going to turn out for the best." The words seemed trite, but it was the best comfort he could offer.

He felt her stiffen against him. "I just don't get how you guys can believe that God is always there to make everything better."

You guys? Nate felt as if someone had punched him in the gut. "Carly, don't you believe in God?"

She pulled away. "We need to find Kim. We can talk about this later."

She was right, of course, and though Nate felt frustrated at their curtailed discussion, he moved along with Carly, putting all his efforts into finding the teenager.

They'd gone a short distance when suddenly Carly grabbed Nate's arm, stopping him. "Wait. Do you hear that?"

Nate held very still to listen. Amid the usual buzz and chirrup of insects, a faint warbling sounded in the distance.

"I think it's a bird or some kind of animal."

"Not that," Carly whispered. "That!" she exclaimed when the faint but distinct sound of someone crying came to them.

"It's coming from that direction." Nate pointed his flashlight. "Kim!"

Relief and anxiety mixed into one powerful surge. He hoped it was Kim and that she cried only because she was lost. They hurried as fast as they were able through the undergrowth.

"Kim!" Carly shouted, and Nate echoed her call.

"Over here!"

Grateful to hear the thin thread of Kim's voice, Nate changed direction toward a ten o'clock angle, increasing his pace and pushing away the shrubbery with a vengeance. Carly hurried behind him. Their flashlights picked up the teen at the same time. She sat cross-legged on the ground, her face stained with tears and clouded with relief, her glasses missing.

Carly rushed to her, hunkering down. "Kim, are you all right? What happened? Oh, my—look at your hands." In concern, she lifted the girl's palms from where they sat face up in her lap. Small red cuts crisscrossed the skin.

"I was trying to find my glasses," Kim said, her voice wobbly and hoarse. "I'm legally blind without them."

"Did you drop them here?" Carly searched the ground near her feet.

"I was running and fell. I swung my head around, and they flew off. My face was sweating—it's happened before when I swing around too fast."

With care, Carly looked through the brambles beside Kim while Nate pulled out his whistle and gave one extended blow.

The shrill noise shocked Kim into jerking her attention his way. "My dad's mad, isn't he?"

"Not so much mad as very worried," Nate assured. "What possessed you to take off like that, alone and off the path? You know the rule about trail mates, Kim."

Carly drew her hand back suddenly with a hiss, lifting her finger to her mouth to suck it.

"Be careful," Kim said. "There are thorns. That's partly how my hands got all scratched up."

"Let me help." Nate moved, careful to shine the flashlight on the ground to catch any possible reflection of the lenses. "Here, you hold the light," he said, handing Carly the flashlight, "and I'll look."

"I was doing okay," Carly muttered.

"Yeah, but my hands are tougher." He dug around through an area she hadn't yet explored. A thorn pierced the pad of his index finger. "Ow!" He pulled his hand away and shook it.

"Tougher, huh?"

He didn't miss her grin. "Just hold the light."

After pulling back a few brambles, he saw a blue earpiece sticking up at an angle. He plucked the glasses out, glad to see them in one piece.

"Here you go. They don't look damaged."

"Thanks." Kim took them from him, cleaning the lenses on her sweatshirt before slipping them over her ears. "It's good to be able to see again." Her words came dull.

"How did you get out here?" Carly asked.

Kim looked sheepish. "I took my gold watch off before I went to get water—I didn't want it getting wet and ruined, even though it is waterproof. It was my mom's," she finished sadly. "I don't wear it much, but today I did, and I had laid it on my backpack. But it must have fallen or something, because when I came back, some animal—I think it was a raccoon—found it and ran with it into the woods. So I chased it." She shrugged.

"In the dark?"

"It was still light then. I didn't know I'd get lost. When I realized the watch was really gone and the raccoon had gotten away, I didn't know where I was. I kept trying to find the path back, but instead I kept digging myself farther into the trees. I heard what sounded like a moose or maybe even a bear. It made an awful grunting noise. I got scared and ran, but I tripped over a tree root or something on the ground here, and my glasses flew off. By then it was dark."

Nate watched as Carly pulled a first-aid kit out of her backpack. "Hold the light while I take care of her hands," she addressed Nate.

This time, he obeyed as Carly washed the dirt and dried blood off Kim's palms with the water from her bottle, then swabbed them with antiseptic-soaked gauze from a foil packet.

"Feel like you can walk?" Nate asked.

"I think so." They helped her to her feet, giving her leverage underneath her arms. Kim hissed as she straightened her leg.

"You think it's sprained?" Carly asked.

"No, I've had those from playing softball. I think it's just scraped."

Still, Kim limped, and Nate slipped his arm around her waist to support her while she gripped his shoulder. It made for a slow trek back to camp, but the teen was already shaking so much, he didn't want to push their pace.

"My dad's going to be so mad," Kim said again, and Carly shared a look over Kim's head with Nate. He sensed her alarm and also wondered why Kim should be so worried about her father's reaction.

"I'm sure it'll all work out fine, Kimmers," Carly assured.

When they reached camp, Frank was already there, along with the others. As Kim nervously limped into the clearing, his face grew stern, his jaw clenched and unclenched, but tortured relief filled his eyes.

Nate let go of her, and Kim nervously adjusted her glasses and moved a few steps toward her father, awkward. "I'm sorry, Daddy."

Tension crackled through the air. "Kim," he said, emotion choking his words. "That was really stupid."

"I know."

He held out his arms to her, and she hurried into them. A flash of pain burned through Carly's heart, and she turned away, toward her tent. At times, she wished she had tried to find her own father. If she'd been sure of his identity, she might have attempted it. When she was little, she used to wonder if he even knew of her existence. According to her aunt, her mother had been wild, and she'd told Carly no one knew her father, least of all her mother. Not that her mother had been around much to ask. Still, Carly wondered...

"Carly?"

Nate's voice stopped her. She looked over her shoulder to where he still stood at the fringe of trees.

"If you're not sleepy, I'd like to talk."

Mentally, she felt wide-awake, though physically her muscles begged for rest. The search for Kim had given her a second wind, yet she didn't feel as if she could drag herself another step.

Against her better judgment, she nodded and followed him to the fire ring several feet away, watching as he relit the wood and wondering why he looked so serious. So this would not be another of their light, friendly conversations. She had a feeling she knew what topic he wanted to introduce, and instantly went on her guard.

Chapter 9

Nate warmed his hands over the small fire, enjoying its warmth and examining Carly in its flickering glow. She took a seat on a log across from him, her face a study of emotions. She may make a habit of tucking herself away in a private corner in an effort to hide from the world, but at times like now, she was easy to read. She acted as if she expected the worst, and Nate found himself in no better frame of mind. He took time to sort out what he wanted to say. When he had collected his words to the best of his ability, he shifted his position. Her gaze jumped from the fire to his face.

"I'd like to resume our conversation from where we left off."

"Yeah, I got the feeling this wasn't going to be a powwow to discuss the absence of the great fireball in the sky and the rain we've been having."

Despite the seriousness of the moment, Nate's lips curved into a faint smile at her choice of words. "What did you mean when you said you didn't get how we believed that God is always there to make things better?"

"You have a good memory." She prodded the dirt with the toe of her hiking shoe, looking at it. "I meant exactly what I said."

"Seems a little odd to have an attitude like that and be a member of Jill's church. On my visits there, I noticed they're a faith-believing bunch."

"I'm not a member of her church."

The words scraped like sharp pebbles in Nate's head. "Then why are you with the church group?"

"Why are you?"

"I was invited—by Ted."

"And Jill invited me." She shrugged. "She knew I needed a break from life and offered it."

"I see." He shut his eyes a moment to get his bearings. "So you don't believe in God." He posed the words as a statement; her attitude made it more than clear.

She eyed him with caution. "If I say I don't, you're not going to start preaching to me, are you?"

He gave her a sad smile. "No, Carly. I'm not going to preach to you. If you want to go get some shut-eye, I won't keep you any longer."

Rather than say good night and retreat to her tent, Carly surprised Nate by sitting motionless, a wistful look spreading across her face as she stared into the flames.

"The truth is before this hike, I could have said those words with conviction. But I don't feel that way anymore. I believe there is a God." Her midnight dark eyes lifted to his. "I'm just not so sure I want anything to do with Him."

At least she was honest and didn't try to fake something she didn't feel; he may not like her words, but he respected her forthright sincerity. His stepmother had woven a web of lies to trap his dad, who'd fallen for each one. Nate pressed his lips together in thought, wondering how to respond, when Carly spoke.

"I did once."

The three words jarred Nate. "What happened?"

She drew her knees up to her chest and locked her arms around her legs. "A little girl didn't get her prayers answered."

He waited, sensing more. He wasn't disappointed.

"When I was little, I used to curl up in my bed at night and pray that God would bring my mama back to me. My aunt never taught me to pray, but I'd seen kids do it in movies, and they always got what they wanted, so I prayed, too. I told Him I'd be good. I begged Him; I made deals with Him, anything to get out of my aunt's house and have my mama back." She grew very still, focused on the fire. "She did come back three times; I was twelve the last time. But each time she only stayed a few days, and she was always going on and on about some new boyfriend or a job she had at a nightclub or something else in her life that excluded me. She rarely noticed me except to ask if I'd been a good girl.

"That last time, I hadn't been, and my aunt let her know about it. My mama talked to me longer than she ever had and really paid attention to me because my aunt threatened to throw me back to her. But I didn't care that she was mad. I soaked up every moment of her sudden interest, and from that incident, I learned that bad girls get all the attention. So I began to live up to the name. If it was wrong, I did it. I didn't care."

She rested her chin on her knees. "Not that it did any good. Mama never came back, and after a while, I quit trying to be bad, quit hoping for something I realized wouldn't happen, and I quit praying to God. My aunt told me He didn't exist, and I figured she must be right."

Nate swallowed over the painful lump in his throat. At her wistful, childlike words and cheerless expression, he wanted nothing more than to enfold her in his arms. To pull her into a hug and kiss her, to let her know someone cared. And that was the problem: He cared too much.

Now that he recognized the truth concerning Carly's lack of faith, he knew that to go to her, to do those things, would invite disaster. He didn't want a relationship like his dad had. Nate had seen the results when what had appeared to his dad like nuggets of gold turned into fool's gold—something not worth all the pain he'd endured. To become involved with a woman who didn't share Nate's beliefs spelled danger.

He cleared his throat, uncertain of what to say. She lifted her head, spearing him with huge eyes that glimmered with unshed tears, and he felt as if his heart had been squeezed so he could barely breathe.

"She was wrong. I feel that now more than I know it. It's not logical after all. But at the same time, I'm not sure where I stand when it comes to making decisions."

He swallowed hard, recognizing the question in her statement. "It's a first step, Carly. Every important decision is arrived at one step at a time."

She chuckled. "Especially when traveling up a steep mountain."

He gave a wry grin. "Yeah, especially then."

She was silent a moment. "Honestly, Nate, I'm not sure what my destination will end up being in the grand scheme of things, but just so you know, I'm not a quitter when it comes to life. I may have given up believing my mother would return and given up on God, but on the things that really mattered—school, work, relationships—I always kept right on going no matter what."

Nate winced at her selection of words, but judging from her history, they came as no surprise. He weighed his reply.

"Carly, in your job as a reporter, you kept yourself well informed before writing your newspaper articles, right?"

"Well, I worked the entertainment section, so there weren't a lot of hot, juicy stories to be had, but yeah, I did."

Sidetracked for a moment, Nate homed in on her words. "If there was a hot, juicy story, would you have grabbed it?"

"What reporter wouldn't?" She laughed. "It's that type of story that gets a gal noticed and gains respect among her peers. Most people would rather read about what evils have hatched deep inside their town than read about who won the blue ribbon for the biggest zucchini or what band played at the Maple Syrup Harvest Festival. It's just human nature." She shrugged. "But Abernathy assigned me to entertainment, and what the boss says goes, so I never got my chance."

"Human nature can be cruel."

"It is cruel. That's just a fact of life. But it's a journalist's job to record all the facts and keep the public well informed."

"So if you still had your chance, would you take it?" The terse question left Nate's mouth before he could think to haul it back.

She seemed a little surprised. "I don't work at the paper anymore."

"There are others."

"But without credentials, I won't get far. Not unless I could present to the editor an exclusive headline story to hook interest. Don't think I haven't tried looking for work already. But Abernathy didn't send me off with any recommendations. Not after the scene I pulled at his office. Stupidity on my part, but what's done is done."

Nate took a steadying breath. He hadn't meant to get off on this track. With her curious nature, she probably felt more intrigued about his curt questions and behavior than ever before. He forced himself to switch back to the initial topic. This wasn't about him; this was about her.

"Like I said, Carly, you have to be well informed before you can make a good decision about anything in life."

She quirked her brows as he again switched the subject. "Okay, so?"

"So you might find the information needed if you attend the nightly Bible readings on a regular basis. I'm not trying to push you, just trying to help steer you where to look." He had noticed from the start that she didn't always show up at their group gatherings and should have realized something was amiss, but he had just assumed she was too exhausted or that she'd had some other logical excuse.

"I'll consider it."

That was all Nate had hoped for; at least she hadn't said no. He released a breath, smiled, and gave her a nod. "Well, it's getting late. I need to get some sleep." He stood up, noticing her expression of surprise, which she quickly masked. "I'll see you in the morning."

"Yeah, okay. See you."

Her words seemed faint, uncertain, but Nate didn't let himself turn around and ask why. The temptation to take her in his arms and hold her was still too strong.

❧

The next morning, Jill insisted she could withstand the hike, though she didn't look much better. Kim seemed subdued, Frank appeared more tense than usual, and Ted acted almost scatterbrained. But the change in Nate baffled Carly more than anything else. He still acted as polite and helpful as ever, but he no longer sought her out. He rarely smiled, and when he did, it seemed almost sad.

She wondered whether his attitude had to do with her confession the night before, with Kim's disappearance, or with something else entirely. Their entire group seemed downcast after last night's frightening event, so maybe that was all that bothered him—the aftereffects and shock of what had happened and of what could have happened but didn't.

Carly still harbored surprise that she'd revealed so much about her past to Nate, since it had taken her months to leak the same information to Jill and Leslie. She'd known Nate a little over two weeks and had brought out every skeleton in her closet for his view, save for one. What was there about Nate that invited confidence? She had avoided this very thing, told herself she wanted to keep him at arm's length, and then, with little prodding on his part, she had revealed a good deal of her story.

Carly tried to ignore Nate and his sudden indifference to her, tried to pretend it didn't hurt. But it did. And she thought it an ironic twist that his distance irritated her more now than his constant shadowing had done during their first days of the hike.

They traveled a short, eight-mile distance that day, surprising Carly since Ted always pushed them. But the tough drill sergeant appeared to have softened around the edges, and Carly sensed he still worried about Jill.

"Tomorrow we tackle the Camel's Hump," he told the group. "It's above treeline, made of steep rock, and is as treacherous as all the stories you've heard. It's one long endurance test; I hope you're up for it."

As usual, Ted was all cheer and optimism as he prepared them for their next climb. Carly's gaze connected with Nate's, and he winked, sharing with her an amused smile. Carly felt lighter, though she hadn't yet shed her backpack.

After Carly deposited her things in the shelter, she looked at the mountain in the distance, which did resemble a camel's hump. Earlier, they'd run across the path of some hikers coming from Canada, who'd just tackled the treacherous mountain; one of the young men had slipped and fallen, banging up an elbow and badly scraping his leg.

"Nervous?" Kim came up beside her.

"About climbing the Hump?"

The girl nodded.

"Maybe a little. But if over three thousand people have tackled it, we can, too."

Kim flashed her a big smile, and that's when Carly noticed the elastic band that now secured the teen's glasses around her head.

"Smart add-on to the specs," she said.

"Yeah, Dad made it. He's good with putting things together from nothing."

Carly hesitated, remembering the night before. "Are things all right between you and your dad?"

"Sure. He was teed off at me; big surprise. But he's the greatest dad there is." Sincerity rang in Kim's voice. "He didn't want me to come on this hike, but I convinced him."

That surprised Carly almost as much as the wide variety of age groups she'd seen among those hiking the trail—from senior citizens to six-year-old twins backpacking with their parents. Kim appeared to be in good physical condition, an outdoor-type of girl. She had told Carly she'd played several sports at school.

"Why didn't your dad want you to come?"

Kim shrugged, seeming nervous. "Just didn't like the idea; I guess he didn't want the added hassle." She fidgeted with her walking stick. "I better go help Dad with dinner. See ya."

"Yeah, see ya," Carly answered pensively as she watched Kim head to the shelter where Frank had just emerged from the trees, hauling water.

"Heyo, what's up with you and Nate?" Jill asked, coming up behind her.

"How are you feeling?" Carly countered. "You still don't look in peak condition for the climb."

Jill answered her sad pun with a groan. "I'm bushed, but I'll live. This isn't the first time I've had to test my endurance beyond reason. The outback may not have as many places to climb, but it does have its challenges, and I managed twenty-three years Down Under. You've seen the movie *Crocodile Dundee?*"

Carly nodded.

"Well, I was more the Dundee type, and Ted the one I saved. From a black snake. . .deadset," Jill said, laughing at Carly's skeptical look and lifting her hand in a Scout's-honor pledge. "Anyhoo, back to my question. What's with you and Nate?"

Carly had hoped she had successfully diverted the topic. "With us?"

"I sensed friction between you all day."

Carly snorted. "I have no idea. I made the mistake of telling him about my whole sordid life last night—well, not the part about Jake—and now he doesn't want anything to do with me." She shrugged. "It's for the best; I don't need any more hassles to complicate life."

"That's not like Nate." Jill looked puzzled. "I was hoping the two of you would be good friends."

Friends. Right. Carly gave a cynical smile. "Well, some things just aren't meant to be, Ju-Ju. I'm hungry. Let's eat while there's still enough daylight to see."

All through her preparation of vegetable stew via a food packet, Carly thought about Nate, wondering what she'd done to put the breach between them. He had seemed sympathetic last night, not judgmental—not that she wanted anyone's pity, either. She only wanted to understand what was going on between them and why she couldn't seem to get the guy out of her thoughts.

Growling to herself in frustration, she grabbed her mini recorder to document her day. Once she finished, she cleaned herself up as much as possible and laid her sleeping bag in the shelter. Tonight, she didn't want to be bothered with pitching her tent; a few in her group shared the idea, since she noticed their sleeping bags also laid on the wooden floor inside. Deciding to make it an early night, Carly settled in, thankful for her warm clothes and the insulation the sleeping bag gave.

A step at the entrance and a shadow alerted her to someone coming inside the shelter. From behind, the firelight glowed where the others held devotions, casting the face of the newcomer in darkness. Carly saw blond strands of hair and noted the curved outline.

"Kim? Is that you?"

"Yeah. Are you sleepy?"

Carly sat up. "Not if you want to talk."

Kim moved to Carly's sleeping bag and knelt down, sitting on her heels and tucking her hands between her knees. "I do, sorta. I feel closer to you than the other guys, and I need to talk to someone."

Carly tensed, thinking she knew what was coming. "Is it about your dad?" she prodded softly.

"My dad?" Kim sounded confused.

Carly bit her lip, not wanting to jump to conclusions. "Why not just tell me what's bothering you."

"I'm sort of scared about tomorrow."

"About climbing the Camel's Hump?" This, Carly had not expected. They had already managed some treacherous climbs, and Kim had never shown one ounce of fear but had always been the one ready to forge ahead.

"Yeah." Kim slumped down to a sitting position. "Remember when I told you the other night I was legally blind?"

"Yeah."

"Well, one day—soon I think—I'm going to be blind."

The shock of Kim's words robbed Carly of a reply.

"This hike was sort of a dream that I wanted to make come true before I lost my sight for good. And I'm glad I came. But the symptoms the doctor warned me about have started up, and now Dad's worried and wants to take me off the trail. But I don't want to go. I want to keep hiking to the border of Canada like my grandparents did. It's like one of those dream-wish sort of things to me."

She hesitated. "The other night when I got lost, the reason I tripped is because all of a sudden I couldn't see. It only lasted a couple of seconds, and according to the doctor, the disease gets progressively worse a little at a time and I won't go blind all at once. I should still have several weeks left. Even months."

"Isn't there an operation that can help you?" Carly forced the words out through a tight throat.

"Nothing that's even half of a guarantee. Or that isn't too risky. I've prayed about it a lot—Dad, too—and I just don't want to take those kinds of risks."

"But if there's a chance, isn't it worth the risk?"

"Hey, are you crying?" Kim sounded baffled. "Don't cry. I'm okay with it all, really. I just wanted someone else to know, maybe so you could be my cheering section. The others here don't know because we're still new to that church—we just moved to Goosebury a few months ago—and I didn't want anyone to know and then start getting all weird around me. People do that; all my friends in Massachusetts did. That's one reason we moved to Goosebury to be with my grandparents. I just want to be treated normal, and you always seem so together. I didn't think you'd get weird on me, too."

Carly didn't feel one bit together, and Kim was comforting her, which further addled her mind. In these past weeks of playing cards with Kim and getting to know her, she'd thought of the cheerful teen as the little sister she'd never had.

"How can you be so strong about all this? Why aren't you even the least bit angry?"

"At first I was. I threw a crying and shouting fit at home after the doctors told me, and I think if I didn't have Jesus to fall back on, I might still be really mad and never have left my room. I didn't for days. Sometimes I still get to feeling sorry for myself. But my relationship with the Lord has actually improved, and He's given me this strange sort of peace I never had before. Even before I found out."

"Kim, are you in there?" Frank's voice came from outside.

"Yeah, Dad, I'm coming," she called, then whispered to Carly, "He's still freaked out about last night, but anyway, now you know why." The teen hurried to her feet, leaving Carly shaken and far from feeling any peace.

Chapter 10

After devotions, Nate couldn't sleep and walked around the outskirts of the camp. He heard Frank call to Kim, saw the two leave the shelter area, and noticed they seemed to be having another heated conversation.

Ted clapped a hand on his shoulder, startling him. "Jill is feeling crook again. I don't want her to take the Hump, but she insists she can do it."

"Sorry to hear she's still sick."

"I'd like for us to pray for her tomorrow as a team. There's strength in numbers."

"Good idea. You want us to do that now?"

"No, everyone but you has turned in for the night." He paused. "So, what gives? Why are you prowling the area?"

Nate blew out a harsh breath, fisting his hands and shoving them into his pockets. "You didn't tell me Carly wasn't a member of your church group."

Ted seemed confused. "I didn't think it would matter."

His words sharpened Nate's disappointment to anger. "You didn't think it would matter to try to hook us up, knowing she wasn't a Christian, knowing what you know about my family and the hellish nightmare we're going through? That my dad's gone through for years?"

"Hey, man, chill out. I didn't know she wasn't a Christian. Jill met her when she was out shopping, but I don't hang with the women. I barely know Carly."

Nate forced himself to calm. "Sorry, Ted. I should've known better."

"But I'm really surprised Jill had a hand in this." Ted shook his head as if to clear it. "It's a good thing you found out before anything could happen. Now you know and can steer clear of entanglements."

"Yeah."

At the mockery in Nate's voice, Ted peered at his face. "Uh-oh."

Nate let out a disgusted laugh resembling a snort. "You can say that again."

"You hardly know her."

Nate leveled a gaze at his friend. "How long did you tell me it took before you felt you loved Jill? Seven days?"

"Love. Oh, boy. Nate, I'm so sorry, man. If there's anything I can do. . ."

"Thanks. I have to work this one out for myself."

The two men parted, but rather than return to his tent, Nate used his flashlight as a guide to walk the perimeter of the campsite, needing to release his frustrated energy. After only an eight-mile hike that day, he didn't feel one bit exhausted, and his Carly-ridden thoughts strengthened when he remained motionless.

All day, he'd avoided Carly to the point of almost ignoring her, but he hadn't failed to notice her confused and hurt glances when she thought he didn't see. Turning a cold shoulder on her wasn't right, not after all the disappointments she'd suffered, and he didn't want to add to them and hurt her. Falling for her wasn't right, not after all the misery he'd endured, and he didn't want to add to that and hurt them both. Could he settle for in-between and just be a friend to her for the remainder of this hike, then part ways and forget about her?

He didn't need the Bible to tell him a Christian shouldn't get involved with a non-Christian; he'd had the proof in his own family and seen the dangers and results of conflicting faiths. Nate blew out a self-disgusted laugh. For the first time, he began to understand his dad instead of judging him. If his dad felt about Julia the way Nate was beginning to feel about Carly, then Nate could see how easy it was to reject what was right and embrace temptation.

Alerted to the sound of someone softly crying, Nate halted in shock. He followed the sound, his heart dropping when his flashlight picked up Carly. Her arm flew up over her eyes, and he dropped his flashlight's beam.

"Carly? What's wrong?" He thought about scolding her for taking off by herself, but curbed his words at the bleak despair in her eyes as they met his. She crossed her arms over her waist, clutching her elbows; she looked so vulnerable, so childlike, so desperate. So alone.

Her anguish tore at his heart until he felt her pain as if it were his. Without saying a word, he laid his hands against her back and drew her close. The dam broke as she let out gasping sobs, muffling them against his shirt. He lifted one hand to the back of her head, his hold tightening around her as he closed his eyes, wishing he could absorb her pain, wishing he could halt her tears while wondering what had caused them.

When at last Carly's tears dwindled to shuddering breaths, Nate smoothed his hand down her hair. "Okay, now?" he asked.

She sniffled and pulled away, wiping the back of her hand against her nose. "Yes, sorry. I should go back to the shelter."

"Do you want to talk about it?"

"I don't want to bother you."

Her words cut like knives, accusing him of his distant behavior. He felt their sharp sting to the core of his soul. No matter his personal feelings, he'd been wrong to ignore her, especially since he'd asked for her friendship.

"It's no bother."

At his quiet words, she looked up as if uncertain. Struck anew, he felt as low as river algae. Had he put that hurt look in her expressive eyes?

"We're friends, Carly. It's okay." He made his decision.

A ghost of a smile lifted her lips. "Maybe I shouldn't tell you—she doesn't want everyone to know—but I can't handle this myself. It's all too much right now." He thought she might start crying again, but she straightened, then shook her head as if to stop it. "It's Kim. She's going blind."

"Blind?" Stunned, Nate watched Carly.

She nodded. "This hike is her dream wish. Nate, if there really is a God, how could He let this happen? Kim believes in Him. I feel as close to her as if she were my little sister; she's so special. When she told me tonight, I felt as if my heart might break. I still feel that way."

Her jumbled words made him swallow hard. He didn't know how to answer. But her grieving for Kim's sad situation made him realize what a sensitive and caring individual Carly was. Her first words questioning God's existence after telling him last night she'd come to believe it, then her next sentence proving she did believe it, showed him, too, that she was seeking. But seeking wasn't finding, and Nate cautioned himself.

"Carly, the answer to your question lies beyond my reach. Right now I'm going through some difficult times myself with my family and have tossed a few of my own questions up to God. I don't understand why some things happen, but I know that without Him, I'd be a lot worse off than I am now. So until I figure the reasons out—and I may never figure them out—I can only rely on Him as the safety harness to get me over the steep cliffs. I know that's the only way I'm going to make it. I don't know Kim well, but she seems tougher than she looks, and my guess is she's going to make it, too."

He didn't often speak of his faith and felt a little uneasy under Carly's stare. She gave a slight nod, her eyes lowering to the ground. Silence stretched between them.

"It's late." Feeling he'd botched things, Nate decided to end this before he made it worse. "We have a hard climb tomorrow. I think we should both try to get some sleep."

Carly rubbed the moisture from her cheeks with both hands in one quick swipe. "You're right. I'm sorry."

"Don't be."

"Between my shedding tears all over you and ripping you with my talons, I've turned into quite a trail mate, haven't I?"

He gave a soft chuckle. "I've done my share of acting just as bad."

She looked anxious again. "You won't tell the others; I don't think Kim wants them to know yet."

"No, I won't tell anyone. It's her dad's place or hers to give out that kind of information."

"I wouldn't have said anything but—"

He sighed, realizing she'd taken his words wrong. "Sometimes heavy burdens need to be shared. Kim did that with you, and now you've done that with me. It's okay."

"Thanks, Nate." Her smile trembled, though her eyes shone and seemed more peaceful. "For being a friend."

They returned to the shelter, and she made her way past the sleeping campers to her bedroll, while he moved to his at the opposite wall. Once he settled inside it, he thought about their conversation and turned to glance at her in the dim lighting, but she'd turned her back to him. He looked away from her huddled form and to the peeled wooden logs above, reminding himself that friends were all they ever could be. He offered up a silent prayer for her, that she would find the answers needed; then he offered up another one for the brave teenager. Carly's words about Kim still stunned him, and he wondered why she'd told no one else of her condition. That she'd chosen to confide in Carly told Nate a lot, and he was glad others saw Carly's worth, too.

For the rest of their hike, he would continue being her trail mate and stow any mushrooming feelings far behind him, abandoning them on some lonely summit. He owed her that much.

⌒

Fog and rain greeted them before they reached the Camel's Hump. Carly welcomed the bite of the stinging droplets on her skin; they helped to remind her she was alive. Kim, poor Kim, so young to go through something like this, too young. . .and Nate. She forced her mind to the treacherous climb of bare, treeless rock before her, but like the persistent droplets, the memory of his embrace lingered. . .his lips in her hair, his soothing voice, both hesitant and quietly commanding. A lifeline to help her pull herself together—she, who rarely fell apart.

These past two weeks had not only challenged her endurance, they'd stripped her of what she'd always considered her strengths, only to prove they were nothing more than weaknesses. Her callused view of life, her tenacity to forget the dull pain of the past while holding on to its brief, sharp joys, laying brick by brick a wall of defense through her mockery of both herself and others. Hardened. Confident. Invincible. . . . Nate with slow persistence chipping away at the mortar that hid her miserable, dark soul—exposing her to light, sometimes without a word, sometimes with just a look. The wall flaking, herself trembling. Uncertain. Frightened. Vulnerable.

Her sole slipped on the slick rock, and she scrambled to get a hold, grabbing the jutting gray stone above to prevent her fall.

"Careful," she heard Nate's caution behind her.

Careful. She had tried to be cautious, to guard herself against him, but that hadn't prevented Nate from seeing through her farce or from her divulging secrets better left hidden behind her wall. Worse, a part of her cruel nature had welcomed the pain of baring her conscience to him, of the need to have him hear her confessions. In an act of self-punishment, she had hoped he might condemn her, might agree with her that her soul was as black as her aunt said, and yet the very thing that would disgust him, she had refrained from airing, unable to bear his judgment or the censure she was sure would chill his eyes. The distance he had put between them yesterday, the distance she had told herself she wanted, had made her heart ache with confusion and regret.

She didn't need this! Had done her best to avoid it. With Jake, she had been in love with the idea of being in love. In the sum total of the six months she had been with him, he had not once triggered the emotions that two weeks with Nate had produced. Had not once stirred, not only her flesh, but the core of her heart and soul, as well.

Carly gasped as the wall that surrounded her emotions crumbled further with the stark knowledge. She didn't want this! If she could, if there was a path, she'd leave the trail now and return to Goosebury. The withering judgment of the town would seem like balm compared to the torment going on inside her.

She told herself as they made the final ascent that she could handle one more week. At the summit, visibility was poor, but as close as Nate stood, their eyes connected, and she wondered if she believed her personal claim.

She loved him.

The wind had picked up speed, battering against them as they stood on the barren stretch of rock and took a break from climbing. But the thirty-mile-per-hour gusts that threatened to push them over the edge seemed inconsequential to the violent jumble of emotions that raged through her mind.

Her recognition of God's existence had somehow sneaked up on her, the awareness slow in coming; the realization that she loved Nate attacked her without warning as she climbed one of the most treacherous mountains on the trail. Both revelations scared her but for different reasons, and her mind felt as shaken as her body, now battered by the wind.

To escape the strong currents, Ted cut their rest short, and with the help of the white blazes on the rocks, they began their descent on the north side. The traction proved difficult, the rocks still wet though the rain had given over to mist. Carly concentrated every effort on where to place her feet and hands, not allowing her traitorous mind to heckle her further or to explore either well of revelation.

Halfway down the mountain, she lost her grip. She grabbed at the steep rock face, scraping her fingertips in a futile attempt to halt her slide of more than six feet on her stomach. Her sweatshirt rode up, the rocks biting into bare flesh. All at once, her soles thudded to a stop on a short ledge and stopped her fall into nothingness.

"Carly!"

She heard more scraping as Nate hurried his descent and landed beside her. "Are you okay?"

"Just a little shaken." More than a little. Her hands, chest, and legs stung with fire, and she trembled as much as her voice. She kept her gaze on the gray rock beneath her, her heart pounding with the fact that, except for one short ledge, she could have hurtled into oblivion.

Oblivion? Or was there more?

With a numb sort of shock, she watched Nate's hand pull her palm up. With him, she looked at the scrapes on her flesh. From the sticky feel, she was sure more of the same abrasions covered her skin below her jeans and sweatshirt.

"Do you need a minute to catch your breath?" His voice came very low, still.

She only wanted off this mountain and down onto level ground. She shook her head, trying to regain her confidence. With a shaky leg, she found a firm footing, beginning a much slower descent. Her body screamed from the pain of each action, and her mind reeled with the knowledge that this could have been more than just another fall. Only when she was again on safe ground did she let her mind continue its course.

Falls came with the territory; she had learned that these past seventeen days, since each of the group had endured their share. But this last fall had sent her close to hurtling off a mountain, and the shock of that made her throat tighten with apprehension.

She had always approached life with a devil-may-care attitude, certain once it ended, nothing else remained. Now she questioned that certainty, and with those questions came greater fears of the hell she'd heard mentioned. Fire and brimstone didn't sound like something she wanted to face, but she feared eternity held nothing more for her. She didn't need a Bible to tell her that her past sins were wrong; she'd known it deep inside. Otherwise, she would have felt no guilt, and she had. Each time.

Nate put a hand to her arm. "Are you okay?" The deep concern in his eyes moved her, shocked her. He looked as shaken as she felt.

"Falls happen." She tried to be glib with her answer, but he offered no answering smile.

"We can take it slower if you need to."

"I'm fine." She forced her lips into a facsimile of a smile. "Really." Without another word, she walked after the others. Yet her knees still shook, and throughout the rest of the hike to the next shelter, Carly revisited her near encounter with death.

⟡

That night after supper, Nate watched Carly and Kim approach their circle as the group prepared for devotions. Cheered that she'd made the choice to join them, Nate kept his expression calm as their eyes connected, and he gave a nod in greeting.

The barest smile touched her mouth before she sat beside Kim, only a few feet from Nate. The teenager was as bubbly and vivacious as ever, and Nate marveled at her strength, especially knowing what he now did about her disability. Both she and Jill had managed the Camel's Hump with few problems, Kim, with her youthful energy, raring to go once her feet touched level ground. Nate knew the prayers before the hike had aided in their success, and he was sure they'd saved Carly. Fresh panic rushed through his heart as he recalled the sound of cloth and buckles skidding on stone and the sight of Carly sliding toward the edge.

Each night, one of the group made a selection, and tonight as Sierra read a passage from the Gospel of John, Nate watched Carly. Her hands, which had covered her knees so loosely before, tensed as her fingertips dug into her jeans. Her expression remained a blank mask, but in the flicker of campfire, he sensed moisture shimmering in her eyes. She whispered something to Kim, then rose and left.

Nate waited for her to return. He didn't think she would wander off, but as her assigned trail mate, he felt responsible. For all her brash independence and womanly strength, Carly had hidden away the hurting little girl from so many years ago, and he felt she'd just come to discover her on this hike. Personal epiphanies could do strange things to people, making them act contrary to their nature.

He gave her a few more minutes, then made his exit as Kim explained her views on Jesus' reactions in the passage. The shelter was dark, a few other campers already inside their sleeping bags. Nate headed in the direction he'd last seen Carly.

He wasn't sure what he expected to find, but when he spotted her sitting on the ground, dejected, her arms crossed on upraised knees, her head buried in them, he hesitated. He didn't think she was crying, but she looked beaten, like the loser of a long battle.

"Carly?" He whispered her name, afraid if he spoke too loudly, he might make her bolt like a frightened doe. A long, tense moment passed before she looked up.

Chapter 11

Carly stared at Nate, resigned that he'd found her. He always did.

"I noticed you left and wondered what happened to you."

She offered a weak smile, the best she could do. Not even one of her usual flippant replies would surface to her brain.

"Is this about Kim?" he prodded, his voice still low as if afraid he might upset her.

She shook her head. "I'm still worried about her, sure, but no."

He moved closer and hunched down before her. "It might help to talk about it."

Why did he have to be so nice? It would have been so much easier if she'd ignored him all along like she'd planned to do, like she'd wanted to do, and if he'd kept his distance. It wasn't too late; she still held the key to drive him away. Once she told him, once she admitted her sins, then he would give her all the space she wanted. Her heart mocked her that now she was lying to herself, but her mind remained firm. She did want distance. She needed distance. Besides, once this hike ended, they would go their own ways. Her, back to Goosebury, and him, to wherever he came from. Suddenly she wanted to know.

"Where do you live?"

Her question took him by surprise; she could see that in the way his eyelids flicked up and how the soft rays of moonlight brought out the whites of them a little more. She was glad she sat in shadow so he couldn't see her as well as she could see him.

"Bridgedale."

"Is it far from here?"

"Southern Vermont."

She heard the puzzlement in his voice.

"Is Bridgedale a small town or a big city?"

"A small town."

"And are the people there as unforgiving as people in Goosebury? Are they as eager and ready to condemn a person for a stupid mistake when they probably do things just as bad?"

He grew so silent, she didn't think he would answer. "Bridgedale has its share of hypocrites. Unfortunately, there isn't a town called Hypocriteville for all of them to move to."

His voice came both tense and light, and she gave a half-amused chuckle at his remark. "But you're not one of them, are you, Nate? You don't judge a person by their faults, do you? No," she answered her own question. "You're not the type. At least I hope you're not the type."

Another tense round of silence. "Carly, where's this heading?"

"Good ol' honest Nate. Fair dinkum, Jill calls you. You're always so straight-forward in your approach. Genuine, cutting straight to the chase. You would've made a good reporter, except you're just too nice. Reporters have to be tough sometimes, aggressive, mean. That's why I would've made a great one if I'd had a chance. I'm all those things. Good stories don't just fall into our laps, Nate, we have to pursue them, like a dog sinking its teeth into a mailman's trousers."

She wished the moon revealed his face better. When he didn't answer, she sighed, folding like a leaf under the weight of the rain. "You want to know where this is heading? All right, I'll tell you. That woman they talked about tonight, the adulteress Jesus saved from stoning? Well, that's me, Nate. Only it gets worse. I fell into that trap with the same guy—twice."

He didn't move, didn't breathe. She wished he would do something. Strike out with sharp, condemning words, clear his throat in nervousness, shake his head in a superior manner—anything!

"At the beginning, I saw the faded mark on his finger and asked about it. But he promised me he wasn't married, that it was from a class ring he no longer wore—he said the stone had come loose—and like a fool, I believed him, or that's what I told myself. Some things just didn't add up—his private calls on his cell when we were together, him living in the next town but never taking me to his home. I wrote our advice columnist at the paper to get some help, telling her he was married, though I didn't know for sure. Jake made me feel pretty and wanted—all lies, of course, to get what *he* wanted. I know that now. I found out a year and a half ago at the museum where I was doing an interview. I ran smack into him and his wife.

"You've heard of the expression 'the fur flew'?" Carly asked, then went on without waiting for an answer. "Once I made it obvious I was more than another art patron with my opening remark to Jake, she hit him with her purse, and he lost his balance and fell into a cordoned area." She laughed through her tears. "At that moment, I both admired the woman and despised her. I got my licks in, too, and threw the guidebook I was holding right at his gaping mouth."

She looked past the satisfying humor of seeing Jake sprawled at the foot of a painting of Mount Vesuvius and Pompeii, then grew serious. "We were both Jake's victims, his wife and I, and I swore I would never have anything to do with him again. But then he came to Goosebury several months ago, all penitent and charming. He told me his wife had left him, that he'd filed for divorce, and like a gullible fool, I believed him a second time. But I found out he had lied again—his wife phoned me at the office. That was the day I lost my job—I was so mad at him I ripped the phone from the wall and threw it on the floor. Later, Jake found me in the park, and we had it out. Our argument was overheard, and the rest, as they say, is history."

Nate's continued silence provoked Carly's irritation. "So there you have it! Now you know the deep, dark sins of Carly; now you can brand me with your scarlet letter or throw rocks at me. There's plenty around, so why not just grab one and get it over with!"

He recoiled as if she'd hit him. "Throw rocks at you? Why would I want to do that?"

"Don't you get it, Nate? I'm that woman Sierra read about tonight. Even Jill doesn't know all my darkest secrets. No one does but you."

"Carly." His voice came very quiet. "Didn't you hear the rest of the passage? About how Jesus forgave and saved the woman, telling the mob that those without sin should be the ones to cast the first stone? No one did. That's because everyone sins and falls short of the mark."

"Even you, Nate?" she mocked. "You're so good. Surely you don't sin."

He sighed, and it sounded almost sad. "Everyone has sinned at one time or another. Being a Christian doesn't mean we do everything that's right and never slip up or miss the mark. It means we're forgiven and continue to allow Jesus to work through us. I still mess things up, Carly; I'm not perfect. But I know I have a Savior who's there, ready to forgive me when I turn back to Him and ask."

She froze, her mind refusing to believe what her heart had begun to hope. "God wouldn't want me, Nate."

"You're wrong, Carly. I think maybe He's the one who brought you here, away from everything else, so you could come to this point. I think He knew it was time, and you were ready to hear His message."

Tears glazed her eyes, and she flicked them away. Why was she always crying lately? This time on the trail she had probably cried more than she had in the last year.

"But if you want to know what I think—you weren't the only one in the wrong. That lowlife boyfriend of yours is the real jerk as far as I'm concerned."

"He's not my boyfriend anymore. I never want to see him again. I may have been pretty loose and wild these past years, but the thought of being with another woman's husband makes even me sick. Especially since my mother did it. That's why my aunt hates me so much. On my thirteenth birthday, she couldn't wait to tell me what trash my mama and I both are and how my mama and uncle had an affair. Sometimes I wonder if I could be his daughter and that's why they took me in when Mama dumped me on them."

Nate became as still as if he'd been turned to stone. Shame washed through Carly at her outburst. If she could bite off her tongue, she would do it. Why had she said all that?

Nate cleared his throat, clearly ill at ease. Who could blame the poor guy? In this world with the slogan of "Do What You Like," her wild lifestyle wasn't a rarity except to the old gossips of Goosebury. And evidently to Nate. She had never been attacked with such fierce guilt before; Carly felt lower than she ever had in her entire miserable life.

"Carly, God hasn't seen or heard anything that will shock Him or keep Him from loving you. He doesn't ask you to clean yourself up before you come to Him; He asks that you come to Him and let Him clean you up."

Despite his calm words, her tears kept falling. She was glad she remained in shadow so he couldn't notice them.

"Nate." She worked to keep her voice steady. "For an entire lifetime, I was told there was no God. Lately, I've started changing my position on that. I appreciate what you're saying, but as the investigative type of person, I just can't accept what you say on blind faith. I need to dig in, to get the facts and see for myself."

"Then do it."

His three words took her aback, mirroring her earlier thoughts. "What?"

"You're a reporter; do what reporters do—dig in. The most realistic place to find out about God is in the Book of old records and documents, the Book that talks about Him. I have a pocket Testament if you want to borrow it. If you have questions, I'm here, and I know either Jill or Sierra would be happy to explain anything, too."

Stunned, Carly asked, "Why do you care so much?"

He glanced down before meeting her gaze. "We're friends, Carly. Friends care."

A painful lump lodged in her throat; she couldn't believe he would still consider her a friend after all she'd told him. "I'm not always a nice person, Nate. But you already know that by my attitude toward you those first days."

"Hey," his voice teased, "I thought we already put that behind us." When Carly remained silent, he went on. "Like I said, everyone occasionally misses the mark, Christian or not. No one here thinks any less of you, least of all me. Everyone has a bad day now and then."

Carly snorted. "That was more than one bad day, Nate."

"Week, then?" Nate flashed her a grin. "Believe me, I understand. I had a bad five minutes beside a creek once, and as far as I can tell, no one's held it against me. Come to think of it, I held her against me."

Shocked amusement chased away the gloom, and she swatted his arm. "I cannot believe you just said that."

"If you want the truth, neither can I. But then, I never said I was perfect."

She chuckled. "Okay, Nate. I accept the offer of your book."

He moved to his feet, holding out his arm. "Need a hand up? I think we should get back now. We don't want to start another panic like the other night."

Carly nodded and accepted his help, surprised she didn't want this talk with him to end. It had been one of the most emotional times of her life, one of the most shameful, one of the most awkward—and one she felt may have been the most important she had ever lived. Despite knowing her past, Nate still wanted her companionship.

He had not rejected her, had not thrown verbal rocks at her, had not eyed her with disgust. He had accepted her and offered his hand in friendship. He might not be perfect, but he came awfully close. And with another shock, Carly realized the only people who knew her secrets and still had shown her kindness were Christians: Leslie, Jill, and now Nate.

What made them different from the gossips in Goosebury, from her stern aunt, from her former coworkers who'd whispered behind her back? Was it their relationship with God? She had watched from a short distance that morning as the group stood in a circle, holding hands and praying for everyone, especially Jill. They'd then prayed for angels to guard their whole group as they hiked up the Hump. Carly thought about her near fall. Had an angel saved her from death, or had it been coincidence that the ledge had been there? Had God really cared enough about someone like her to assign a guardian to take care of her, despite all she'd said against Him in the past?

Once so sure she'd possessed all the logical answers, Carly now floundered at the unexpected questions.

⌒

The next day, the climb loomed as hazardous as before, and the early morning rain didn't help. Whoever named the stretch of land a *trail* must not have known that *trail* implied something that could be hiked, whereas this northern section had to be climbed most of the time. Nate had expected it, though as a former section-hiker, he'd never traveled this far.

It was an obstacle course, the trail going up one side of a mountain, over nearly upright slabs of rock, then down the other side—dangerous for anyone, but especially an inexperienced climber. At one point, they had to descend a forty-five-foot ladder to get down a cliff. The going went much slower, everyone taking more care how and where they stepped. Nate forgot to breathe when Kim's foot slipped on the rung twenty feet above ground, but she managed to hold on and found a foothold, continuing the descent. Nate's heart pounded as Carly took the ladder. Every time she approached a dangerous descent, he held his breath, praying she would make it.

As she stepped onto safe ground—however "safe" ground could be on a mountain—he let out the breath he'd held. The last one down, he grabbed the ladder and began his descent. He never knew what happened. One minute, he had about six more rungs to go; the next, he lay sprawled on the ground, pain shooting through his backside.

"Nate!" All of a sudden, Carly knelt beside him, her hand on his shoulder. "Are you okay?" Concern flashed through her eyes.

"Yeah." He moved his legs to experiment. "Nothing feels broken." Except he felt like he'd fallen fifty feet and not five. "Just bruised."

Ted approached and offered him a hand. To Nate's surprise, Carly took his other arm, and they helped lift him to his feet. He winced and doubled over at the sudden pain shooting through his hip, but after a while, it faded to a degree that he felt he hadn't fractured it and could walk.

"Think you can continue?" Ted asked.

"What choice do I have?" Nate joked back. Secluded in the middle of the wilderness as they were, the only choice was to go forward.

As they continued their trek, he leaned on his walking stick until the fire eased into a sting. He noticed Carly's frequent glances over her shoulder, as if she were afraid he might suddenly fall off the mountain, and he recognized the irony that now she worried about him.

He hadn't been able to stop thinking about her when she was out of his sight, and when she was within sight, walking in front of him, it was worse. Every day, his feelings for her increased; every day, he wanted what he couldn't have.

Stupid, Nate. Really stupid. Hasn't your experience with your family taught you anything at all?

But. . .would it really be so bad? Carly was nothing like his stepmother. He'd never felt this strongly about anyone; even Susan had injured his pride more than she'd hurt his heart. But Carly. . .she was sincere, even if she did have some rough edges; compassionate, funny, smart, beautiful. . .would it really be so bad?

Nate already knew the answer, but his heart defied logic. Carly's story didn't shock him as much as she'd thought; he'd sown some wild oats before becoming a Christian, ones accepted by society as a whole but rejected by God. He hadn't been pure either, not until Jesus forgave him and washed away his sins with His saving mercy. And as Nate had told her, he still wasn't perfect. What shocked Nate had been the unspoken message she'd revealed through her rush of words—*"I'm not worthy of love or forgiveness; I'm trash because my aunt says I am, because I had a relationship with a married man, because my uncle might really be my dad. . . ."* The unspoken words had hit him harder than the spoken ones. In her mock indifference, as the tears glistened on her cheeks, he had glimpsed her genuine hurt and vulnerability. And at that moment, he'd known without a doubt: He loved Carly.

Since he'd come on the trail and reflected on the beauty of nature all around him, since he'd taken part in the Bible readings and devotions each night, Nate had rediscovered the peace missing inside him for months, as well as a channel back to his Creator. He relied on that channel now.

"God," he said under his breath. "She's almost to the point of finding You; I can feel it. Maybe by dating her I could help be a better witness to her than I am now. Because if it really is so dangerous, if I could fall away from You by dating her and backslide, like losing my grip and falling down one of these mountains, then You're going to have zap these feelings I have for her out of me or send a chariot from the sky to sweep me off this trail."

Being with Carly every day—and her trail mate to boot—was slowly killing Nate's steadfast ability to resist temptation. Last night, as she'd sat there so sweet and lonely, all the while trying to act so strong and courageous, he could barely restrain himself from showing her just how much he cared by taking her in his arms and initiating another kiss. Their first kiss burned itself into his memory each night before he fell asleep and reminded his heart when he was awake and their eyes would by chance meet.

If only he'd known then what he knew now, he would never have let this happen; if only he'd known she wasn't with the church group and didn't share his faith, he would have been polite, yes, but certainly never kissed her. Yet he hadn't known. And that made him feel as if he'd been tricked—though he wasn't sure who to blame. Was it his fault he'd been ignorant of the facts and drawn close to her vibrant personality, seeking friendship? Was it his fault that he was a man, with all a man's feelings, and attracted to a very beautiful woman?

But you know now.

Nate shut out the small whisper and concentrated on the next climb.

Chapter 12

Carly didn't know what was wrong with her; she felt restless even after having just hiked up a mountain with gusts of wind at gale force almost knocking her down. They'd had to stop at points so as not to be blown off the mountain. Her respect for hikers intensified each day she spent challenging "the beast" as Bart had dubbed the precarious path of steep mountains. At Profanity Trail, it hadn't taken three guesses to know why it had been given such a name. She looked, stomach plummeting, at what had been termed so carelessly the Chin. Devil's Drop might have been a more accurate name for it.

The trail descended straight down the side of a mountain, with treacherous sections that stood perpendicular, each of them at least fifteen feet wide. One slip of the foot and her near miss of the other day would become a reality.

"And I came on this hike, why?" she wryly muttered to herself.

"You okay?"

She looked at Nate. His face bore a look of concern as if he could read her mind. "Well, I always wanted an adventure; I got one."

He cracked a grin. "A little adventure can be fun. You'll do fine. And remember, I'm right behind you."

For some reason, his words gave Carly the added boost she needed, though if she fell into him, they would both go hurtling off the mountain. Still, to know he was behind her, supporting her, helped.

It took their group over an hour to ford the Chin, no more than half a mile in length. Everyone made it without mishap, and a lot of backslapping and smiles floated around. Jill offered a short prayer of thanks. Carly had grown accustomed to hearing them pray for each other, for the group, for the hike, even for other campers each morning and evening. What once made her uneasy and desire an escape now made her watch with frank interest. She'd read some of Nate's New Testament the night before and couldn't wait to get Nate alone. She realized she could ask her questions of the group and they wouldn't mind, but she didn't feel comfortable with that idea yet. First she wanted to see how Nate responded to her queries. Jill still looked too shaky and pale, and Carly worried that her friend continued to fight the lasting effects of whatever virus had attacked her. At the shelters, Jill often excused herself early and crawled into her tent to rest, so Carly didn't want to bother her.

Once they arrived at Sterling Pond Shelter, Carly felt they'd reached the proverbial calm oasis after the steep barren stretches of windy mountain. The tranquil area was a treat for the eyes and a balm to the soul. The pond, a shimmering glacial lake, sat atop the mountain and seemed almost surreal, a pleasant dream after the day's nightmare of a climb.

Carly shrugged off her backpack and ate, feasting on healthy snacks rather than exerting more energy to cook a meal. Day after tomorrow, they would reach another predesignated food drop, and Carly had ended up packing too much food, as she'd been told many hikers did.

She sat by the pond, enjoying the cold breeze that ruffled her hair and the white cirrus clouds in the blue sky before dusk. Nate joined her. She lifted a slim packet from her backpack.

"Want a protein shake?" she asked innocently. "I'm trying to cut down on what's in my backpack."

His brows lifted. "Are you sure you aren't trying to kill me, then hide the body to create your own headline story?"

Laughing, she choked on a sip of her shake. "Oh, come on, Nate. It's not that bad."

"You're right. It's worse." He grinned. "So, after experiencing the Chin, you ready for tomorrow? Whiteface Mountain is a tough climb."

"Worse than what we've already been through?" Carly doubted it could get much worse.

Nate shrugged. "So I've been told. Ted and I only section-hiked it years ago. I've never hiked the whole trail at once."

Knowing he was also a first-timer at thru-hiking made Carly smile. "I read part of your book last night."

"Oh?" Evident interest lit his eyes, but he didn't push, instead waiting for her to offer information. Carly liked that about him, though she was just the opposite.

"There's something I don't understand. Well, more than one thing, really. If the Father—God—is so good, why would He want to kill His only Son? Why did He allow that to happen? That doesn't seem like a good thing to me. Weren't there other ways to work things out?"

Nate hesitated, as if gathering an answer in his mind. "Jesus freely gave up His life, since His Father willed it of Him, and He loves the Father, just as the Father loves Him. Men loved sin, and that separated us from God. Blood is sacred to God, and a perfect sacrifice was the only way to save us so we could be with Him."

He hesitated. "I don't want to sound like I'm preaching."

"No, please, go on. I asked." Carly wasn't sure why, but she didn't mind Nate explaining things to her.

He smiled. "Okay, then. God loves us, but sin kept us away from Him and from every good thing He has for us. Sin is like a chasm between mountains, with no way to the other side. It's like we're stuck on one steep and windy mountain with its sheer drop-off to death, but we're unable to reach the next mountain to find cool, refreshing water."

Carly nodded, glancing toward the peaceful pond, then back to Nate.

"Despite the wickedness of men, God looked beyond that and wanted His creation—us—with Him. He loved us that much. But He is so good, so holy. And just as where light is, there can't be darkness, where He is, there can't be sin. So He formed a plan from the foundation of the world, knowing what would happen to us, how sin would claim us. . . . Have I lost you yet?"

She shook her head, entranced. "Not at all. Go on."

"Jesus became the blood sacrifice, sacred to God. In the Old Testament, they sacrificed unblemished goats and sheep—that was a foreshadowing of Jesus yet to come. He was the ultimate sacrifice; only His death didn't just atone for people's sins, like the sheep's did; His blood washed the sins away like a pure, strong rain causes the dirt to wash from the rocks and makes them gleam when the sun comes out. Because He was pure and without sin, His blood was pure. There's a verse in Isaiah I learned that helped me when I was a new Christian: 'Though your sins be as scarlet, they shall be as white as snow.'"

His quiet words fascinated her, bringing a catch to her throat and the sting of tears to the backs of her eyes. "Thanks, Nate. I think I understand a little better now."

They talked more about it until dusk darkened the clouds. The group began to gather in a circle for devotions. Nate stood to join them and held out his hand to Carly, an open, silent invitation. She glanced at the calm, refreshing water, then back at Nate and gave a little nod. Taking his hand, she allowed him to help her to her feet.

Nate listened in amazement as Carly drilled the group with question after question about the reading Bart chose. She wanted to know why the Jewish rulers condemned Jesus when there was so much proof He was a "good guy" because of the healings He'd done and the people He'd brought back to life. She wanted to know why His own hometown didn't accept Him since they'd seen all His works and wondered how they could explain such evidence away. She wondered how His own brothers and sisters couldn't tell who He was when their mother so obviously knew and probably had told them. Once someone would answer, she'd pop back with another question, not to start a debate, but in a candid desire to get all the facts.

Some of her questions were brilliant, others might have seemed ignorant or silly to some who'd been in the Christian faith for a while, but to Nate they were all significant evidence that she was searching and trying to understand.

He didn't treat her or her questions with anything but the utmost respect, as the entire group did. Devotions forgotten, she continued popping the questions out until long after dark.

Ted brought a halt to the evening, reminding them they had another difficult climb tomorrow, and many groaned.

"I warned you sluggards what you were up against at the beginning of the trip," he said, and Nate felt sure he wasn't the only one who would like to give their cheerful drill sergeant a good dunk in the glacial pond.

Ted looked at Carly. "If you're ever interested in joining our Bible studies once we get back home, we meet at our house on Wednesday nights. I'll bet you could bring a whole new perspective to things and get all of us in the Word digging for answers. You sure know how to make a person think."

She shrugged. "I guess it comes with the territory of being an ex-reporter. We're pretty hard-nosed. We don't give up until we find the answers we're looking for."

Her words twisted inside Nate, giving him yet another good reason to write off Carly Alden as a potential girlfriend. If he were smart, once this hike ended, he would create distance instead of tossing around the idea of asking for her e-mail address. She'd always wanted a headline story to secure a coveted position as a journalist at a newspaper office—at least that's what she'd told him. And a one-on-one, exclusive interview with the stepbrother of the juvenile felon who'd burglarized a convenience store and killed the town's most beloved cop, along with wounding two other policemen and several civilians during his car chase getaway, would be too juicy a morsel for her to pass up, Nate was sure.

Forget about her, Nate. Pray for her, hope the best for her, but forget about her.

Again, his heart wouldn't listen.

Chapter 13

Carly wasn't sure if the climb up Whiteface Mountain seemed so rough because they were all weary from climbing for days or if it really was one of the worst mountains they'd encountered. At least the sun had dried the rain from the rocks, and a number of handholds jutted out for them to grab onto. No mishaps occurred, and the group breathed a collective sigh once they made their descent on the other side.

"Only sixty-two miles to go," Nate said.

Carly twisted to look back at him. "Go where?"

"The Canadian border. We're nearing the end of the trail, Carly."

"I can hardly believe it." Had they really come so far? Mixed feelings of relief, jubilation, and regret swept through her, leaving her almost dizzy. Or maybe that stemmed from the aftereffects of the climb.

And what of Nate; would he shake her hand and return to Bridgedale once they reached trail's end? Of course he would; it was where he belonged, just as she belonged in Goosebury. They would wish each other well and go their separate ways. Once apart from him, she would get over this ridiculous, mad, "swoonable" desire for Nate to take her in his arms and kiss her as he had that day in the rain and then tell her he wanted more than friendship.

The altitude must have finally gotten to her head for her to entertain such crazy thoughts. What the rocks and mountains had done in battering her body, her mind had done to her heart, thinking up all manner of ridiculous scenarios. Once she found level ground again, things would settle back on an even keel. At least she could hope.

At Bear Hollow Shelter, Nate pitched his tent and found the spring so he could retrieve some water. Jill was already there for the same reason. She straightened when she heard him approach.

"Heyo." She smiled, though he noted the strain around her mouth. It had been a hard trail for her, for all of them. "You all right, mate?"

He withheld a wry chuckle at the idea of being "all right" and filled his containers. "How long have you known Carly?"

"Half a year. Why?"

"This Jake character." Nate could barely get the name out without clenching his teeth. "Is he a threat to her?"

"Other than hounding her to death, no. He's a mongrel, that one, the most despicable person alive." Jill studied him, her gaze intent.

Nate came alert. "He's come after her? Stalking her?"

"I wouldn't say stalking, but he won't leave her alone." Jill bit her lower lip, then let it loose. "Nate. . ."

"That's not good." His jaw tensed. "She's looking for answers. I hope she joins your Bible studies once you return to Goosebury."

"What's going on between you two?" Her voice was very quiet.

Mockery made him raise his brow. "Going on between us?"

"Carly never would have told anyone about Jake. . .unless. . ."

"Unless she had good reason to?" he finished for her.

She inhaled a swift breath. "I never meant. . ." She didn't finish.

"Never meant what, Jill? To push us at each other? To make us trail mates so we would have to spend time alone together? Or you never meant that I should fall in love with her?"

"Oh, Nate."

He shook his head. "You knew better. And still you did it."

"I just wanted you to be good mates. Carly needs them; she's so lonely, though she won't admit it, and I felt you two would get along. As good mates, only that."

He gave her a steady look, and she lowered her gaze as if ashamed. "I guess I overshot my mark."

"Maybe just a bit." His voice was grim.

"I never dreamed Carly would want more than friendship, what with the way she feels about blokes right now and all she's been through, and I knew you'd just broken up with a sheila, so I didn't think you'd be interested. . . ." She bit her lip again. "How does she feel about you?"

He sighed, looking at the water. "I haven't asked and don't feel I should. But one thing's clear: She no longer rejects my company."

"I'm so sorry, Nate. I should've told you about Carly from the start. It's just I never thought. . ." Tears trembled in her voice. "What will you do?"

"Do?" Bitter irony twisted his words. "Well, as I see it I have two options. I can toss everything I know is right to the wind and do what my dad did and pursue this, hoping against hope it doesn't turn out bad like it did for him. Or I can cut my heart out of my chest and walk around half empty, hoping God'll somehow fill the void."

She gasped. "You've known her less than three weeks."

His gaze shifted to hers, somber. "And you knew Ted less than that. Deadset?"

"Deadset," she whispered.

Seeing tears glisten and one drop down her cheek, Nate felt like a worm, but he was too upset to withhold his words. He just managed to keep his tone quiet. "I've never felt about anyone the way I do about Carly. And now, no matter what decision I make, I'll suffer for it, and Carly will, too."

"Nate, I don't know what to say. I'm sorry. I'm sure if you ask, God will help you over this hump, too."

He only looked at her, and she lowered her head. "I'll pray for you."

"Thanks." Again, he couldn't keep the mockery out of his voice, and when she turned and hurried away, he felt like a heel.

It wasn't all Jill's fault. He had seen a few warning signs—Carly's absence from Bible studies the first few nights, her lack of participation when she did join the group. He just hadn't looked hard enough to recognize those signs for what they were.

"Nate?"

Hearing her voice, he tensed. She walked toward him, her expression concerned.

"Is Jill okay? I just saw her coming from this direction, and she seemed to be crying. Before I could ask her, she went inside her tent."

Worm and *heel* were words too nice for Nate. Algae worked better.

"I may have said something to upset her."

"You, Nate?" Her full lips tilted into a soft, incredulous smile and drew Nate's eyes to them. "Somehow I doubt that. You're too nice a guy."

His mind already wrapped up in Carly, who now stood so close, Nate didn't return her smile as he again looked into her dark eyes. "You wouldn't say that if you knew what I was thinking right now."

Her smile faded as her lips parted, her expression one of dawning shock and revelation. Her night-dark eyes glistened with a mix of anticipation and fear. She lifted her face, just a fraction, and he realized with a jolt that she wanted him to kiss her.

The awareness made withdrawing that much more difficult. Nate struggled within himself, his jaw flexing hard, the pull toward Carly strong. . .too strong. His fingers lifted to brush her satin cheek, stopping at her jaw, and he slowly leaned in toward her.

"Carly!"

Jill's voice broke them from the spell. Carly jumped and turned as Nate dropped his hand to his side.

"I need your help, luv. It'll just take a few minutes."

"Sure." Carly appeared confused and again looked at Nate. She opened her mouth as if to say something, then just shrugged with a little smile and hurried away.

Nate closed his eyes, realizing how close he'd come to the brink. His mind knew profound gratitude, his heart only anger that Jill had pulled him back just in time. He couldn't go on like this, torn between right and wrong from moment to moment, tempted on a twenty-four-hour basis. The newfound peace he'd discovered with God these past weeks seemed to shatter into fragments inside him.

In the Bible passage they'd read when they first started this hike, the apostle Paul wrote that he waged war against the law of his mind, making himself a prisoner of sin and allowing sin to work in his members, saying what a wretched man he was since he desired to do what was right, but his body kept doing what was wrong. Nate now understood the man's plight. He seemed to have no control over his body, over his heart, regardless of his spirit's warnings of what he knew to be acceptable. And no matter how hard he tried to pretty the picture of having a relationship with an unbeliever, the canvas remained bleak and gray.

"I can't keep this up, God, not for another week. And I don't see any chariots coming from the sky to cart me away, either. Give me what I need to do Your will, since You haven't killed these feelings inside me like I asked. If anything, they're stronger than ever."

He couldn't help his bitter prayer. Right now, he hurt, and he'd always been open with God, never hiding or pretending. His Creator knew him inside out. He knew just how much Nate wanted Carly, knew just how much he desired to take her in his arms and show her. . . .

And Nate knew the next time an opportunity came, Jill might not be around to stop it.

Sierra approached Carly as they readied for their hike the next morning.

"I just want to tell you how much I enjoyed meeting you and getting to know you, Carly. When we reach Johnson today, Bart and I are leaving the trail. That tumble he took yesterday hurt his ankle, and he can barely walk on it, it's so swollen."

"You're not finishing the hike?"

"We just can't. I don't think he can make the next fifty-four miles, and he's happy to call it quits. I'm thrilled we made it this far; it's been an experience I'll never forget. We came to find a better connection with nature, with God, and with each other. And I think we did all that and more. We may be newlyweds, but we've known each other forever, it seems." She laughed. "We were high school sweethearts. And even though we only got married a few months ago, we were already comfortable around each other, maybe too comfortable. We took each other for granted, and this hike has helped us to better appreciate each other."

"That's great, Cat. I'm happy for you." Carly was but couldn't help feel a twinge of jealousy. She would love to have the kind of relationship Sierra and Bart had, if she ever did decide to start a relationship with someone again. Unwanted, an image of Nate came to mind, and she shut her mental blinds over it. "I wish you the best. Be sure and come to the Native American art exhibit

I told you about next month."

"Bart and I talked about it, and we definitely want to go. And Carly, you really should consider coming to one of the Bible studies at Jill's. We have such fun there. We read, we discuss, we pray. But we have dinner before that and end the night shooting pool in Ted's game room. We have a sort of running challenge—the guys against the girls in eight ball. Losers wash the dishes. Of course, we girls always win."

Sierra winked, and Carly laughed. The idea didn't sound as distasteful to her as it might have weeks ago. These people had become her friends, and she welcomed the opportunity to see them again.

"E-mail me anytime. Jill has the address. Maybe we can do lunch sometime, too." The women hugged, then along with everyone prepared to leave the campsite. When the group gathered to pray for a safe day's hike, Carly decided to join them. No one looked shocked, and Carly felt grateful for that.

Nate seemed tense, but he smiled when she greeted him. She yearned to ask about his bizarre behavior the night before, her heart leaping at the memory of the kiss he'd almost given her, but instead she made a silly remark that soon she would resupply her protein shakes and had plenty to spare any time Nate wanted one, to which Nate gave a taut chuckle. She didn't understand the sudden friction she sensed between them, though he still conversed with her in an easy manner.

Their hike seemed to go faster, cheerier, or maybe the group's general mood had changed, knowing they would soon reach civilization if only for a short time. They trekked four miles to the trail turnoff at the main road and made it into Johnson early in the afternoon.

At the sight of a supermarket, Laundromats, a drugstore, and other welcome beacons of civilization, each of the group went their own way to tackle priority lists. For Carly, that included food—real food—and picking up new batteries for her mini recorder. While inside the drugstore, she noticed Nate head for one of the outside pay phones, probably to call home.

A thread of guilt wound around her conscience that she hadn't done the same, and she grabbed a couple of postcards to put with her purchases, intending to jot notes off to Leslie and Blaine, and even her aunt, while she took advantage of the local Laundromat. Not that Carly felt Aunt Dorothy would care if she fell off a mountain or made it back to Goosebury in one piece, but she should at least send a postcard for the sake of her young cousin, who didn't treat her like ragweed and often enjoyed sneaking up to Carly's attic room at night and talking with her. Maybe that's why she felt so attached to Kim; though Trina had a more somber, detached personality, almost gothic, the teenagers were close to the same age and had both latched onto Carly.

After paying for her purchases, she took her bag and juice and left the building. Her attention shifted to Nate, who stood tensed against a phone stand, clutching its metal side with a white-knuckled hand. His other hand gripped the receiver to his ear; his eyes when they met hers seemed apprehensive.

"Nate?" she whispered. Without thought, she shifted the bag to her other hand and touched his arm in concern.

He shook his head, showing he couldn't yet talk, and continued to listen to whoever was on the other line.

"Just how bad is he?" He waited, his jaw clenching. "Well, what can you tell me, Julia?" He rolled his eyes closed then open in barely concealed patience. "Yes. . .yes, I understand. No, I won't. I'll be there as soon as I can catch a bus back." He blew out a rapid breath. "No, Julia, I'm sure you weren't to blame for any of it. I need to get off the phone now so I can make arrangements. Good-bye."

Nate hung up and looked at Carly. Her heart beat fast at the pain in his eyes. "It's my dad," he said, his jaw flexing. "He had a heart attack three days ago."

"Oh, Nate. . ." Her hold on his arm tightened. "I'm sorry. Is it bad?" She winced at her stupid question; of course it was bad for Nate to be looking this white.

"He's in critical condition. Complications developed. I need to get back to Bridgedale."

She nodded. "Anything I can do to help?"

His expression softened as if shocked and amazed by her offer. "Yeah. If you would let Ted know, I'd appreciate it. I heard him say he was heading for the supermarket. I need to make arrangements to find a way out of here."

"Sierra and Bart are leaving the trail today, too. They might be able to help."

"I'll meet up with them." Still, he stood there, his expression blank.

She set down her bag and offered him her drink. "You look like you could use a perk."

He took the drink she offered with a measure of wary curiosity.

"It's just orange juice. No seaweed in it. Promise."

"Seaweed?"

"Kelp."

"Ah." His manner distant, he nodded one brief time as if figuring something out. "Seaweed." He spoke as though not aware of what he said, as if his mind operated in some other realm.

He took a few thirsty swallows, then handed it back to her. "I need to go make plans for finding a way back home."

"Plans can wait a few minutes," Carly said, injecting calm authority into her words. "You still look shaky. What kind of trail mate would I be if I let you go off like this?" she joked. Not spotting any type of bench, she took his arm to move with him to the curb. "Just sit down awhile, until you feel more grounded." She didn't give him the chance to refuse. She sat by the side of the street, pulling him down beside her. Lowering his head, he propped his forearms on his widespread knees in dejection.

"I should have been there for him, Carly," he said after a moment, his voice husky. "He came to see me at my apartment the day I left for the hike; he needed me then, but I couldn't take hearing more of the same. I walked out, actually left him sitting there on my bed, and told him to lock the door before he left." He shook his head. "I didn't want to hear anything he had to say."

She hesitated, considering the action, then slid her arm around his shoulders. "Nate, you couldn't have known this would happen. If you had stayed home, it probably still would have happened."

When he didn't respond, she continued. "You told me a few days ago this hike has done a lot for you and has blown away the cobwebs from your mind—reenergized your spirit. I think that's how you put it. If you hadn't taken this hike, you might still be in the position you were then. Now you've got more clarity of mind and maybe could be a better help to your dad and your family than you would have been had you stayed."

He sat still a moment before turning his head to look at her.

"Thanks."

A wealth of emotion infused his simple word, and Carly nodded.

They sat in silence for a few minutes, sharing her orange juice. When he again stood, Carly was grateful to see more color in his face.

"I need to get started."

"I'll go find Ted."

Nate nodded, and Carly wondered if this was the last she would ever see of him. Somehow, it didn't seem the right time to ask.

Thirty minutes later as the group convened for good-byes, she received her answer. Bart, Sierra, and Nate shook hands and accepted hugs all around. When Nate stopped in front of Carly, she looked up, wondering which form of farewell he would choose. He did neither, only stared into her eyes. The others moved away as if to give them time alone.

"I'll never forget this hike, Carly, or you."

His words rang clear with a final farewell and answered another of her unspoken questions. She had expected this, always knew the end of their trail together would come; she just never realized the reality would hurt so much.

Swallowing over the lump in her throat, she foraged around in her backpack and pulled out his pocket Testament, handing it to him.

"Thanks for the loan."

His eyes lowered to the black book, stayed there a few seconds, then lifted to hers again. "Keep it. And, Carly?"

She tilted her head, waiting, her heart speeding up at the intense but gentle expression in his blue-gray eyes. Nate hesitated as if trying to make a decision about something. Then, with a touch barely there, he clasped her arms and leaned down to press his warm lips to her forehead.

"Never give up your search."

Unable to find her voice, she gave a slight nod. With a tight smile and answering nod, he turned away to join Bart and Sierra. As Nate hoisted his backpack up and walked off with the couple, Carly stared after him, a film of tears clouding her vision.

"Good-bye, Nate. I'll never forget you, either," she whispered.

Chapter 14

The hike didn't become any easier, but it did grow less crowded on the northern section of the Long Trail. In the evenings, Carly took out Nate's New Testament, running her fingers along the worn edges and over his name that he'd penned on the first page. Holding his book helped her feel close to him. Two days had passed since he'd left, and she felt as if her heart had a hollowed void. She missed their lively banter, his teasing grin, the breathless way her heart caught when their eyes met. Even those first few frustrating days with him had mellowed into a pleasant memory, often bringing a chuckle or making her pulse race when she remembered those moments by both streams. . .and their kiss. A kiss that had caused her heart to pound, making her feel warm and alive, yet protected and cherished.

By the beam of her flashlight, Carly read the tiny print. Being a fast reader, she started at the beginning once more and whipped through all four Gospels in two nights. Some of the things Jesus told His disciples and others sent a shiver of awareness down her spine. His ancient words mirrored the way events happened in the twenty-first century, bringing the book to life in a way Carly never would have dreamed that documents written over two thousand years ago could do.

Fascinated to see the parallels, she soaked up the words of and about Jesus, not understanding the entire message but able to grasp a good deal of it. Each time she reached the Crucifixion, the manner in which the people treated Jesus appalled her. The account of His Resurrection sounded too far-fetched to believe, yet the words tugged at her, not allowing her to discredit them so easily.

She joined in the group discussions and asked pointed and deep questions as if she were interviewing Ted and Jill, Kim and Frank. They answered to the best of their ability, often pacifying Carly, sometimes confusing her.

The third night on the trail since they'd left Johnson, Jill approached Carly as she closed the pocket Testament and stared into the fire. Jill winced as she sat down.

"You okay?" Carly worried because Jill had never regained her rosy complexion.

"Between you and me? No. I'm bushed. Only God's grace is getting me through this hike. I'm still crook. Ted wants me to see a doctor once we get back."

"Good for him. At least we're almost at the end of the trail."

"Too right." She looked at the Testament in Carly's hands. Carly followed her gaze, then smiled at Jill.

"Nate gave it to me."

Jill nodded, a somber expression in her eyes. "You miss him, don't you?"

"Am I that transparent? I need to work on that. I used to be as solid as a brick wall."

"Not all walls are good to have, Carly."

Carly snorted and looked into the fire, shaking her head. "Ju-Ju, if I told you my deepest, darkest secrets, you'd be sorry you even knew me."

"I doubt that. Give me a fair go."

And suddenly tired of hiding, Carly did. She told Jill everything she'd told Nate...and more. She confessed her disgusting attitude and her despicable acts, going as far back as high school. She admitted her hatred of her aunt and uncle, and why, and also her bitterness and hatred toward her mom. Strangely, baring those restricted feelings from her past to her friend brought satisfaction. The words were dark, but she felt lighter.

Jill stared at her, her expression unchanged. "And you think that makes you unlovable how?"

Carly blinked. "Didn't you hear a word I just said?"

"I heard, but it's you who needs to listen."

"What?"

"Carly, before I became a Christian, I was a bartender in my poppy's boozer—not enough to make a quid, but I didn't care. I was, shall we say, more than mates with some of the blokes there. I drank, I smoked, I raged on till all hours of the night and often past them. . . ."

As Jill continued recounting her life, Carly stared, unable to link the wild girl described with the quiet one who sat before her now.

"So you see, no one lacks a past, even Christians," Jill concluded. "Some pasts are nastier than others, but it takes one step to forgiveness—asking for it and accepting Jesus as your Savior. The day that happens, God wipes the slate of your life clean, and you start fresh with no past as far as He's concerned. No worries."

"So, after all that's done, you stop making mistakes?"

Jill blushed. "No. I made a doozer of one just this month, but I know I have a loving Father who forgives and waits for me to ask Him to step in, and I have. I've prayed that He somehow fixes my blunder to His satisfaction."

"What blunder?"

Jill shook her head. "Maybe I'll tell you someday; not yet."

⟶

Nate sat beside the hospital bed and watched his dad open his eyes. Relief surged through him.

"You know, Dad, if you really didn't want me to go on the hike you could have just told me."

At Nate's light words cloaking two days and nights worth of worry, his dad let out a faint laugh, then grimaced.

"Sorry. After you've just had triple-bypass surgery, I shouldn't crack jokes. How are you feeling?"

"Like someone took a can opener to my chest."

"Not far from the truth." Noticing his father's eyes dart past him and around the room, Nate added, "Julia left to get something to eat."

"I'm surprised she stayed. A couple of days before I collapsed, she threatened to leave me."

That didn't shock Nate, and he felt briefly remorseful that he wished the woman had walked out of his dad's life. He talked a bit more before his father grew less lucid and closed his eyes again.

Throughout the next few hours, Nate tried to read a sports magazine, tried to watch news on TV, and consulted with doctors and nurses who slipped inside to tend to their duties. His mind seesawed between thoughts of the man in the hospital bed before him and thoughts of the woman he'd left behind on the trail. He prayed for Carly often, asking the Lord to open her eyes to the words in his pocket Testament. He hoped that, with time, his feelings for her would fade. If she did become a Christian, he would renew their acquaintance in a heartbeat, but that was a dangerous road for his mind to travel. He couldn't plan his future on a possibility.

The next time his father awoke, they engaged in brief conversation before Julia swept into the room. Nate tried to give her the benefit of the doubt, tried not to judge too harshly, but he couldn't help comparing her superficial, self-centered conversation to Carly's worries about Kim and others. Two nurses came in, asking them to leave for a few minutes, and Julia and Nate walked into the corridor. She surprised him when she clutched his arm, worry lines apparent on her face. For the first time, he wondered if her calm demeanor in the room had been an act so as not to upset his father.

"Do you think he'll be all right, Nate? He told me heart problems run in your family."

"His doctor is one of the best; with a lot of attention and prayer, I think he'll be fine."

She averted her gaze and scoffed. "Prayer. For the life of me, I can't understand why he prays to a God who obviously doesn't care. He didn't care about Brian getting beat up by his dad all those years or later having no dad."

Nate felt an odd sense of déjà vu, remembering a similar conversation with Carly. He hesitated, not wanting to spend more time with Julia than he had to, but the sense that he should talk to her remained, and he led her to a private waiting area. He told her much of what he'd told Carly, surprised when Julia not only listened but then quietly asked him to keep praying for all of them. Her request was brief and tense, but he felt she'd meant it.

Later, in his dad's room, Nate realized with shock that sharp edges no longer bordered his thoughts concerning Julia or even Brian. Something had happened to Nate on the trail to eliminate the anger, and he attributed the reason to knowing Carly.

"Are you all right, son?" his dad asked when Nate continued staring into space.

Nate lifted his brows. "The question seems reversed. Shouldn't I be asking you that?"

His dad smiled.

"I'm sorry I wasn't here for you." Nate's guilt weighed heavily on his heart.

"Here for me?"

"When this happened."

"Nonsense." His dad shook it off.

"No, really. I should have been here."

"Nate, I've thought a good deal about our last conversation. You're a grown man. I expect you to live your own life and not feel as if you have to stay in Bridgedale to watch out for me."

"Stay in Bridgedale?" Nate was shocked. "What are you talking about?"

"I've sensed for some time you would like to spread your wings, like Nina has done. You always were the type to get restless if you stayed anywhere for long, probably because we made so many moves when you were a boy."

"Yeah, but move away from Bridgedale?"

"You don't like it here; that's obvious. So don't stay. There are plenty of nice cities and towns in Vermont; you don't have to go far." His dad grew reflective. "I especially liked that small town we lived in when you and Nina were in high school—Goosebury. Now there's a name if ever I heard one." He chuckled, then winced.

An odd sense of fate led Nate to say, "Strange you should bring up Goosebury. The group I hiked with was from there."

"Really? Anyone I know?"

"Ted Lizacek and his wife. . .you remember, I went to school with him."

"The name does ring a bell."

It should; Nate had practically lived at Ted's home.

"A honeymooning couple that lives outside of Goosebury, and some newcomers to the area—a man and his teenaged daughter. And Carly Alden."

"Alden." His father's eyes brightened. "The same Alden that formed the Covered Bridge Society there?"

"I don't know. I guess. She lives with an uncle and aunt."

"I seem to remember him mentioning a niece." His father peered at his face. "So are you interested in this girl?"

Nate's shock vibrated to his spine. "What makes you ask that?"

"She's the only one you mentioned by name besides Ted."

His dad was too keen. "It wouldn't matter if I was."

"Oh? Why is that?"

"You told me not to make the same mistakes you did, and I'm taking your advice."

"I see." Understanding filled his father's eyes. "I'm sorry for you but am glad to hear it, son."

"Actually, as long as we're on this subject, I need to get something off my chest." Nate hesitated, not wanting to upset his father but knowing he needed to acknowledge past mistakes. "I judged you for marrying Julia; if nothing else, my experience with Carly taught me that what we're so ready to condemn others for, often without understanding the situation firsthand, can wind up being our own personal temptation."

"Unless you've walked a mile in a man's shoes, don't fault him for stumbling when the path gets rocky?"

Nate chuckled in wry agreement. "Yeah, something like that."

He felt better for having spoken, and the two men shared an understanding smile.

Chapter 15

After a steep and rocky trek, Carly and the others made it to Shooting Star Shelter. Surprised to see another hiker there when the trail had seemed abandoned by all but them, they eagerly welcomed the older gentleman into their circle. From his radio, they learned that the man who'd murdered the two hikers had been found and brought into custody, and everyone rested easier that night. All except Carly.

She wandered the fringes of the camp to seek some solitude and realized with a wry twist that she missed the way Nate always found her. Taking a seat on the ground, she stared up at the starry sky, intent on spying out the constellations. Even they weren't random but formed pictures, appearing to tell a story. She remembered how Sierra once said that God wrote His story in the heavens at the very dawn of creation. For a moment, Carly wondered about her ancient ancestor, chief to the Abenaki, and if he'd sat on this very mountain studying the stars, pondering their story.

She thought about her own story: abandoned, misplaced, ignored. Was it any wonder she felt separated from everyone else, that God wouldn't want her either? Years ago, she had stopped feeling sorry for herself. She had attributed her breakdowns with Nate to utter exhaustion. Yet while these weeks had broken her, they had helped build her up, too. The book Nate had given her. . .the words seemed to niggle inside whatever was left of Carly's wall, urging her to come out from behind the old bitterness, the old pain, and to accept the teachings on the pages.

With absent movements, she shuffled the book's edges with her fingers, listening to the pages riffle. She thought about the message the book held that made more sense than she would have believed possible; she thought about her friends who showed such courage through their problems and attributed their strength to their relationships with God; she thought about Nate, who'd become more than a friend and had been forthright in his answers, never pretending something he didn't know. But most of all, she thought about what Jesus had said in Matthew when He instructed His disciples before He left them: "I am with you always, even unto the end of the world." Nate felt it; Kim felt it; Jill felt it; Leslie felt it. All of them were assured of the message and harbored no doubt. They trusted God's Word.

Jill told her last night that the Lord had never let her down, and when—just as a child who didn't understand a parent's decisions or rules—she felt God had failed her, He always comforted her, showing His love in different ways. Carly thought about what life might have been like if her mother hadn't dumped her on Aunt Dorothy. She'd been raised without love but had never wanted for anything material. She'd been given a good education, along with her younger cousin. For the first time, Carly acknowledged that if her mother had kept her, she may have suffered a much worse existence than she had. Now she could see it was better for her that her childish prayer had never been answered.

How long she sat there before she heard footsteps, Carly didn't know. Possibly hours.

Kim sat down beside her. "Is everything all right?" Her eyes were sleepy behind the glasses, and Carly realized the teenager must have just woken up. Once Kim had confided in her regarding a very personal matter; now Carly chose to do the same.

"Kim, how does one become a Christian?"

Taken aback, the girl blinked. "Well, um, okay. You pray and ask Jesus to come into your heart. And you should also ask Him to forgive you for your sins. That's what I did."

Heart pounding, Carly nodded. She needed no further contemplation. Ever since she'd sat down tonight, she'd known this moment had arrived. Tomorrow would take them to the end of the trail, but on this night, Carly decided to travel a new path to what she sensed would be the start of a lifelong adventure.

"Will you help me?"

At Carly's soft question, Kim smiled and took hold of her hands as the group had always done before prayer; while above them, the stars glimmered in a peaceful sky, silently telling their Creator's story.

❦

Nate spent most of his time at the hospital until the day of his father's release; then he went home to sort out his own life. Looking around his shabby apartment, he realized his dad had been right. Nate was tired of Bridgedale, but he wasn't sure where to go. Not Goosebury, that was a given.

As the weeks slid by, the pain of losing touch with Carly grew less intense. He still missed her and prayed for her, but he felt assured God would give him the strength needed to go on. He felt emotionally weary, like a survivor of a battle or as if he'd passed some sort of endurance test. In hindsight, that he had passed gave him relief. Twice, he almost e-mailed Ted to ask about Carly but resisted, deciding it better not to invite heartache or temptation back into his life.

The townspeople hadn't changed their views toward him and his family, though their words and looks were less aggressive. His church seemed more sympathetic; and though he hadn't spent time in outside activities with its members, tonight he planned to attend a singles' dinner.

He looked over his stack of mail, curious when he saw a letter from Jill. He tore into it and withdrew a sheet of paper. On it were all the names, addresses, e-mail addresses, and phone numbers of everyone who'd been in their hiking group, along with a brief note from Jill about how she thought it a good idea if they all stayed in touch.

Nate spotted Carly's name immediately, followed by numbers that told how to reach her. He ran his finger along the line of them, finding that he had sudden trouble breathing, and he stared at the paper a long time. His hands shook as he crumpled the page into a ball and tossed it toward the wastebasket. Tossed it and missed.

Rather than pick it up, he grabbed his jacket and keys and left his apartment as though a fire alarm had gone off in the building as well as inside his brain.

"Rack 'em." Sierra gave Bart a wicked grin as she rolled the eight ball down the table his way.

"That's right. Rub it in," he muttered.

Carly chuckled as she chalked her cue stick, bending over the table and poising herself to break for their second game against the guys. At the loud smack, the colored balls scattered, sinking a solid in the corner. She scoped out the table. "Three in the side, six in the corner," she said before hitting the cue ball with expert precision. The red and green balls shot to their respective pockets.

"Good one!" Jill cried.

"Well done," Leslie agreed.

Carly again ran the table. Ted groaned, and Jill laughed.

"If you weren't before, you blokes are sooo lost now," she teased. "We have a pro on our side, and we're going to cream you!"

Jill literally glowed. All in their group had been shocked and excited to hear upon their return to Goosebury that her bouts of illness had been due to being pregnant. Carly realized more than ever how God had protected her friend, since Jill had only endured minor falls on the trail.

"If only Nate were here," Ted grumbled. "Talk about a pro; he was a pool shark in high school. We won many a game in those days."

Upon hearing Nate's name, Carly lost all concentration and missed her mark. The cue ball smacked into the wrong one and bounced off the rim, narrowly knocking the eight ball in the corner pocket and losing them the game.

"Careful, Carly," Leslie said from her stool by the wet bar, where sodas and chips had been laid out.

"Too right," Jill added.

Carly walked over to Leslie. "I slipped." She shrugged.

"Yeah, and I bet I know why." Leslie cast a look at Blaine, who stood busy, selecting a cue stick from a rack on the wall. "Jill told me about you and Nate.

I'm not sure what surprised me more—that you fell so hard and so fast for him or that Nate was the guy I had a crush on in high school. We went to the same one, you know."

"You never told me that." Carly looked at Leslie, amazed. She had been four grades behind Leslie so had never known Leslie or her classmates.

"I didn't know her Nate and my Nate were the same. Anyhow, it wasn't something I wanted to broadcast. Nate and I were the innocent parties to the brunt of a practical joke set up to hurt me by another girl who liked him. Actually, just about every girl in high school liked him. It was a black day when his family moved from Goosebury." Leslie laughed.

"I figured he was popular." Carly watched Blaine take a shot, though her mind didn't follow the game.

"Have you e-mailed him?"

"Why would I do that?"

"How about because you like him? And there are no longer any obstacles—" Leslie cut short her words, as if she shouldn't have said what she did.

"Obstacles? What do you mean?"

Leslie wet her lips. "Maybe I shouldn't have said anything, but now that you're a Christian, you should know. The Bible warns us not to have a relationship with anyone who doesn't share our faith—simply because it can pull us back and make us fall away from God. It's not to be mean or anything, or like we think we're better than others. We just have to be careful so as not to lose what we've found."

Carly's mind swam at Leslie's words. She had thought that Nate hadn't contacted her because he wasn't interested in anything more than friendship; his farewell had been final enough. It had hurt, still hurt, but Carly was learning to accept it. Thinking back, she realized his distance and odd behavior came after she'd told him she didn't believe in God. Now Jill's remarks about a recent blunder and about her wanting Carly and Nate only to be "good mates" made sense, too.

She had come so far since that night. If she'd known about the peace and satisfaction that came once she accepted Christ, she might have searched for answers long ago. Then again, she'd always been pretty hard-nosed. It had taken quite a few knocks on the trail to shake her up enough to get her to listen.

"Oh!" Leslie pressed a hand to her distended stomach.

At her sharp exclamation, Blaine scratched, his cue stick skidding across the green felt and sending the eight ball into the corner pocket.

"Leslie?" He approached his wife, his face white.

She nodded with a small, scared smile. "It's time."

"But you're not due for another two weeks." Blaine looked as if he might pass out or be sick. He put a shaky hand to her back. "Maybe it's just false labor pains, hon, like last time."

Carly glanced down, noticing the material of Leslie's brown jumper had darkened. "Not this time, Blaine. Her water just broke."

Blaine's face went almost gray. Everyone jumped into frenzied action, and somehow Blaine found the strength needed to keep it together and assist his wife upstairs and into their car. Jill called the doctor, and Carly took the house key Blaine pushed into her hand to go and grab Leslie's things and bring them to the hospital, while Sierra called the church prayer team on her cell phone.

Once Carly made it to Blaine and Leslie's house and found the already-packed case in the front room, she hurried back to her car. By the time she arrived at the hospital, she noticed Ted and Bart doing their level best to try to keep Blaine from losing it. She had a lot of time to think about all Leslie had revealed, and in between prayers for her friend, she made her decision.

Chapter 16

The next morning, after a night of little sleep in an uncomfortable chair, Carly drove home, tired and cranky. She let herself in the front door.

"Where have you been all night?" Aunt Dorothy asked sternly. "Up to no good. I'd stake my life on it."

"Then you would be dead." Carly had noticed her cousin's bike missing from the garage, so she felt it safe to speak. "I was at the hospital; Leslie went into labor last night and had a baby this morning—a girl. Seven pounds, eight ounces." Carly delivered her words in a monotone, her thoughts jumping ahead. "Now I have a question I'd like answered."

Her aunt's facial muscles tensed.

"Why do you hate me so much?"

Aunt Dorothy closed her mouth, looking away. Hearing footsteps, Carly turned to look as her uncle came from the kitchen, his newspaper still in hand.

"Is it because I'm his daughter?"

Her aunt gave a sharp intake of breath, but her uncle's expression told Carly what she needed to know. Shock, followed by a strange mix of remorse and relief gentled his brown eyes.

Carly gave a stiff nod. "I thought so." Without another word, she trudged upstairs to her attic room.

She sat on the bed and stared at the wall, barely aware of the tap at her door. She turned to find it slowly opening, her uncle on the threshold. They stared at one another as the old-fashioned clock on her bedside table ticked away the seconds.

He stepped inside, looking awkward. "We thought it best not to tell you until you were grown. Later, we decided not to tell you at all."

Numb, Carly hugged herself and nodded.

"We didn't think Dorothy could have children; when your mother asked us to take you in, she agreed."

"And you?" She nailed him with a look. "Did you even want me?"

"I caused so much pain to both Dorothy and your mom; I only wanted what was best for everyone involved." He hesitated, then walked closer to sit down next to her. "But especially you. You were the innocent in all this."

Carly snorted. "Not according to Aunt Dorothy!"

"She's very bitter, and I honored her wish that you not be told. But Carly. . ."

217

He moved as if he would take her hand, then sat back as if he'd changed his mind. "I have always cared and wanted what's best for you. I know I've been stern with you and not the best of uncles—we don't see eye to eye a lot of the time because we're too much alike. But if I hadn't cared about you all these years. . ."

"It's okay. You don't have to say it." Carly felt uneasy at this switch in their relationship, though she'd always suspected it.

He blew out a heavy breath. "That may be, but it's something I should have said long ago. You're special to me, Carly, my firstborn. I even had a hand in naming you, more or less. Even gave you my surname when your mother dropped you at our door to raise."

Carly had always wondered about that, assuming they'd unofficially adopted her since she'd had no last name of her own. She wasn't sure how much longer she could hold herself together and didn't respond, hoping he would go away. Yet this had been something she'd always wanted, to know her father, to talk to him.

He must have read the pain-filled indecision on her face. "It appears to me this isn't a good time, but now that you know the truth, we need to talk. We can go to Milton's Pantry and discuss things over dinner this weekend."

She had to know. "Were you ever planning to tell me the truth? Or would you have been content just to go on pretending you were my uncle?"

"As a matter of fact, Dorothy and I have argued about this for a long time. I felt you should know when you hit twenty-one, but I refrained from saying anything then. Now, at least that disagreement between us has been settled."

"I don't want Trina knowing." Carly made the decision. She didn't want her little cousin's hatred, too.

He sighed. "Let's just take this as it comes. This past hour has been full enough already."

Carly nodded, watching distantly as he patted her hand, then rose and left the room. She swiped away the tears that dripped down her cheeks. Though she felt tired, she needed action, and she knew she would never be able to sleep.

Moving to her desk, Carly turned on her computer to check her e-mail. A brief, lighthearted post bursting with smiley faces, hearts, and dancing animated kittens and puppies came from Kim, and Carly smiled. When they'd crossed the Canadian border at the end of the trail, even as weary as all of them were, Kim had thrown off her backpack and done a series of cartwheels, exuberant that she'd made it to the end—that she'd lived out her dream.

Carly dashed off an equally silly reply to the teen's post, sent it, and tapped her finger against the keyboard, deep in thought. Biting the corner of her lip, she looked at the folded page Jill had given her at church weeks earlier.

"Come on, Carly girl," she muttered to herself. "Where's your backbone? You just braved your aunt with a question that's revolved inside your head for years and discovered the truth. This could never be as bad."

She hoped.

Smoothing out the page, she spotted Nate's address and began to type.

༄

Nate packed up the last of the moving cartons, glad to be getting out of the dump he'd called his apartment for a year. He was taking to the road, uncertain of his destination and planning to wing it. Once he found a place he liked, he might settle. He winced when the telephone rang—again—and Brittany left her sixth message. He'd met her at the singles' dinner weeks earlier, had taken her out twice, but knew it wouldn't lead anywhere and had tried to tell her so. But she wouldn't listen. Nor, it seemed, would Susan, who now wanted back in his life and called just as often.

Glancing at his laptop, he wondered if he should boot up one final time and check his e-mail in case anyone had contacted him from the hiking group. He mocked himself.

"What for? You don't need to hear from her; you don't want to hear from her. Remember?" Besides, if she did contact him and he learned she still hadn't found Christ, it might kill him. He wondered just how long it would take for these feelings to dissolve.

Spotting a library book he'd checked out during his quest of deciding where to go—one filled with information on Vermont's towns—he groaned. He should drop it off before he forgot and maybe pick up a fast-food meal on the way. After all that packing, he was hungry.

Twenty minutes later, library book in hand, he approached the front desk. The young librarian smiled at him as he handed her the book.

"Yoo-hoo, Nate!"

At the loud stage whisper, he looked into the adjoining glassed-in room where a few computers sat at a long table—and also Mrs. Greenwich, the keyboard player at his church.

"I'm so glad to see you. Be a dear and watch this for me, will you?"

Puzzled, Nate pulled his brows together. "You want me to watch a computer?"

"Yes, I have to make a quick trip to the ladies' room, and those school boys over there jump on whenever a computer is unmanned and no one's looking. We're on a scheduled time with these you know. I don't want to lose my slot or my article."

"Sure, okay." He glanced at the open screen of the Internet article she'd been reading about crochet patterns.

"Feel free to use it while I'm gone—just don't lose my window."

Once she'd left, he stared at the screen, tempted to look at his e-mail account. Loud whispers and muffled laughter drew Nate's attention to the three boys—brothers, judging from their red hair. They pretended to pore over a book, and as Nate watched, one of the boys made spitwads from his notebook paper on the table and stuck it in a straw. Nate shook his head as one of the paper cannonballs went flying into an unlucky bystander's hair. The boys fairly fell over themselves with quiet laughter as the woman continued to peruse the books, heedless that a white glob sat in her teased, sprayed hair. A stern, elderly librarian approached the table, and the boys quickly behaved like docile angels, again poring over the book.

Nate shook his head at their antics and glanced at the computer screen again, then at the keyboard. As long as he was here and the thing was sitting in front of him, why not look?

He opened a new window and brought up his e-mail account, his eyes going wide when he saw he had a post from Carly. His heart tapped out a crazy dance, and he felt as if he were caught up in some slow-moving dream as he moved the mouse to click her message open.

"I told you I'd be back in a flash," Mrs. Greenwich suddenly said as she approached him.

Nate quickly closed the window and rose from the chair.

"Thanks for watching things. Will we be seeing you at church this Sunday? It's so lovely you could make it to the singles' outings. My Joey enjoys them so, and from what he said, it appears to me that girl Brittany likes you."

He refrained from wincing at her obvious attempt at matchmaking. "No, actually I'm leaving town tomorrow."

"Is that a fact?"

Nate smiled. "I'm going to see a little of the world—Vermont anyhow. I need to get back to packing. Good-bye, Mrs. Greenwich."

Nate moved toward the front doors, his curiosity heightened by Carly's post. If he hadn't wasted time watching those unruly boys, he would have had a chance to read it. What could she have to say to him? What did she want? It had been almost a month and a half since they'd parted ways, and she'd never written before this.

Nate toyed with the idea of signing up for some Internet time to check it out. But he didn't want to get sucked into a lengthy conversation about Brittany or his family with Mrs. Greenwich, and Mrs. G was, as Jill would say, a real ear basher. The woman loved to talk up a storm.

Exiting the library, Nate shook his head at his stupidity of how easily he'd almost fallen into the trap of reopening contact with Carly.

Chapter 17

Bases are loaded," Carly whispered to Kim. "This is a sure thing; don't sweat it. Remember, she pitches low and fast."

Kim nodded, adjusted her cap, and took up the bat. In the past three weeks, her vision had worsened, but the kid was a fighter and determined to enjoy life, even, she'd told Carly, after the blindness struck. She'd taught herself Braille and confided to Carly that with the new Braille deck of cards her father had bought her, she would continue whipping Carly at their games. In turn, Carly taught Kim expert tips in shooting pool after Wednesday night Bible studies and assured Kim that somehow she would help her learn to knock the right balls in their pockets and obliterate the guys each game, even after her sight was gone.

Now an assistant softball coach for her church's team, Carly watched Kim step up to the plate to practice her swing. Ted, the real head honcho, employed his usual tactics to whip the team into shape at practice.

"Come on, Sasha," Carly yelled to the nineteen-year-old who ran for second base once Kim hit the ball far outfield. "Come on! Pick up those heels, woman! This isn't a turtle race."

"I see our drill sarge's bad habits rubbed off on you."

Carly froze at the voice she'd thought never to hear again.

As Marissa slid into home plate, barely missing being tagged as the third out, Carly gave the girl no more acknowledgment for her nimble feat than a dazed nod. When she felt she could turn around, Carly looked beyond the fence.

Nate stood there, a few feet away, as attractive as ever in a blue T-shirt and jeans. His eyes reflected the sky; his smile was as calm as the breeze. Carly had to remind herself to breathe.

"Carly—watch out!"

Before she could move, what felt like a boulder struck between her shoulders. "Oof!" This time she really fought for breath as she bent over double, grabbing her knees, and Sasha, along with Kim and a few other team members ran from their places on the field and surrounded her. "You okay, Carly?" Kim asked.

"Whoever called it a 'soft' ball didn't know what they were talking about," she muttered when she could talk.

"Sorry, Carly!" Loretta, an outfielder and one of the worst ball players in all of Goosebury, called out.

All at once, large, warm hands grasped Carly's shoulders, and he was there with her. "Come on and sit down." Nate led her to the ballpark's row of bleachers. "Looks like your trail mate is to the rescue—again."

She almost laughed but for the pain it caused. Leslie handed her baby girl, Marena, to Blaine and hurried Carly's way. "I saw the whole thing from the car. We just got here. Let's go to the restroom and take a look at the damage."

Carly hesitated, looking at Nate.

"I'm not going anywhere."

His intense blue-gray eyes sent a shiver of expectation through her, and minutes later, his steady words rang through her mind while she stood before the sink. Leslie pulled up her shirt and studied her back. "Ouch. You're going to have quite a bruise, but I think you'll live. Do you want me to get some ice?"

"And just how would I hold it there?"

"Good point. Maybe you should call it a day and go home. Soak in a tub?"

Carly heard the teasing in Leslie's voice. As many times as Carly had tormented Leslie when she'd dated Blaine, Carly deserved her friend's treatment. Their eyes met in the mirror.

"Why do you think he came back?" Carly questioned.

"Why don't you ask him?"

"Would it bother you much?"

"What do you mean?"

"Since you liked him in high school. I mean, on the off chance something did happen, I wouldn't want you to be uncomfortable around me, us. With all that happened with you two." Good grief. She was blabbering like a smitten kid and making no sense whatsoever.

Leslie laughed. "Nothing happened. I doubt he even remembers me; we shared a few classes, that's all. But those days are long gone, Carly. I'm a happily married woman, in love with my husband, not a jealous teen sulking over an old high school crush." She winked. "I say go for it."

Carly grinned. "If I don't hyperventilate this time or have the dugout fall on top of me, I just might. But first, I want to hear what he has to say. He has a lot of explaining to do."

Leslie chuckled, shaking her head. "I sure don't envy Nate right now."

⁂

Nate perched on the bleachers, awaiting Carly's return. He had opened her e-mail message two days ago, unable to resist knowing what she had to say. In her brief message, she had inquired after him and his family and stated that she hoped his father was well. She had added in a postscript—"Oh, by the way, I dug into your book and found all the info needed. With Kim's help, I accepted Christ the day before we hit Canada. Thanks for all your patience and help. Without you as my trail mate, I would have never reached that end goal."

Blown away, Nate had stared at his computer screen for endless moments before scrambling for his cell phone to call Ted, who confirmed Carly's words and that she'd also joined their church.

A flash of bright red brought his attention to Carly and her friend walking his way. The woman spoke to Carly, then joined a man holding a baby. Nate studied Carly. As beautiful as ever, she approached him. His heart beat as if it weren't a part of his body, just as it had done when he'd first spotted Carly near home plate giving Kim advice.

Washed in bright sunlight, her flawless skin held a healthy glow, and he detected a sparkle in her dark eyes. She had pulled her hair back in a long, messy ponytail and stuffed it under the red ball cap.

"Is everything all right?" he asked when she took a seat on the bleachers beside him.

"After a month of mishaps on the Long Trail, this is nothing."

He looked into her curious eyes, recognizing her reference to their time together as a question, an invitation to proceed with what had brought him to her.

"I got your e-mail, Carly. I'm glad you made the choice you did."

"So am I. I'm sorry to hear your service is so slow, though."

"Slow?"

"Your e-mail account. I sent that post weeks ago."

He bit back a wry grin. So that's how it was going to be. "I moved out of Bridgedale and have been on the road for weeks, not always near a computer. I had a lot of decisions to make; a lot of praying to do."

She mulled that over and smiled, her expression relaxing. "I understand. I've done a lot of that lately, too."

To hear proof of her practicing her faith cheered him.

"You look good. Are things going better for you?"

"Some things. I discovered I was right about my uncle—he is my father. We had a rough few days, but we're sorting it all out. Jake visited a few times while we were hiking. I think he decided I'd moved away; he hasn't bothered me since."

"That's good to hear."

"And I've been writing my guidebook. I'm still not sure if I'm going anywhere with that, but I directed Cat to a magazine publisher who showed interest in some of her poems."

"That's terrific. So, do you like this church?"

"I love it. I felt as if I belonged from the moment I stepped foot inside the door with Les."

"Les?" Alarm shot through Nate.

"Leslie Cartell, my friend." She motioned to the woman with the baby. "A nickname I call her."

"You and your nicknames." Relief made him smile. "Do you have your mini recorder with you?"

"It's in my car," she said, her tone confused.

He nodded, thinking. "So do you need to stay until the game is over?"

Her eyes grew wider. "No, I can leave. This is only a practice game." She glanced at the coach, and Nate looked, too. Ted caught their looks and made a sweeping, umpirelike motion with both arms, pointing to the parking lot.

Carly chuckled. "Mr. Subtlety has spoken."

Nate grinned. "Let's get out of here." He noticed Carly wince as she stood up. "Maybe you should have that looked at."

"I'm okay, just sore."

"Have you eaten?"

"I had an apple before the game."

"Let's get something to eat. I haven't eaten since breakfast." She looked at him, her eyes brimming with questions, but he needed to do this his way.

They stopped at her car first so she could grab her recorder from the glove compartment. Nate opened the passenger door of his car, not failing to note her confusion before she slid inside. Neither of them spoke during the five-block drive to a fast-food restaurant. Nate pulled into the drive-through area and looked at the menu.

"Nothing much for a veggie lover, but they have a cucumber salad."

"I'll just take French fries and a vanilla shake." She pulled off her ball cap, setting it in her lap.

Nate heard the quiver in her voice; his own insides shook, and he wondered if eating a hamburger was a wise choice. Once they received their order, he drove to another area of the park. They shared a bench and small talk while they ate and watched the ducks glide on the quiet, glassy pond.

As Carly gathered her trash and stuck it in the bag, she winced.

"Turn around, Carly."

"Why?" she asked but did as he quietly ordered, swinging her legs to the edge of the bench.

Nate slid closer and pushed her long ponytail over her shoulder, then lifted his jumbo cup of iced soda to the middle of her upper back. She gave a sharp intake of breath as soon as he touched her, and he sensed it wasn't the extreme cold against her T-shirt that caused her sudden shortness of breath. His own pulse had sped up at the silky texture of her hair against his fingers.

"Better?" he whispered.

She gave a weak response that sounded like confirmation.

"I imagine you're wondering why I'm in Goosebury," he said after a moment, knowing the time had come to speak.

"The thought had crossed my mind."

"I came to give you an interview. An exclusive."

"An interview?"

He sensed disappointment in her puzzled question.

"Ted told me you still haven't found a job. This will guarantee you a top position in the best newspaper office in all of Goosebury. A hot and juicy headliner, just like you always wanted."

She remained so quiet he wished he could see her face.

"Turn your recorder on, Carly."

He noticed her hand shake as she did.

"My name is Nate Bigelow. Brian Bigelow is my stepbrother. My father adopted him when he married my stepmother."

She gave another sharp intake of breath.

"I see you recognize the name." He let out a soft snort. "For months the local press, the national news, the news magazines have hounded my family for the inside scoop, but we've managed to avoid them. Now I want to give you the story. Everything you want to know."

He lowered his drink from her back as she slowly turned on the bench to look at him. She switched off the recorder button. "Why, Nate? Why me?"

"That's a question I'd prefer to answer after the interview. Shall we continue?"

She nodded, still dazed, but he saw her journalistic brain move into gear as her eyes grew more alert, and she began to call the shots.

"First, why don't you tell me about your relationship with Brian, how long you've known him, and anything else you feel might be significant?" she suggested, switching her recorder back on.

For the next fifteen minutes, Nate recounted everything from the time he'd met his troubled young stepbrother when his dad dated Julia to the time of the crime. Afterward, he answered each of Carly's soft questions, more often about him than Brian, until she could think of nothing more to ask. She turned off the recorder and studied him. This had been the part he'd been dreading ever since he'd decided to do this interview.

"Now that you know the truth about my family, how do you feel about me, Carly?"

"Feel about you?" His question clearly baffled her. "No different than usual... why?"

Nate's heart skipped a beat at her answer and then began to pick up speed. "And what is 'usual'?"

He was asking a lot from her, and he knew it by the cautious look that entered her eyes. She remained silent, but her silence was all the answer he needed.

"My stay in Goosebury is permanent," he admitted. "I moved here a few days ago."

Her eyes widened, her lips parted. "Oh."

225

"And if you're willing, I'd like for us to become more than trail mates."

"Oh." The word left her mouth in a whoosh. He didn't miss the way her eyes lit up. He waited for her to say more.

She swallowed and moistened her lips. "Since you've avoided interviews for so long, why'd you give me the story, Nate?"

"Isn't it obvious? What other information do you need to figure it out?"

"I'm a bit slow on the uptake today," she whispered. "Maybe you should just tell me?"

He skimmed his fingertips down her cheek. "How about if I show you instead? I love you, Carly; I have for some time."

He lowered his head and caught her gasp with his mouth as he gave in to his overwhelming desire to kiss her. His own breath wedged inside his throat when she softly whimpered in relief and clutched his shoulders, eagerly returning his kiss.

With great effort, he drew away, having wanted this for so long and now realizing she'd wanted the same. "And I trust you," he whispered. "I know you won't twist my words, that you'll do the right thing with this interview."

Carly blinked several times as if to collect her thoughts, then gave a slight nod. To Nate's shock, she ejected the microcassette and dropped it into what was left of her vanilla shake.

"Why'd you do that?" His mouth dropped open.

"There's no garbage can nearby, and I don't want to litter." She shrugged as he continued to gape at her. "I could have just erased the tape, but I have a box of fifty at home, so losing one isn't so bad. And I wanted you to get the message."

"What message? That you like your mud shakes better than vanilla ones?"

She chuckled. "That you can trust me, Nate. With anything." When he only stared, she explained, "I haven't often done the right thing. Now that I have a clean slate, I don't want to muddy it up with a lot of dirt."

"Dirt?" She had completely lost him.

"Dirt. My own experiences showed me that some stories shouldn't be broadcasted. Sometimes the public doesn't need to know all of the gruesome details or the dark background facts, and I think this is one of those times." She smiled.

"But what about the job you've always wanted as a top journalist?"

"If I can't get a job on my own merit and instead have to rely on someone else's pain and tragedy to further my career, then I'm not interested in pursuing it. I'd already planned to ditch the story halfway through our interview."

Dumbfounded, Nate expelled a confused, exasperated breath. "Then why'd you let me go on like that? Why'd you ask all those questions?"

"Isn't it obvious?" she teased, using his words from earlier. "I want to know everything there is to know about you, even the imperfect skeletons in your closet. After all, it's only fair." She grinned impishly. "You know mine."

"Carly." Nate shook his head in mystified amusement. "Will I ever understand you?"

"Probably not. But who knows what the future might hold?" Her eyes sparkled as she linked her arms around his neck. "Then, too, I've heard it said a little adventure can be fun." She pressed her lips to his.

All confusion fled Nate's mind as he wrapped his arms around her. He may never figure out this unpredictable, exciting, maddening woman, but he sure looked forward to the challenge of trying!

Epilogue

Spring of the following year

Carly waited at the back of the church, her heart in her throat as she watched Kim carry her spring bouquet of pastel flowers down the aisle after Sierra. Kim had practiced the slow march for days, so as to make the procession without faltering and without the aid of her white cane. As she reached the front and turned gracefully to the left, Carly exhaled a relieved breath and silent cheer for her lovely young friend. She noticed Chris, a cousin of Nate's and the youngest of the groomsmen, watching Kim with the same intensity mixed with awe, and Carly smiled. Kim was now fifteen, Chris seventeen. From what Carly had witnessed these past weeks, she sensed young love in bloom. Kim's blindness hadn't deterred Chris one bit; he sought her company and acted very protective of her, though Kim's bubbly and confident nature seldom warranted such care.

Trina followed Kim, her head held high. Aunt Dorothy had just about died when Trina colored a violet streak in her dark hair to go with the rose dress, but Carly liked it. It suited her. Months ago, their father had decided to tell Trina that she and Carly were half sisters. For a few days, Trina had withdrawn, but she later approached Carly in her attic room and asked, "Since we're really sisters, does that mean I can have your CD collection when you die?" She had cracked a joking smile, and from that day forward, the two had grown even closer than before.

Jill squeezed Carly's arm. "No worries, luv." She winked in encouragement before taking her turn down the narrow aisle.

Leslie turned from her seat in the pew and smiled at both of them. She held Jill's infant son, Titus, and Blaine sat beside her, holding baby Marena, who was teething and gnawing on her daddy's shoulder. The dark-haired little beauty raised her head, catching sight of Carly in the floor-length, ice white gown shot with iridescent sequins, and smiled, letting out a gurgling squeal. Blaine jiggled her to shush her, offering an apologetic look to Carly, who chuckled under her breath. Bart sat next to Blaine and gave her an emphatic thumbs-up. She felt so grateful to have all her friends there, and family, including her new one.

Carly's eyes went to the couple in the first pew. The trial pending, the Bigelows had visited Goosebury for a month's rest, and after meeting the distinguished lawyer, Carly had seen where his son had picked up many of his good traits, including his consideration for others.

As Jill moved down the aisle, Ted watched from where he stood at the front as best man. The drill sergeant, tough-as-nails coach made a surprisingly gentle and compassionate father to his son.

She had worried over whom to choose as her matron of honor, Jill or Leslie; both women were her dearest friends and had done so much for her. But when Leslie confided she was again pregnant and battled morning sickness, the decision became apparent.

Leslie had talked to her step-grandfather, who'd relented and allowed Carly a third chance at the *Gazette*. Within months, Carly proved her merit to Mr. Abernathy and became a top journalist assigned to some of the best stories. She had left the news office the first time ignorant but had returned with wisdom that gained favor with all those she interviewed—tenacity mixed with mercy.

Her father squeezed Carly's arm. "Are you ready?"

She smiled. "Are you kidding? I've been waiting for this day forever," she quipped, quoting one of Kim's lines.

Last night, her father had talked with Carly into the wee hours. With all subterfuge banished, the two of them had developed a close bond. She'd even witnessed to him about Christ on a few occasions, and he'd listened, showing interest. When she was little and dreamed of her Prince Charming, she'd wished she could have a daddy to one day walk her down the aisle, too. Now her dreams had become a reality. All of them.

The organist began the triumphant chords of Wagner's "Bridal Chorus" from *Lohengrin*, and Carly looked Nate's way, meeting his eyes. She worked to steady her suddenly rapid breathing and returned his expression of awe with a slight smile as she glided up to the altar to take her place beside him.

When Nate had asked her weeks ago why she'd never come up with a nickname for him, Carly had put her arm through his as they'd rocked on the porch glider. "I tried. But I never could settle on just one name because you're so many things to me. My Friend. My Trail Mate. My Rescuer. . ." At this she had rolled her eyes, and he had laughed. "My Brother in Christ. My Confidante. My Expert Pool-shark Partner." They both grinned, and then she grew serious. "My Love, and soon to be, My Husband. How can I come up with a nickname for all that?"

As the ceremony progressed and they spoke their vows to one another, Carly looked into Nate's sky-colored eyes glowing with love and wondered how she had ever gotten along without this man.

The minister pronounced them husband and wife, and the organ pealed a triumphant refrain. As Nate's mouth covered hers in a warm, intimate kiss, which sent her heart to the summits, Carly thanked God that from this day forward, she would have Nate as her lifelong trail mate.

And to her, that was better news than any headline story.

Sweet, Sugared Love

Dedication

Much thanks to Therese Travis, Theo Igrisan, and my mother for all their help. For my sons—thank you for your suggestions, Brandon, and to Joshua for his idea of a prank. To my Lord, who may not always give us what we think we want—but never fails to keep His promises concerning a better future and the dreams He has for us.

Chapter 1

M "*aybe if you pray hard enough, Jared, God will drop your future wife on your doorstep.*"

As he drove his horse-drawn wagon along the one-lane dirt road rimmed with white pines, Jared Crisp shook his head at the memory of his brother Brandon's teasing words.

On a day like this, he'd decided against taking the car. The invigorating air felt good against his face as he made his bimonthly deliveries of his family's maple syrup. Besides, tourists got such a kick out of his old-fashioned mode of transportation, especially the children.

On these late spring mornings, the local kids often gathered on sidewalks or played games in their front yards. The *clip-clop* of Tamany's hooves along the asphalt of the main road drew them forward, flocking to him as if he were the ice-cream man. He patted his pocket to assure himself he'd remembered the treats to dole out to small, eager hands, then withdrew one for himself and unwrapped it, popping a maple candy disc into his mouth.

Buttery and sugary, the candy melted on his tongue, the sweet creamy flavor a time-honored blend his great-grandfather had dreamed up when he first started making and canning maple syrup. Perhaps his family was a bit on the old-fashioned side, and some of the teenage boys did look at him with raised brows as they drove past in their sports cars, but there was steadfastness in family tradition that the entire Crisp family upheld with staunch regard.

And that included Jared finding himself a wife.

He had begun to wonder if God forgot His promise to him years ago. His three married brothers—all younger—taunted him mercilessly about his desire to hold out until God brought Jared the woman He had chosen especially for him. In high school, he'd dated, nothing serious or steady. A tragedy in his senior year involving a troubled classmate committing suicide over another friend of Jared's had brought him closer to His Savior. And one day during deep prayer, he felt as if God told him not to seek a wife, but that He would bring the woman Jared was to marry to Goosebury. Some of the women who'd grown up with Jared had shown interest—Jared wasn't blind—but he saw no sense in dating if it could never lead to anything serious. Why get mired in a relationship that involved deep emotions and could only inflict pain when it ended? When Jared met his future wife, he would know; the Lord had shown him that. And he wanted his heart to be whole, not scarred from past love interests.

Let his brothers scoff; Jared didn't care. He knew the wait, though at times trying, would be well worth the effort when the day came. Yet he didn't want to be as old as Abraham when that glorious day arrived.

"I'll be hitting thirty-three come December," he said under his breath. "But you already know that, God. So any time you're ready to set me up with a life mate will be fine with me."

A shout from up ahead made Jared crack a smile as the first of his young friends spotted him. He brought the wagon to a halt and soon bright, smiling faces and eager pleas surrounded him. When he'd filled all eight of the outstretched hands, the children talked with him, a few petting Tamany, who bore their sticky hands and awkward pats like a real trooper, flicking her ears and giving a little toss of her head now and then as if in agreement with the conversation. Jared sensed the old bay loved the attention.

"My mom had to take me to the dentist the last time you came," said Jimmy, a seven-year-old ne'er-do-well who'd captured the town's heart as easily as the cartoon character Dennis the Menace. Jared had heard a number of whispers labeling the boy "Jim-Jim the Peril."

"I chipped a tooth. See?" Jimmy opened his mouth and pointed to an incisor. "The doc had to file it down. Does it look sharper?" he asked with the hopeful tone of one who took pleasure in pointing out his physical battle scars, much like a pirate with a peg leg and eye patch.

"It sure does," Jared agreed, at which the boy's face beamed. "But better be more careful in the future, Jimmy. Those candies were made to be sucked on and enjoyed, not bit into so they end up breaking all your teeth."

"Oh, it's okay. Mom said she needed a good excuse to get me to the dentist anyway."

Jared shook his head in amusement. He had a feeling Jimmy's munching days wouldn't end. He said good-bye to the children and continued on to his aunts' souvenir store. The citizens of Goosebury dearly respected and loved both of his father's elderly sisters, even if they were somewhat senile and had a habit of finishing one another's sentences, at times creating confusion.

He pulled the horse and wagon up before the small log A'bric & A'brac store, which also fronted their home. Once he tied Tamany to the post, Jared easily hefted the last carton of Crisp's Maple Syrup from the back of the wagon. He often made his aunts' store his last stop, since they always invited him to the noon meal, and Jared never declined their great cooking.

As he opened the door, the silver chimes tinkled a greeting to all within. He saw no sign of his aunts. Behind the counter, a woman faced the wall of shelves, her back to Jared. Light blond hair escaped out of some contraption holding her hair up high and letting it hang down in thick, messy waves that appealed.

Jeans and a pink T-shirt clad her trim figure. Of average height, she turned as he walked closer and assessed him with startling blue eyes.

"Can I help you?"

Jared stared, dumbstruck, as a jolt ripped through his heart. He set the carton on the counter with a swift thump as realization struck him such a forceful blow he didn't bother curbing the words that spilled from his mouth.

"You're the woman I'm going to marry!"

Sharon Lester eyed the tall, hulking man with alarm. He winced after blurting the disturbing words, but she backed up regardless.

"Um, excuse me a moment. I'll be right back."

Without awaiting his reply, she strode to the curtain shielding the dining room as fast as could still be considered normal. Sharon had recently moved to Goosebury at her friend Leslie's urging, thinking the town peaceful and safe. She had temporarily stayed at her friend's renovated barn near Leslie and her husband, Blaine's, home until half a month earlier when she found her present job and rented Loretta Crisp Mallory's larger house. This month had been the first time she'd relaxed in years.

Now she wasn't so sure that this town didn't have its own brand of crackpots.

Catching sight of plump and gentle Loretta, she hurried toward her. Tall and bubbly, Josephine Crisp, Loretta's sister, stood nearby as they both inventoried a delivery of mementos. Sharon had learned during her first day in their employment that Loretta was a wartime widow who'd moved into their parents' old home with Josephine, a spinster. They had converted the huge front parlor into a small souvenir shop that also specialized in antiques. The only one in town like it—the only one Sharon had ever heard of—the hominess of the atmosphere gave an old-fashioned, mid-twentieth-century flair to the place. Open at ten o'clock, A'bric & A'brac closed its doors at five sharp, when the sisters retreated to the back of the house to carry on with their daily lives.

"Whatever is the matter, dear?" Josephine asked. "You look like—"

"You saw a ghost," Loretta finished for her.

"There's some weirdo out there," Sharon explained. "A real crackpot. He said something, well, pretty suggestive. . .in a way. It sort of rattled me."

"Oh, dear." Loretta set down the miniature of a ceramic covered bridge. "We can't have that. It must be a tourist. Everyone in Goosebury is reasonably sane. Perhaps—"

"We should investigate," Josephine concluded.

"Yes, please. I hope you don't mind."

"Nonsense," Josephine said with a smile, putting her arm around Sharon.

"We take care of our own," Loretta confirmed.

The two women bustled toward the shop. Unable to quench her curiosity, Sharon followed and peered through the curtain.

To her astonishment, Loretta hugged the candidate for the asylum. "Jared! It's so good to see you. I'm delighted you're feeling better. It's always lovely to see Thomas, but—"

"We missed you," Josephine finished with a welcoming smile. "Colds can be such nasty things. I do hope you enjoyed the spiced cider we sent with Thomas?"

"It was great. Even if it was out of season."

"Oh, pish," Josephine scoffed. "Just because it's a Christmas tradition doesn't mean it can't—"

"Help heal one's bones all year round," Loretta finished with a smile.

The man they called Jared looked over Loretta's shoulder and spotted Sharon peeking through the drape. Before she could retreat, the sisters turned to look.

"Sharon, dear, the crackpot must have left. Jared here is the only one in the store—"

"So all's safe now."

Sharon felt the burn of her face and wondered if it had achieved the glow of maroon. She saw the corners of the man's mouth twitch. Aggravation that he found the situation amusing made her square her shoulders and step forward.

"Come here, dear. We'd like you to meet—"

"Our nephew Jared Crisp. His father—our brother—is head of Crisp Maple Syrup. It's a family-owned business. Have we told you? Our great-grandfather by many generations—"

"Started making maple syrup years ago, but all the family has a part in it, however small."

"Jared, meet Sharon Lester," Loretta said, oblivious to the tension between the two. Jared and Sharon continued to observe one another—Jared working hard to contain his amusement, Sharon with narrowed eyes. "She moved to Goosebury, what was it—two months ago?"

"Almost." Sharon was surprised at how calm her voice sounded. "A month and a half."

"So, you just moved here. . . ." A wondering note touched his words, the reason for which Sharon didn't care to speculate. She eyed his offered hand as suspect, but with the two sisters watching, she had little choice but to receive his greeting.

His hand felt warm, strong; his fingers long, encasing her much smaller hand. Uneasy, she withdrew hers before he could fully shake it.

So this was the nephew about whom she'd heard nothing but glowing reports during the evenings she and the children shared his aunts' table. Curious, she took inventory since he seemed unable to take his eyes off her face. His hair, dark and thick, grew a little long to his collar. His face was strong, lean; his nose straight and long; and his eyes. . .

She felt her heart give a strange flutter as she met his eyes, which had not stopped gazing into hers. She hadn't noticed his eyes before. A mixture of gray, pale green, even silver combined with black lashes and dark brows, his eyes were striking.

Disconcerted, she averted her gaze to Loretta—another mistake, because the woman beamed at her as if she possessed a secret. Josephine's expression matched her sister's. The two had done nothing but extol the virtues of their extraordinary nephew to Sharon for weeks, and she sensed matchmaking imminent in their plans. Jared was out of the ordinary, all right—and granted, he could turn a number of heads—but he was also clearly insane. Besides, she never planned to marry again.

She was saved by the bell—literally—as the door swung open and two of her children stampeded inside, breathless.

"Mama! Mama!"

With satisfaction, Sharon noted Jared's startled expression of disappointment. Maybe she didn't have to worry about his pursuit of her after all.

"Kitty—Mindy—walk, don't run. Where's Andy?" Sharon looked beyond them for sight of her twelve-year-old son.

"He's with the moose," six-year-old Kitty exclaimed, her eyes bright with excitement.

"The *moose*?"

"The mama moose got hit by a car or something," her ten-year-old explained. "And left a baby moose behind. Andy's with it."

"Oh, dear," Loretta said. "Wild moose—"

"Can be dangerous," Josephine finished.

Alarm chilled Sharon's blood. "Where is he?"

"Near the crossroads by the interstate," Mindy said.

"The interstate." Sharon struggled not to let her fear show. "I told you children not to leave the main square."

"My wagon's out front," Jared said, his tone concerned, sober, "if you need a ride."

Sharon owned no car; neither did Loretta or Josephine—not one in working order anyway. Still, she hesitated. Walking had never presented a problem; most everything she needed stood within close range of the shop. Yet she must get to Andy quickly. Since Jared was the sisters' nephew, Sharon hoped that made her acceptance of his offer of a ride safe and that he wouldn't resort to any hidden psychopathic tendencies.

She gave him a slight nod and turned to her oldest daughter. "Mindy, you come with me. Kitty, stay here."

"Mama!"

"Do as you're told."

"We have milk and cookies," Loretta coaxed.

"Would you like some?" Josephine added.

A somewhat pacified Kitty nodded, allowing Josephine to herd her to the back and the kitchen.

Sharon remembered she was supposed to be on the clock. "You don't mind me leaving?"

"Of course not. You go with Jared and get your son."

Loretta's sympathetic eyes comforted Sharon, and again she felt the peculiar warmth to know someone cared for her.

Outside, her abrupt pace halted when she saw the horse and wagon. "You mean this? I thought you meant a station wagon."

"Tamany can get us there fast," Jared assured. "I know a shortcut. Most cars can't travel it because it's a dirt road and uneven.

"Neat!" Mindy exclaimed, needing no persuasion to jump into the back of the old-fashioned vehicle.

Sharon said nothing, ignoring his helping hand as she climbed onto the seat. She reminded herself that this man was the sisters' nephew and that they knew of her location and that she was in his company. Really, though, it shouldn't come as a surprise that someone with a few screws absent in his noggin would be driving a horse and buggy in the twenty-first century.

Chapter 2

Jared drove Tamany to the area Mindy directed him, extremely conscious of the silent woman sitting on the other end of the wagon seat. Accustomed to the ribbing he received from his brothers and having learned to laugh at himself and take things in stride, he hadn't let his aunts' mix-up regarding the identity of Sharon's "crackpot" embarrass him too much. He'd found the whole thing rather amusing, though Sharon obviously did not.

Frustrated, he crunched down hard on the sliver of his candy disc. He would have offered Mindy a piece, but her mother would probably insist on inspecting it first to make sure he hadn't laced it with cyanide.

How could he have been so stupid to say what he had to her? Granted, the surety that swept through him had floored him, but such a first impression hadn't won him favor. Still, seeing two of her three kids bound through the door convinced Jared he must have gotten some wires crossed and been mistaken at the connection. He still could hardly believe the children were hers; she looked as if she were a college girl in her early twenties, not a mom with a brood of kids.

Knowing this was no time for small talk, he curbed his desire to learn more about this family and struggled to keep his questions inside. Where was Sharon's husband? His aunts had seemed pleased to introduce Jared to her, or had he misread their actions, as well?

Near the turnoff to the interstate, Jared spotted a dark-haired boy off the side of the road. He stood a few feet away but alarmingly close to a pale, dusty-brown moose calf.

"Andy," Sharon called out at the top of her voice as the boy turned upon their approach. "Get away from that animal!"

At the clopping of Tamany's hooves, the moose calf turned its ungainly head to look. To Jared's surprise, it remained still, and he wondered if seeing the horse, another creature on four legs, had helped to ease any panic the animal must feel; had he driven a noisy car, the moose would have fled, Jared was sure. That it stood on tall, skinny legs near the boy and had not run away amazed him. He imagined the little fellow felt lost without its mother and uncertain of what to do.

"Mom!" the boy cried out as Jared brought Tamany to a halt and Sharon jumped down. "Look what I found. Can I keep her?"

A girl moose, Jared mentally corrected.

"Of course not." Sharon approached boy and moose with caution. Jared also left the wagon, unsure. The calf was young, no more than a couple of weeks old he would guess, but it was still wild. At this stage of life, the calf resembled a baby deer, stockier in build, and stood as tall as the boy's waist. If it panicked, it might get hurt.

"But she's got no one else. Her mama got hit by a car or something." He pointed. "Over there."

Jared looked in the direction Andy pointed. In the distance, a massive carcass lay at the side of the road.

"And just why you're out this far from the shop is what I want to know," Sharon said, her voice grim.

The boy quirked his lips to the side but didn't reply.

"Why did the mama go into the road?" Mindy asked curious.

"Probably to lick the salt from it, if there's any left this late in the season," Jared responded. "They need it for their diet."

"There's salt in the road?" The girl's eyes grew round. "Why would anyone salt the road? It's not like people are going to eat it or anything."

"Mom, please," Andy begged. "We could put her in that old barn at the back of the house. We can't just leave her here for a grizzly bear or a wolf or some other killer animal to find. We just can't!"

"The boy has a point," Jared said, earning him a sharp glare from Sharon. "The calf is still nursing. Most calves stay with their mothers through the first year of their lives and aren't able to fend for themselves or understand all the dangers of predators."

"And just how do you know so much about moose calves, Mr. Crisp?" she asked, her words quiet but no less barbed.

"My sister-in-law works with the wildlife reserve."

His steady answer curbed a further reply, and he watched as her mouth formed a silent "oh."

"I have some rope in the back of the wagon. We can lead the calf to your barn, and I'll call Becca, my sister-in-law, to inform her of the situation."

"Please, Mom," the boy pleaded again. Within his narrowed eyes, a darker blue than Sharon's, Jared sensed both desperation and the prelude to angry resentment should she refuse.

"Oh, all right," she said at last. "But only until someone from the wildlife department can come and cart it away."

"Do you have a cell phone?" he asked Sharon. "I can call Becca right now."

"I'm sorry. I don't."

With no means to contact his sister-in-law, Jared saw no alternative but to try to lasso a moose.

As he retrieved the rope and the small family stood on the sidelines to watch, he knew he looked foolish and felt more than a little ridiculous. Sharon must already think him a dolt, but he wondered what Becca would say to his plan. He hoped he wasn't breaking any laws connected to wildlife. He knew leaving the young untouched was vital to their well-being, but in the case of an orphan, he felt there must be extenuating circumstances.

Knowing that moose had poor eyesight, which could work in his favor, he asked Andy to talk to the calf in quiet tones while Jared approached it from behind. Its long ears flicked back, as if it heard him, and Jared sensed that coming up and suddenly slipping the lasso around its neck might scare it worse and cause it to bolt.

He considered what he was about to do, knowing it would forever mark him as a lunatic in Sharon's mind, with no hope of rectifying his earlier mistake—but it was the only solution he could think of at the moment.

" 'Amazing grace! How sweet the sound,'" he sang in a gentle tenor, hoping not only that it would help calm the calf and alert the animal to his presence but also work as a silent prayer heavenward for help. " 'That saved a wretch like me. . .'"

He moved closer; the moose remained still.

" 'I once was lost, but now am found; was blind, but now I see.'" As he sang the last line, he gently dropped the large noose over the compact head and long snout. The animal lumbered a step forward in shock, but Jared tightened the rope, keeping a firm grip on it. He stood very still and sang another verse to quiet the calf, even reaching up to lay his hand on its bristly hide in reassurance. It must have been too young to consider humans a threat.

Mission accomplished. Now Jared wondered how he would lead the animal to the wagon.

"Andy, grab some twigs with fresh green leaves and bring them here please." He hoped Sharon wouldn't mind his ordering around her son. The youth gave him a narrow-eyed glance but moved to do as he asked. "Walk slowly, so as not to scare it," he said when the moose gave a nervous jerk once the boy turned.

"What do you want with twigs?" Mindy wanted to know.

"Moose are herbivores. Do you know what that means?" She shook her head, and he continued. "They eat plants. From what Becca told me, moose start eating solids early, and they have some of their teeth, so I think this might work."

Andy returned holding a handful of twigs.

"Great, now hold it out to the moose and slowly walk toward the wagon."

"I don't think so." Sharon stepped forward. "If that animal has teeth, it may bite. Didn't Loretta say wild moose are dangerous?"

"Mom, the twig is really long. I'll be careful."

Jared understood the boy wanting to take part in what he must consider a big adventure, but he also understood Sharon's fears. Rather than interfere, he let them work it out. Andy convinced his mom, while Jared stood, with as much patience as he could muster, hoping the calf wouldn't become nervous and bolt.

"First let it have a taste," Jared instructed, "but no more."

Andy held the tip of the long twig under the moose's nose, a leaf brushing its nostril. The animal sniffed the branch, its huge upper lip opening to nibble the tender leaves.

"Start walking backward," Jared instructed.

Andy did so, and the moose also moved, craning its neck for another bite. The boy kept the leaves just out of reach, and the moose continued to follow him with Jared keeping a loose rein on the rope.

Once at the back of the wagon, he tied the moose's rope to it and they took their places inside, Jared with a silent prayer of thanks. Both Andy and Mindy sat in back, to "watch" the calf as if afraid it might dissolve into thin air should they look away for a moment.

Jared picked up the reins and clicked his tongue for Tamany to walk. He kept up a slow and steady pace that the moose calf could follow. Mindy soon grew tired of watching and positioned herself between Sharon and Jared, leaning over the back of the seat.

"How come you sang to the moose?" she wanted to know.

"That must have seemed crazy," Jared admitted with a smile. He noticed Sharon didn't deny it. "When my grandfather was alive, he had an ornery horse that always quieted when he sang or hummed church hymns. I remembered him doing that when I was a boy, so I decided to try it, too."

"Why church hymns? Do other songs work?"

Jared shrugged. "Don't really know. Never tried before, and that's all my grandfather sang back then. He was in the church choir."

"Are you in the choir, too?"

"Well. . .yes." His face and ears grew warm at her personal questions.

"I didn't see you when we went last week."

"Mindy, that's enough," Sharon said quietly. "Maybe Mr. Crisp doesn't go to our church."

"Do you?" Mindy asked.

"I go to the same church that my aunts go to—Grace Fellowship—but I was out of town last week, and I was sick before that."

"That's the same one we go to!" the girl exclaimed, eager. "Me, Mama, Andy, and Kitty."

He noticed the omission of her father. "Your dad doesn't go there?" he asked.

He felt more than heard the seconds of significant silence. "Daddy died last year."

"Oh." Stunned, Jared refrained from looking Sharon's way. "I'm sorry."

"Do you know anything else besides church songs?" Mindy asked in a bright voice, as if unfazed by her admission of her father's death.

"I, uh. . .sure."

"Do you know 'Row, Row, Row Your Boat'?"

"Yup."

"Will you sing it with me? I'll start, and you follow."

Jared grinned. "Well now, it seems to me that song doesn't really fit our situation. How about we revise it a bit? Drive, drive, drive your wagon along the winding road. Horse and harness, moose and rope, a sight to behold."

He heard Sharon chuckle at his silly parody of the popular melody.

"Okay!" Mindy giggled. "But you start."

One following the other, they sang countless rounds of the song, though he noticed neither Sharon nor Andy joined in. When Jared neared the road intersecting with the town's main square, he stopped the wagon. "You'll have to tell me where you live," he explained to Sharon.

"We're renting Loretta's old house."

He nodded and headed about a mile down the lane that ran behind the shop to the yellow-shingled home nestled in the wood.

"How come we haven't seen you in town before?" Mindy wanted to know.

"This is a busy time of year on my family's farm."

"What do you do there?"

"Oh, plenty of things." He pulled the wagon into the drive in front of the barn and tied off the reins. "I'll tell you about it sometime. Right now we should take care of the moose."

To Jared's relief, getting the animal into the empty barn didn't present a problem. The calf followed Jared as he led it by the rope and tied it to a post inside.

"Do you have to tie her up?" Andy's sulky tone matched his mutinous expression.

"I do if you don't want the moose bolting any time the barn door opens." His answer seemed to pacify the youth.

"I'll give you a ride back to the shop," he told Sharon, "and I'll call Becca from there."

"I want to stay here," Andy said.

"No." Sharon's reply to her son was abrupt. "I don't want you alone with that moose."

"Aw, Mom. She's not going to hurt me. I was alone with her a long time before you got there."

"Yes, and we'll talk about that later," she said, her tone promising discipline. "Now come along."

"I wanna stay." He crossed his arms, rebellion clear in his wide-legged stance.

"I'm not going to argue with you, Andy. You're coming with us."

"No."

Uncomfortable with the rising tension between mother and son, and feeling in part responsible since he had a hand in delivering the moose, Jared cleared his throat. "The calf will need to eat. Maybe Andy could gather some horsetails, water lilies, pondweed—any other woody plants from the pond over yonder."

Sharon whipped her irritated gaze to his; Andy's narrowed eyes simmered with instant resentment aimed at Jared.

"It was just a thought," he explained, realizing he'd overstepped the mark again.

To his surprise, Sharon gave a slow nod of agreement to his plan. "All right, Andy. You can stay, but I don't want you going anywhere near that moose while I'm gone. Gather the food, as Mr. Crisp suggested, since I don't want the thing starving before help gets here, but that's all. I get off work in two hours. If a worker from the preserve hasn't arrived by the time I get home, we'll both go in the barn to feed it."

The boy didn't respond, but Sharon turned to the wagon as if she considered the matter closed and was confident he would obey her instructions. Noting the boy's sultry expression, Jared wasn't so sure.

❦

That evening, everyone sat at Loretta and Josephine's dining table, clasping hands and bowing heads as Josephine said grace. Sharon closed her eyes and for a moment relaxed, as her action blocked out the sight of the man sitting across from her.

It hadn't surprised her that Josephine asked Jared to stay to supper since he'd missed lunch because of the moose; the man *was* the sisters' nephew. And it didn't surprise her that the sisters increased their efforts to interest Sharon in Jared—and for the same reason. What did surprise her was that he seemed more uncomfortable than she felt. The realization that she was a widow with three children must have played a large factor in his unease.

Loretta and Josephine merrily ordered the supper conversation, playing off each other's sentences as always, seemingly unaware of the tension between their guests. As for the children, Mindy ate her food with silent, single-minded concentration, Kitty played with hers, and Andy wolfed his down like the place was about to blow up and he had to get out of there before it did. Sharon had only taken a few bites when Andy rocketed up and headed for the door.

"Andy!" she called after him. "Finish your supper."

"I am finished," he said without turning around. "I'm going outside."

Before Sharon could correct his manners or behavior, he disappeared from sight, and the door slammed, announcing his departure.

"I apologize," she said to the two sisters. "I have no idea what's gotten into him lately."

She squirmed at the half truth. Andy hated his father and what he'd done to them, but until several months ago when Sharon received the phone call from prison with the news of Mark's death, Andy had always nurtured his animosity with quiet deliberation. Since then, he had become sullen and rebellious.

"That's perfectly all right, dear," Loretta said. "Boys—"

"Will be boys," Josephine finished. "Why I remember Jared was quite the handful." She chuckled. "Such a prankster. You never knew—"

"When he'd hit next," Loretta ended. "There was that time in the root cellar with the flour—"

Jared choked on his iced lemonade. "Aunt Loretta, I doubt Sharon and her girls would be interested in hearing that story."

Sharon eyed his reddened face and decided to take pity on him. "If Mr. Crisp would rather we not know—"

"Well, I wanna know," Mindy jumped in. "What did he do, Mrs. Loretta?"

Loretta looked at Sharon, uncertain, then at Mindy. "I suppose that's something you'll have to ask him yourself, Mindy."

Mindy turned pleading eyes his way, and Jared let out a resigned breath. "I covered myself in flour and scared my cousin into thinking I was a ghost. She ran into the kitchen, banged into the table, and knocked over the jars of applesauce my mom was canning. Three crashed to the floor—none of them had lids on them yet."

Kitty giggled.

"Tell them the rest, Jared," Josephine urged, a twinkle in her eye.

"The rest. Yeah, right." His eyes, bearing a gleam of sheepish amusement, moved from Kitty to Sharon. "My mom turned around, saw me in the doorway, and took a step back in shock. When she did, she stepped on the cat's tail. It yowled and scratched her ankle. Mom dropped the pan of hot applesauce and bent over in pain to grab her ankle or the cat—no one knows which. The cat raced away and knocked over the broom. The handle hit mom in the head."

Sharon felt her mouth twitch.

"Go on, Jared. Finish it."

"There's more?" Mindy asked with a squeal of delight and the thrill of discovering another's humorous scrapes.

"Yeah, unfortunately there is." Jared smiled at Mindy. "My aunt—my mom's sister—came running into the room to see what all the commotion was about. She slipped and fell in the applesauce. When Susie—my cousin—ran screaming from the cellar where I'd scared her, she opened the front door and let the dog inside. It came bounding into the kitchen, saw the cat, and gave it a merry chase through the kitchen. The dog and cat slid and ran through the applesauce—then into the parlor and over Mom's newly covered chairs."

Sharon could no longer contain her mirth. She laughed, tears filling her eyes. Jarred grinned at her amusement.

"My dad came in, caught the dog, and hauled it outside, and that was the end of that."

"Did you get in trouble?" Mindy wanted to know through her giggles.

"Uh, yup. You could say that."

"Almost every day of the week," Josephine finished for him. "You might say our dear Jared was always in the thick of things."

He gave an embarrassed grin and shook his head.

The atmosphere had lightened considerably. Loretta wiped tears of mirth from her eyes with her napkin.

"Say," Josephine began. "Jared, you mentioned earlier that you had to go into the city this week, and, Sharon, you mentioned yesterday how you haven't been able to find any slim-size jeans in town to fit Andy or clothes for Kitty. Wednesday's your day off. I'm sure Jared wouldn't mind taking you into the city."

She beamed at Jared, who looked as trapped as Sharon felt.

"I wouldn't want to impose," Sharon said quickly.

"Nonsense. It would be no imposition, would it, Jared?" Loretta asked, aiding Josephine's cause.

His uncertain smile flickered. "No imposition at all." Sharon realized he said the only polite thing he could under the circumstances.

"Really, it isn't necessary." Sharon fidgeted with her napkin, wiping her mouth though it didn't need it.

"Well, dear, to be honest, I have no idea when the coupe will be fixed to run such a distance without stalling—"

"And you did mention all of Andy's jeans had holes in the knees," Loretta reminded.

Sharon withheld a sigh. Lately, her son whisked through a pair of jeans in less than a month, and the small children's-clothes shop contained a very scant selection of size 6X clothes for Kitty when she'd shopped there.

"I really don't mind." Jared's eyes were kind, his tone softer, more sincere as Sharon looked up at him.

"Neatness," Mindy said. "Will you drive the horse and wagon?"

"I hadn't planned on it." He looked at Sharon. "I *do* own a car. I take Tamany when I make my rounds because tourists get such a kick out of seeing an old-fashioned horse-drawn buggy."

Feeling pushed into a corner but not wanting to be rude or disappoint Jared's aunts since they'd done so much for her and her family, Sharon gave a slight nod. "All right. Thank you." She squeezed the words from a tight throat.

She still thought the man a lunatic, but he didn't appear dangerous. When he'd sung one of her favorite hymns to the moose calf, he'd floored Sharon. But when he explained his motive later, she'd understood his reasoning. His actions and the gentle way he'd handled the orphaned moose as well as his ability to laugh at himself and make others laugh with him made Sharon realize the man did possess some admirable traits.

But dating him was out of the question, and she would need to get that across to the two sisters as soon as possible once he left.

She had a feeling it would be easier to lasso a moose.

Chapter 3

Sharon eyed the pleasant young woman who was inspecting the moose calf for possible injuries. She noted Becca's teasing affection for her brother-in-law, whom she treated as a beloved family member.

"I hope I didn't break any laws," Jared said in worry as he hunched down beside Becca.

"Hmm." Becca deliberated. "She's such a young one. A couple of weeks old at the most." She let out a sad little sigh, but her brown eyes danced with mischief as she glanced at Jared. "Feeding her wasn't the best of ideas, but I understand the situation, and I really do think it ingenious how you got her here. I wish I'd been a bird in a tree to see that. You singing to a moose." Becca laughed.

"At least I had a captive audience," Jared joked back.

"Yeah, well, with your voice, you always do. Believe me, if I hadn't been out of town, I would've come here straightaway. I'm sorry you had to keep the moose overnight."

"So are you saying we shouldn't have fed her?" Sharon asked. "Were the plants not good for her stomach since she's so young?"

Becca directed a look to the door, glimpsing where the children gathered around her truck. Andy had left the barn only at Sharon's insistence. She hadn't wanted him in the vicinity when they discussed the moose's fate.

"What you did won't hurt her," Becca assured. "Jared was right about that. But when a person feeds a moose, it can present a problem. The animal can grow to expect it from everyone, and later, when it's grown, it can attack a person if not offered food. Some moose have had to be killed because they presented that very danger."

"That's terrible," Sharon said. "Neither of us meant to do anything wrong; Andy was only trying to help." She didn't mention that when she'd found his bed unslept in that morning, she'd hurried to the barn to find Andy tucked in a sleeping bag a few feet away from the moose. Sharon's heart had almost stopped, though the scene she'd stumbled upon had been docile. Her son had slept while the moose calf opened its eyes at the squeak of the barn door and lifted its head. The calf had grown more alert, probably hoping for more of the leafy treats they'd fed her the previous evening.

Becca looked at Sharon with an understanding smile. "Andy did fine. This little girl will need a lot of care before we release her to the wild, if that's Hugh's

248

decision. It depends on how she responds while in captivity."

"Then you've found someone who will take it?" Jared asked.

Becca nodded. "I talked with Hugh MacFarland last night on the phone, and he said to bring her in. He's a retired game warden who now works as a wildlife rehabilitator. His farm is ten miles from here."

"You're not taking my moose away, are you?"

No one had noticed the shadow that filled the barn door, blocking out the sunlight. Sharon sent a concerned glance to her son.

"Andy, we talked about this earlier—"

"I can take care of her," he interrupted, walking forward. "I can take real good care of her."

"I'm sure you can, Andy." Becca's tone was soft and sympathetic. "But wild moose don't make good pets."

"But she likes it here!" he insisted. "I want to keep her."

"A baby moose calf like this is fun to have around." Becca agreed in understanding. "But they grow fast—and get bigger every day. In the animal kingdom, they're the fastest to grow."

"The barn is big," he shot back. "She'll have room."

"Right now she needs formula that you don't have," Becca explained. "She needs to be bottle-fed. Later she'll need approximately forty-four pounds of food a day to stay alive, but her stomach, when full, can weigh well over a hundred pounds. She'll need feedings around the clock, medicine administered, her pen cleaned. And moose get big. As they grow older, they can also become dangerous."

"She won't hurt me; she likes me. And I can give her milk from a bottle just like anyone else."

"Andy, that's enough," Sharon admonished. "You knew yesterday we couldn't keep the calf."

"But it's not fair!" He scowled, tears in his eyes. "I found her! She belongs to me!"

Becca stood from her kneeling position. "Hugh is wonderful with animals, Andy. He has over forty years' experience. His father worked with the wildlife department as a vet, and Hugh has been around wildlife ever since he was a kid. His farm has a lot of wide open space for wild animals to move around. Tourists have visited and looked at them through the fence, so I'm sure Hugh wouldn't mind if you visited the moose."

"Her name is Caramel."

Sharon's stomach clenched as she heard in Andy's voice the extent of his attachment to the animal.

"And anyways, we don't have a car, so how am I supposed to get to the farm?" Andy's words were terse.

"Maybe Jared will take you if you ask." Becca directed a brief teasing smile toward her brother-in-law, and Sharon noted his shock at her suggestion. A significant look passed between them.

"Sure, I can do that," he said looking at Andy, then Sharon.

Already feeling like a leech for intruding upon Jared's time with the next day's forced shopping trip, Sharon opened her mouth to respond. But Andy spoke first, hurling angry words at Sharon.

"You never let me have anything!" Angry tears filled his eyes. "I've always wanted a pet, but I never could have one because of Dad—and now, when I can have one, you won't let me. You hate me!"

He whirled around and sped out the door.

"Andy!" Sharon prevented herself from running after him. She knew he needed time alone, but her son's pain pierced her heart. "I'm sorry," she said in embarrassment to Jared and Becca.

"That's all right," Becca sympathized. "I understand."

"It must be tough raising kids alone," Jared added quietly.

"Lately it's been no picnic, that's for sure." Sharon attempted a weak smile his way as Becca led the moose calf to her trailer. Mindy and Kitty watched with sad interest as Becca situated the animal in the back; Andy was nowhere in sight.

Before she slipped behind the wheel of her truck, Becca gave Jared a hug. "Josh and I will see you at supper this Friday?"

"Sure will," Jared agreed.

They watched as Becca drove away. The girls looked after the moose with woebegone expressions.

"I can take you to visit the moose," Jared assured.

The morose frowns evolved into grateful smiles. "Can we go tomorrow?"

"Next week might be better," Jared hedged. Though he didn't know for sure, he had a feeling Hugh would want to get the moose settled into a routine before bringing outsiders to visit.

Once he'd given his promise, the girls scrambled off, chattering about a tea party and dolls.

"You two are close," Sharon said. "You and Becca, I mean."

"Becca is like a little sister to me, though when we first met, she wanted more of a relationship."

The admission didn't surprise Sharon in the slightest. She'd seen the admiring glances Becca gave Jared.

He glanced her way. "I introduced her to one of my younger brothers, Josh, and it was love at first sight for both of them. They're a matched set."

It was on the tip of her tongue to ask why Jared hadn't been interested in Becca, who seemed pretty, intelligent, and kind, but she decided silence would serve better. She didn't need to broach a discussion on personal relationships, which could become embarrassing if it led to what happened between them in the shop yesterday.

As though he'd read her mind, his expression grew fixed. "I gave the situation over to God years ago, about me finding a wife. I haven't dated since then, and I don't plan on doing so." His eyes continued staring into hers, affecting her clear to her spine so she had trouble gaining a breath.

"Well"—the mood broke as he gave her a slight grin—"I need to get back to the farm. I'll pick you up at noon tomorrow." Sharon gave the barest of nods, and he strode away to his car. His somber words clutched her heart like a vise, and remembering his opening remark at their first meeting, she stood and watched as he drove away.

"I'm not that woman, Jared," she whispered. "I never can be."

❧

Jared almost laughed at the relief that crossed Sharon's face when he arrived to pick her and her children up for their shopping trip. She hadn't really imagined he would drive a horse and wagon down the highway into the city, had she? He had told her it wasn't his regular mode of transportation; she'd seen his car. Then again, she already considered him a polite psychopath, so who knew what she thought?

They barely spoke during the twenty-minute ride, and Jared sensed Sharon had something on her mind. Noticing the friction between Andy and his mother, it didn't take a lot of speculation to determine its cause. To help ease tension, Jared turned the radio on to a Christian soft rock station and got a glimpse of Andy in the rearview mirror rolling his eyes skyward at Jared's choice. He wondered if the boy disapproved of the mild music or its message.

Once he found a parking space near the department store Sharon pointed out, he hurried around to her side of the car. She held on to the latch, her focus turned toward the backseat as she imparted last-minute instructions to her kids, and when Jared opened her door, she gave a surprised start. She eyed him with suspicion as she emerged, again ignoring his offered hand as if she suspected a practical joke, and he wondered if no man had ever opened a car door for her... any door for her, he thought, as he also opened the glass door of the department store and she gave him another odd look.

An elderly woman laden with bags nodded her smiling thanks as Jared kept the door open for her, as well. When he joined Sharon, she eyed him as if he were a goldfish in a birdcage.

"What?" he asked.

"Nothing." She shook her head as though unable to figure him out.

They headed toward the escalator to the second floor. An excited pair of small children raced ahead to be the first up the rising metal stairs, and Jared pulled Sharon out of their path and harm's way. She tensed and withdrew her arm from his grasp, stepping away from him at the first possible moment. He said nothing as the children's mother approached. She made a quick apology, brushed past them, and hurried to the escalator in pursuit of her young ones.

Upstairs, Sharon looked at her son. "Over in that far corner with the sailboat suspended from the ceiling is the boys' department. Your sisters and I will be over there"—she pointed to the other side of the store—"in little girls'. Like I told you earlier, Andy, now that you're older, I'm giving you more freedom by letting you choose your own clothes—but nothing with rips, tears, patches, or hems undone."

"But it's in style."

"I don't care what's in style." Her soft-spoken words brandished the rod of authority. "It's hard enough to keep you in clothes that don't unravel within weeks and that still follow the dress codes, so I don't need you choosing jeans and shirts that already have wear to them. And Andy, please make sure they cover *all* the areas they're supposed to, not just parts."

"Aw, Mom, can't I be like all the other guys? It's bad enough being the new kid on the block."

"Then save up your money and buy whatever ripped clothes you want to wear. But I won't invest in them. Are we clear on that?"

"Yeah, right, whatever."

He didn't move.

"The clothes aren't going to grow feet and walk to find you, Andy," Sharon urged.

"What about *him*?" He directed a glare Jared's way, doing nothing to hide his animosity.

"Mr. Crisp was kind enough to bring us to the mall so we could buy you clothes," she said in a quiet but firm undertone. "Please treat him with the respect due him and watch that attitude."

"Is he going with you?"

Sharon sighed. "I imagine he'll do whatever he wants to, since he's an adult and has the option of making his own decisions. You on the other hand, don't." She seemed to relent a bit. "I'll be okay. Now get hopping. I want to get home before Christmas," she exaggerated. "Be sure and stay on this level—don't go anywhere else."

Andy stomped off, and Jared wondered at her strange message to the boy, that she would be okay.

Sharon watched him go, her brow wrinkled with worry, before turning to her youngest with a smile. "Okay, Kitty, let's see what they have for you."

Jared stood in place, uncertain of what to do or where to go. Kitty looked up at him, her big blue eyes including him in their group.

"You'll come with us, too, won't you, Mr. Crisp? I really do need a man's opinion," she added.

At the six-year-old's remark, which came with all the simper and attitude of a full-grown Southern belle, Jared noticed Sharon wore the same shock that must cover his face.

"Uh, sure," he answered, and Kitty turned with a satisfied whirl of her plaid skirt. She headed the line to the girls' department, as if they, her entourage, were to follow.

"I really have no idea where she picks up these things," Sharon said from beside him. "I would guess prime-time TV; I had to work the late-night shift this past year before moving to Goosebury, and who knows what my kids watched in the babysitter's company while I was away."

Her statement bore self-condemnation, which Jared felt misplaced.

"Don't be so hard on yourself. You've done well by these kids. It's easy to tell you're a good mother and only want what's best for them."

"Thanks." She gave him a sidelong glance as if he didn't know what he was talking about. After the altercations with Andy, he understood her hesitance.

"It must be difficult to raise them without a man around to help."

He had intended his statement as sympathetic, but once he heard his words aired, he realized she could take them wrong.

She got that worried look again and darted him another glance. "Listen, you and I both know this outing was a lame attempt on your aunts' part to get us together. But let me tell you from the beginning, I'm not interested in getting married again. Ever. And that includes dating. So if that in any way interferes with your future plans—as a remark you made the other day leads me to believe—it would be best if you and I don't connect again after this shopping excursion is over. I appreciate your taking the time out of your busy schedule to bring us here, Jared, don't get me wrong, but I want to avoid any misunderstandings right from the start."

He chuckled and gave a wry shake of his head. "That was some speech. Did it take long to prepare?"

She stopped in the aisle and blinked at him in shock.

He smiled to show he was teasing. "Sharon, it's okay. Relax. I don't have ulterior motives, and if it's okay with you, I'd like to start over again and pretend our first meeting never happened. Just as friends—nothing more planned or hoped for." He didn't want a ready-made family and felt he must have been mistaken on hearing from God about Sharon being the wife for him.

He held out his hand to her. "Jared Crisp, moose catcher extraordinaire. Nice to meet you."

She let out a short laugh, glanced down at his hand, then back into his eyes. She shook his hand and released it, though the sparkle in her eyes told him she again felt at ease, perhaps for the first time that day. "Sharon Lester, overworked and underrated mom, but only one of many of my kind. It's nice meeting you, too."

"Mom, are you okay?" Mindy stood in the middle of the aisle, her expression a study of confusion. Kitty stood at one of the endcap displays, sliding dresses and outfits over the circular rack and selecting them with all the excitement of a new starlet bearing a charge card with zero credit limits.

"You're not planning to try all those on, are you?" Sharon asked, picking up on Jared's train of thought at the humongous pile hung over Kitty's skinny arm. Numerous clothes racks stood throughout the area, which was twice the size of a tennis court. Two hangers with outfits that looked as if they were made of blue handkerchiefs slid from the pile Kitty held and to the floor by her white sneakers.

"You big dummy," Mindy said. "You're only supposed to pick from this section, in your size."

"I'm not a dummy. The sign says 6X."

"No, it says $6. Don't you even know how to read?" her sister shot back.

Kitty's brow wrinkled when she realized her mistake. In disappointment she looked at the small section of the rack Mindy motioned to, which amounted to no more than three inches width, mostly of the same outfit in the same color.

"Mindy, no name-calling. Kitty, there are plenty of clothes to choose from in your size, with a lot more racks still to look through. This is a big store." She helped her daughter hang the oversized clothes back on the rack between their proper number holders and directed a look toward Jared. "Are you sure you're up for this?"

At her impish but innocent look—the first time she'd ever relaxed around him enough to tease—he grinned. "Well, it'll be a new experience, anyway. I feel a little like Lewis and Clark on the verge of exploring a new world."

"Oh, yeah." Sharon laughed. "You have no idea."

He didn't miss the wicked twinkle in her eyes or the way her lips twitched at the corners as she turned from him. Suddenly, Jared felt a lot like that goldfish in the birdcage. . .or maybe a songbird in a goldfish bowl. He felt the strangest need to gulp down a massive supply of oxygen.

A gullible male caught in the shopping trap of a feminine clothes-world experience, that's what he was. What had he been thinking when he agreed to what surely must be every man's daymare? He couldn't call it a nightmare since the sun was still out.

"Second thoughts?" Sharon asked sweetly, catching his eye as he edged toward the aisle. Kitty squealed as she spun a second rack of dresses, whirling the poor holder around like a Looney Tunes Tasmanian Devil.

At the challenge in Sharon's eyes, he squared his shoulders and forced his shoes to stop sliding inch by inch over the flat gray carpet toward the aisle floor.

"Just lead the way, Lewis," he muttered.

"Sure thing, Clark."

Again, she gave him that all-knowing smile.

⚜

Sharon could almost laugh if she didn't feel so sorry for the poor guy. Kitty was acting true to form and insisting on modeling every outfit to pirouette and gain advice. It concerned and saddened Sharon that her youngest daughter sought Jared's opinion each time. Kitty yearned for a father figure in her life; she was too young to really remember the continual threat Mark posed, and only desired what many other girls her age had—a father.

Sharon felt Kitty was too young to tell of the past she would prefer they all forget, though one day she knew she might have to. Of their family, Kitty was the only member who'd not been targeted by Mark's outbursts; she must have forgotten the nightmares that woke her, crying, during those dark days.

"What do you think of this one, Mr. Crisp?" Kitty asked with a smile, holding out the hem of the latest blue number.

"I'm beginning to feel like a potato chip as often as you girls call me that," he said. "So why don't you call me Jared instead?"

"Mom?" Both girls looked her way, and Sharon hesitated, then nodded her permission. If he didn't mind the informality, she wasn't going to insist on decorum.

"So, Jared," Kitty insisted, "you like?"

Sharon glanced to where he leaned against the counter, his stance a bit awkward. His eyes appeared to have glazed over as though his brain had turned to mush, and she hid a smile. "Maybe that's enough, Kitty. You have plenty of dresses to decide from."

"But Mom, this is *important*. I want to try out for children's choir like it said we could in the bulletin, and I have to look just perfect."

"I should think it's your voice that you'd be concerned with," Sharon said, noting Jared's sudden alert expression; the first sign he'd come back to the land of the living since Kitty had started her fashion show twenty minutes before. Andy finished his shopping in half the time, and now stood with his hands in his coat pockets, impatiently waiting for Sharon to go to the boys' department and approve his choices. To his credit, he said nothing to hurry his little sister along, but he'd always adopted favoritism with Kitty, as a protective big brother.

"Jared, do you like this blue one better or the green one?" Kitty insisted.

His shifting eyes reminded Sharon of a cornered animal. "I'm not sure I remember which is which," he admitted.

"I'll try the green one on again." Kitty headed for the dressing room.

"The yellow!" Jared called out. "The yellow was best."

"Which one? The one with flowers on the skirt or the lacey things on it?"

He looked like he might start to hyperventilate. His face went a shade red. "Uh. . .the lace?"

"I liked that one, too," Kitty said with a decisive nod. "Okay. Which shirt did you like? I can't wear a dress every day—Mama won't let me."

"Kitty," Sharon said, noting the panic that had sparked to life in Jared's eyes again, "they're having a sale on the shirts. We can get all three."

"Really?" Her eyes went wide. "Yea!"

"Keep it down," she said to her daughter, but Kitty had already raced toward the dressing room.

"Thanks," Jared said, and Sharon smiled.

"Not a problem."

Andy looked back and forth between them, then bridged the distance to stand beside Sharon. "Can we get my stuff now?"

"Patience, Andy. I can't leave Kitty here by herself."

"Mindy's here."

Yeah, a lot of help she would be. Sharon looked to where her older daughter thumbed through a table display of filmy scarves, beaded bags, and other accessories.

"Five more minutes," Sharon promised.

She wished she could buy all their purchases at one register, but store policy prevented it. Or maybe something about their actions or appearance made the store clerk nervous and afraid they would shoplift, so she'd told Sharon she had to purchase the clothes in that department when it really wasn't necessary. Then again, maybe she was just being paranoid. Sharon had no way of knowing, but she did note the young girl's frequent glances in their direction.

Sharon's mind drifted back to the past, to pre-Christianity days—when her husband forced her to steal from mini-marts and even stores like this one. To refuse had been to face a worse punishment than what any policeman could mete out.

"Sharon?"

She looked at Jared and tried to compose her face into a blank expression. He looked at her as though she hadn't succeeded.

"You okay?"

"Sure." She gave a careless smile and shrugged. "Just thinking."

He hesitated as if doing some of his own thinking. "I asked if you'd like to get a bite to eat after this. The mall has some good restaurants."

Sharon hedged, not sure how to respond. She knew her kids must be hungry; she was hungry. And Jared must be to have suggested a meal. But she couldn't let him pay, and she didn't dare tell him she couldn't afford a restaurant outing, not after this clothes shopping excursion.

She bit so hard on the corner of her lip she felt she'd almost bit through it. If she canceled out the weekend trips to the video rental store for a month—her one concession to paid family entertainment—she could swing lunch today.

"Mom, can I have these two scarves? Both would look really cool as a belt with my tops."

Sharon noted the cost of each of the long, embroidered, fringed accessories— one turquoise, the other black. Even on sale, their prices ranged in the two digit numbers. Already she sensed a permanent hole resided in her pocketbook, and she hadn't added in the price of the clothes Andy had selected yet.

"No." Sharon felt a twinge of pain at Mindy's hurt look. "I bought you clothes last week; this is Kitty and Andy's turn." She hated having to say no to her kids, hated their looks of disappointment even more. They had endured so much disillusionment and pain in their young lives. "I'm sorry, Min."

"It's okay." She shrugged but didn't make eye contact.

Sharon didn't feel as if it were okay at all; Mindy rarely asked for anything. She wished now she hadn't lashed out her answer and wondered if there was a way she could add the scarves.

"Maybe we could put them on layaway for school," Sharon suggested, knowing autumn would roll around before she knew it. Mindy's eyes grew hopeful, then clouded when Sharon questioned the salesclerk, who told them they couldn't put sale items into layaway.

She sensed Jared struggling with the idea of offering to front her the money. She had learned in her years of being married to Mark to home in on body language. Jared straightened from the counter, intent on the conversation, his hand going to his back pocket. To avoid possible embarrassment for either of them should he offer and she would need to refuse, Sharon gave in to Mindy.

"All right. Put them with the jeans on the counter," she told her daughter. "It means no movie rentals for at least a month and a half though."

"Okay," Mindy said, too jubilant with the idea of gaining the scarves to consider future Saturday nights sans viewing entertainment.

"Did you know the local library has movies you can check out?" Jared asked. "On tape and DVD."

"Really?" Sharon and Mindy said in unison.

He nodded. "My brother's family takes advantage of it every Wednesday— you can check out up to three new releases per card and keep them for a week, free of charge."

"Thanks for letting us know." Sharon gave Jared a smile. He really wasn't such a bad guy. Now that she'd said what she needed to say, and more importantly, he'd agreed, she could relax around him and consider a simple friendship.

"I'll bet they're crummy movies," Andy muttered, shooting a glance of disinterest at Jared before looking Sharon's way.

"They have new DVD releases from as recent as this past winter. I saw that Narnia movie that's so big with kids on the shelf there, too."

"Really?" Mindy's eyes got big. "Mom?"

"We'll check it out later," she promised.

Kitty flounced out of the dressing room. "Are you sure the dress isn't too fancy to wear to choir tryouts?" she asked no one in particular, suddenly worried. "Should I pick a different dress?"

"The dress is perfect," Jared hurried to say. "But I'd save it for Sundays or special occasions. You can wear anything you want to the tryouts, Kitty. What's important is that you bring a well-rested voice."

"How would you know?" Mindy asked, her brows pulling together in curiosity.

Sharon watched Jared go a deeper shade of red. "Well, the fact of the matter is, I'm the children's new choir director—just a volunteer till they can find someone better qualified."

Everyone stared at him, no one speaking.

"Sorry, guess I should have mentioned that before."

If he had worn a tie, he would be pulling at it about now. Sharon worked to hide a smile. Suddenly, the pressure of money problems faded away. "Well, to be fair, I guess you weren't given a chance. Kitten, you heard the words from the man himself. So what say we buy what we've got and then go have some lunch?"

A rousing chorus of affirmatives met her suggestion, though Sharon knew she'd have to make a few cuts to the budget to pay for today's little overexpenditure, but she figured one splurge couldn't hurt.

They lunched at a café in the mall, and Jared picked up her ticket before Sharon could stop him.

"Jared, no," she said, but he'd already risen from the table and headed to the register. He sensed her lack of funds and didn't want to make things worse.

Upon his return, he confronted her grim expression with composure, waiting for the fire to fall, but it didn't. He assumed it was because her kids were there.

"I talked you into this," he explained. "It only seems right I treat."

"I don't like the idea of you buying our meals," she said in an undertone. The girls were busy discussing friends, and Andy, who had wolfed down his chicken, now frowned and picked at his chocolate cake with his fork.

"Take it as a token of our new friendship," Jared replied, wishing she wouldn't make such a big deal out of a simple gesture. "Friend to friend."

"I'm not a pauper, either." Her eyes burned into his. "I pay my debts."

"Okay." He wasn't sure what she wanted. "If you insist on returning the favor, you can pay me back by letting me take you to the library after we leave here and check out a movie I can watch with you and your kids."

Her shock matched his own. Had he really suggested such an idea? He enjoyed her company but hadn't planned on prolonging the day. Not until the words came flying from his mouth.

Andy's fork clattered to his plate. "I don't wanna see a movie. I wanna see my moose."

"It's only been a couple of days." Jared sighed at the unwanted change of subject. "I'll give Hugh a call later to find out if a visit is okay this weekend. I could take you on Saturday after my work is done at the farm."

"I want to see her now! And I don't need your permission or your ride."

"Andy," Sharon admonished. "Watch your tone, and apologize to Jared this minute."

He turned his glare on his mother and then dropped it to his plate, offering a mumbled "sorry" to the chocolate cake.

Sharon sighed, but when she looked Jared's way, he sensed her irritation had tempered toward him by the apologetic smile she gave. "Saturday sounds good. I suppose we could make a full evening of it. Library, moose, and a movie."

His lips twitched at her witty reply. "That sounds okay by me."

Andy grunted.

"I get off work at five," Sharon said, ignoring her son's response, "so I'll have to trust you to select something decent since the library closes before then. Something family oriented that we could all watch together."

He looked at the faces around the table. The girls' eyes were bright, eager; Andy again frowned at his plate.

"Okay, I can do that. Saturday it is then."

He wondered why her words should make him feel good, especially since Andy detested the idea. All Jared sought was Sharon's friendship. . .so why was he already anticipating Saturday's approach so much?

Chapter 4

Jared spent the next few days avoiding the issue, but in his quiet time with the Lord, he felt God made the matter very clear to him. He hadn't misunderstood. Sharon was the one.

"But I hadn't planned on taking on a ready-made family, Lord," he argued the first morning.

God reminded him of Joseph, who took Mary as his wife after she became pregnant.

On morning two, Jared offered another argument. "She doesn't seem to like men, especially not me, and she says she never plans on getting married."

The Lord reminded him of Hosea's story and led him to turn there. Though Gomer ran away from Hosea and to an immoral life, God urged Hosea to find her and take her back as his wife.

"Her son despises me," Jared countered the next day, though the words sounded lame.

The Lord reminded him that he hadn't chosen Andy for Jared's wife.

After three days of struggle, Jared gave in and again turned the situation completely over to God.

"Okay, Lord, if it's really Your will then You're going to have to open doors to make it happen. She slammed them all tight and padlocked them in my face. So I'll just stand back and watch You work as locksmith, if You don't mind."

At least Sharon was willing to enter into friendship with Jared and hadn't written him off as a complete psychopath due to their first meeting. As for himself, Jared felt at odds. Before he'd met her, he thought he would want a speedy engagement after long years of waiting for this moment to arrive. But now he found he didn't want to jump into anything and to take it very slow remained the best course, especially given the fact that Sharon was totally against the idea of marriage.

He felt at odds with his own goals.

Jared picked up Sharon from work on Saturday, much to her evident surprise.

"Since I was coming to your house anyway, I thought I'd swing by and spare you the walk."

"I like to walk."

Great.

"But thanks for the offer. I'll just get my purse." She offered him a doubtful smile.

Outside, when he put his fingers to her elbow to steer her to his car, she pulled away from him as if his skin were red-hot and he'd burned her.

At the question in his eyes, she explained with a feeble shrug, "I don't like being touched," then yanked open the passenger door and slid inside.

Even better.

Jared rolled his eyes heavenward and wondered if God was into practical jokes.

Didn't like being touched? Never wanted to marry again?

Like Hosea had to do with Gomer, Jared had a feeling he would need to learn and exert extreme patience with Sharon if she was part of God's plan for his life; he certainly didn't consider her promiscuous as Gomer had been, far from it. But he'd always assumed the woman God had for him would be, if not excited by the prospect of Jared as a husband, at least somewhat open to the idea. Not posting warning signals into every word or gesture or look she gave him.

The drive to her house took only a few minutes, but the tense silence seemed to triple the time it took to get there.

She fidgeted and looked at him. "I'm sorry. About what I said back there."

He gave her a sideways glance. "Don't worry about it. My family was never much on personal space. I grew up with a lot of hugging and touching involved, so most of the time I'm not even aware I'm doing it."

She grew quiet, turning her gaze to look out the windshield, and he realized that sounded bad.

"Not meaning I touch people a lot, or that I touch just anyone—I don't." He felt his face heating. "Except for family and friends. And when I touch someone, I'm usually sincere about it."

Okay, that sounded worse.

"I mean—"

"I know what you mean." She offered him an understanding smile, getting him off the verbal hook upon which he'd impaled himself. "I grew up in a hostile environment and couldn't wait to get out of the house when I was old enough. I ran away from home and married at sixteen. I had Andy six months later. I'd just turned seventeen." She again turned her attention to the windshield. "I guess you could say I jumped right out of the frying pan and into the fire. But I didn't know it then."

Intrigued by her comment, Jared was preempted from asking more when Mindy appeared on the road, racing toward the car, Kitty far behind her.

Sharon rolled down her window. "What's wrong?" she called.

"Andy said he's going to see his moose and doesn't need Jared to take us there."

Sharon's mouth tensed. "A ten-mile walk is not something I'm going to attempt after a full day on my feet; I'll talk to him."

"But Mama, he already left."

"When?"

"Five minutes ago," Mindy rushed to say as a breathless Kitty finally joined her. "After his cartoons were over."

"Get in the car," Jared said, sure Sharon wouldn't want to detour to her house. "We'll catch up to him."

The girls piled into the backseat. Once they buckled themselves in, Jared took off. They soon spotted Andy. Jared pulled closer to where the boy walked alongside the road and eased his foot off the accelerator.

"Get in the car, Andy," Sharon said out the open window, her tone brooking no refusal.

Andy tensed and faced her off as Jared hit the brakes. The boy seemed about to argue, but something in his mom's expression must have stopped him. He did as she said, slamming the door harder than necessary.

And now off to begin this fun outing.

Somehow Jared didn't think a medley of car tunes would help ease the tension this time.

❧

Sharon had just about had it with her son; there was no excuse for his surly behavior. Once they reached Hugh MacFarland's farm, Andy took off running to the chain fence.

"Andy, wait!"

He refused to listen and twined his fingers through the iron links as he scanned the area.

A strapping giant of a man with gray hair and crinkles around his eyes came from a building outside the gate to greet them.

First he shook Jared's hand. "Nice to finally meet you. Becca talks a lot about her 'big brother.' She explained the situation, and while I don't normally allow visits at this stage, I decided to make an exception for the boy." He looked at Sharon and the two girls, his confusion evident.

"I'm sorry. Andy is really eager to see the moose," Sharon said, motioning behind her to where Andy stood at the fence. "I'm Sharon Lester, and these are my daughters, Mindy and Kitty."

Hugh gave them all a welcoming smile. "All right then." He led them toward the fence where Andy stood. After introducing himself, he explained to Andy in a firm but gentle voice, "I prefer as little human interaction with the moose calf as possible. But you're welcome to watch her through the protective fence."

Andy nodded, though he didn't appear happy. Sharon gave him a warning look, and he gave a little quirk of his mouth. "Thank you, sir."

"Sure. Well, come along then. I hear you're eager to see her." He led them to another enclosed area, this one smaller and cut off from where other animals roamed.

As they approached, Sharon saw the baby moose drinking from a bottle hooked to the fence.

"Wow, she's gotten big," Andy said, his surliness forgotten.

"She sure has. She looks like she's weeks older and not days," Sharon added.

"Moose grow very fast," Hugh said. "We still hope to release her to the wild at some point, though she wouldn't take the bottle at first and had to be hand fed. She's young enough that we hope it won't present a problem."

At the sound of their voices, the moose stopped feeding and turned her head to look at them.

"Here, Caramel." Andy's fingers wiggled through the fence. "Here, girl."

"Andy, don't," Sharon warned under her breath.

The moose looked Andy's way and pricked its ears.

"Can I pet her?" He turned hopeful eyes toward Hugh.

"Andy, you heard what he said about human interaction."

"Please?" He ignored his mom, his eyes still on Hugh. "We're friends. She knows me."

"I'm not so sure, Andy. Moose—or any wild animal for that matter—don't tend to be friendly or trust—"

The moose warily picked its way toward them and stopped at the fence between Andy and Jared.

"Well, I'll be. . ." Hugh's words trailed off.

"Maybe she wants you to sing to her again, Jared," Mindy said, and Sharon noted the embarrassment on his face.

The moose craned its neck to sniff at Andy's fingers. Its tongue came out to lick once, before it stepped back.

"She's thanking you, Andy," Kitty squealed in delight.

Hugh didn't look as pleased. Yet when Andy glanced his way, he managed a smile. "Looks like you did make a friend."

"So can I pet her?"

"I'd rather you didn't. It's for her sake, son. Too much human interaction can make her dangerous and unfit to release in the wild."

"At petting zoos they let us pet the animals," Mindy argued, not helping matters any.

"Yes, but those animals will never again be released to the wild. They'll live out their existence in a zoo, always dependent upon people to give them food and never able to learn to forage on their own."

"Elsa did," Mindy argued. "So why can't Caramel?"

"Elsa?"

"The lion in the *Born Free* movie. They had her for a pet, then released her."

"Ah, Elsa. Of course." Hugh's mouth twitched, and Sharon wondered if he had children of his own to be so patient with hers. "That was a vastly different situation. The owners understood wildlife, and though I don't remember the movie to the letter, it seems to me as if they encountered a great number of problems reacquainting Elsa to the wilds of Africa. She almost died before they were successful. Wildlife, for the most part, just aren't meant to become house pets. Animals of the wild were created to know and live the life God meant for them to have."

His answer seemed to pacify the children, though none of them looked happy. Sharon had never been able to give them a pet; her husband wouldn't allow one, and then when she and the children lived on their own, the apartment they rented had a no-pets policy. She wondered if the sisters would mind if she bought the children a dog or a cat.

They remained twenty minutes longer, neither Andy nor Mindy wanting to leave. At Sharon's lure that Jared had checked out a movie for them to watch, both Kitty and Mindy were ready to go, but it took some prodding to pull Andy from the fence. Rather than order him to come, Sharon cajoled him, saying they were having his favorite that night—creamy chicken Alfredo.

Andy looked at Hugh. "Can I come back and visit her again?"

At first Sharon thought the man might refuse, and who could blame him, but instead he gave a kind nod. "Sure. As long as you follow my rules, I don't mind your visiting. I have other animals on my farm, as you no doubt noticed. Goats, calves, rabbits, a few dogs, and several cats. You're welcome to visit with them, too. Some would enjoy the company and the attention, and you can pet most of them at will."

"Can we, Mama?" Mindy turned eager eyes her way.

"Well, I don't see why not."

"Will you bring us again, Jared?" Mindy asked, giving Sharon a turn at blushing. She didn't want him to think they assumed him to be their permanent personal chauffeur, which was how it was beginning to look.

He glanced at Sharon as if reading her mind and grinned. "Sure, I'd love to."

Andy stalked off to the car without another word.

Chapter 5

Jared never thought he would hear Sharon squeal like a little girl. The shine in her eyes and the glow of her face made him glad he'd chosen this movie and not the other one about toys that came to life. The Narnia one had been checked out.

"I take it you approve?" he asked with a grin.

"I haven't seen this movie since I was a kid. When I was a little girl, I used to dream Chitty was my car and would take me places far away, like 'Hushabye Mountain'—to happy places where all was safe."

Her wistful words seemed to cover a great deal more, and Jared felt as if an invisible fist closed around his heart.

From behind Sharon, Andy glanced at the cover of the Disney DVD she held. "It looks stupid. And what a dumb title: *Chitty Chitty Bang Bang*. Who thought up something retarded like that?"

Even her son's taunts didn't wipe the smile from Sharon's face. "Don't knock it till you've tried it, champ."

They'd enjoyed a reasonably friendly supper—at least Andy didn't glare at Jared from across the table the entire time. He had been too busy gulping down the delicious meal Sharon had prepared. Jared hoped the boy's animosity toward him wouldn't spark up again, now that they had consumed the last of the apple pie.

By the time the actor who played Caractacus Potts had gone to the candy factory with his invention, the children, including Andy, were absorbed in the story. Even Sharon sat like a child, a delighted smile on her face. Andy sat between them—he had plunked himself in the middle cushion the moment Sharon sat down. Jared realized it was Andy's way of putting distance between Sharon and Jared.

"It would be so neat to make candy." Kitty's expression grew wistful as she lay stretched out in front of the TV, her chin propped on her hands.

"We do that very thing at my family's farm," Jared said.

"Really?" Kitty turned wide eyes his way.

"Sure do. Maple sugar candies. I usually have some hard candy on me, but today I don't. I'll bring you a sample next time I see you."

"Sh!" Andy said. "I'm trying to watch the movie."

Jared caught Sharon's apologetic look on her son's behalf but wasn't surprised at the youth's curt remark. The boy had labeled him an enemy from the start, and by the manner in which he always seemed to insert himself between Sharon and Jared, whether by words or actions, it wasn't difficult to figure out why.

The movie ended with a rousing sing-along of the theme song, which both girls began to croon, and Jared thought he heard Sharon hum. But Kitty hadn't forgotten Jared's previous comment.

"Do you really own a factory and make candy?"

"Well, not a factory like in the movie, no, but we do have a building set aside with workers—most of them family members—who boil and prepare the syrup, getting it ready for distribution. From the syrup we make candy using a family recipe."

"Wow." Kitty's eyes sparkled.

"Neatness," Mindy added.

"Do you know where maple syrup comes from, Kitty?" he asked.

She thought hard. "From cans?"

Andy laughed, and Sharon shot him a mild warning glance. He quieted and smiled at his sister with friendly tolerance, putting out his hand to tousle her hair. He seemed to have a strong tie to both his sisters.

"Well, to begin with, no," Jared said. "But it does wind up in tins. It comes from inside trees."

He didn't think it possible for her huge eyes to go wider. "Trees?"

Jared nodded. "Maple trees. We tap the trees in the springtime, capturing the sap, and then boil it to make syrup. We travel by horse and wagon to collect the sap from the buckets of those trees within easy reach, in what we call gathering."

"Wow, that's so cool," Mindy said.

"You don't use a tractor?" Andy asked.

"No, our family holds to old-fashioned ideals whenever possible. Tourists love the horse and wagon bit, and we even put a picture of Tamany on the cans."

"Really? I want to see!" Kitty shot like a cannonball for the kitchen. Soon creaks and slams of cabinets flying open followed.

"Kitty, don't wreck the place," Sharon called in alarm. "We ran out of syrup yesterday, and I threw the tin away already."

"I'll bring some of that next time I come, too," Jared promised.

"We don't need any of your lousy syrup," Andy said. "It's awful."

Mindy rolled her eyes and ran to the kitchen.

"Andy!" Sharon stared in shock at her son. "Apologize to Jared."

"Because I don't like his stinking syrup?"

"No, because that's not how you treat a guest, and with the way you wallowed your French toast in syrup at breakfast yesterday, I should think you like his syrup very well. It's because of you we ran out of it."

Andy scowled. "I'm going to my room."

Before Sharon could say another word, he pivoted on his heel and stormed down the hall. She seemed to wither as Jared watched her.

"I'm sorry about all that." She glanced at him.

"It's okay; I understand. He feels like I'm a threat."

Her eyes seemed to sharpen with comprehension at his comment, and she cast a nervous look toward the kitchen, where both girls were.

"Can you stay for coffee? I know it's late, but I think explanations are in order. I have to get the girls to bed first, and I don't want them to hear what I have to say."

"Sure." He felt cheered that she wanted him to extend his visit for whatever reason. "Want me to start the percolator?"

"If you'd like. It takes about a half hour for their baths; they like to play in the bubbles. But I can cut playtime shorter. Then there are bedtime prayers. Often Kitty requests a story afterward, but they can do without a story for one night."

"No, you do whatever it is you usually do. Don't cut things short on my account."

Her expression softened with something like wonder before she turned away. "You know where the kitchen is. Let them know Mom said it's bedtime." She said the last a little more loudly.

Jared watched her disappear down the hallway and into what he assumed was the bathroom before he entered the kitchen.

Mindy rolled her eyes and grinned. "We heard." She shot a look to her sister. "I get dibs on Mr. Suds," she said and ran out of the room.

"No fair! You had him last time." Kitty chased after her sister.

Jared chuckled, wondering why children always felt the need to run and where they got such energy. Sharon's children were beyond energetic; around them, he felt his years, even if they were only in the tri-decade. Again, he wondered if he had what it took to tackle such a feat. Most men started a family from scratch; he would get the full deal all at once.

God, if this really is Your plan, then You're going to need to equip me to be the kind of man they need in their lives.

Jared easily found the coffee and went about making it. The rich aroma permeated the kitchen by the time Sharon made an appearance. She seemed a little flustered.

"Everything okay?"

"Yes, they flew through their bath in record time. Really strange." She seemed preoccupied, worried. "They asked me to ask you something."

He lifted his brows, waiting.

"They want you to read them their story tonight."

"Oh." Jared hadn't expected that. He stood up from the table. "Do you mind?"

She shrugged as if she didn't care either way, but the troubled look in her eyes didn't match her supposed indifference.

༺☙

Sharon stood in the doorway of the girls' room and watched as Jared sat on Kitty's bed, a book in his large hands. Both girls sat on either side of him and cozied up to him as though he were their father. Kitty propped her elbow on his leg, leaning in to him, and Mindy craned close as though interested in the opposite page.

A sharp twinge pulled at Sharon's heart. They had never known the love of a father, though since she'd become a Christian over three years ago, she'd been trying to teach them about the love of their heavenly Father. Still, for two little girls not yet at an age to understand so much about life and death, or even about God, she knew it wasn't always enough to be told they had the affection of an invisible being.

They wanted visible arms of strength to hold them, an audible voice to comfort and assure protection in a way only a father could. She shared the girls' dilemma; she'd never known the love of an earthly father. Her birth father had died before Sharon was born, and her stepfather had been a beast; her mother too troubled with her own worries to care about the needs of her two girls. In all honesty, at times Sharon still felt disassociated from the world, and so very lonely. Lonely enough to yearn for a pair of strong, gentle arms to hold and comfort her, too.

She listened to Jared's low, soothing voice as he read the silly story of a lady-bug and a grasshopper, one that Mindy had long outgrown but now responded to with smiles and giggles as if it had been her choice.

Once he closed the book, the girls made it clear they weren't ready to let him go just yet.

"Tell us how you make candy," Kitty implored.

"And how you get the syrup out of the trees," Mindy added.

"Do you use straws?"

"Do you saw the trees in half?"

Under their sudden and fervent stream of questions, Jared looked a little taken aback. He caught sight of Sharon and gave a lopsided "how'd I get into this?" grin.

"Tell you what. Next spring, when it's sugaring time—what we call the time to collect syrup from the sugar bush, the maple trees—how about if I take you to the farm and show you how it's done?"

Kitty squealed. "Really? You mean we get to ride in the wagon with Tamany?"

"Well, Tamany will be leading it," Jared corrected, amused.

"Honest?" Mindy asked.

"If it's okay with your mom." All three looked at Sharon with pleading expressions. But a mischievous smile lifted Jared's mouth, and she detected a twinkle in his eyes, too.

He knew what position he'd placed her in. She should be irritated that he would force her to make such a decision in front of the girls. How could she say no when they looked at her with such big, pleading eyes, like little kittens in their fuzzy white robes? Yet how could she say yes, when further attachment to Jared could only hurt them since he could never be the father figure they clearly expected? With a slight smile and an even slighter shake of her head, she narrowed her eyes, promising him a future reckoning.

"That's still pretty far in the future to make plans about now," she said at last.

"I know, I know," Mindy replied. "Live each day that comes without wondering or worrying what the future has in store."

The flip way Mindy spouted the mantra that Sharon had clung to and repeated during the most horrific days of her life made her feel a little sick inside. She glanced away, unable to look in their eyes as she tucked her daughters into their beds and kissed them good night. She sensed Jared watch her as he stood to the side the entire time.

Once she flicked the light switch and closed the door, he again looked at her. "You okay?"

"Sure. I just need to say good night to Andy. Go ahead and pour us some coffee—if you don't mind?"

"Of course not." He moved down the hallway, and Sharon watched him a moment before heading to her son's room. She tapped on the door. When he didn't answer, she nudged it open a few inches.

"Andy?"

Paying no attention to her, he sat on the bed, his back to her as he thumbed through a comic book. So that was how it was going to be.

She approached him. "I'm not going to get into a big recitation of what you did wrong out there—you already know. But what I want to know is why you're acting this way." She sat next to him, putting her hand on his shoulder. "What's bothering you, son?"

Her gentleness broke Andy, and he bowed his head, trying hard not to cry, then burrowed his head against her shoulder.

"I'm sorry, Mom. I just don't want him here. Why did he have to come, anyway?"

His answer confirmed her suspicions. "We're just friends, Andy. Nothing else. Everyone needs friends, and Jared is a nice guy." With the words aired, she realized how true they were.

"Yeah?" He pulled back and eyed her with suspicious anger. "And how long'll that last? How long till he hurts you like Dad did?"

His words made her wince. Not for herself, but for her son. "Andy, not all men are like your father—"

"You said Dad was nice, too, when you first met. That's what you told us."

Sharon drew a sharp breath. She'd been fooled by Mark's charm and sweet talk, but their marriage hadn't been bad until he mixed with the wrong crowd after losing his job. He'd started taking drugs and drinking more heavily.

"What do you want me to do, Andy?" She withdrew her arm from around his shoulder and studied his face. "You want me to be without friends?"

"You have us."

She hugged him to her again. "Yes, I do. And I love you guys bunches. But you're my children; when I say friends, I mean adult friends."

"What about Leslie and Jill and Carly?"

"You're right. They're my friends, and I'm thankful for them. But they're also married women with lives of their own and new babies to take care of, besides. Babies are wonderful blessings from God, but they can be a handful and take a lot of a mother's time. I talk to Leslie and the others on the phone and see them at church, and that's great. But sometimes I enjoy having someone my age to hang with, too."

At first, it hadn't mattered; her children were everything to her and still were. But in the last year, Sharon had begun to feel the loneliness sharpen and produce within her a strong desire for adult companionship.

He scowled. "Like Mr. Crisp."

Sharon sighed. "Jared has shown our family nothing but kindness, Andy. Taking time out of his life to help us, to drive us where we needed to go, even helping to save the moose calf." It was the wrong thing to say.

"It's because of him I lost her!" Andy shot back, his eyes burning with hatred again. "If he hadn't called his stupid sister-in-law, then she would've never taken Caramel away."

"That's enough, Andy." Sharon rose from the bed. "We did what was right and what was lawful. We've talked about this before, and you know how I feel. End of story." She bent and kissed his brow, but he didn't respond. "Lights out. Tomorrow is another day, and it'll be here before you know it."

She exited the room, turning back at the door to see him sitting in the same position. Sighing, she clicked off the wall switch, leaving him in the glow of his bedside lamp, and shut the door.

Their conversation escalated her agitation coming so soon after watching the happy picture of Jared with her girls. As she walked into the kitchen, Sharon reached a decision, one made no easier with the friendly smile Jared beamed her way.

Chapter 6

Jared knew something was wrong when Sharon didn't return his smile. She seemed edgy again, offering him only a fleeting look before heading to the cupboard to pull out a box of powdered sugar doughnuts.

"Want some?" she asked.

"Sure. I poured the coffee," he added unnecessarily, since she had already seen the mugs.

"Thanks." She set the box on the table between them. "I'm sorry I only have prepared foods to offer you. I don't cook meals from scratch anymore."

"Do you hear me complaining?" He studied her, puzzled. "As long as it's good, I'm happy. And the meal was great."

Still, she seemed distant as she pulled a doughnut from the box, dunking it in her black coffee. Jared did likewise with his sugared coffee, then wished he hadn't once he took a sip; the powdered sugar made the coffee too sweet. He took another sip anyway, trying not to wince.

Sharon's mouth twitched. "You don't have to drink it, Jared. I can get you a fresh cup."

Before she could take away his coffee, he wrapped his fingers around the handle. "It's all right."

"I know it's not the best coffee, but it was on sale—"

"Sharon." He set his mug down. "Will you please stop apologizing? There's no reason to."

She seemed surprised by his gentle request and looked into her mug a moment. He wondered if she always beat herself up over inconsequential matters.

"About Andy. . .again, I want to apologize for his behavior. To understand what's going on with him, you'd have to know what he's been through these past few years." She ran her finger along the inside loop of the mug's handle, her eyes intent on her action. "My husband died in prison. He attacked a woman—a friend of mine now, actually—who writes a local advice column. Mark arranged a meeting with her in a park a few towns away and stabbed her there."

Jared sat still, dreading what was coming but, at the same time, needing to hear it.

"I'd written her for advice. Mark found out and. . .well, let's just say he wasn't happy. Things came to a head, and I left with the kids. He pretended to

271

be me, to lure Dear Granny to the park—that's the pseudonym she uses for the column. To honor a promise, I can't tell you her real name, though you probably know her. Anyway, I called the police when I read the newspaper account and realized it had to be Mark. He was convicted and sent to prison for his crimes, which included not only attempted homicide, but also possession of narcotics, firearms, and a few other tidbits the police found when they searched the house. I wasn't there; I'd gotten away from him long before that."

Jared briefly closed his eyes and swallowed. Things were falling into place.

"I visited him in prison, though. He was still my husband, and I was raised to believe that you don't just ditch a marriage. More than anything, I wanted Mark to change. Those last years with him, when things got bad, I kept hoping he would, but it never happened. Each time, he promised he would, but he never did."

Her words came fast as if she needed to get them out before she lost her nerve. "I visited him twice a month for almost five years. But it was the strangest thing—a Christian ministry also visited the prison and brought literature, books, and magazines. One of the cons even headed a Bible study. He persuaded Mark to join—they were cellmates—but it took a while before Mark agreed to try it. I'd talked to him about God, too; I was a new Christian at the time, thanks to Dear Granny." She smiled secretively. "And I wanted my husband to find Christ. Despite all he'd put us through, I didn't want him to burn in hell. And I knew he was fast headed in that direction."

She shook her head, giving a small, humorless chuckle. "The irony of all this is that he *did* come to accept Christ through his cellmate. And during that last year I saw a real change. I began to hope life could be different for us, even though he'd be in prison a long time. Next thing I know, I get a phone call about a prison fight and that Mark got stabbed. I talked to his cellmate after I collected his personal items, and he told me Mark had nothing to do with the outbreak but was just in the wrong place at the wrong time. That the last thing he whispered before he died was to let me know how sorry he was and that he loved me and the kids."

Sharon swiped at her eyes with an impatient, brisk motion. "Sorry. I promised myself I wouldn't do that." She cleared her throat. "Anyway, Mark died last year, and Andy is still dealing with hard issues concerning all of it. At this point, he resents male interference. He's been the little man of the family ever since I left Mark. A daunting responsibility for such a young boy but I never expected him to do that. He took on that responsibility himself."

Jared wanted to respond with sensitivity, but a probing question intruded. "Did your husband, did he. . ."

"Hit me?" she asked when his words trailed off. At his brusque nod, she took another sip of coffee. "Yes, when things got bad after he lost his job. I used to not be able to talk about it; that I can shows progress."

Her slight smile hinted at an undergirding of strength. "I attended a Christian-based support group for abused wives, even before Mark went to prison. Through that, I've learned some things. Among them, that I don't deserve to be a punching bag to anyone, that God made me, that He loves me, and that I'm important to Him. In the past two years, I've begun to heal and have grown closer to the Lord. I've put the past behind me and moved forward, but for the kids, it's harder. I left the very day Mark started taking out his anger on them, so they didn't get a lot of it. But Andy is the oldest, and he remembers. Everything. Mindy, I'm not sure sometimes what she's thinking, and Kitty was only a baby. But now and then with the things she says, I think she must remember something."

Sharon bowed her head and shook it. "I can steer them in the right direction, but that's it. I can't force anything—either their forgiveness of their dad or for them to let go of the pain and the past."

Jared nodded, thinking how much she'd taken on her shoulders. "When we met, I thought you were a good mother. . ."

Sharon's head jerked up, as if she expected a verbal blow, and he wondered if she received criticism from others for the decisions she'd made.

"Now I know you're a superior one."

She went a shade of rose, and with the way she averted her eyes, he knew he'd embarrassed her with his praise. "I'm glad you feel that way, Jared. It makes what I have to say a little easier."

Jared tensed.

"I have to keep my daughters' best interests in mind, and I've seen some things that disturb me." She fiddled with her doughnut, dunking it but not eating it. "They've become attached to you, in such a short time. That worries me, because I think. . ." Her dunks became more frequent, her doughnut smaller as sodden chunks fell away; still she didn't meet his gaze. "I think they expect more to come from this association than will happen. And I don't want them hurt." Her eyes lifted to his. "You understand my position, don't you?"

"I'm trying to." Jared watched her closely. "So you think we should talk to them? Explain things?" He had numerous nieces and nephews but didn't really know the first thing when it came to dealing with children.

"Actually. . ." She looked down at her coffee again. "I think it would be better if we just stop this before they get hurt."

"Stop this?" Jared didn't look away from her. "You mean stop seeing each other?"

"You make it sound like a whole lot more than it is," Sharon accused, and Jared looked down, acknowledging the truth of what she'd said. "This was supposed to be all about friendship, Jared. Nothing more."

"You're right. I'm sorry. That came out wrong."

God had told him one thing; Sharon told him another. Free will had everything to do with a person's future. He couldn't force Sharon to change her mind; he wasn't that type of person.

"So since we hardly know each other," she continued, "and since upon knowing each other, things haven't always worked out well. . ." Her words trailed off, and he knew she meant Andy. "I think it best if we just keep our distance from now on."

"That sounds almost hostile."

Her eyes flicked up, and in them he saw what looked like disappointment. For the first time he realized her pain and also the surprising hurt he felt.

"Sorry, I didn't mean to come across as sounding obstinate," he amended. "I don't want to make waves in your family, Sharon. Not when you're working so hard to make things right again. So I'll get out of your hair." Now that she'd made her wishes known, he felt like an intruder. He scooted his chair back from the table.

"You're leaving?"

The plaintive surprise in her voice shocked him. She averted her gaze a moment as though flustered by what she'd said.

"I mean, you don't have to go right now. Since you're already here and all."

"Suddenly I don't feel much like talking." He tempered his stiff words with a semismile. "Supper was great. You're an excellent cook, and I had a good time. I'll leave the movie here. The kids may want to watch it again. I know my nieces and nephews are like that. It's due back a week from today."

Sharon's expression remained troubled. "Thank you."

"Not a problem." He forced himself to relax. She couldn't help the way she felt; she only put her kids first, like any good mother. He wondered if she ever took the time to think about herself. "Take care of yourself, Sharon." He hesitated then held out his hand for her to shake.

She looked at it a moment, and too late he recalled that she didn't like being touched. That made sense now, too. But before he could pull his hand away, she placed her hand inside his.

Her hand was soft, warm, and Jared wished he could hold it forever. She didn't withdraw as quickly as she'd done on previous occasions, seeming hesitant to break contact with him.

Their eyes met, but before Jared could do something he would regret, he slid his fingers away. She began to rise from her chair, but he shook his head. "No need to walk me to the door. Finish your coffee."

Before he left the kitchen, he cast one last glance over his shoulder, noting she had barely moved and still stared into her mug. As he reached for the door, he sensed she had turned to watch him, but this time he didn't look back.

"You look awful," Carly said to Sharon as she jiggled her baby daughter, Mali, who fussed in her mother's arms.

"Carly's right, luv," Jill intoned in her Australian accent. "You don't look as if you've been getting enough sleep." Her own daughter, Jolene, napped in the shaded stroller in a froglike position that made Sharon wonder how babies didn't get cricks in their necks.

Sharon eyed her friends with a grimace. "Wow. Thanks." She turned to Leslie. "Anything to add to the collection of compliments?"

Leslie laughed. Paula played with a doll rattle on her mom's lap as the four women sat on a bench outside the ball park, one of the rare moments they'd forged to get together for a day out, even if it included their children. The mild, sunny weather had been perfect for their noonday picnic.

"I'm worried about Andy," Sharon admitted, watching her son toss a softball around the field with Kitty and Mindy. The three played with caution around the younger children—Leslie's girl, Marena, and Jill's boy, Titus, who chased like an excited puppy after the softballs that outstretched gloves missed.

"What's the matter with Andy?" Leslie studied him. "I hadn't noticed anything."

"I don't think he's taking everything that happened with Mark well."

"Who would?" Leslie sympathized. "It's a lot for a boy his age to handle. For anyone to handle."

"I know, but it's more than that." Sharon sighed and shifted position, propping her heels on the bench with her arms around her legs. "He's become entirely too protective of me—which is strange, since we've been arguing lately and he's so angry with me. Especially about that moose calf."

"The one Jared captured with a song?" Carly asked with a chuckle.

"Yeah." Word had leaked out about the moose calf's containment, though not from Sharon, and now Jared singing to the moose was the town's latest joke.

Besides spotting him at church from a distance, Sharon had rarely seen him in the two months since they'd said good-bye, but she noticed he took the ribbing very well. More than one local had teased him about serenading the moose calf. He and Sharon made brief eye contact—no more than a nod in greeting—but she'd felt his gaze clear down her spine. On those occasions, her breath caught, and she'd quickly focused her attention on something else. Or had tried to.

Carly leaned over and looked at her a little too intently. Mali's head rested on her mom's shoulder, her huge dark eyes observing Sharon as Carly patted her back.

"It wouldn't be just Andy you're upset about, would it?"

"Well, Mindy and Kitty have been moping around the house, too." But she knew the cause for their doldrums. They missed Jared and told her so at every opportunity. His presence did seem to brighten a room, as lighthearted and funny as he could be.

"Hmm. What about you?"

"What about me?"

"Have you been moping?"

"Why should I be moping?" Sharon felt herself getting defensive.

"Why, indeed?"

Carly's smile made her uneasy, and she averted her gaze to watch the kids toss the ball.

"I hear Jared is teaching both of the girls in choir this year," Carly said after a moment.

At her words, Sharon almost snapped her neck with how fast she turned it. "Along with ten other children, yes, he is. He volunteered till someone else comes along." Too much; she'd said too much, and Jill's surprised glance in her direction told her so.

"You spoke with him about it?" Carly pursued.

"We, um, spent a couple of days together a while back." At their intent expressions, she hastily added, "His aunts offered his services to drive me and the kids around on errands."

"Oh." Carly seemed disappointed. "I thought you meant like a date."

Sharon's face warmed at the memory of inviting him to supper. She and Jared knew she had made the offer in friendship, but her friends would see it differently. "No, not a date. I don't date."

"Too right," Jill said. "And neither does he."

"I know; he told me."

Carly's eyes widened.

Stupid thing to say, Sharon. Really stupid.

"You talked about his love life—or rather his decision to go without one?" Carly asked. "That conversation must have gotten rather personal."

Sharon slid her feet to the ground and rubbed her hand down her jeans, uneasy. "He told me about waiting for the woman God handpicked for him— after I said I wanted to keep our relationship friends-only." Her face reddened more as Jill's mouth dropped open. Leslie also stared.

"Meaning I warned him in advance, before he got it into his head that anything could go further—but this was before I knew about his feelings on dating." She didn't dare tell them what Jared had blurted out the moment he saw her. She hadn't been able to get that first meeting out of her mind. "You know how I feel about all this; I've told you I never plan to marry again. So. . ." She attempted a bright smile. "Can we just change the subject? Carly, you never did tell me how that book deal went down."

Carly hesitated as if she might pursue the topic, then shrugged. "I'm not sure yet, but the editor seemed interested in seeing more. *A Short Guide to the Long Trail* might just find a home after all."

"How does Nate feel about it?" Sharon asked, relieved that the spotlight was off her.

"He's already debating on whether we'll buy a summer beach house in Hawaii or a small chalet in Switzerland." Carly rolled her eyes and laughed. "I tried to explain that the career of a writer and bars of gold bullion don't necessarily go hand in hand. But he says he has faith in me, obviously more than I have in myself."

"I'm glad things have settled down for him and his family," Leslie said. "He deserves a vacation to both places. Blaine and I were talking the other night, and we think it just isn't right for a community to show hard feelings toward an innocent relative of a convicted criminal, no matter the situation."

Of the three women, Sharon felt closest to and admired Leslie the most. Sharon's husband had stabbed Leslie in the park upon learning she was the advice columnist, Dear Granny. Since Sharon had met her to apologize on the day of Leslie's discharge from the hospital, the two women had grown close, and Leslie had been the one to lead Sharon to the Lord.

"I agree," Carly said. "Things have quieted down since Nate's stepbrother was convicted. But I'm really thankful to be living in Goosebury and not in Nate's hometown, so Nate doesn't have to deal with any of the flack there; his dad wrote that some in town still treat them badly, though Nate's stepbrother was sent to prison for his crimes."

At the word prison, something tightened inside Sharon, and Carly drew her brows together. "Sorry. That was a bad slip."

"It's okay." Sharon shrugged. "It's been over half a year."

Several seconds of uneasy silence passed before Jill spoke. "I seem to remember once, Carly me mate, when you were quite fed up with your hometown and ready to fly the coop."

Carly let out a sheepish laugh. "Yeah, well, that was before I found you guys. And before my dad and I got to know one another. And before I met Nate, and he moved up here. Life has taken a definite upswing since those days. And in ways I never imagined." She peered down at Mali's rosy face. The baby slept, content on her mama's shoulder. "Even my aunt has softened around the edges with Mali's arrival."

"And who could blame her? Mali's a little gem," Leslie said.

Something clutched Sharon's heart as she looked at the sleeping baby, who had her mama's eyes and thick black hair. Sharon had never had the big, happy family she'd envisioned, but she didn't dare go too far down that trail of thought.

She had miscarried her fourth child months after Mark's arrest, and though years had passed since that time, the loss still stung.

They talked fifteen minutes longer about home, husbands, children, and work before Leslie said she had to go. The others also needed to get home for one reason or another, and Sharon's own laundry awaited, as well as the recent lists of school supplies she'd received. She couldn't believe summer was almost over and the kids would be back in school within two weeks. For her children, it would be a new adventure, a new school, and again she worried about Andy. He had become so withdrawn and somber. She had thought at Jared's absence Andy would have perked up, but that hadn't happened.

"You know I'm here for you, right?" Once she'd buckled the still-sleeping Paula into her infant seat, Leslie turned to Sharon, who stood between their cars. "Any time you need to talk, just pick up the phone. I miss having you for a neighbor."

"Me, too. But I needed something within walking distance of my job and a bigger place, especially since Andy needs his own room now. I can't believe he's almost a teenager."

"You could still call."

"What with your answering all your readers in your column and taking care of your family, I didn't want to intrude with my problems."

"It wouldn't be an intrusion, Sharon. I still make a habit of getting together with Nana on Tuesdays to sort through the reader mail, but even Dear Granny needs a break." She winked at the use of the moniker that she and her nana cowrote under. "I wish you would join us for the Bible study at Jill's."

"If I had a car, I would. It's my next planned purchase. But I can't borrow Loretta and Josephine's car on Wednesdays because they go out for bingo night."

"Blaine is putting our car in the shop, and we're hitching a ride with Carly." Leslie thought a moment. "Did you ask her for a lift? They just bought that minivan."

"I don't want to be a pain. I still don't know her that well to ask for favors."

"Are you kidding? Carly thinks you're great. Believe me, she doesn't think of you as a pain. Do you want to go next week or not?"

"Well, yes, but—"

Before Sharon realized what Leslie had in mind, her friend called across the parking lot. "Carly! Can you give Sharon a lift to Jill's house Wednesday night?"

"Leslie!" Sharon argued under her breath.

"Sure," Carly shot back with a smile. "The more the merrier."

"See how easy that was?" Leslie's eyes twinkled as she turned back to Sharon. "Though her clichés sometimes get a little hard to take." She grinned. "To be fair, she comes up with some original lines, too."

"I think Carly's and Jill's gung ho attitudes have rubbed off on you."

"I hope you're not upset?" Leslie's smile faded. "It's just that we both know you need Christian fellowship outside of church, and I've been wanting to get you over there for some time. We make a regular party of it, you know. After Bible study, we talk, eat, even shoot pool. The girls against the guys."

"I haven't shot a game of pool since Mark and I were dating," Sharon mused.

"Then you play? Great!"

"Well, I am a bit rusty." Sharon laughed.

"I'm sure you'll pick it up again in no time."

"Mom?" Kitty impatiently called from the rolled-down window. "Are we going soon?"

"I'll let you get back to your kids," Leslie said with a grin. "And I need to get home, too. Blaine gets off work early today, and I don't want him coming home to an empty house. See you on Wednesday night!"

"Okay." Sharon slid behind the wheel of Loretta and Josephine's car.

"Are we going to Jill's?" Mindy asked before Sharon had a chance to slip the key into the ignition.

My, what big ears we have, she thought with a wry shake of her head.

"I'm going this Wednesday night, but you'll stay with a babysitter."

"Aw, Mom," Kitty said.

"Will anyone else be there?" Andy asked from the front seat.

Sharon darted a look his way, noting his intent expression. "Yes, since it's a Bible study I'm sure other people will be there."

She didn't elaborate, though she felt she knew to whom her son referred. But Jared must not be one of the regulars, or Leslie would have said so.

⌒⁓

"Hey, buddy," Nate said as he came up to Jared and slapped him on the back. "Been serenading any sweet moosies lately?"

"Funny," Jared said without looking up from sorting the different music printouts into folders. Choir practice had let out twenty minutes before, but he had some things to organize.

"So how were things at the kiddie zoo?"

"You're beginning to sound like your wife."

Nate laughed, and Jared glanced up, a grin edging across his features. It had been a difficult practice; "zoo" about defined it, what with Jim-Jim the Peril instigating all manner of pranks, yanking Kitty's ponytail, and getting into more mischief besides. The kid had a voice that should accompany a halo, but sometimes Jared wondered if horns hid beneath his red hair.

"You look like you could use a reprieve," Nate said, taking a seat on the bench. The sanctuary where they practiced every Saturday almost echoed in the afternoon quiet. No more cries of "I'm telling," giggles, or chattering filled the white-steepled church.

"Brother. And how!" Jared exclaimed, sticking the folders in his briefcase.

"You should come to Jill's this Wednesday. We're following a schematic of New Testament readings the pastor sent different groups, and just between you and me, we could also use another good hand at the pool table afterward."

Jared laughed. He'd shot pool over at Nate and Carly's a few times before. The pool table had been a housewarming-wedding gift to the couple from Nate's father.

"I thought the Bible study at Jill's was mainly for young married couples."

Nate looked at him as if he'd swallowed a minnow. "What gave you that idea?"

"Well, could be because the group is composed of couples, all who've been recently married."

"I didn't start going there until after Carly and I married, but Carly attended before that."

"Oh yeah?" Jared mulled it over. "I might give it a try, then."

"Need directions?"

"No, I've got it covered." Jared picked up his briefcase. "I better scoot. I'm expected at Tom and Carol's for supper."

Nate walked with him through the front doors, and Jared pulled out his keys to lock the church, noticing that it had started to rain again. Outside, under the eaves, he saw two children with their backs to the wall.

"I'll catch you later," Nate said with a wave. He took off at a jog for his car.

"Mindy, Kitty, what are you girls still doing here?" Jared asked, holding the door open.

"Mom didn't come," Mindy said.

"She must be running late," Jared assured. "Come inside, out of the rain."

The girls hurried through the door, obviously glad he'd found them.

Sprinkles of water darkened their T-shirts, but they didn't look as if they'd been outside too long. He hoped the rain would pass soon. A streak of lightning followed that thought.

"I'll bet she forgot about us," Kitty said to Mindy. They stood, hugging themselves, their noses pressed to the glass on each side of the door.

"I doubt she forgot you," Jared said, wondering where they'd gotten such ideas.

"She's been acting weird for weeks," Mindy argued. "All spacey, and sometimes I have to say her name a few times before she answers."

"She probably has a lot on her mind." Jared thought about Mindy's words and wondered if Sharon's behavior had to do with Andy. "You two should help her out whenever you can. Do your chores and do what she tells you. Don't give her a hard time." He tempered his words with kindness.

"We don't." Mindy's eyes were wide with sincerity. "Honest."

"How come you stopped coming over?" Kitty wanted to know. "Don't you like us anymore?"

"Sure, I like you. I teach you songs every Saturday, don't I?" Jared felt put on the spot and peered out the window, hoping to glimpse his aunts' coupe.

"But how come you don't come to our house anymore?" Kitty insisted.

Jared paused; he didn't want to say anything that would make it worse for Sharon. "The supper your mom made me was a payback for the trip to the mall. That's all."

"She never paid anyone else back like that," Mindy said.

"What do you mean?"

"Whenever Leslie did us a favor, she never made her food. And she never used her best dishes, except when you came over."

That bit of news intrigued Jared. He had thought his chance with the girls' mom had ended with her announcement that they shouldn't see one another again, even as friends. Now he wondered.

At the sound of a horn honking, the girls spun around to the window. "She's here!" Kitty squealed, and they ran outside. Mindy tore open the passenger door, Kitty the back door, and in that moment, Sharon and Jared made eye contact.

Jared raised his hand in greeting; Sharon paused and then did the same before saying something to the girls, then returning her attention to the rain-spattered windshield, which the wipers worked to keep clear.

Jared watched the car pull away, the tires making wet sounds along the pavement. The girls waved to him, their faces almost pressed against the glass, and Jared smiled.

Maybe, just maybe, he had heard God right after all.

Chapter 7

Sharon helped Jill and Leslie prepare the food, setting it on the counter buffet-style. Everyone had brought a dish, and Sharon's french-fried onions over creamy green beans had garnered quite a few approving glances. As she shoved ice into cups and set them along the bar, the doorbell rang.

"A late arrival," Jill murmured. "I wonder who it could be. Hon?"

"I've got it," Ted answered his wife. Sharon heard the sound of the door opening in the next room. "Jared! It's good to see you, buddy. Come in and join the party."

The moment Ted said his name, Sharon dropped the cup. A good thing she'd held it poised over the ice chest and it only hit the cubes. She fetched it out and, with trembling hands, resumed her task.

Jared had come? Had Leslie known he would when she invited Sharon to the Bible study last week?

A glance toward her friend showed Leslie's surprise at seeing Jared walk into the kitchen, where the group had gathered. Sharon felt his presence without needing to look. The sound of his rich voice greeting the others brought chill bumps over her arms that had nothing to do with the frozen air of the chest. She pulled out the cup and carefully set it at the end of the row, next to the other six. Wiping her hands on her jeans, she turned.

Jared seemed just as shocked to see her. His blue jeans and maroon pullover seemed to make the other men fade into the background. Something in his eyes flamed to life as he looked at her, making it difficult for her to swallow.

"Hi, Sharon."

"Jared."

He held her gaze a few seconds longer, then, as if sensing her unease, focused his attention on the men's discussion of the upcoming football season.

Sharon forced herself to concentrate on her task as she filled an extra cup with ice for the new arrival.

After Ted said the blessing over the food, they ate. Sharon took a seat at the table between Leslie and Carly, who told them news about a young friend of hers with excitement. Jared joined the other men in the den, making it easier for Sharon to relax, though knowing he sat only a room away made her tingle with a strange awareness of his presence. His warm voice rose above the other men's as he joked and laughed with them.

"I was floored when Kimmers told me the news," Carly said. "A friend I met on the trail years ago. You might have seen her at church. Pretty, going on nineteen, walks with a white cane?"

Sharon nodded.

"She's been blind for a few years now, and they thought it would be permanent." She looked at Jill. "This new procedure isn't as risky as the ones she could have gotten years ago. She and her dad decided against them, and the doctor told her she's the perfect candidate for this one."

"I think it's amazing," Jill said. "Technology and medicine certainly have advanced in this past year alone."

"When is Kim's surgery?" Leslie asked.

"Nothing has been scheduled yet. I'll let you know when."

"Are she and Chris still going out together?" Jill asked.

"Oh, yeah. He's head over heels in love, has been ever since he was a groomsmen at our wedding and Kim was my bridesmaid. From what she told me, she feels the same about Chris. Chris is Nate's cousin," Carly explained to Sharon. "And Kimmers is already like part of the family. She came with Chris to Nate's family reunion this past summer. Everyone adores her."

"So they're that serious?" Leslie asked. "They're still so young."

"It wouldn't surprise me if they ended up marrying sometime in the future. They're rarely apart."

The women expressed their delight at such an idea.

"I got an announcement card from Sierra and Bart the other day," Jill said. She smiled at Sharon. "Good mates of ours who joined us on the Long Trail and came to our Bible studies. They moved to Phoenix two years ago. Anyway, Sierra had twins! Can you believe it?"

"I know," Carly enthused. "I got a card from Cat, too. I think it's fantastic!"

Sharon smiled at Carly's use of nicknames for her friends. The talk evolved to the children.

"Great news," Jill said. "Ted's niece agreed to come over and babysit on Bible study nights. Not only that, but they'll have their own Bible-incorporated playtime and teachings. She works in the children's church and is full of ideas." She smiled at Sharon. "So be sure to bring your kids next time."

"Thanks, I will. The sisters were thrilled to spend time with them tonight. They're making chocolate chip cookies."

"The sisters. . .you mean Jared's aunts?"

"Yes." Sharon took a quick bite of fruit salad, glad for something on which to focus her attention. "They dote on the kids as if they were their grandchildren."

She didn't miss the pleased looks that Leslie, Carly, and Jill exchanged, but to her relief, no one raised questions about Sharon and Jared or a relationship.

If he overheard any speculation like she'd endured at the park, she would have burned with mortification.

Once the women stored the food in the refrigerator, they gathered in the next room for Bible study. Sharon wondered if it was mere coincidence that the only available seat for her was beside Jared on the sofa.

She sank to the cushion beside him, and he gave her a friendly smile.

"How have you been, Sharon?"

"Great." She returned his smile. "Helping the kids get ready to start a new school. Their first day is just around the corner." *The girls miss you, and I don't know what to do about it, since I feel the same but don't want to feel this way.*

"I've seen the girls at choir practice, of course, but how's Andy?"

"As well as can be expected, I guess." Her smile wavered; she tried not to show concern.

His expression gentled. "What's up? Has he been giving you problems?"

From anyone else, Sharon might have taken offense at the inquisitive remark. But she felt relief that Jared had opened the door for her to talk about Andy. She assumed it was because Jared knew about their past. She'd told very few people.

"I worry about him. He's been so distant lately, hardly talks to me anymore, and he spends too much time in his room."

Jared thought a moment. "Have you taken him to see the moose calf?"

"Why, no. . ." Sharon wondered if something so small could have had such a big effect on her son. Remembering his behavior the first few days after they rescued the animal, she realized it must. "I'd completely forgotten I promised the kids we'd visit again; I've been so busy. But then, he didn't bring it up, either," she added in confusion.

"I guess he figures if he did you might ask me to drive you there again."

"And so he picked the most appealing scenario of the two choices—to stay away from the farm," Sharon agreed. "I'm sorry." She winced as she realized how bad that sounded.

Jared shrugged. "It didn't take an anvil to fall on my head for me to figure out Andy doesn't like me."

"Not just you, Jared. I think he'd be that way with any man."

"I know."

Their conversation ended as Jill began the study. Everyone opened their Bibles to 1 Corinthians. With amusement, Sharon noticed that handwritten notes and fluorescent highlights marked the pages of Jared's Bible, as well as her own. The study continued, the reading concluded, and Jill opened the floor for anyone to express what they'd gained from the reading. New to the study, Sharon kept quiet, wishing to observe this first time. Jared had no such compunction. She listened, amazed by his perception, inspired by his fervent and beautiful expressions of what the verses meant to him. She agreed with so many things he said; other remarks of his took her mind along new paths and struck a chord deep within.

After the study concluded, Jill and Leslie grabbed snacks while the others went down to the basement game room. A refrigerator there contained sparkling sodas, and Carly filled orders behind the wet bar, opening liter bottles and pouring sodas into glasses. Sharon helped and handed Jared the fruit spritzer he'd ordered—fruit juices and club soda combined.

"Thanks." His gray-green eyes connected with hers as she handed him his glass.

A rush of warmth she couldn't explain swept over her face. "Sure."

He lifted his glass a few inches as if toasting her before he moved toward a high, round table. He set the glass down and went in search of a cue.

How? How did he do that? Jared possessed the ability to stir something deep inside her without even touching her. He'd made no physical contact with her since his arrival, not even to shake her hand in greeting or share in a hug as he'd done with the others.

"Sharon!"

"What?" She jumped at the shock of Carly's voice near her ear, louder than usual.

"I asked what you wanted to drink." Carly's dark eyes gleamed in amusement as they darted to Jared, then back to Sharon. "But you seem to have your mind on other things at the moment."

"I think I'll have a fruit spritzer, too," Sharon said, making a point to ignore Carly's blatant teasing.

"A popular choice tonight." Carly's mouth quirked at the corners.

"I happen to like fruit," Sharon insisted. Both women glanced at one another, then burst out laughing. Sharon couldn't help herself; Carly's gregarious personality might at times set her on edge, but for the most part, her warmth put Sharon completely at ease.

"Well, that's terrific, Angel. Fruit is good for you."

"Angel?"

"My new nickname for you. Besides the fact that you look like one, I happen to know you sing like one, too."

"Not anymore. I don't sing anymore," she elaborated under her breath, hoping Carly would leave it at that.

"Hmm," Carly studied her a moment, then smiled. "Well, I could always call you Fruit-jitters, since you're so jittery and 'happen to like fruit.'"

This brought on another gale of laughter from both of them, and before Carly walked away, she said with a wink, "I think I'll just stick with Angel."

The game commenced—guys against the girls. As she'd warned the other women, Sharon hadn't practiced, and only after a number of turns did she pick up old skills.

"Want a few pointers?" Jared asked from across the table as she practiced in between games.

"Sure." Sharon had relaxed in the past fifteen minutes, joining in the fellowship and laughter, and her earlier uneasiness around him had disappeared. She expected verbal pointers, so when he came around the table to stand behind her, her heart beat a little faster.

Without touching her, he showed her a better way to hold the cue and crouched with her to eye the balls.

"Hey!" Blaine complained, his Texas accent strong. "What're you doin', Jared—goin' on over to the opposition's side? They sure don't need any tips."

"Sh!" Leslie gave her husband a playful swat on his chest, then reached up to whisper something in his ear. Blaine's eyebrows rose as he glanced in Sharon and Jared's direction, and she wondered what Leslie had said.

"The light above casts the ball's shadow onto the table in the direction you want to hit it." Jared's breath warmed her ear. Sharon shivered and closed her eyes for a moment.

"Steady," he said. "Keep your arm steady. Direct your shot as if to hit the shadow, but always keep your focus on the middle of the cue ball. If you hit the edge, it'll miss the mark and could go into a spin. You want to position yourself behind the ball so as to aim for that shadow. You have a good shot for the 2-ball from here. See how the shadow slants toward the corner pocket? Go ahead and try for it."

He stood so close she felt his body warmth, and that made her a bit lightheaded. One fraction of a move on her part, and her back would touch his chest.

"Steady, Sharon," he said. "Now, pull your arm back in one smooth move. Let the stick slide along your fingers, and keep it smooth."

Sharon swallowed and shot, but her arm jerked. She tipped the ball at the bottom, sending it into a jump.

"All right, good try. Let's give it another shot." Jared reached across the table for the white ball and repositioned it. "You need to relax more. You're holding the stick too tight." He paused. "Would you like me to show you what I mean?"

At her bare nod, he moved behind her again. This time, his large hand covered hers, unclamping her stiff fingers and positioning them until they loosely cupped the area near the bottom of the stick. With his other hand, he positioned her hand so that it formed a loose O near the top of the stick. He leaned into her, keeping his warm hands on hers, and pulled the stick back and forth in two graceful moves, the second much more swift. With a loud smack, the cue ball hit the red ball, which zipped toward the corner pocket and plummeted downward.

Sharon caught her breath the moment he touched her, stunned by the sudden awareness that she wanted this. She wanted Jared near. Even more shocking, she wanted him to turn her around and gather her into his arms.

The unexpected image of herself in Jared's embrace made her tense against him; he released her hands, stepping quickly back.

She straightened and licked her bottom lip before she looked up at him. He lifted his gaze from her mouth to her eyes.

"Anyway," he said at last, his voice a bit strained. "That's how it's done."

"Thank you for showing me," she whispered.

A clatter of footsteps on the stairs saved them from further conversation, as those who'd gone upstairs returned, and the second game began. Throughout the game, Sharon felt Jared's eyes on her a few times, but when she looked his way, he averted his gaze.

When his attention focused elsewhere, she watched him, admiring his attractive face and form. His features were strong and masculine but kind; she couldn't remember once seeing his face twisted in an enraged scowl, though he'd had good reason to be angry with her and her kids plenty of times. His body was lithe, trim, strong; she could see the muscles of his back and shoulders ripple beneath his pullover each time he bent low to take a shot. But protectiveness grounded his strength. She knew he would never hit a woman.

She wished now she hadn't told him they couldn't be friends. Twice before the party broke up, she almost told him so, almost asked his forgiveness, almost asked if he would try again. Both times she chickened out, and when everyone said good-bye for the night and went their separate ways, Sharon nursed a heavy heart.

"Jared, yoo-hoo, Jared!"

Jared turned outside the church steps to meet his aunts. They each gave him a hug, and he noticed they seemed to bristle with excitement. Their blue eyes sparkled.

"We wanted to invite you over—" Loretta said.

"For Sunday dinner," Josephine finished.

"We've cooked all your favorites."

Josephine nodded. "Roast beef and potatoes with cooked carrots—"

"And creamed corn," Loretta ended.

"Pumpkin pie. . ."

"And pecan, too."

Jared laughed, spreading his hands out as a sign for them to stop. "All right, already, you've convinced me. But as wonderful cooks as you both are, did you really think I'd need that much persuasion?"

"Oh, you are such a charmer," Loretta said.

"A real sweetheart," Josephine added.

Jared smiled. "Only telling it like it is. What time should I come over?"

The sisters looked at one another, then at Jared.

"Why, right now of course," they said in unison.

He chuckled. "I just need to talk to the pastor about the Christmas program, and I'll be there."

"There's still almost three months to go, isn't there?" Loretta asked.

"You must be excited," Josephine added.

Excited wasn't the word. Everything that could fall apart so far had, and Jared didn't want to fail in his first attempt as a choir director. Because many families went out of town at Christmas, the church held the program the week before the holiday, and he found himself wishing for that extra week. One of his leads and three others had recently come down with chicken pox; even though it was too early to worry about a lack in his cast, he knew winter often brought an outbreak of all manner of viruses. Sharon hadn't been at the Bible studies at Jill's for the past four weeks, and Leslie told him that one by one her children had succumbed to another bug going around. Today, he'd seen her and her family across the aisle in the back pew and had given thanks that everyone was well, but he couldn't rid himself of the feeling that something would go wrong with the program.

Once the service ended, he had headed toward Sharon to say hi, but another church member approached her, and he'd backed off.

He missed her. This past month had been harder than he'd expected. At Ted and Jill's, as he'd given Sharon pool tips, when he'd leaned toward her, so close he could smell her flowery perfume, his pulse rate had increased and he'd wondered if she could hear his heart beating. It had taken a great deal of self-control not to pull her into his arms and kiss her. He wondered what she would have done if he had. Of course, with the others looking on, giving them no privacy, it hadn't been an option.

After discussing set and performance issues with Pastor Neil, Jared drove to his aunts'. Kitty answered his knock.

"Jared!" She threw her arms around his hips and hugged him hard, burying her cheek in his stomach. "You came back."

Staggered by the unexpected welcome as well as by the identity of the welcoming party, Jared felt tongue-tied.

"Jared!" Mindy rounded the corner of the foyer. "Neatness! Are you eating with us?"

Us?

"Come in, Jared, come in," Loretta said, walking behind Mindy.

Jared had little choice even had he wanted to hold back. Kitty grabbed his hand and dragged him inside, as if impatient with his sluggishness.

"What perfect timing. Dinner's ready," Josephine said, coming behind Loretta.

"You didn't tell me you had other company," he said under his breath to his aunts.

"Oh, Sharon?" Loretta asked.

"She and her family always eat with us on Sundays," Josephine added. "Now come along before the food gets cold."

Having received nothing but welcomes, Jared prepared himself for Sharon's reaction. As he entered the dining room, she turned from setting the table.

She smiled a welcome, her eyes reflecting her delight as though she'd expected him. The afternoon sun highlighted her pale blond hair with golden-white highlights and reminded him of an angel. She wore a simple blue dress with no frills or decorations. It made her eyes even bluer.

"Hi."

For a moment Jared could only stare. This was the first time he'd been this close to her since the Bible study more than a month ago.

"Hi."

A string of questions from Kitty and Mindy forestalled anything else they might have wanted to say to each other.

Dinner progressed much like the first time he'd eaten there with Sharon and her family. Kitty and Mindy asked for more stories from Jared's boyhood, and his aunts embarrassed him by bringing up more of his immature pranks, which he then had to explain and expound upon. Andy glowered at him, wolfed down his food, and ran outside. The aunts fed off one another's sentences and continued to spur everyone on to other topics.

Once the meal concluded, Sharon began removing the dishes from the table, taking them to the kitchen in what he assumed had become her regular after-dinner chore. After she cleared the table of everything but Jared's setting, Loretta and Josephine smiled at him, and Josephine tilted her head toward the kitchen in a blatant sign that he should join their other guest.

"I think I'll take a breather on the porch while the weather's still nice," Loretta said. "Sister, won't you join me?"

"Why I'd be delighted to, sister."

Jared rolled his eyes at their obvious ploy and grinned. "If you two were any clearer, they'd have to mark your foreheads with masking tape so no one would walk into you," he joked.

Josephine tittered as she followed Loretta outside.

Jared finished the last bites of his meal, picked up his empty plate and glass, and carried them to the kitchen. Sharon filled one side of the sink with sudsy water, the other with clear rinse water. His aunts didn't use their automatic dishwasher, claiming it left ugly spots, and weren't willing to try newer models with the no-spot guarantee. So the dishwasher's sole purpose had become the drying rack.

He set his plate on the countertop and moved next to Sharon. She glanced at him, smiled, and continued her task. From the open window over the sink, a mild breeze wafted inside the room, which felt hot and stifling from dinner preparations and the cleanup involved.

"I hope you don't mind if I come in and pester you," Jared joked.

"Pester me? Are you kidding? It will be nice to hold a conversation with another adult for a change. I'm just about burned out on the topics of cartoon characters, comic book heroes, and the back-to-school blues the girls have been singing."

She swiped a plate clean with a sudsy rag and let it sink into the clear rinse water without letting her hand touch it. Though more steam rose from its surface than the side Sharon worked out of, Jared stuck his hand down to grab the plate. He winced as the liquid scalded, and snapped the plate up and to the bottom dishwasher rack in one swift, circuslike move, almost losing his grip.

"Maybe you'd better wait until the water cools," Sharon suggested with a half-concerned, half-amused smile. "Or your aunts might be minus a few dishes."

She had a point.

He cradled his hand beneath his armpit.

"Are you okay?" she asked.

"Never better."

Not sure of what to do with himself, but wanting to remain in her company, he moved behind Sharon to the opposite counter that angled with the counter-top where she stood, making an L shape. He shook his hand a few times but saw no burns of any degree, though the skin had reddened. His back to the counter, he braced his hands against the Formica and hoisted himself to sit on top.

Sharon turned her head to look at him, her eyebrows lifted.

"What?" Jared spread his hands wide.

With a little smile of disbelief, she shook her head and plucked another dish out of the soapy water. "Nothing."

He watched for a while, admiring the outline of her face.

"Do you really do all those pranks they said you did?"

He gave a sheepish grin. "Yeah, and worse."

"Worse?"

"Taping the kitchen sprayer's lever down so that when my sister turned on the water, she would get it—full in the face."

Sharon chuckled. "Now that was bad."

"You haven't heard the worst part yet," Jared said with a pained smile. "My mom was the one who turned on the water, not Amy. Amy got sick, so Mom took over Amy's chore of washing the dishes that night."

Sharon laughed. "Your poor mom."

"I like it when you do that," Jared said his tone soft.

"Do what?" Puzzled, she glanced at him.

"Laugh. It's good on you. You should do it more often."

Her face was already rosy from standing over a steaming sink, but with the way she looked down, he felt she might be blushing. Knowing he'd embarrassed her without meaning to, Jared slid down from the counter and returned to the rinse water. Skimming his fingertips over the top, he realized the temperature had cooled enough for him to pull out the clean dishes. He cleared the sink, setting the tableware in the dishwasher racks to dry.

"You know," she said after a minute, "this old-fashioned way of doing this is nice when it's shared. More, I don't know—homey? Instead of just quickly done and over with. It takes longer, but it gives people a chance to talk."

"My family is very old-fashioned when it comes to. . .well, just about everything," Jared admitted. "Though on the farm we've made some modern adjustments for convenience' sake."

Sharon spent an inordinate length of time cleaning out a glass, and Jared realized she had something on her mind.

"Kitty and Mindy really want to see your maple sugar farm next spring," she said after a moment as she handed the glass to him.

He rinsed it. "The invitation is always open. We get tourists year-round, and my family would love to meet you. I've told them a lot about you." He cut off his words, wondering if he'd said too much.

She cast him a sideways glance along with another smile, this one self-conscious.

"When we talked before the Bible study at Jill's, I said some things. . . ." Her words trailed off, and he kept himself from urging her to continue, patience never a great asset of his. "Truth is," she said as she washed another plate, "maybe I was wrong."

"Wrong?" He tried to follow her.

She quit rubbing the washrag in repetitive circles and looked at him straight on. "About us being friends. If the offer still stands, I'd like to take you up on it again."

Jared felt a twinge of disappointment. She only mentioned friendship, nothing more personal. But he realized a friendship with him was a major step for her. And he'd always known he would need to take things slow.

"Of course the offer still stands. I'm glad you changed your mind." He wondered if he should take it a step further, and decided honesty was always best. "I've missed you."

"I've missed you, too," she whispered, peering shyly up at him.

"Well then. . . ." He wanted to suggest another outing but refrained and let his words trail off. He should let her take the lead since she'd opened up negotiations between them again.

"Well then." She smiled and pulled her lower lip in her mouth in contemplation. "I'm taking the kids to Hugh's farm this coming Saturday; he's about to release the moose calf to the wild, and I promised Andy he could say good-bye. Would you like to come with us? Afterward maybe we could grab a bite to eat at a restaurant the kids enjoy."

She expected him to wait a whole week? Jared corralled his impatience to see her before then. Until that moment, he hadn't thought he'd spend time with her again at all.

"That would be great," he said. "I look forward to it."

Chapter 8

Mindy opened the door to Jared's knock.

"Hi, Jared. Mom's not home yet. She called and said she's running late, and to just come in and make yourself at home."

"Thanks." He smiled at the girl as he stepped inside. "Have you been practicing your lines for the program?"

"Yeah, but I gotta get back to my homework now before we go to your aunts' to be babysat. Mom said I have to finish before then."

Before he could say another word, Mindy ran to her room. Her door slammed, and Jared exhaled a long breath, looking around the empty den. Since their second trip to see the moose a month and a half before, Jared had taken Sharon and the kids out twice, to the movies and to eat at a kid-oriented restaurant. Tonight was the first night he would be with Sharon alone. Not a date, he reminded himself. You couldn't call Christmas shopping a date, and Sharon had shown no interest in crossing the sole-friendship sector. No matter, tonight would be the first occasion he and Sharon would spend time with one another, without the children, without his aunts, just the two of them alone. He wondered why he should feel so nervous.

Jared shed his jacket on the ottoman and walked into the kitchen as he'd done three Saturdays ago when he'd asked for a glass of water. Whenever he came here, he'd asked for water, due in part to the dry mouth he got each time he saw Sharon, who seemed more beautiful every time he saw her. Sharon had been busy the last time and had told him to help himself. He didn't think she'd mind him repeating the act, since she'd conveyed through Mindy the message to make himself at home.

He pulled a glass from the cupboard and turned on the faucet. A stream of ice-cold water hit him full in the face. Dropping the glass in the sink, he brought his hands up to shield himself from the watery assault. With one hand he groped for the faucet lever and turned the tap off. He grabbed the hand towel from where it hung and wiped water from his eyes.

A quick study of the sprayer showed duct tape held down the lever and a clamp that looked like it came from a children's toy set had been rigged into position straight toward Jared's face.

Andy's snicker heralded his entrance into the kitchen. "Did you have an accident, Mr. Crisp?"

Before Jared could answer, he heard Kitty squeal in glee and her running footsteps from down the hall. "Jared's here!" She turned the corner into the kitchen and stopped in her tracks, her eyes going wide.

With his hair dripping into his wet face and his blue shirt plastered to his shoulders, he knew he must look a sight.

The sound of the front door opening and closing made them all turn toward the doorway. Within moments, Sharon entered. Her mouth dropped open.

"Jared! What happened?"

Jared glanced at Andy, saw the bitter challenge in his eyes, and resumed toweling dry. "I had an accident."

"An accident?"

"Yeah, an accident."

Andy broke away from Jared's stare, looking uncomfortable.

Jared smiled at Sharon. "Are you ready to go?"

"I just have to get out of these work clothes and into some jeans. I'll be right with you." She cast a curious glance between Andy and Jared but left without another word. Kitty followed her.

Jared rubbed at the dampness on his shirt. Without looking at Andy, he spoke. "I take it you were eavesdropping on us while your mother and I did the dishes at my aunts' house several weeks ago."

"What do you mean?" The boy's words were wary. "I didn't do nothin'."

"The window was open, we were talking, and you'd gone outside. It doesn't take a mathematician to put the pieces together, Andy." He pulled the tape from the sprayer and held it up.

Andy narrowed his eyes, lifting his chin.

"This doesn't look like something either Mindy or Kitty would do." Jared undid the clamp that kept the sprayer nozzle aimed high. "And this, unless I miss my guess, is from a sci-fi toy set of a popular movie. My nephew Billy has one like it."

Surprise lit the boy's eyes a moment before the usual cynicism took over. "So if you knew I did it, why didn't you tell Mom?"

"Because this is just between you and me. I don't want to get your mother involved. She has enough worries right now."

The boy crossed his arms and scowled at Jared. "Yeah, well maybe you should just leave, and she wouldn't have any more worries."

"Have I done something to hurt you, Andy?"

"What do you mean?"

"Have I done anything to make you dislike me? I helped you save the moose calf, I took you to see it; I try to help you guys out whenever I can."

"Yeah, well, we don't need your help! So you can just stop helping us to make me like you because I'll never like you."

Jared laid the towel on the countertop and placed his palms against the edge, leaning his weight on them. "Let's get something straight. I'm not helping you for any reason other than I want to. Life is a whole lot nicer when there's not so much hate involved, Andy. Did you know it's easier to smile than it is to frown? The muscles work harder when you frown."

Disregarding his words, Andy's scowl grew even blacker. "You're not my father!"

"I didn't say I was."

"Yeah, well, don't try to be. Because you'll never be my father!" Andy raced from the room, and soon a door slammed down the hallway.

Jared sighed, wondering if he would ever make peace with the boy. Sweeping his hands through his damp hair, he tried to bring it to order. He had to chuckle. He supposed it was fitting that after years of instigating childhood pranks he should get his own dose. The Bible did say that you reap what you sow.

The sprayer safely disengaged, Jared pulled the glass from the sink, glad to see it hadn't chipped or cracked. He filled the glass with water and drank down half. Sharon appeared in the doorway, now in a cozy-looking gray fleece shirt and blue jeans, and Jared set down the glass.

"You look great." And she did. No matter what she wore, she made the outfit. Her choices always brought out the sheen of her hair, the startling blue of her eyes, and flattered her slender figure.

She smiled but seemed uncertain.

"Is everything okay?" he asked.

"I don't know, is it?" She moved toward him, her eyes taking in the strip of duct tape and the clamp at a glance. She raised her eyebrows as she looked at him. "An accident?"

"Yeah. I should've never turned on the water."

"Funny, Jared." She didn't look amused. "You shouldn't shield him like that. He doesn't need to think he can get away with this kind of behavior."

"I didn't want to upset you."

"I'm his mother."

"I know. But we talked, and I handled it." Jared winced when he thought of what a mess he'd made of things. "As a former prankster, I recognized that's all this was."

"Was it?" She shook her head. "I'm not so sure. But let's get one thing straight right now—no more deception. Even little white lies."

"You're right, and I'm sorry. I wasn't thinking."

"I know. You were just trying to get him off the hook." She sighed. "I'm not sure we should do this tonight. It's a good sale, but there'll probably be another. Maybe I should call your aunts and cancel; I'd hate for him to pull another of his stunts."

"I wouldn't worry about it; he'll behave for them. And my aunts love spending time with your kids. They told me so. Loretta doesn't have grandchildren, and they both dote on your kids. Besides. . ." He grinned. "They rented the new *Oliver Twist* movie. I'm sure they would be disappointed if they couldn't watch it with the kids."

"Well, a good dose of Oliver may be just what Andy needs," she mused. "It might help him be thankful for what he has and stop pouting about what he doesn't have."

Jared nodded, pleased that in the past few weeks she'd grown comfortable enough with him to discuss personal issues, at times asking for his viewpoint.

"All right," Sharon agreed. "Let's do this."

Once they dropped off the children at his aunts' house, Jared drove Sharon to the same mall they'd visited months earlier. Sharon noted the outside Christmas decorations though Thanksgiving was still a week away. Inside, holly and tinsel decked the stores, and piped Christmas music from an earlier decade played over hidden speakers.

"Leslie told me the toy store is located near this department store, but I guess we should find a directory."

"I guess." Jared shoved his fists into his jacket, nervous, as if he feared another experience like last time, and she chuckled at the memory of Kitty her clothes diva.

Outside the department store, they located a guide. Sharon found the toy store in the green grid, and noted it was twelve stores down. Quite a walk, but she'd worn athletic shoes, having expected the exercise. She noticed Jared glance with interest into each store's front window, as if he'd never seen the items on display before.

"Any time you want to stop and look, let me know," Sharon said. "I know you need to do your Christmas shopping, too."

"Well, no. I don't shop."

"You don't shop?" She gave him a curious, sidelong glance.

"Boxes of Crisp's maple fudge and other maple sugar products from our line to my friends. Gift certificates that I buy online for the family." He shook his head. "I'm not really into store shopping."

Sharon stopped walking and turned to stare at him. "Then why. . . ?"

"Why what?" His brow lifted in question.

"Why did you say you wanted to go Christmas shopping with me when I brought it up the other day?"

He grinned and grasped her elbow to steer her back into a walk. "Let's head for that toy store, shall we? Before those sale items are gone."

Sharon allowed him to steer her, noticing he moved his hand from her arm to the small of her back as they walked through the crowd. What surprised her wasn't that he touched her but that she welcomed his touch. Yet she feared that allowing such actions now could only cause problems in the future.

With relief and regret, she felt him drop his hand away as they entered the toy store.

The front display featured a huge, tabletop electronic building game encased in plastic, set up for shoppers to test. Jared's attention riveted to the beeping rubber-and-steel construction machine that a young boy worked hard to manage, using the lever on a control box to manipulate a steel claw.

Sharon's mouth twitched when she saw the light of boyish interest sparkle in Jared's eyes. "Go ahead and watch. It shouldn't take me long."

Without waiting for his answer, she picked up a shopping basket and studied the aisles, easily locating the doll section. She pulled a clipping of the sale ad from her purse and surveyed shelves with the help of the photograph. Soon she found its match. Three left, and two boxes dented, the film of plastic broken. She was glad now she hadn't put off the shopping trip another day.

All year, she put a little into savings each paycheck to make sure her children would have a Christmas. She would never forget the Christmas when she was married to Mark and the kids had woken up to nothing. She had planned to go shopping Christmas Eve but had discovered Mark had disappeared on one of his weeklong jaunts, taking the money with him. She had dipped her hand into the jar, which should have been filled with bills from the tips she'd earned at work, and found only pennies, nickels, and dimes. Mark had even taken the quarters.

A kind neighbor, Mrs. McGraff, learned of the incident when she saw Mindy sitting on the porch, crying that Santa had forgotten her. Thirty minutes later, the elderly woman appeared at the front door with boxes of hard candy and a batch of homemade cookies for the children to enjoy. Also in her arms had been a stuffed toy lion, used but still in good condition, a drawing set, and some unused coloring books and crayons. She explained to the children that Santa must have left them on her doorstep by mistake and that she'd heard the reindeer's harness and had peeked out of her window for a "look-see."

Mindy, then three, stared with huge eyes at the gray-haired woman, but Sharon would always remember the smile on her daughter's face as she grabbed the stuffed lion and hugged it to her heart. Mrs. McGraff later explained to Sharon that she kept toys for when her grandkids visited and hoped Sharon didn't mind them being used. Sharon, unable to talk at first for the happy tears, had squeezed the woman's hands in gratitude, calling her a Christmas angel.

Now that Sharon was a Christian, she wondered if God had sent Mrs. McGraff to them and had been looking out for Sharon and her kids even before she'd learned of His existence. As many times as she could have died from Mark's outbursts of anger, as many times as she and the children escaped, miraculously running into others who'd helped them, Sharon knew God must have been watching over her family from the start. At the women's shelter, Leslie had once told Sharon someone must have been praying hard for her. Remembering her grandfather in Ohio—whom the family had rejected upon his Christian conversion—Sharon wondered if he prayed for them.

She went down another aisle and located a football for Andy, hoping to steer his interest in sports and provide an acceptable outlet for his anger. A children's confectionery-bakery set for Mindy seemed a good choice. Since watching the flying-car fantasy movie and hearing about Jared's occupation, Mindy's interests revolved around joining a candy-making factory the first chance one opened in Goosebury. Adding several small, inexpensive toys for stocking stuffers to the basket, Sharon completed her task. For Jared's aunts, her friends, and the kids' teachers, she planned to make homemade batches of cookies or fudge, a tradition she'd started with the children two years ago and one Mindy would be even more enthused about this year.

Unable to fit the bulky bakery-set box into the basket, she wrapped her arm around the carton, holding it to her side. She walked to the front and stopped at the end of the aisle, astounded at the sight that met her eyes.

The boy who'd operated the electronic gizmo had gone; Jared now sat on the stool, his tall, trim form leaning forward, with the soles of his shoes on the rungs and his knees pressed against the table. His long fingers wiggled the lever of the hand-control box as he manipulated the steel claw to pick up a toy log. A lock of dark hair, usually swept back from his forehead, dangled across his brow. The tip of his tongue touched his top lip in a picture of studied concentration, and Sharon stood still as she watched him without his being aware.

A smile spread across her face. Jared was unlike any man she'd ever known; from the moment of their bizarre meeting, he had stunned her, confused her, and intrigued her. Her initial anxiety in his presence disappeared within twenty-four hours of knowing him, and now she saw another side to him she'd never realized existed. The heart of the little boy still lived inside the man.

"Excuse me," a woman said behind her.

Sharon apologized for blocking the aisle and moved aside. She would have loved to watch him longer and didn't want to disrupt his fun, but he caught sight of her, so she moved toward him.

"I always thought of going into construction." With a semibashful smile, he set down the control.

"Was this before or after you became an employee at your family's maple-sugar farm?"

"Well, I do run pipelines between trees and clear fallen branches from the paths," he said in mock defense. "That could be considered construction."

"It's certainly constructive," she laughed.

He noticed the box under her arm for the first time and stood. "Let me take that. Too bad this store doesn't have carts."

Unaccustomed to receiving help from a man, she felt a bit strange letting him take the huge box from her. It wasn't heavy, but it was awkward. "Thanks. My arm feels as if it's going numb."

"How long have you been holding this?" He easily hefted it beneath his arm, carrying it on his hip. "You should have asked for my help earlier."

"I didn't want to bother you."

"Bother me?" He seemed confused. "Sharon, I'm here for you. If you need my help, ask."

"I'm just not used to that sort of thing, Jared, asking for help or expecting it. My stepfather wasn't well-bred, and Mark certainly wasn't; I doubt either of them knew any manners at all. They expected their women to wait on them and be their slaves—the cavemen of the twenty-first century," she joked.

"Well, I'm not like them," he said, his expression serious.

"No, you're not. But then, I'm not your woman," she said before she thought.

The words hung between them, and she wished she could retrieve the tactless remark, even though it was true.

"No, you're not," he agreed quietly. "But I'm no Neanderthal, either. A woman like you deserves to be treated like a lady."

Uneasy with the personal direction his remarks had taken, she lifted her basket a fraction. "I should pay for these." He nodded.

Once they left the toy store, they remained quiet, and she hoped she hadn't offended him. Catching sight of one of her favorite kinds of stores, she grabbed his arm to stop him. He looked at her in surprise.

"Have you ever been to a Dollar Store?" she asked.

"Uh, nope, can't say that I have," he said.

"Well, you're in for a treat. Come on."

He answered her smile with a lopsided grin. Thankful the ice had again thawed between them, she led him through the crowded store, crammed with numerous baskets and bins of assorted merchandise. They maneuvered the aisles like little children let loose in a candy store. Jared slipped a reindeer puppet over his hand and made it talk to her in a high squeaky voice and "kiss" her nose. Sharon giggled both at his antics and at the anxious expression of the woman shopper who approached the aisle, studying Jared as if he belonged in a straitjacket.

Sharon couldn't remember ever having such fun with a guy. She held up cheap, dangly earrings to her ears for his advice, and he shook his head at each one, which she then replaced with another. His smile grew wide at a pair of long tasseled rhinestones. "Perfect." He grinned, then insisted on buying her a rhinestone tiara to go with them, placing the silver crown on her head and calling her "princess." She didn't even object to wearing it through the mall, despite the odd looks she received from other shoppers. Jared's fun-loving nature was contagious.

At the glass door leading out of the mall, he opened it for her and swept low in a bow. He straightened once she swept past and nodded his head in greeting at two elderly ladies who tittered behind their gloves as he kept the door open for them.

"Young love," Sharon heard one of them say to the other as the two women walked away. "So crazy, so sweet."

Sharon knew Jared must have heard, though thankfully he didn't bring up the woman's comment.

At his aunts' house, they rounded up the kids, and he drove them home.

"What's that on your head, Mama?" Kitty wanted to know.

"Hmm? Oh, just a crown," she said as if it was an everyday occurrence for her to wear a piece of jewelry from a children's play set.

In the rearview mirror, she saw the girls shrug at one another, though Andy looked less than pleased. Once Jared pulled his car into her drive, he cut the ignition and got out, going around to her side. To her shock, Andy bolted out of the backseat and opened her door before Jared could get there.

"Thanks, sweetie," she said, peering at him, curious.

The girls ran into the house, but Andy seemed intent on loitering. Sharon gave him a pointed look, but he pretended not to understand.

"Andy, it's bedtime," she reminded.

"Aren't you coming, too, Mom?" he asked, sending a baleful look Jared's way.

"In a minute. Go on."

With a scowl that had become common for him, he took off for the house.

"I had fun tonight," Sharon said when she and Jared were alone.

"So did I. I didn't know shopping could be that much fun."

Only with you. She had always considered it a chore before.

He came close to her, so close she saw the moon's reflection in his incredible eyes, making them shine almost silver. For one breathless moment, she felt sure he would kiss her. Her heartbeats escalated as she stood motionless. Her gaze dropped to his slightly parted mouth, which lowered a fraction toward hers.

The inhuman *yowwwwl* of a cat made them both jump away, and Jared's chuckle sounded self-conscious. Taking her hand in his, he bowed low over it, as if addressing royalty. His soft lips brushed her knuckles, and this time her heart jumped at the tingles that remained when he straightened.

"Good night, fair princess. The time has arrived that I must ride off into the black evening on yon charger, as daybreak shall, in due course, commence."

At her raised brows, he added, "Mrs. Beldon's literature class—Shakespeare, sophomore year."

Sharon laughed as she waved him off. "You nut. Off with you. Find some other lady to beleaguer with your questionable charms." She remembered a bit of Shakespeare from high school, too.

He clasped his hands over his heart in a dramatic pose. "Oh, the arrows of disdain doth pierce through my heart. Have you not a drop of mercy, dear lady?"

"None. Motherhood sucked it all out of me." She grinned. "Begone with you then."

"Alas and alack, I fear my words are of little merit here." He winked. "And so I shall make my fondest farewells."

"Isn't that what you've been doing for the past five minutes?"

He laughed at her quick comeback, saluting her with a more modern, pilot-type gesture, two fingers away from his brow. "G'night, Sharon."

"G'night, Jared."

She was still smiling as his car pulled out of the drive, and he stuck his hand out the window in a wave, one she returned.

The silence that settled in around her once his car disappeared down the lane seemed lonelier than ever. And in that moment before she turned to enter the house, she realized she hadn't wanted him to go.

"Jared, what are you doing to me?" she whispered.

A movement at Andy's bedroom window caught her attention. Her son's face stared out at her, his expression in shadow, and she frowned when she realized he'd been spying.

Chapter 9

At the Crisp farm, the onset of the holidays meant a huge boost in workload, with hundreds of orders for Christmas gifts readied and shipped to customers. The advance of autumn always brought more tourists to the farm, as well. But on the actual holidays, the family took time to rest and enjoy each other's company.

After Thanksgiving dinner, the men congregated around the TV to watch football, while the women clustered in the kitchen to talk while they cleaned.

Jared tried to get interested in the game. Normally, he liked football, but today he had too much on his mind. At halftime, he slipped on his coat and wandered outdoors onto the porch, studying the view.

Forests of snow-flocked sugar maples hemmed in all sides of the farmhouse, and in the background, he saw the rooftops of the buildings they used to make the maple syrup and store it, as well as that of a small gift shop. A thick blanket of snow covered the ground, and Jared wondered what Sharon would do if he drove up in a horse-drawn sleigh. She might enjoy the experience a lot more than the first time she'd ridden behind Tamany.

After their Christmas-shopping excursion, he'd almost kissed her. If the neighborhood cat hadn't picked that moment to start a screeching operetta, he would have. But in hindsight, friends didn't kiss friends, and he worried that if he tried again he might scare her away. He knew she was the one God had chosen for him, but she hadn't experienced that epiphany yet; until and unless she did, they must remain just friends. His mouth twitched at a bumper sticker he'd once read—"God, I need patience—now!" Still, in retrospect, he couldn't call a wait of over ten years impatient.

The door opened behind him. "Jared?"

His mom walked up to him, wearing her pink pullover sweater, her arms crossed over her chest.

"You shouldn't be out here without a coat, Mom," Jared quietly scolded.

She chuckled. "Are you kidding? It's nice to leave that hot, steamy kitchen." Her green eyes, almost lost between her laugh creases, studied him. They weren't laughing now. "Are you all right, son?"

"Sure. Never better."

"Didn't you like dessert?"

"What a thing for one of the best cooks in Goosebury to ask." He laughed.

"With a wall of blue ribbons to prove it." He pulled her up against him in a one-armed hug.

"In jams only. But you didn't ask for seconds of pumpkin pie. And you always ask for seconds."

"Maybe I'm trying to watch my weight?"

She slapped his stomach hard.

"Ow!" he joked.

"Tight and flat as an ironing board. You're not Tom. Your brother, now he does need to shed a few pounds."

"He must like Carol's cooking." Jared winked as he mentioned Tom's wife.

"Hmph." She studied him closely. "Mrs. Moorehead's niece has come to Vermont to visit over the holidays. She's staying through Christmas."

"That's nice. I'm sure Mrs. Moorehead will love her company since she doesn't get out much," Jared replied, ignoring his mother's obvious insinuation.

"I could introduce the two of you."

"I met Mrs. Moorehead back in fifth grade when she flunked me in spelling."

His mom struck him again.

"Ouch." He laughed. "Hey—now that did hurt."

"So tell me, would it hurt anything for you to go out with her niece one time? She's a nice Christian girl. I met her, and she's very sweet. I know you're waiting for the right woman to come along, but honestly, did God tell you that your mom couldn't give a little nudge?"

"Yes, it would hurt things, and no, He didn't. But I might as well tell you." He paused, wondering how much to reveal. "I found her."

"What?" His mom's eyes grew wide. "Who? What's her name? Does she live here in Goosebury? You cruel, heartless son—why don't you tell your poor mother these things?"

He laughed at her spiel of questions and raised his hand as if to calm a wild filly. "Whoa, easy there. Calm down, Mom. Nothing's set yet, but I'm sure she's the one."

"Well, hallelujah, I never thought I'd see the day. Does this blessed wonder have a name?"

"Sharon Lester."

"The woman with three kids, who works at Loretta and Josephine's shop?"

"That would be the one."

She tilted her head, watching him, as if considering something. "Why didn't you bring her over for Thanksgiving dinner?"

"I invited her, but she'd made other plans."

"Hmm. So when *do* you bring her home to meet the family?"

"I'm working on it. I'm still figuring out a way to broach the subject of a more personal relationship; she's going to take some careful handling."

"What's wrong with her?"

"Wrong with her?" He drew his brows inward, confused.

"That she doesn't see what a treasure you are."

He grinned. "And you wouldn't be just the least bit biased, would you?"

"Not a bit." Her words came sincere. "Just ask the rest of the single women in Goosebury who have, at one time or another, tried to capture your heart. Even your own sister-in-law, before you introduced her to Josh."

Jared chuckled dryly. "Yeah, well, this time I'm the one trying to capture Sharon's heart. I have to go slow; she's been through a lot, especially in her marriage. She's a widow by the way; I wouldn't even think of pursuing a married woman."

"As if I thought you would," she scoffed. "Your character would blind someone if the sun struck it; it's plated in twenty-four karat."

"Thanks, Mom, but I have my flaws. Remember all the practical jokes? Now and then, I still like to pull a few on my brothers."

Her eyes narrowed. "I'd forgotten about those. Hmm, maybe brass plated."

"And I had to go and remind you," he said with a mock groan. "I promise you'll meet Sharon soon. Her kids want to see how the maple-sugar farm is run, so I'm going to use that as a lure during the sugaring season, scoundrel that I am."

A smile of wonder tilted his mom's mouth. "You love her."

"Yeah," he admitted for the first time aloud. "I do."

☙

"I hate this stuff." Mindy frowned, her head buried against one hand, her elbow propped on the table. She poked at the mound of mashed potatoes and lifted her fork, letting what was on the tines plop to join the rest of the white mass.

"You loved mashed potatoes a week ago," Sharon said with fast dissolving patience. She had worked hard to prepare this Thanksgiving meal, even making from scratch the potatoes Mindy criticized.

"Why couldn't we have gone to Jared's?" her daughter plaintively shot back.

Kitty also looked up, her expression lackluster. "Did Jared ask us over?"

Mindy had overheard the conversation when Jared invited Sharon last week; Kitty had been in another room.

Andy grabbed his fourth roll, his appetite not the least bit affected. "We don't need to go anywhere else," he said to his sister. "We're a family, right? Just Mom and us, like it's always been. We don't need anyone else."

Just Mom and us. Sharon sighed. "Always" to a child could mean a matter of a few years, which was all it had been. In truth, she hadn't wanted to refuse Jared's invitation to spend Thanksgiving with him and his family. But lately, she'd felt confused by her feelings while in his company. The confusion made her wish to retreat, but when she did, she found all she wanted was to be with him. A vicious cycle she couldn't satisfy. Neither way made her completely happy.

"Why's the turkey all dry?" Mindy complained.

Sharon shoved the gravy bowl her way. "Put some of this on it."

"I don't like gravy. It has black dots floating in it."

"That's pepper."

"I don't like pepper."

Sharon had just about had enough of Mindy's dislikes. She rose from the table and carried dishes to the sink. "Fine, you don't have to eat. And you don't have to eat any cake, either."

"Cake?" Mindy perked up. "What kind of cake?"

"Carrot cake with cream-cheese frosting." Sharon smiled, glad to see she'd interested her cranky daughter at last. "I bought it at the bakery."

"Carrots in cake?" Kitty asked. "Yuk."

"What dork put cheese in icing?" Mindy agreed. "And whoever heard of carrot cake for Thanksgiving?"

Sharon threw down the trash she'd just gathered onto the bar. "Well, that suits me just fine! You don't have to eat any carrot cake." Tears rushed to her eyes, and the children stared at her, agape. "I'll eat the whole cruddy thing myself!"

They didn't respond, and Sharon, humiliated that she'd had a brief emotional meltdown in front of the kids, ran to her room and slammed the door.

She threw herself on her bed, knowing she had acted as much like a child as her kids. She felt horrible for sinking to their level, but she couldn't help herself right now. She felt empty, her heart so heavy it actually hurt to breathe. She did this for them. Couldn't they see that? If she and Jared did grow closer, when it ended—and it must end—his absence would only hurt the girls.

Her arguments against considering a second marriage failed to stir her resolve as they always had before. She knew Jared would never hurt her, would never ask anything of her she wasn't willing to give. He lived out his Christianity, and in the short time she'd known him, almost from the beginning, he'd found a door into her life she hadn't realized she'd left unlocked. Or perhaps his laughter and tenderness had been the key—

"Mom?"

Sharon jumped a little at the unexpected sound of Mindy beside her. She hadn't heard the door open.

"I'm sorry. I ate my potatoes and turkey, but do I hafta eat the cake?"

Sharon let out a laughing sob and rolled over to embrace her daughter. Mindy's arms squeezed her back just as hard.

"I guess I should've known better than to expect my kids to do cartwheels about a cake with vegetables in it, huh?"

Mindy giggled.

"Maybe there are some pudding cups still in the fridge."

"Chocolate?"

"Unless Andy found them, all that are probably left are the swirls."

"I like swirls!"

At last, Sharon had hit upon something her daughter liked.

"Moppet?" Sharon addressed Mindy by her special nickname. "Mama's sorry, too. It's been a rough week, but I shouldn't have taken it out on you guys."

"I understand." Mindy looked at her with wise eyes, and Sharon believed she understood more than Sharon was willing to say.

"Let's go get those pudding cups, shall we?"

"Yeah—let's!"

They were all sitting around the table in harmony as a family again, giggling over a joke Kitty had just told and halfway through the plastic pudding cups when the doorbell rang. Kitty rocketed off the chair before Sharon could stop her.

"I wonder who could be here on a holiday," Sharon mused aloud. "Everyone I know had plans."

Kitty came to the kitchen door, her eyes sparkling and her smile as big as Christmas morning. Jared entered behind her, his eyes just as lively, his smile a bit uncertain. A thought startled Sharon's mind: Now, her Thanksgiving was complete.

———

Chapter 10

Jared hoped he wasn't intruding on their holiday, but he saw by the food on the plates they had just finished dinner. At least the family, except for Andy, looked happy to see him.

"I just swung by. I gave the nieces and nephews a ride in the sleigh earlier and thought that while we still had daylight, you guys might like to take a ride."

He barely got out the last few words amid the little girls' squeals. Both girls shot up from the table and clustered around their mother.

"Can we, Mom?" Mindy begged.

"Can we?" Kitty repeated.

"Pleeease," both of them cried, before beginning another round of begging.

Sharon laughed and shook her head. "All right, all right, just give me room to breathe."

"Yea!" they shouted in unison before darting from the room. "Let's go see the sleigh!"

"Coats, hats, and gloves!" Sharon called, but they disappeared out the door.

"Once the outside air hits them, they'll remember," he assured. "What about you?" he asked when she remained seated. "Aren't you coming?"

"I probably shouldn't be getting out right now. I woke up with a tickle in my throat and can't afford a cold."

Jared felt disappointed; he had looked forward to this since he'd gotten the idea to hitch up Tamany and Treacle. He wondered if the suggestion that she wrap her neck in a thick scarf would sound too selfish and decided it would.

"That's too bad. I hope you feel better soon."

"I'm feeling better than I was. I just don't want to make it worse."

In the background, the door slammed, the sound of running feet and laughing complaints about the cold heralding the girls' reentrance. A door creaked open in the background, and Jared assumed they were fetching their outerwear.

He glanced at Andy, already sure of the boy's answer but feeling he should ask. "Would you like to take a ride in the sleigh?"

"Do Martians inhabit the earth?"

His gaze steady, he sensed a rude refusal. "No."

"There's your answer." The boy's eyes glimmered with their usual dislike.

"Andy," Sharon warned.

"No. . .thanks," he added, grudgingly.

Jared withheld a sigh, wondering what it would take for Andy to cease considering him as the enemy. "I talked to Hugh yesterday." He directed his words to Sharon while Andy started his third pudding cup. Two empty cups sat in front of him. "I was at the store picking up a few things for my mother and I ran into Hugh. He asked about you guys, said he wouldn't mind some help at the farm. Mentioned Andy and asked if I thought he'd be interested."

"He got rid of Caramel," Andy said sulkily.

"Well, he did say she seems to be doing fine. Apparently, she's been visiting the farm recently."

This got the boy's attention.

"My moose calf?" he asked, though Jared could see it was killing him to talk in a sociable way with him. "Caramel's been coming around Hugh's farm?"

"Yup, according to Hugh. He's been monitoring the calf's progress and still feeds it when it comes around. With winter coming on, he's short of help."

"Mom? Can I?"

Sharon's brow creased in worry. "He's only twelve," she said to Jared.

"I'm almost thirteen, Mom."

"And Hugh's farm is ten miles away," she continued as if Andy hadn't spoken. "What can Hugh be thinking?"

"Twelve-going-on-thirteen isn't so young," Jared assured, thinking of some of the jobs he'd had at that age. "It's only for several hours on the weekends."

"Mom, please?"

"What about school, Andy? That comes first."

"I'll study real hard and ace all my tests. I already have been, and the stuff we're learning now is so easy, it's boring. Please, Mom."

She sighed. "I'll have to think about this, Andy. I can't give you an answer right now."

Andy didn't argue with her, his expression that of a boy walking on thin ice. He rose from his chair, picked up his dishes, and stacked others on top, then took them all to the sink.

Jared acknowledged he probably should have discussed the matter with Sharon in private. If nothing else came from this, at least she wouldn't have to deal with Andy's misbehavior, what with the buttering-up job he witnessed. He watched Andy gather the garbage in preparation for taking it out, and from the perceptive smile of amusement Sharon sent Jared, he understood the boy's voluntary help wasn't a normal occurrence.

The girls appeared, bundled like miniature green and pink snowmen, and Jared escorted them out to the sleigh. First they insisted on petting Tamany and the matching bay, Treacle, their mittened hands stroking their velvet noses and necks. Tamany nickered and gave a slight toss of her mane, enjoying the attention.

Once he'd tucked them under the blanket and they took off, the girls squealed to hear the sound of the bells on the harness jingle, and Jared chuckled at their excitement.

"You girls act like you've never been on a sleigh ride before."

"We haven't."

Their answer surprised him. He was so accustomed to the sleigh that the novelty of the event had worn off long ago. But through the girls' eyes, he experienced the ride as if for the first time.

Mindy and Kitty squealed and waved to any passersby they met, those on foot and in their cars, as if they were princesses in a parade acknowledging their devoted subjects. Jared noted that cheerful smiles and amused waves always answered their exuberant welcomes. The holidays brought out the best in everyone. Their town was friendly, but especially around the holidays, Jared felt like he inhabited a Norman Rockwell town in a Currier & Ives setting.

He drove Tamany and Treacle past their white-steepled church, which stood amid the snowy landscape near a backdrop of twilight blue sky. A huge evergreen, over two stories tall, stood like a sentinel at the front and toward the side of the building. Strings of golden Christmas lights glimmered in its boughs, repeating the soft yellow glow of the church's windows.

He had hoped to share such a peaceful, romantic setting with Sharon and chuckled wryly that his plans, again, had backfired. But he enjoyed her girls' company and took them away from the buildings of town and over the hills of Goosebury.

"If you girls don't stop all that squealing," he said with a smile, "you might not have voices for the Christmas program. It's not all that far away, remember."

His mild, amused warning didn't faze them one bit.

"Let's sing a song!" Kitty insisted.

"What kind of song?" Jared asked.

"A sleigh song!"

"Yeah! Like the one you made up the day we met you," Mindy added.

"A sleigh song," Jared muttered in reflection. "Okay, how about this? Drive, drive, drive your sleigh, over the ice and snow—two squealing girls, giggling and waving, a-sleighing we will go!"

The girls giggled again, and soon they both joined in at the top of their lungs in countless rounds, broken up by even more giggling. And Jared had thought his nieces were bad when it came to uncontrollable laughter!

He grinned at their silliness, glad they were having such a fun time. He didn't regret following through with the sleigh ride, even if it hadn't gone according to plan.

Once he delivered the girls safely home, they jumped out, thanking him, and hurried inside. They left the front door wide, and unsure if he should go inside or not, he peeked his head around the partition.

"Hello?"

Sharon caught sight of him as she came from the kitchen. Laughter sailed down the hallway.

"Come in. It sounds like they had a good time."

"Yeah." He stepped inside and shut the door against the cold. "So did I."

Her eyes stayed on him a moment, looked away, then back. "Would you like some coffee? I have carrot cake, too."

"I've never tried it, but sure."

They headed to the kitchen. Kitty and Mindy ran out from the hallway, minus coats and mittens, and almost mowed Jared down.

"Thank you," Kitty said, wrapping her arms around his middle. "I had the bestest time!"

Sharon shook her head in amusement and popped the girls' overlooked stocking caps off. "It's time for both of you to get ready for bed."

"Can't we stay up since it's vacation?" Mindy pleaded. "Please!"

With a tolerant smile, Sharon let out a resigned breath. "One hour. But go play in your room. I need to talk to Jared alone."

"Yea!" The girls squealed and raced away.

"Quietly!" she called after them.

Jared noted the sound of their bedroom door clicking softly closed and couldn't prevent a grin. A grin that disappeared the moment he caught sight of Sharon's more somber expression.

"Am I in trouble?" he half joked.

"Maybe. Let's talk in the kitchen."

Jared followed, now almost dreading the next few minutes.

⌒☙

Sharon poured them both coffee. She cut them each a slice of cake and sat down across the table from him, setting the plates down as she did.

"Jared, I know you're only trying to help with Andy, but next time, please wait until you can discuss it with me. I'm not sure what to do about that job situation; Andy has been a handful lately, but now. . ."

"You're right; I made a mistake in doing that. I didn't think before I spoke, and I'm sorry."

Amazed, Sharon studied him. She had never known a man who admitted to being wrong. When she had tried to talk to Mark about similar matters, he'd gone on the defensive and then, too often, the offensive.

"But now that we're alone, I'd like to continue our discussion," he went on.

She realized he was asking her permission, and she nodded.

"I think this job would be good for Andy. I know"—he raised his hand as though to curb a comeback—"I'm one to talk since I don't have kids. But I speak from experience. I was about Andy's age when my dad had had enough of my pranks, which had really gotten out of control by then, and he made me get a summer job. I threw newspapers—not much, but it helped me learn to be responsible and kept me out of trouble. I still had chores on the farm, but this gave me a sense of independence, and earning some of my own money helped me better appreciate what I had. I had a lot, but at age twelve, kids often don't realize that."

She appreciated his sincerity. "You make a good case. I'll admit once you left I had pretty well decided the answer would be a no, but I'll rethink my decision."

"Glad to hear it. If you decide in favor of the idea and ever need someone to give him a lift—if my aunts' car fails or you have to work—give me a call."

Jared never failed to astonish her with his thoughtfulness. It was too bad Andy didn't realize what a support he had in Jared.

"I'll remember that."

He smiled and took a bite of cake. He looked at it, his expression neither delighted nor disgusted.

"You don't have to eat it if you don't want to. It hasn't been the flavor of the day here."

"It's okay."

"Are you sure? I can get you some doughnuts to go with your coffee instead." She had half-risen from her chair when he reached across the table and put his fingers to her arm to stop her movement. The contact, though brief, burned through her sweater.

"Sharon, it's fine." He studied her. "This is the second time you've worried about my reaction to the food. What gives?"

She opened her mouth to speak, then closed it and took a sip of coffee, sorting out her thoughts. "Mark was very demanding when it came to his meals. If something was the least bit off, he let me know he didn't like it. It's one reason I quit cooking from scratch." She left it at that, and from Jared's expression, he understood what she didn't say.

"Sharon, I'm not Mark."

"I know that." She attempted a smile. "You're nothing like him. It's just that sometimes. . ." She looked down at her cake. "I can't help it if memories interfere with the present. I've received counseling, and I have a support group. But it takes time to heal. It's been years, I know, but I really thought when Mark accepted the Lord and I saw that change in him, that once he got out of prison we'd have that second chance at the life I always wanted." She detested the tears that rose to her eyes and brushed them away, giving Jared a bright smile. "But obviously it just wasn't meant to be."

"I'm sorry it didn't happen like you dreamed it would." His eyes were nothing but sincere, and she believed he really meant it. "But sometimes when we lose sight of a dream we hoped for, God ends up giving us something better."

"I know. That's what Leslie said." She gave a soft laugh. "I have my friends, my kids, a good place to live, and a job I love, with employers who are more like surrogate grandmothers than true managers." She laughed again. "A lot of women would love to live my life."

He grinned, though his eyes remained serious. "You do have a lot, but I feel God has more for you."

His words made her a bit nervous, and she focused on her cake, eating a bite. She wondered if he meant himself, and if he still harbored some pipe dream that she would consider him as more than a friend.

"Can I ask a question?" He sounded hesitant.

She gave a noncommittal nod for him to go on.

"Tell me if it's none of my business, and I'll understand. But something has been bothering me, and I'd really like to know. Why'd you stay with him all that time?"

"You mean, why didn't I leave after the first time he beat me up?"

He winced. "Yeah."

She exhaled a deep sigh, drinking more of her coffee before trying to explain. "My stepfather was abusive to my mom, too, and verbally abusive to me and my sister. By the time I met Mark, I'd already formed a low opinion of myself. So when he added his insults along with the smacks, I grew to believe I really did deserve everything I got."

She shrugged. "You probably think that sounds crazy, but when you're told lies about yourself all your life, before long you believe them. When he'd come back, repentant and in tears, I felt like I had no choice but to take him in, that it really was my fault that I'd made him so angry, and that I was the one who needed to do most of the changing. Of course, I know differently now. But it took a lot of patience from some dear Christian friends to help me see that I wasn't at fault and that Mark was the one with the problem."

"I'm glad you sought help and have grown from the experience," he said. "You're an amazing woman, Sharon."

Her heart quickened at the quiet manner in which he said the words as well as the way his gaze grew so intent on her own.

She stood suddenly on the pretext of going for napkins, needing to break away from his soul-shaking eyes.

"I should go."

She pivoted in surprise to see he'd also risen from his chair. "You just got here."

"Yeah, but it's late, and I have plenty to do over the next few weeks both at the farm and with the program. I called a practice for both this Friday afternoon and Saturday, in case the girls didn't tell you."

"They did." She hesitated. "I'm not sure why I never asked before, but do you live on your parents' farm?"

"Not exactly, not in their house. I have my own place close by, on the land. Nothing much to talk about. A cabin, to sleep; I'm not there often." He chuckled. "I'm usually at Mom's to eat, or at my aunts' or at one of my brother's or sister's houses. They all insist on keeping me well fed."

She smiled at the thought that his family took good care of him; she wondered if his compassion was a hereditary trait.

"Thanks for the coffee." He stood watching her, as if undecided about approaching for a handshake or a hug—she didn't know which, but she saw the desire in his eyes and sensed he waited for a signal from her. Uneasy, she lowered her gaze to the napkins she held, then looked back up at him. He gave her a slight, almost disappointed grin. "No need to walk me to the door. Good night, Sharon."

She watched as he left the kitchen. Everything in her ached to call him back, but she only returned to her chair and stared at her cake. The front door clicked closed, and silence settled thick around her.

Chapter 11

Sharon sat on the pew next to Leslie, who held Marena on her lap while Blaine held a sleeping baby Paula over his shoulder. Carly sat on the other side, with Nate next to her, his arm around his wife.

"Just think, in a few years, I'll be one of the proud mamas watching my little girl perform." Leslie kissed Marena's hair. "Time goes so fast."

"Yes, it does," Sharon agreed. "And after having to whip up an angel costume and a wise-man costume, it seems to go even faster. It's a good thing I had Loretta's help. She's an expert when it comes to getting sequins to stay on the material *and* look decent."

"Those two really love you and your kids, Angel." Carly's eyes gleamed. "And unless I miss my guess, I'm certain someone else does, too."

Sharon knew she referred to Jared and looked his way. He caught sight of her from where he stood at the front and gave a friendly nod. Feeling the blush clear to her toes, she returned the greeting.

"Like I said," Carly mused, leaving the statement unfinished. Her eyes danced with mischievous delight.

Sharon quickly changed the subject, pointing out costumes as more children approached the stage. The heavenly chorus, she assumed from reading the program in her hand, though they wore silver robes and didn't have wings like the angels. She had spent the greater part of one day off from work, making the gauzelike, sequined wings she'd wrapped around wire hangers and trying to get them to fasten right and not hang lopsided on Kitty's costume. Mindy's wise-man outfit hadn't been half as difficult to put together.

The lights went down, the only electric light remaining a soft spotlight above where the pulpit usually stood. At the edge of three steps that led to the altar, candles glowed and flickered in tall, ornate golden stands. The wooden stable Ted and a few other men had built stood in the center as the shepherds flocked around it.

Jill played the organ, and the program unfolded without a hitch. Mindy almost forgot one of her two lines but recovered after only seconds. Kitty looked adorable in her angel costume, and Sharon smiled with pride as she watched her daughters perform.

"Did you make those wings?" Leslie asked.

Sharon nodded.

"They look like they could have been bought from a craft store. That's some amazing work."

"I've dabbled in crafts ever since high school," she whispered back. "That's one reason I applied for a sales position at A'bric & A'brac. When I saw they dealt in homemade crafts, I fell in love with the place."

The finale began, and the wise men bowed before the baby Jesus, played by Carly and Nate's baby Mali. No boys had been born in the congregation within the last year to take the role, and Carly's baby was reputed to have the best temperament. Tonight, however, she presented another side to her personality.

Mali squealed and grabbed one of the wise men's fake beards, bringing it to her mouth. The band holding it behind the boy's ears stretched. He leaned far into the manger as his wise man companion, Mindy, tried to disentangle Mali's fingers from the cottony wool.

"See." Andy leaned up from the pew behind Sharon to whisper in her ear. "I told you they shouldn't have gotten a girl."

At that moment, Mali let go of the beard, and the elastic band snapped back into place, stinging the poor wise man in the jaw.

"Ow!" he cried, rubbing his chin.

Jared's reaction came immediately, as he directed the heavenly chorus to begin the final carol of "Gloria."

Sharon tried hard not to laugh. By the way their shoulders shook, a number of the rest of the congregation dealt with the same problem.

The burst of singing made Mali cry. The children froze, uncertain what to do. They looked back and forth from the baby to Jared, who silently directed from the wings, and then to the audience. Mindy suddenly bent down and picked up Mali, holding her close and jiggling her while the chorus ended their final *gloria*s.

"Trust Mali to steal the spotlight," Carly said in an aside to Leslie and Sharon after the lights went up and everyone had been dismissed. "That girl is going to be an actress. Mark my words." She hurried up to the front to collect her daughter.

Mindy and Kitty ran up to Sharon, their eyes gleaming.

"Did you hear me sing, Mama?" Kitty wanted to know.

"I messed up," Mindy said, "but then I remembered my line. Do you think anyone else noticed? Did you like it?"

"Both of you were wonderful," Sharon assured, hugging her daughters.

"They really were," Jared said, and Sharon looked up in surprise, not realizing he'd joined them. "I was proud of both of them, and did you notice how Mindy saved the program?" He winked at the girl.

"Sorry about Mali's theatrics," Nate said, shaking hands with Jared. Jill and Ted joined them.

"Well, when a baby is part of the cast, I imagine you have to expect such things." Jared shrugged it off with a grin. "But unless any new babies are born between now and next year, I imagine they'll have to go back to a doll."

"As a matter of fact. . ." Jill's face went pink.

Sharon looked at her. "Jill? You're not serious."

"Too right. Remember when I thought I couldn't have kids, before Titus came along?"

"I remember! And now God is giving you a triple blessing," Leslie enthused, hugging Jill.

"Too right," Ted echoed his wife's Australian slang, beaming like he'd just been given the news.

Everyone laughed, and the couple received congratulations all around. Sharon was thrilled for Jill but couldn't help feel a twinge of envy. She'd always wanted a lot of children and would have loved to have another baby. But that meant marriage, and she wasn't ready for that. She corrected the surprisingly vague thought—*never* would be ready for that.

"So I might become one of those stage mamas," Jill laughed. "Be warned, Jared."

"Well, that's great—I think," he joked. "But I'm resigning as children's choir director."

"What?" Sharon asked. "How come?"

"I only volunteered for the job until Pastor could find someone more qualified, and I just don't think I'm cut out for it."

"Sharon could always take over," Leslie said.

"Sharon?" Jared glanced her way in confusion.

Sharon sent Leslie a sharp look, and Leslie glanced at the floor. "Oops. Sorry. I forgot."

"Do you sing?" Jared asked.

"No," Sharon said. "I don't," she stressed, looking at Leslie. "And I have no experience teaching choir, either."

"What's this I hear about you quitting, Jared?" A young man similar to Jared in looks came up and slapped him on the back.

"Hello, Brandon. Where's the family?"

"Darla's helping Rex out of his costume, and Mom and Dad are talking to the Abernathys."

Leslie perked up. "I need to talk to Nana before she leaves. I'll talk to you guys later."

The newcomer looked directly at Sharon. "Since Jared seems to have misplaced his manners—hi, I'm Brandon, Jared's brother. You must be Sharon. I've heard a lot about you."

"Hello." She shook his hand, not failing to notice the glint of mischief in his eyes and how Jared's face suddenly flushed.

"Sorry, I was about to do that," Jared said.

"I just came over to tell you what a great job you did with the program," Brandon told him. "You deserve whatever you put on your Christmas list this year, and I imagine I know what'll be at the very top." He chuckled as if sharing a private joke.

Jared turned even redder. "They're serving hot cider and cookies in the kitchen. Why don't you go fill your mouth with some?" he suggested.

Brandon laughed as if Jared had told a big joke, but Sharon saw Jared wasn't amused. And suddenly she understood what was number one on his list. Brandon's curious glances in her direction, along with Jared's focus elsewhere, convinced her Brandon's comment had to do with her.

"We should be going," she said, putting a hand on each of her daughters' shoulders.

"You're not staying for the party?" Jill asked.

"Not tonight."

"Mo—omm," Mindy complained.

"You still have school tomorrow. School doesn't let out for vacation until the end of this week." She wondered if she appeared as nervous as she sounded.

"But it's still early!"

"Sorry, Min. Not tonight. You and Andy both also have homework. Night all." She included the entire group in her hurried good-bye, while herding her girls to the door and Loretta and Josephine's car, which was finally in good running order. "Come along, Andy," she called to her son, who talked outside with a boy his age. She felt a little foolish for making such a fast escape, but couldn't help herself.

Feeling bad for denying Mindy and Kitty a well-deserved party, she stopped at a fast-food place and bought everyone a hot chocolate with whipped cream. Once they arrived home, she pulled out a bag of chocolate chip cookies, and they had a short, private celebration before she shooed Andy and Mindy off to finish their homework and Kitty off to bed.

The girls seemed satisfied with the substitute party, but Sharon couldn't stop feeling on edge.

"What's wrong with me?" she muttered, threading her fingers through her hair, her elbows on the table as she rested her head in her hands.

She couldn't even be sure Brandon implied Jared still hoped for a relationship with her; she'd only assumed it. She had known how Jared felt from the start, though he agreed to her stipulation of "just friends." Sometimes, though, when she looked into his eyes, she sensed he desired more. What had scared her and made her run like a frightened doe that evening was that she had begun to desire the same.

"Thanks a ton," Jared mumbled to his brother the moment Sharon fled.

"Hey, I didn't mean anything by it. I didn't realize she'd be so fidgety and would take off like that; I'm sorry, dude." Brandon looked the slightest bit uneasy, and Jared relented. After all, he'd never told any of his brothers the details of his and Sharon's strange relationship, or more accurately, their lack of one.

"Let's get some of that cider and I'll explain things. But only if you promise not to use it against me in the future, especially when we're in public."

"Now, would I do that to you?"

"Yup," Jared came back without hesitation. "I'm surprised Darla lets you out in public."

"I really thought you two were together, or I wouldn't have said a word."

Their trek to the church cafeteria was slow; many parents and their excited future stars stopped Jared to congratulate him on the program's rousing success. They'd either forgotten Mali's finale, or maybe they thought her impromptu performance added to the program.

Once they collected cups of cider from a smiling Mrs. Moorehead, Jared told his brother everything since his first meeting with Sharon. He didn't divulge those things Sharon had confided in him, except to say she'd endured some tough situations that made it difficult for her to trust.

His brother stared at him.

"What?" Jared asked.

"I'm still trying to get past the fact that you have *finally* found The One." With two fingers of each hand, he made quote marks in the air.

"Forget I said anything." Irritated with what he felt would result in another round of ribbing, Jared shook his head and took a sip of cider.

"No, wait. I meant that in a good way." His brother's expression *seemed* earnest. "You always stuck to your guns in this, unaffected by anything the family had to say, and Tom, Josh, and I have given you a hard time, even if it was all in fun. But hearing you tell how it happened—and that it all went the exact way you felt God said it would—right down to the smallest detail—man, Jared. That's awesome."

"It is, isn't it? Now I only have to convince Sharon," he reminded dryly.

"Yeah, well, I don't know. You've trusted God all this time, so why stop now? I don't think He'd let you down after bringing you this far."

"I know. I just have to be patient." He sighed. He was certainly getting a lengthy lesson in patience.

"You could always use the old 'absence makes the heart grow fonder' bit."

"What are you talking about?"

"I did it with Darla. She acted like she wanted nothing to do with me at first, though our friends made me think otherwise and I'd catch her looking my way. So I got the idea that if I acted disinterested maybe she'd change her tune.

Even when my buddies told me she kept searching for me and asked questions, I stayed hidden. After a month, she caved." Brandon grinned. "I still hide from her at the pool hall or at the lake fishing with the guys, but now it's only when I need to get away."

"Not only does the whole concept sound immature, it sounds cold-blooded." Jared eyed his brother in disbelief.

"It worked." Brandon shrugged.

Jared shook his head, always amazed to what new lows his youngest brother would stoop. No wonder his parents tried to keep him away from the tourists. "Well, I won't have time for socializing after tonight. Things are getting busier on the farm, and you won't have time for any games of hide-and-seek from Darla either."

"Okay, okay. So what do you plan to do about Sharon? You going to take my advice?"

"Giving her a little space might not be a bad idea with the way things have gone between us lately. But the last thing I plan to do is hide from her."

Chapter 12

Sharon wondered if Jared was hiding from her. That idea seemed preposterous when she considered it, but since the night of the Christmas program, she'd barely seen a trace of him. She assumed he'd been busy with work, but except for the two times she'd called asking him to give Andy a lift to Hugh's farm when the sisters' car died, Sharon hadn't seen Jared much at all.

She told herself it was silly to feel wounded by his lack of company; the two times she did see him, he was as friendly as always, and she knew she was being ridiculous to view his absence as a slight.

On Christmas Eve morning, she and the kids took the two-hour bus ride to her mom's. Her stepfather was gone for the day, something for which she was grateful, though her mom didn't mention where he was.

"You look good, Mom," Sharon said as she helped her mother make turkey sandwiches. The girls sat planted in front of the television in the next room, watching an animated Christmas special, and Andy stood outside tossing a ball to Brambles, her stepfather's mutt.

The dark circles under her mom's eyes made her appear tired, but she did look better than the last time Sharon had seen her, at Mark's funeral. On that day, she'd had bruises.

"I didn't want to say anything with the kids in the room," her mom murmured under her breath, "but Garth is in rehab."

"Rehab?" Sharon almost dropped the mayonnaise jar as she set it down.

Her mother nodded. "After what happened with. . ." She hesitated, her eyes darting to Sharon, then to the slices of bread laid out, as if realizing she had brought up a touchy subject.

"It's okay, Mom," Sharon assured her. "You mean after Mark was killed in prison."

"Yes, well, not long after that, he came to me after one of his drunks and told me he wanted help. I'd never seen him like that. He cried—actually cried like a baby. He didn't seek professional help until last month, though. He tried quitting on his own. It didn't work."

"Why didn't you tell me all this before?" Sharon stared at her mom in disbelief.

"I didn't want to bother you, what with all you've been through." Her mom bit her lip, uneasy.

Sharon withheld a sigh, recognizing the old feeling of unworthiness in her mom's eyes, a feeling Sharon was conquering in her own life with the Lord's help.

"I'm glad Garth woke up and is getting the help he needs," she said, forcing a smile.

She tried not to feel cheated but felt a twinge of selfishness. Why couldn't Mark have sought help before he threw his life away by stabbing Leslie with his vengeful plan of getting even with Dear Granny? That he found help during his last year in prison brought some comfort. Nor could she look at her life with him as wasted. It had brought her the blessings of her three children.

"Will you come home with me to Goosebury?" Sharon asked. "You shouldn't be here alone."

"This is my home, Sharon. I can't leave." Her mom smiled. "I'll be fine."

Sharon didn't doubt that; her mom was made of strong stuff, though Sharon wished she would open her mind and heart to talk about God. So far, she'd shown polite disinterest the few times Sharon had brought up the topic. She hoped her mother wouldn't be upset with her gift.

That night as they opened presents and the children soon became immersed in playing with the toys their grandmother gave each of them, Sharon's mom looked at the book in her lap. Along with it, Sharon had given her a blue cashmere, button-down sweater, which her mom had immediately draped around her shoulders. But she only stared at the jacket cover of *God's Answer to a Life without Fear*, her expression blank.

"A very kind woman gave me that book a few years ago, not long before the police arrested Mark. She helps her granddaughter, a friend of mine, write an advice column for my local paper," she added when her mom didn't respond. She omitted Leslie's and Mrs. Abernathy's names, knowing they wanted their cowriting profession as the advice columnist Dear Granny to remain secret. "That book has helped me, and I want you to have it now."

"Honey, I can't take your book."

"No, Mom, really, it's okay. When this woman gave it to me, she told me someone first gave it to her, and it helped her face her fears. She said she thinks it's a book that should be passed along, which is why she gave it to me. And now I want to do the same. With you." She omitted saying it also brought her closer to God. Such an admission might cause her mother to lose any possible interest in reading it.

"Something like a chain book?" Her mom lifted her brows and smiled, showing the first bit of spirited amusement she'd exhibited all day.

Sharon chuckled. "I guess you could call it that."

The remainder of the evening went well. The kids seemed more relaxed and happy than on previous visits, and Sharon didn't doubt Garth's absence made them more secure. His verbal abuse had created general unease, and Sharon ended each visit within a few hours. This evening, however, she accepted her mom's invitation to stay the night.

The girls giggled at the spontaneous decision and thought it a great adventure that they had no clothes and each had to wear one of their granny's gowns, which hung on them like angel robes. After minutes of bouncing up and down on the feather mattress with a pillow fight following, Sharon read them "The Night Before Christmas" and at last got them calm enough to sleep.

Their heads nestled in their pillows, both girls looked up at Sharon from the guest room's double bed. Their golden hair was tousled from their play, their eyes drowsy from the fun they'd had.

"What do you think Jared is doing for Christmas?" Kitty wanted to know as Sharon tucked the thick down blanket around her and Mindy.

The mention of the man she'd been trying to forget made Sharon's heart give a strange little leap.

"I imagine he's with his family, like we are."

Kitty thought a moment. "But he *is* like family. So why didn't he come over, too?"

Sharon studied her daughter with concerned alarm. "Honey," she said gently, "Jared's not family. He's just a good friend."

"That's not what I heard Mrs. Loretta and Miss Josephine say," she insisted. "They were all happy that Jared found the woman he was gonna marry." Then, as if Sharon wouldn't understand, she went on. "They meant you, Mama."

Sharon felt her heart catch. "They told you that?"

Kitty averted her eyes. "Well, no. I just heard them."

"You were eavesdropping," Sharon scolded. "What have I told you about that?"

"I wasn't trying to be bad," Kitty insisted. "I went to get some cookies, and they were talking in the kitchen. I heard them."

"Are you gonna marry Jared, Mama?" Mindy wanted to know.

Sharon's mouth dropped open in shock at the blatant question. Both the girls' eyes sparkled with hope. The sooner she got such dancing sugarplum ideas out of their heads, the better. Best to squelch all visions concerning any such notion.

"Goodness, no. I never plan to marry again."

"Why not?" Kitty wanted to know. "Miss Josephine said the Lord said man shouldn't live alone."

"She told you that?"

"No, she told Mrs. Loretta."

"Well, I'm not alone; I have you two. And Andy."

"And then Mrs. Loretta answered that she agreed with the plan God gave Jared, since Paul said in the Bible young widows are supposed to marry," Mindy shot back. "It's in the Bible," she repeated for good measure.

"You were listening, too?"

"I went to see what Kitty was doing."

Sharon crossed her arms over her chest, unsmiling, and surveyed her two mischievous matchmakers. "I've raised you girls better than that. You better watch out with this disobedience, or Santa might just decide to skip over our house tonight." She'd already told them Santa wouldn't come to their grandmother's; the sleepover had been a spur of the moment thing, and the kids' presents were at home, still unwrapped.

"But Mama," Mindy insisted, not fazed by the mild threat, "if God says you shouldn't stay single, doesn't that mean you're supposed to marry someone? And God's a whole lot more important than Santa. That's what you said. So doesn't that mean you're not obeying God? And isn't that even worse?"

This conversation was spinning out of control too fast for Sharon's peace of mind. Both girls now looked worried, and Sharon realized Mindy wasn't trying to be disrespectful.

"Okay, that's enough chitchat for one night," she said, managing a smile. "Tomorrow is Christmas, and it'll be here before you know it."

"But Mama. . ."

Sharon rose from the mattress, deposited quick kisses on their brows, and turned out the light. In the attic room, she found Andy sound asleep on the recliner in front of an ancient TV that aired an old black-and-white Christmas movie. Relieved that she wouldn't need to field any additional questions, she turned off the set. She tucked him snugly inside the blankets and kissed his forehead, then headed downstairs to work on a scenic Christmas puzzle with her mom. Hundreds of colorful pieces lay scattered across the dining table. Soft instrumental Christmas music played from the stereo. Her mom was so involved in working the puzzle, she barely spoke, which meant Sharon had a lot of time to think.

As Sharon tried to interlock matching colors, Mindy's fears wouldn't vacate her mind. Did such a verse exist in the Bible, or were the girls just creating more mischief? Sharon hadn't read enough of the New Testament to know, though she'd read bits and pieces here and there, centering on the readings Pastor Neil taught his congregation. For her own private worship time, she used a devotional that directed her to certain scriptures each day.

What if such a verse really did exist? Jared was everything Mark hadn't been: sweet, funny, kind, affectionate. She enjoyed spending time with Jared and missed him. Yet even if he did still have interest in her—although his absence seemed to prove otherwise—and even if the verse Mindy cited was genuine, even then, Sharon wasn't sure she could break her resolve regarding her decision never to marry.

As days passed into weeks, Jared remained busy on his family's farm. The winter had been quiet, with the usual blizzards that snowed them in and chores that multiplied. Jared enjoyed his assigned task of tending to the farm animals, keeping them snug in the barn, while outside the snow fell often and deep. When none of the family was present and Jared was the sole human occupant of the barn, he often found himself singing. At least the animals seemed to enjoy his performances.

The days had grown warmer at spring's approach, the nights frozen, the perfect time for sugaring. The process could last from a matter of days to weeks, depending on the weather. Each spring, new tapholes needed to be bored into tree trunks, taps and hollow tubes needed to be inserted, and Jared, along with many of the men in his family, had spent the past days readying trees for gathering sap.

For the trees within easy access, they used the old-fashioned, bucket-collecting method. But for the sugar bush on the hillsides, they attached plastic tubes to the taps, which formed a network of tubing that allowed the thawed sap to flow to a huge storage tank near the sugarhouse. Today, Jared sang under his breath, not caring that he had company.

"You seem in a good mood," Tom said as Jared brushed Tamany, readying her for the day's ride, along with Treacle.

"I'm bringing Sharon and her kids to the farm. They want to see how the sugaring is done."

"And of course that's your sole reason for playing chauffeur," Tom joked.

"You know," Jared said with a good-natured grin, "you're not so big now that I can't whip you, little brother."

"Don't be so sure." Tom patted his big stomach, which hung an inch over his belt. "I can still wrestle you to the ground any day."

"Well, it's fortunate for you we won't see that theory tested. I have to make tracks. I told her I'd be there by noon."

"All joking aside, how'd you get her to change her mind about meeting the folks?"

"I don't really know. I saw her at church last Sunday, and when she asked what I'd been doing, I told her it was sugaring time. Kitty asked if she could come and see, and Sharon said they could. I have to admit, I'm still baffled, since I wasn't expecting her to agree."

"Maybe you're getting to her."

"Uh, yup. Sure." He waved his brother's comment off and hitched Tamany and Treacle to the wagon. After three months, eight days, and twelve hours of hardly seeing Sharon, he looked forward to the prospect, but he doubted she had missed him. As he drove to her house, however, his brother's words reverberated in his mind, and Jared wondered if Tom could be right. Had Sharon thawed toward him? She had seemed happy to see him and talk with him outside of church.

Once she opened the door to his knock, the thought entered his mind that she looked like a breath of fresh air. Wearing white and a shade of blue that matched her eyes, she dazzled. The girls jumped at him, hugging him. Andy stood nearby and stared at Jared, and to his surprise, Jared sensed less animosity in the boy. Ever since Sharon had bought a used car, she'd been toting Andy back and forth to his weekend job, but Andy had the day off since Hugh's family had gone out of town. She had offered to drive to the farm, but Jared insisted he would pick them up in his horse-drawn sleigh instead.

This Saturday's weather was perfect for a sleigh ride. The sun shone from a pale blue sky, the days had warmed, and the snow of a few hours ago had stopped falling.

Once they drove onto his family's land, past the sign that announced Crisp Sugarwoods to welcome them, Sharon stared in wide-eyed shock. The closer they came to the farmhouse, the more stunned she appeared as she looked around at the distant hillsides of snow-flocked trees.

"Everything okay?" he asked.

"I thought you meant your family had a farm. You never told me you meant a *farm*. I had no idea your parents' place was this big." Her voice squeaked in her nervousness. "How big is it, anyway?"

"It's five hundred and twenty-five acres," he said, wondering why he hadn't brought it up before. His family's wealth and his own interests in the maple sugar farm had never been a problem or something he broadcasted. It just—was. He had mentioned tourists visited year-round, so he'd thought Sharon would have figured out the place was big. "Crisp Sugarwoods has been in the family for generations, since the 1800s."

His parents' two-story farmhouse appeared in the distance, and he sensed by her jittery behavior that Sharon wanted to bolt from the sleigh.

"Sharon, it's okay," he said in an undertone so the kids in the back couldn't hear. The girls were busy pointing out to each other the different features of the farm. "My family members are good, plain country folk. Nothing scary about them—well, except maybe for my brothers." He winked, and she seemed to relax a margin.

"I'm surprised with a house that big you'd want to live in a cabin all by yourself," she remarked, her eyes taking in every inch of the wide brown house which stood out against the snow-covered surroundings.

"Let's just say I'm a man who likes my independence."

"So." She cleared her throat. "Where's your cabin?"

"On the other side of the sugarhouse, beyond those trees," he added when she craned her neck to look. "My parents keep their farmhouse private from the area where we let tourists roam. I'll show you my cabin later."

"Oh, I didn't mean—" Her face grew redder, but the sight of a few members of his family coming out of the house to meet them interrupted whatever she'd been about to say.

For the next few minutes, Jared introduced Sharon and her family to his mom; two of his sisters-in-law, Darla and Carol; and some of his nephews and nieces. His brothers and father were busy on other areas of the farm, and once he and Sharon entered the house, Jared saw a majority of his small nieces and nephews sat at the huge dining table, finishing lunch. Bless his mom, she took Sharon and her kids right into her heart, making them feel comfortable with her easy conversation. In relief, Jared watched Sharon relax, her smiles becoming more natural.

"Jared has a big day planned for you, so I won't keep you any longer." His mom included both Sharon and Jared in her smile. Her green eyes twinkled, and he sensed her approval. She looked from Mindy to Kitty and crouched down, her hands on the knees of her slacks. "And when you get back, we'll have a real Vermont treat. Ever hear of sugar on snow?"

Both girls shook their heads, their eyes wide, and his mom chuckled.

"You will."

Chapter 13

Once Sharon had gotten over the initial shock of Jared's family "farm" and how massive it really was, she allowed herself to relax. His family put her at ease with their friendly smiles and conversation, treating her and her kids as if they'd always belonged to the family. At first she found that a bit strange; most folks in Goosebury showed a reserve toward newcomers, and it often took time to work toward acceptance. Sharon wondered if the Crisp family treated everyone with such friendly welcome, or if Jared had told them so much about her they felt like they knew her.

That thought brought heat to her cheeks, welcome in the cold, crisp air as Jared took them along the thickly wooded trail.

"This is my trail," he told the girls. "Every afternoon I collect tree sap from the buckets." He pointed to several sugar maples, huge in diameter, with two taps instead of just one.

With a few well-aimed words to garner Andy's interest, Jared let her son take a few turns at carrying the buckets and dumping the sap inside the barrel at the back of the wagon. Of course, Kitty and Mindy then insisted they have a turn, and Jared had little choice but to allow it—that or hear their constant pleadings. Sharon watched him lower the bucket suspended from the hook of the spout and place it into Mindy's hands, instructing her to carry it to the wagon. He then hoisted her up so she could pour it into the barrel.

"There sure are lots of trees," Mindy said as Jared rehung the bucket from the spout. "Do you have to get the sap from all of them every day?"

"Yup. Every day. Me and my family. There's too much here for one person to do, though we don't have to worry about the trees on the hills. They have tubing that takes the sap right to the tank." He pointed to the nearest hill, and the kids stared, openmouthed.

"Dad assigned trails to us when we started helping with the gathering," Jared said. "For the next three to six weeks, depending on the weather, I'll collect the sap from buckets on my route so those working in the sugarhouse can boil it to make maple syrup. We start the process after a few sunny days when it gets warm—in the forties—but the nights are still freezing. That's the best time for the sap to flow."

Kitty peered into the bucket Jared had just positioned. "Look, more is starting to drip out of the tree," she said. "But it's so slow."

"A tree that size, from one tap, will yield about fifteen gallons of sap a year. It takes almost ten gallons to produce one quart of maple syrup—the size of the jugs we sell."

"Wow," Andy said under his breath. "That's a lot of sap."

Andy's interest in Jared's informative words cheered Sharon. Since Jared had picked them up at the house, Andy hadn't shown animosity toward him, and Sharon hoped those days were over. She had seen a change in his attitude since he'd started working at Hugh's farm, though she still didn't feel comfortable with his attachment to the moose calf, which had strengthened through the months.

As the horse-drawn sleigh whisked over the crisp snow, still deep for early March, the sun beamed down from high above, making the snow on the limbs glitter like diamonds in a crystalline world.

Once they collected all the sap, Jared took them to the sugarhouse to watch the sugaring process. Inside the warm room, the sweet smell of maple sugar permeated the air.

First he showed them an evaporator, a machine that stood a few inches under Jared's height and three times as wide. He introduced them to the man who worked it, his brother-in-law, Greg.

Kitty edged closer to try to get a better look, and Sharon called her back before she hurt herself. She had seen the quantities of steam billow from the chimneys before they'd entered the building.

"They use a very hot fire to dissolve the water from the sap," Jared explained as if reading Sharon's mind. "That's what this machine does. The sap has to be boiled right away, or it begins to spoil. I'll let Greg tell you more." He slapped his brother-in-law on the shoulder.

The three children as well as Sharon listened to Greg's detailed explanation of what happened to the sap in the evaporator as it took a winding path along different pans, becoming denser with the process. He then introduced them to another man, who showed them the hydrometer, where the sap was checked for proper density, then passed along to a pump which filtered out what he called sugar sand. The result was a fine golden syrup he called "liquid gold." This they stored in a steel drum until ready to be packaged in small containers for distribution.

"Wow, all that just to make syrup," Mindy said in awe.

Sharon noted the rapt expressions on her children's faces. Even Andy appeared intrigued, and she was glad she'd agreed to come. She had enjoyed the tour so far, more so because Jared led it. The past months without him had been difficult, and she'd reached the point of admitting she needed his presence in their lives.

Next Jared took them to the confectionery kitchen, where three women were hard at work. He moved to a dark-haired young woman who stood at the end of a counter and gave her a one-armed hug as he looked into the huge, stainless steel bowl she stirred. "What are you making?"

She shook her head and rolled her eyes with a smile. "You know exactly what I'm making, and yes, you can have some." She spooned a bit of the close-to-a-peanut-butter-consistency spread off onto another spoon and from there onto her finger, slipping it into his mouth.

"Jared's always loved maple cream," she explained to Sharon, who had watched, wide-eyed, the whole exchange with the mystery woman. "Ever since he was a tot running around in diapers."

"Thank you so much for that informative comment, Amy," he drawled. "Sharon, my sister, Amy. The oldest of my siblings, but by no means the wisest." She swatted his arm, and he pulled away in mock pain, grinning all the while.

"It is so nice to meet you," Amy said, her brown eyes alight with friendliness. "When Jared was born," she explained to Sharon, "he was the first boy, and Alice, Andrea, and I spoiled him rotten. Oh, fools that we mortals be." She looked up at the ceiling as if addressing the heavens, and Jared gave her hair a gentle yank.

"You love me, and you know it," he shot back.

"Ah, yes," she said in mock despair. "Like I said—fools and mortals."

Enjoying their banter, Sharon smiled with relief to learn they were siblings.

"And these are my cousins." He continued the introduction as he smiled at two young blonds. "Emily and Grace."

The women nodded shy hellos, which Sharon returned. Using fancy-shaped leaf molds, both women cut candy. At Jared's nod, they offered a sample piece to each of the children, who grabbed the sweets up from the platter with eager thanks.

"This entire farm really is all family operated, isn't it?" Sharon asked, thinking of all the cousins, brothers, and sisters she'd met. "When your aunts said all of the family takes part in some way, they weren't joking."

Jared laughed. "Yup, just about everyone has a hand at the Sugarwoods, though a few, like Becca, have become traitors and work outside the farm," he joked. "To be fair, she takes a hand with the tourists once in a while, especially helping out at the petting zoo."

"Petting zoo?" Kitty asked, her eyes wide.

"We open it in April. You'll have to come back then," he added and looked Sharon's way. Her heart gave a little jump at the idea of returning. What had been a frightening prospect now appealed.

"For the most part, it's all family here," Jared continued from where he'd left off. "My dad has ten brothers and sisters, so when you figure out the generations, that does amount to a lot of workers. Even the small kids have chores to help out."

"Does all of your family live on the land?" Sharon asked in shock.

"Not all of them, no. Most of those who do have their own places."

"It's like your own little community," she mused.

"I suppose so. My grandfather left an equal share in the farm to each of his sons and daughters, and smaller shares to us grandkids. We all have a part in its operation and in voicing opinions during family meetings. Case in point—we recently voted in favor of a reverse osmosis machine that will help speed up the evaporation process. We still stick to old-fashioned ideas and methods but have allowed room for more modern technology in some areas.

"Would you like to see the Crisp farmhouse store and the items we sell?" he asked the girls.

"Sure!" Mindy responded.

The small tourist shop, with its bottles, jars, and tubs of maple syrups, creams, and candies was inviting. A few tourists stood at the back of the store, trying to decide between two packaged gift sets. Sharon recognized products that Jared's aunts sold in their souvenir-craft store, as well.

Jared's cousin behind the counter seemed as nice as the rest of the Crisp clan, though she watched Sharon the entire time with curious interest. Sharon had begun to see a pattern. At the mention of her name upon Jared's introduction, many looked at Sharon with recognition, and she recalled Jared once told her he'd spoken about her—but she didn't realize he meant to his entire family! She wasn't sure how she felt about that. He'd been quite verbal about his interest in her when they'd met last summer, and these past months without him had given her a lot of time to think. Even before discovering that the Bible instruction to young widows to marry was true, Sharon realized she'd lost her heart to Jared long ago.

Counseling with the pastor's wife and some heart-to-heart talks with Leslie had helped Sharon reach a new stepping-stone in her bridge to healing. She no longer allowed old, painful memories from years before to pull her away from the desire for Jared's touch. Now she anticipated it, though she had no idea how to tell him so. Still, despite these new feelings, she didn't know if she was ready for more.

"You guys want to celebrate a springtime sugaring tradition?" Jared asked.

The girls answered with eager squeals, and they returned to the farmhouse where his mom, sister, and nieces greeted them with smiles. Three boys and girls also joined them, and Sharon learned they were Amy's kids.

His mom led the troupe to a huge kitchen, where Jared, Sharon, and the children sat around the large table. His mom heated a pot of syrup, using a candy thermometer. After a few minutes, she nodded to Jared. He grabbed an empty pan and went outside, grinning mysteriously. The children and Sharon looked at the Crisp women puzzled, but only more mysterious smiles greeted them.

Jared's sister Alice set out a bowl of dill pickles, and his teenage nieces, Tamara and Beth, poured coffee and put out yeast doughnuts. Jared returned minutes later, the pan full of snow.

"Why'd you bring snow inside?" Kitty wanted to know. "Won't it melt?"

"Watch, and you'll see." He set the pan on the table and scooped snow into individual containers Alice set out. His mom brought the hot syrup from the stove and drizzled a light helping onto each mound of pure white snow. The children's eyes grew wide as the maple syrup formed lacelike patterns across the top of the snow and quickly hardened. His mom handed a container and fork to each of them. The children wasted no time in sampling the sweet.

"Mmmm," Kitty said. "This is better than a candy factory!"

"What do you mean?" Mindy asked as she bit into her own golden brown serving. "This *is* a candy factory!"

Many of them laughed along with the girls, who began to sing the "Toot Sweets" song from the *Chitty Chitty Bang Bang* movie they'd seen the previous year, broken up by a good deal of giggling from Kitty as she tried to whistle through the candy.

"Silly girl." Caught up in the fun, Sharon wrapped her arms around Kitty, who sat beside her, and sprinkled her cheek with kisses.

"Stop it, Mama," Kitty laughingly protested. "They're all sweet and sugared!"

"Well, darling," Jared's mom said with a smile, "that's what love is. Sweet as sugar."

Without meaning to, Sharon's gaze met and locked with Jared's across the table. His eyes held a wealth of emotion, though his face remained blank. A strange, sort of hopeful expectation cornered her thoughts, and warmth suffused her face before she tore her gaze away from his and tried to concentrate on her treat.

"Now eat a bite of pickle," Jared's mom suggested to the girls.

"A pickle?" Kitty's nose wrinkled. "Yuk."

"Try it," Alice urged. "It's really good. It takes the edge off the sweetness. Doughnuts are good with it, too."

Sharon had to agree as she forked some of the extremely sweet taffylike candy into her mouth and followed it with a bite of juicy dill pickle. Andy wolfed his down in no time and asked for seconds. Sharon would have corrected him, but Jared's mom already held the ladle poised over the snow, and Billy, Amy's son who was around Andy's age, also held his bowl out for more.

The group broke up after a relaxing time of conversation while they all enjoyed their treats. Amy's girls asked Mindy and Kitty to join them in playing a board game, and Billy asked Andy if he wanted to see his CD collection. Sharon nodded for her kids to go ahead. A few minutes of conversation ensued among the adults before Jared turned to Sharon. "Would you like to take a walk?"

After her recent thoughts, Sharon's heart leaped at the prospect of spending time alone with him, but she nodded. Thanking the rest of the Crisp family, she walked with him out the back kitchen door that led to the mudroom, and from there, outside.

Jared walked with Sharon across the snowy yard. He wondered if he imagined the hope in her eyes when his mom talked of love, but now that they were alone for the first time in months, he didn't want to scare her away by asking.

"How have you been?" He glanced her way.

"Good. Andy had a birthday last month, so now I'm the mother of a teenager."

"That's hard to believe," he said admiring her youthful face. "You don't look a day over twenty-one."

She laughed. "Sometimes I feel twice that. Having kids is great, but they can wear a person down."

"Single parenthood must be tough."

"It can be."

Their words held a host of unspoken thoughts regarding their situation, and a moment of awkwardness passed between them.

"I guess you heard about Kim?" she asked after a minute.

"The girl from church?"

"Yes."

"I've been busy at the farm and am behind on current events. What about Kim?"

"She had surgery in January. Her sight was restored."

"That's terrific! You don't seem happy." He noted the lines between her brows. Jared led her through a patch of trees, pushing a low twiggy branch aside and clearing the way for her to pass.

"Oh, I am. I'm thrilled for Kim. But Carly told me just a few weeks after the operation Kim started having problems. When the doctor examined her, he said there's a chance she might go blind again; that these results won't last."

"That's hard." Jared felt a twinge of sympathy for the brave teenager.

"Chris is more upset than most—Chris is the guy she's been dating, Nate's cousin. He asked her to marry him after he graduates from college in a few years, but she refused and broke up with him. Carly said it's because she's afraid she'll go blind again and doesn't want to be a burden to Chris. Which is ridiculous, since he's loved Kim from the day they met—and she was blind then."

"One-sided love can be a tough situation. I understand his pain."

At his telling words, she stopped and looked at him sharply. "Oh, she loves him; she's just scared and isn't thinking straight right now."

"And I'm sure he's just as scared. Of losing her." He stared into her eyes, his expression as intent as hers. "Especially since she told him to leave, and she's run from him, closing him out."

"She can't help the way she feels. She's been through a lot."

"I understand that, but she has to come to a place where she realizes she doesn't need to go through those feelings alone."

"She's a private person, afraid to open up."

"But she won't be happy until she allows love back into her life and allows herself to love again. He's there for her and wants to grow old with her, to share a life with her and her kids."

"Her kids," Sharon whispered. "Who are we talking about here, Jared?"

He withheld an answer, but he saw the knowledge in her eyes, the affirmation that they had been discussing the same thing.

"I'm afraid."

"I know."

"Not of you." She gave a slight shake of her head.

"I know that, too." He lifted his hands to cradle either side of her head, his eyes searching hers.

She blinked up at him, but no fear touched her expression, only an uncertain hope. She glanced down at his mouth and moistened her lower lip.

All restraint dissolved when he realized she hadn't pulled away, had, in fact, swayed closer.

He lowered his head and brushed his lips against her soft ones. Slow, gentle. More than once. His heart felt as if it might race out of his body, and his breathing grew unsteady. He didn't deepen the kiss, though he wanted to. Instead, he lifted his head to look at her.

She opened her eyes as if awakening after a long sleep, her own chest rising and falling faster than before. They stared at one another a long moment.

Like a woman coming out of a trance, she lifted her fingertips to touch his lips, her gaze on his mouth.

He took her hand in his and dropped a gentle kiss on her fingers, before lowering it so he could speak. "Sharon, I love you. I want to spend my life with you."

"I don't know if I can give you that." She looked up at him, her eyes vulnerable and concerned. "I might end up disappointing you, and I don't want to. I just don't know if I can marry again."

"We don't have to jump into anything. Let's just take this one step at a time."

She hesitated. "Why did you stay away so long? Why didn't you call before today?"

Her quiet words gave him hope. "If I could have come earlier, I would have. Funny thing, my brother suggested I stay away to give you space; I didn't intend to though. Things have been so busy here. Though to be honest, with the way you ran out of church after the Christmas program, I didn't think you'd mind the break away from me."

"I did mind." She lowered her eyes, her lashes fanning her cheeks. "I missed you."

Her admission made Jared want to kiss her again, but he refrained.

"I want to show you something."

"What?" She looked confused at the change of topic.

"You'll see."

He kept her hand in his as they spent the next five minutes walking through the trees to the other side, sharing glances now and then.

She exhaled, startled, as they reached a small clearing. "Is this your cabin?" she asked, looking with approval at the log building against a backdrop of trees. At his nod, she went on, "It's so cozy." She studied the entire area. Through a clearing, the distant Green Mountains rose in gentle slopes. "And so peaceful," she breathed.

"In the evenings, you can see the sun set over the mountains." Intent on her reaction, he watched her.

"It's beautiful here, Jared. Thank you for showing me your home."

He had wanted to show her this spot for months. "My grandparents left me this plot of land, from beyond those trees"—he motioned with his arm in the distance—"to over there, where those two white pines stand close together. I own the cabin, too. Remember when I joked with you at the mall and said I thought I might go into construction when I was younger?"

His revelations made her eyes go wide. "Yes," she whispered.

"Well, I had a hand in building this cabin. I always thought some day I might add on to it, if the need ever arose." He left his meaning unsaid but saw by her dazed nod that she understood. And by her averted gaze, he knew when to stop.

He held out his hand to her. "One step at a time, Sharon. That's all I ask."

She nodded, her eyes alight with hope, and took his hand. Together they walked back to the farmhouse.

Chapter 14

Months later, Sharon paced the den, about to go out of her mind. At the sound of a knock, she hurried to open the door and pulled Jared inside, out of the early morning darkness.

He drew her close, and she melted against him, taking comfort in his strong arms. "I don't know what to do," she said against his shirt, trying not to fall apart.

He cupped the back of her head and smoothed his hand down her hair. "Tell me what happened."

"Yesterday Hugh told us he's selling the farm; he's retiring as a wildlife rehabilitator, too." She tried to calm down. "That was bad enough, but then Andy and I argued about bringing the moose here—I told you her leg got wounded somehow a week ago and Hugh's been taking care of it?"

"Yes."

"Well, Andy hasn't been happy with me about any of that. . .and other things." She sighed. Ever since she and Jared had started seeing each other on a more personal level, she and Andy had butted heads.

"We had something of a shouting fest. He ended up locking himself in his room. I had a bad dream and couldn't get back to sleep. So I got up and found Andy had gone. His backpack is missing, and a carton of pudding cups is gone, too." She realized in her panic, her words rambled. "Kitty's still too sick with the flu to leave her alone, and I don't know what to do."

"Did you call the police?"

"No, only you."

He held her from him, his hands clasping her shoulders. "I'll find him, Sharon. It's going to be all right."

The strength of his words and sincerity in his eyes helped her believe him, and she nodded. His smile encouraging, he bent to deposit a gentle kiss to her lips before retracing his steps out the front door.

Anxious, Sharon stood in the entrance, hugging herself, bereft of Jared's consoling warmth and fearful for her son's safety. She watched Jared pull a flashlight from his glove compartment. He beamed the glow onto the pavement while striding toward the lane, then turned and saw her standing in the doorway.

"He walked through the lawn and tracked mud down the drive," Jared

335

called as he moved to his car. "His footprints lead south. I'll drive that way; he couldn't have gotten far."

Sharon nodded, though she doubted he saw her. She watched his headlights cut through darkness as he reversed and swung the car south along the road.

"Mama?"

At the sound of Kitty's weak voice, Sharon closed the door against the chill and turned to her youngest daughter.

Kitty's eyes still shone fever-bright, and she trembled in her bed gown, her feet bare on the cold floor.

"What's wrong, Kitty?" Sharon approached and knelt before her. Out of habit, she pressed her forearm to Kitty's brow to check her temperature and found it still flame hot. "You should be in bed, honey."

"Did Andy run away?" Her voice grated hoarse from a sore throat.

"Andy'll be fine," Sharon reassured, smoothing her hand down her daughter's hair, much as Jared had done with her. Sharon put her hand to Kitty's shoulder, pushing her daughter back along the lit hallway and into her darkened room.

"Was Jared here?" Kitty asked as she crawled into her bed and Sharon pulled the covers up over her. Mindy lay sound asleep in the next bed.

"Yes, he came over for a little while." Sharon didn't want to worry her daughter.

"It'll be okay, Mama," Kitty said, her eyes drowsy. "Jared will find Andy. He always helps us."

Sharon stared with amazement at her youngest child. She wished she possessed even half of Kitty's unwavering and unconditional trust, the ability to accept another's words without question. But a lifetime of hurt had drained trust from Sharon with slow persistence.

Two weeks before, Jared had officially proposed. In the months they'd grown closer, Sharon had wanted to spend every moment with him, but her fear to trust in full held her back from giving him the answer he desired. She'd been blind when they first met, blind to what an incredible man Jared was, and later, blind to her feelings regarding him. Since then, she'd opened her eyes to the truth and accepted the knowledge that she loved him, but she couldn't fight the persistent niggling of doubt that to marry again, to entrust her life to another man, could be a mistake. Even to a man as wonderful and kind and patient as Jared. Her mind's logic argued the point while her heart's vulnerability embraced the idea of a lifetime with him, of having children with him. If only she could get her head and her heart to agree.

Tense, Jared drove the car slowly down the lane, his foot barely touching the pedal as he watched for signs of movement on both sides of the road. About four miles farther, he exhaled a sigh of relief when his headlights caught Andy's hunched figure. The boy trudged along with his hands in his jacket pockets. Jared could tell he was tired.

Slowing the car to a crawl, he rolled down the automatic window on the passenger side. Andy looked over, as if hopeful for a ride, and Jared prayed the boy hadn't considered hitchhiking. When he saw Jared, Andy frowned.

"What do you want?" he asked, his breath coming fast.

"Ten miles is a long walk," Jared replied, realizing it best to proceed with caution.

Andy's expression registered surprise that Jared would figure out where he was headed.

"Yeah, well, I can handle it."

Jared inched the car forward next to Andy while the boy stomped onward.

"Hugh installed one of the best security systems on his farm last year. Did he tell you? A burglar broke in last summer and took off with some expensive equipment." Andy kept walking, ignoring Jared. "Even if you make it there without keeling over, you won't get far, Andy. The police will be there before you can get to the moose, and then they'll have to take you to jail and call your mom. You don't want to put her through all that, do you?"

"What do you care?" He stopped walking and turned on Jared.

"She's frantic now," Jared replied, keeping his tone calm. "Why not get in, and I'll take you home? You two can talk about it there."

"I don't need you to tell me what to do!"

"Well, the road you're headed down will only make you more exhausted than you probably already are, and you'll wind up in jail besides."

The boy seemed about to argue, then, to Jared's surprise, wrenched open the door and ducked inside.

Andy remained quiet on the return drive, and when they pulled up the lane, he hauled out of the car before Jared could say a word. Instead of entering the front door, where Sharon appeared, the boy ran to the barn.

Now what's he up to?

Jared turned off the car and got out. "I'll handle it," he quietly called to Sharon, whose face seemed a mask of distressed confusion.

She hesitated, then nodded and closed the door.

The moment he entered the barn, Jared spotted Andy. The boy sat with his shoes flat on the ground, his back against the wall in the same corner the moose had inhabited.

Jared stood just inside, leaving the door ajar so the moon gave them some light. Under the circumstances, he debated whether or not he ought to speak.

"I know it's hard to let go of something you care about," he said at last. "But you want the moose happy; Hugh's a trained professional and wants the best for her, too. He's not going to let her go before she's ready to survive in the wild."

The boy scowled, remaining silent.

"Even if the law allowed you to keep Caramel, she wouldn't be happy here. And I doubt you would be happy seeing her unhappy." Jared gave a cursory glance around the cramped barn. "She's not a moose calf anymore. She's a yearling—almost her full size now—and she needs the wide outdoors to run and play and roam. She needs to be around others of her own kind."

"What do you know?" Andy yelled, tears shining in his eyes. "She got hurt once already. She's not safe out in the wild. There are predators and hunters and other people who can hurt her. She needs me! I have to protect her."

"What happened to her was a fluke, Andy. Hugh said it looked as if she got stuck in some barbed wire. I'm sure she'll be fine."

"No, she won't! She doesn't know what mean people there are out there. But I do. Men who can hurt her and kick her and hit her, again and again and again. . . ." As he spoke, he struck his fist against his palm, each smack harder and bringing with it more tears, until he was sobbing. "She needs me to protect her. I have to save her. . . ."

Stunned by Andy's behavior, Jared felt out of his depth as he realized they were talking about more than the moose.

"Andy," he said, trying to sound reassuring, calm. "Little boys can't be expected to stop big, strong men from hurting the people they love."

The boy looked up at him sharply.

Jared took a chance, hoping it wasn't a mistake. "No one blames you, least of all your mom. It wasn't your place to protect her. Children aren't meant to protect their parents; it's supposed to be the other way around."

"What do you know about any of it?"

"I don't. But I do know your mom has let go of the past and, in doing so, found peace. She trusts God to protect her now."

"Will He protect her from *you*?" Andy sneered.

Jared regarded him with surprise. "From me?"

"Yeah, I'll bet you want to marry her just so you can start beating up on her like my dad did!"

Faced again with the horror of what Sharon had gone through, Jared winced. "Andy, I love your mother. Marriage is about sharing love and trust and being committed to doing all you possibly can to help one another. It isn't about creating violence and hate." He realized from what Sharon had told him that her stepfather had done the same to her mother. No wonder the boy resented Sharon's relationship with Jared and despised him! He'd witnessed abuse in marriages all of his young life.

"What happened to your mom isn't how marriage is supposed to be, Andy. God intended for two people—a man and his wife—to become one. To be a team, but more than that, to love and care for one another, to offer each other support. Hatred only divides and tears down. Some men. . ." He trod with caution, not wanting to squash any feelings Andy may have for his dad. "Some men never understand what a real marriage is. Their selfish desires or wrong ideas they've learned cloud the issue. I only want the absolute best for your mom—she deserves all the happiness she can get. All of you do. And if I thought making her happy meant that I should leave you guys alone, I'd do it. Even though it would hurt me to let her go. Letting go hurts. But if you really care about something, like you do your moose, or love someone, like I do your mom, then you want what's best for them. You don't want them to live in cages—forced into an existence that you want so you can be near them. You want them to live the life they were meant to live, that God meant them to have. The life that will make them happiest."

The boy remained quiet, and Jared wondered if he'd even been listening.

"You'd really go away if you thought that would make Mom happy?" he asked, his eyes watchful.

Jared sighed and nodded, not surprised that of all he'd said, Andy would latch on to that. "If I thought your mom would be happier without me, I'd leave right now. I never want to see her hurt and never would do anything to hurt her. When she hurts, I hurt." Jared took it a step further. "My dad raised me to respect women, to protect them and help them if they need it. Women are supposed to be cherished. God highly favored them; He gave them the gift to produce life and bear children."

Silence, thick and heavy, stretched between them. Andy stared at his shoes, and Jared wished he could see his expression. He wished Andy would speak, felt the desire to urge him to, but at the same time dared not force him.

"She cried," Andy broke the endless span of silence.

"What?" Taken aback by the sudden words and surprising switch of topic, Jared peered at the boy. His scowl had disappeared; his manner was resigned.

"Mom. She cried when you quit coming around after Christmas. She didn't know I heard her in her room, but it was because she missed you."

⌒⌒

Sharon had walked to the barn earlier, but upon hearing Jared speak to her son, she remained outside, loath to interfere yet unable to leave. She leaned against the barn's doorjamb, feeling her son's pain, but she knew he needed to hear Jared out before she stepped forward. At Andy's admission of her feelings for Jared, she clapped her hand over her mouth while tears rushed to her eyes.

She thought she'd fooled everyone with her apparent indifference, but she'd ended up fooling only herself. Through the lesson of the moose, Jared had reached Andy in a way Sharon never had, and Andy had opened up to him. Jared's sincere explanation of marriage and his admission of his love for her warmed Sharon's heart to overflowing. She didn't want to live another day without such a man. She desired to spend each year with him, working beside him on his farm, living in his cabin, raising their children, both the ones she now had and the ones she hoped to give him.

She was weary of being single, weary of living in a web of doubt related to the past, a past that she'd long ago put behind her. In the year she'd known him, Jared had shown that he deserved her trust. He loved her, loved her kids, and his actions proved it.

Unable to prevent herself, she entered the barn. Jared turned in surprise, his curious expression changing to awe as their eyes met and held and he read the message she felt sure must beam from her face in the moon's glow.

Andy stood up. Sharon sensed him glancing from her to Jared, before moving forward. His arms went around her shoulders in a strong hug, and she looked at him in surprise. A pang went through her to realize how tall he'd grown this past month alone; he possessed the husky build of a young man and stood almost as tall as she did now.

"I'm sorry I was such a pain, Mom," he said, a catch in his voice, which also had begun to crack with the disappearance of childhood. "I don't mean to be."

"You're not a pain, son. I just want you to be happy. I want that for all my children, and when I can't give them what they need or want, it hurts. I'm sorry about Caramel, believe me."

"I understand about the moose," he said quietly, bowing his head. "I really don't want Caramel living in a dark barn that's too small for her. I want her to be happy in the wild. But is it all right if we visit her tomorrow before Mr. MacFarland sets her free again? Even though it's a weekday?"

Sharon hesitated.

"I just want to say good-bye. I won't do nothin' wrong. Honest."

"Okay." She hugged him close, rubbing her hand up and down his arm.

"And maybe, sometime, can we get a dog?"

Sharon laughed. "I think that would be a great idea, Andy."

"As a matter of fact," Jared said, "one of the collies on the farm had pups this spring. How would you like first pick of the litter?"

"Cool." Andy smiled for the first time that night. "I like collies."

Sharon glanced up at Jared in gratitude, and again their eyes held.

"Well," Andy said, sticking his hands in his jacket pockets, and looking back and forth between the two, "I guess I'll head back to the house. I'm sure you guys want to talk about all that sweet, sugared stuff."

Sharon glanced at him in surprise, realizing by his words, he finally approved.

"Don't stay out too long, Mom," he said with a cheeky grin. "It's way past your bedtime."

Andy left, and Sharon shook her head. "I guess he'll always be protective, but I wasn't expecting that!" The same startled amusement was apparent on Jared's face.

"He's growing up," Jared said. "It's good for him to hold on to those protective qualities, since it's all part of learning to be a man, as long as he doesn't let it interfere with his being a kid."

She regarded him, her smile tender, and he walked close, his expression just as soft.

"About what he said, is that what you wanted to talk about?" His brow lifted. "The sweet, sugared stuff?"

For an answer, she pressed her hands to his waist and lifted herself on her toes to kiss him. She saw the surprise in his eyes when she pulled back.

"What was that for?"

"To thank you for being you, for your help with Andy. . ."

He raised his brow as her words trailed off, unfinished.

She took a breath. "And to let you know I'm ready to take that final step." As her comment sunk in, his eyes grew a little bigger. "You mean. . . ?"

"Yes, Jared, I want to marry you."

He threw his arms around her and picked her up off the ground with a victory cry. She squealed, laughing, as he spun around with her one time, and linking her wrists behind his neck, she lowered her head and kissed him.

༺༻

A month later, Sharon stood in a room at the back of the church, adjusting her short veil over her head. Neither she nor Jared had wanted a long engagement, both of them certain this was the road they wanted and should take. No more doubts had visited Sharon since the night she'd agreed to marry Jared; if anything, every day brought further confirmation that this was God's plan for a new future. A better future.

Denied a wedding dress for her first wedding, which had been a quick ceremony in front of the justice of the peace, Sharon defied tradition for a previously married woman and wore an ice white, ankle-length wedding gown covered in tiny flower patterns of crystals along a round neckline.

"I can't believe you made that," Carly said, fluffing Sharon's dress as she looked at the crown that held Sharon's veil. "You have loads of talent, Angel."

Sharon smiled, wondering if Jared would think her sentimental action silly. She'd taken the Dollar-Store tiara he'd bought during last year's Christmas shopping excursion, his first gift to her, and with lengths of gauze and fancy cording, created a veil that matched the gown in a way that didn't look gaudy, but professionally made. Not only had she broken tradition by wearing white for a second wedding, but also she'd chosen to do something else out of the ordinary. A surprise, and her wedding gift to Jared.

"I hope I don't let you down," Leslie said. "It's been a long time since I played, back when I was living with my mother."

"Don't worry, Leslie, you'll do fine." Sharon had asked Jill to be her organist, but her tiny daughter, Lila, had decided to make an appearance into the world the day before—a month and a half early. Jared had promised Sharon that before they left for their honeymoon in Cancun, they would drop in to visit Jill and her new daughter, both of whom were doing well.

"Are you ready?" Leslie asked Sharon.

She nodded, thinking it ironic that her friends seemed more nervous than she was.

As she took her short and long-awaited journey down the aisle, she noticed Kim at the back, sitting beside Chris, both of them smiling, their arms linked through one another's as they held hands. Chris had never given up on Kim and finally convinced her that he wasn't going anywhere and would always love her, come what may. Whether she went blind again or not, he'd made it clear he wanted always to be a part of her life.

Jared had done much the same with Sharon; from the start he'd been there for her when she needed him. Sharon loved and trusted him, though she knew he was fallible and didn't always make the right decisions—like in staying absent this past winter and not calling her, no matter that he had a viable excuse; she really must teach him how to use a phone.

Life had no guarantees; troubles came, bad things happened. But she'd reached the knowledge that she couldn't hide from a personal future, fearing its outcome. Instead she must trust God. He would never let her down. The Lord had confirmed to Sharon that marrying Jared was His will; He'd just confirmed it for Jared a great deal faster. She grinned with fond remembrance when she thought about their first meeting, when Jared had blurted out that she was his future wife and she'd thought him a crackpot. Now here she was, joining him at the altar to unite with him for the rest of their lives.

Her three kids sat beside her mother in the front pew. Even her stepfather had come, and Sharon had to admit she'd noticed a change in his behavior; she only prayed it would last. Her mother had read the book and just the other night had asked Sharon questions about God; a good sign. Sharon could only hope and pray her mother's interest would continue.

Looking like fairy-tale princesses in their long pastel dresses, their blond hair perfectly styled, Mindy and Kitty appeared as if they might start bouncing up and down in the pew from barely contained excitement, and she winked at them. In his black suit, Andy looked like a young man. Sharon felt a catch in her throat at how fast her son was growing up. He had released his animosity toward Jared, though their relationship was still a bit rocky at times. But Andy was coming along, and for that Sharon felt gratitude.

Every pew on Jared's side of the church was filled, half of them by family alone. And now his family was her family.

As she took her place beside Jared, she smiled, her heart beating fast at the awe and love in his eyes. She'd never seen him in formal attire; he looked so handsome. The ceremony commenced, and the time arrived to present her gift to him. Her palms moist, she brushed her fingertips across them, keeping her hands down at her sides.

Leslie played the organ while Sharon faced Jared and sang for him the vow of love she'd written, to express all he meant to her. He watched, amazed, the delight on his face evident. Before today, she'd never sung for him. Before today, she had never felt she could.

Once they exchanged vows, once Pastor Neil pronounced them husband and wife and they kissed to seal their promise to one another, Jared linked her arm through his and covered her hand with his own. They smiled at one another, then retraced their steps up the aisle and to the back of the church while pleased family and friends looked on.

Outside the church doors, Jared drew Sharon close for a rare moment of privacy before the guests could congregate around them with congratulations and well wishes.

"My princess—you look like a princess today." His expression was tender. "And at last, my wife. You're one gorgeous woman, Sharon."

"You recognize the crown?" she asked, a bit shy at his praise.

Taken aback, he glanced at the top of her veil. "That's the same one I bought you last Christmas? You made that?"

She nodded.

He shook his head in wonder. "You're amazing; God's blessed you with so many talents, and the voice of an angel besides. No wonder Carly calls you Angel. I never knew you could sing like that."

No condemnation traced his voice, only curiosity.

"For a long time, I haven't been able to sing. I didn't even want to. The sorrow of the past few years sucked the desire right out of me. But you gave music back to me, Jared. You replaced that spark of life and resurrected old desires, and not just the singing. You've helped me to rediscover *life*."

His fingertips traced her cheek. "Now we have our entire life before us, to discover together."

She nodded with a smile, and as they shared one last tender kiss before the guests' arrival, she anticipated learning the future with him.

Epilogue

Two-and-a-half years later

A rm in arm, Jared and Sharon strolled through the vast acreage of the
Sugarwoods. Ahead of them, Mindy and Kitty sang as they skipped,
jogged, and ran—walking was not in their vocabulary. Andy held a
branch, which he tapped on tree trunks as he passed them, and Sharon winced
when she remembered his latest declaration that he wanted to be a drummer.

Now that both she and Jared taught the children's choir at their church, she
supposed it shouldn't surprise her that her son's interest had gravitated to music,
but the thought of banging and cymbals all hours of the day didn't appeal. Still,
in Andy's basement room, perhaps the noise wouldn't be too deafening, and
Jared did assure Sharon he could soundproof the room.

Sharon had quit her job at A'bric & A'brac not long after she and Jared married, and she'd been working alongside the Crisp family ever since while learning
about life on a maple sugar farm. She loved it. Often she accompanied Jared on
his deliveries, and they stayed to dinner at his aunts'. In the spring, she helped
make candy and enjoyed mingling with the tourist children at the petting zoo.
She and Becca had become fast friends—she'd become friends with all of Jared's
sisters, brothers, and in-laws, but she and Becca had known each other since the
shared "day of the moose," and she felt closest to her.

With the impending snows, they enjoyed these lingering days of warm
weather. As their walk continued, the girls ended their song, and Andy stopped
slapping his stick against the trees. For a few brief minutes, Sharon treasured
the silence of a Sunday afternoon, though she wished she could find a moment
to speak alone with Jared.

They turned with the bend of the path and came into view of a cow moose
and her calf about fifteen feet away. Jared's arm tightened around Sharon.

"Girls, move back toward us, nice and slow," he ordered, his voice tense but
hushed. "Andy, you, too. No, don't turn around," he warned when Kitty started
to pivot.

Terrified, Sharon stood still, wishing her children were far behind her. She knew
how deadly a cow moose could become if she believed her calf endangered.

Andy stared at the moose a moment before he walked toward it. It lifted
its head, its action abrupt.

"Andy! Stop, don't go any closer," Jared said.

"Dad, it's okay. It's my moose." Still, he did as Jared told him, and Sharon was grateful that Andy's rebellious days were in the past. Jared's loving but strong influence had brought her son in line like nothing else could.

"Caramel," Andy called. "Here, girl."

"Andy!" Sharon warned. "No."

The moose cow's ears went back, her eyes on Andy.

"Jared," Sharon whispered. "Do something!"

Kitty and Mindy had backed within reach. Jared moved Kitty behind him, and Sharon did the same with Mindy. Andy stood about ten feet ahead, too far for Sharon to grab without alerting the moose. Moose had bad eyesight, but she didn't know how bad and didn't want to make any sudden moves that might incite it to attack.

The moose snorted, tossing its head, and Sharon's adrenaline rocketed. "Jared," she pleaded under her breath.

" 'Amazing grace! How sweet the sound,' " Jared sang. Sharon glanced at him in shock. " 'That saved a wretch like me!' "

As he continued the verse, she joined him. Mindy's hand pressed against Sharon's back as she also began to sing; it gave her a strange comfort, the sense that all would be okay.

Her breath caught as the moose cow ambled toward them, its steps slow, wary. She watched, helpless and amazed, as the animal halted a foot from her son, and Andy stretched out his hand to its muzzle. Words of warning caught in her throat.

"Hey, Caramel," he said as if to a beloved pet. "How you doing, girl?"

She sensed Jared's amazement matched her own as they watched Andy's hand make contact with the moose's snout, then travel up along her head. She stood, quiet, and allowed him to stroke her.

"I don't believe this," Jared murmured in wonder.

Neither did Sharon. After such an extended time, she couldn't believe the moose would remember Andy. And obviously it was Andy's moose; the scar tissue from its tangle with the barbed wire on its front leg proved it.

For this miraculous window of time, God had not only protected one of His children; He'd allowed him to connect with one of His magnificent wild creatures in a manner Sharon doubted many people had before. No more than a few minutes passed before the moose nodded once, as if in farewell, and retraced its steps to the moose calf. Both animals walked out of sight and into the trees.

"She was thanking you, Andy," Kitty said, stepping from behind Jared, who stood as still and shocked as Sharon did. "For saving her and for taking care of her."

Jared smiled down at their daughter. "Maybe she was at that."

"And now she has a baby moose all her own to take care of," Kitty ended with a smile.

The soul-stirring moment left a sense of wonder behind, a sense of the miraculous in the atmosphere. As Jared and Sharon held hands and retraced their steps, Sharon realized the perfect time had arrived. The children ran ahead, quieter but just as playful. Andy's voice teasing his sisters floated back to them.

"Jared?"

"Hmm?"

Sharon leaned up to whisper in his ear. "The moose isn't the only one with a baby to care for."

The shock on his face rivaled his reaction to the moose's interaction with Andy. Jared stopped on the path, swinging to face her.

"You're not. . . ?"

"I am." Her grin stretched wide. For two years they'd tried and failed. Early in the year, they at last came to a decision just to enjoy each other and the family God had already given them.

Jared shook his head, his eyes full of wonder, his mouth opening and closing but without words. He cradled her waist with extreme tenderness, as though afraid he might break her.

"You're okay?" he whispered.

"I'm fine."

"You're sure? I mean, about. . ."

Understanding his amazed disbelief, for it equaled what she'd felt when the doctor told her, she clasped his arms. "I had an appointment yesterday. I wanted to tell you as soon as I got home, but you were busy with the pipelines, and then when I finally got to bed last night after helping Mindy with her report, you were already asleep."

"I'm just so. . ." Moisture shone in his eyes. "God has taught me a huge lesson on the meaning of patience these past years and how, when I don't give in or give up, the promise is that much sweeter when it does come. But I'd thought we finally understood His answer about this." He shook his head, bemused. "I—I just can't believe it."

"God is full of surprises," Sharon agreed softly, so in love with her husband and with life.

"You sure you're feeling all right? Not too tired or anything? Maybe we should head back to the cabin or—"

Taking his face between her hands, she reached up and kissed him, cutting off his sweet concerns and showing him just how all right she truly was.

A Letter to Our Readers

Dear Readers:

In order that we might better contribute to your reading enjoyment, we would appreciate your taking a few minutes to respond to the following questions. When completed, please return to the following: Fiction Editor, Barbour Publishing, Inc., P.O. Box 719, Uhrichsville, OH 44683.

1. Did you enjoy reading *Vermont Weddings* by Pamela Griffin?
   ❑ Very much—I would like to see more books like this.
   ❑ Moderately—I would have enjoyed it more if _____
   _____
   _____

2. What influenced your decision to purchase this book?
   (Check those that apply.)
   ❑ Cover   ❑ Back cover copy   ❑ Title   ❑ Price
   ❑ Friends   ❑ Publicity   ❑ Other

3. Which story was your favorite?
   ❑ *Dear Granny*   ❑ *Sweet, Sugared Love*
   ❑ *Long Trail to Love*

4. Please check your age range:
   ❑ Under 18   ❑ 18–24   ❑ 25–34
   ❑ 35–45   ❑ 46–55   ❑ Over 55

5. How many hours per week do you read? _____

Name _____

Occupation _____

Address _____

City_____ State _____ Zip _____

E-mail_____

If you enjoyed

Vermont WEDDINGS

then read

OKLAHOMA *Brides*

by Vickie McDonough

Sooner or Later
The Bounty Hunter and the Bride
A Wealth Beyond Riches

Available wherever books are sold.
Or order from:
Barbour Publishing, Inc.
P.O. Box 721
Uhrichsville, Ohio 44683
www.barbourbooks.com

You may order by mail for $7.97 and add $4.00 to your order for shipping.
Prices subject to change without notice.
If outside the U.S. please call 740-922-7280 for shipping charges.